THE BONE PICKERS

DOUBLE MOUNTAIN BOOKS

Paul H. Carlson, *Series Editor*
Double Mountain Books is dedicated to reintroducing out-of-print
classics of the American West. Primarily facsimile reproductions, these
include recognized works of continuing value in literature,
archeology, history, and natural history

AL DEWLEN

THE BONE PICKERS

INTRODUCTION BY W. U. McCOY

TEXAS TECH UNIVERSITY PRESS

The Bone Pickers is reproduced from a 1958 McGraw-Hill Company, first edition copy and is published as part of the special series Double Mountain Books—Classic Reissues of the American West.

New introductions by W. U. McCoy and Al Dewlen, and editor's note by Paul H. Carlson copyright © 2002 Texas Tech University Press.

The paper used in this book meets the minimum requirements of ANSI/NISO Z39.48-1992 (R1997). ∞

Cover design by Brandi Price
Printed in the United States of America

Library of Congress Cataloging-in-Publication Data
Dewlen, Al.
    The bone pickers / Al Dewlen ; introduction by W. U. McCoy.
    p. cm. — (Double mountain books—classic reissues of the American West)
    ISBN 0-89672-479-4 (paper: alk. paper)
    1. Petroleum industry and trade—Fiction. 2. Amarillo (Tex.)—Fiction.
3. Poor families—Fiction. 4. Ranch life—Fiction. 5. Rural poor—Fiction.
I. Title. II. Series.

PS3554.E93 B66 2002
813'.54—dc21   2002017360

02 03 04 05 06 07 06 07 08 09 10 / 9 8 7 6 5 4 3 2 1

Texas Tech University Press
Box 41037
Lubbock, Texas 79409-1037 USA
1-800-832-4042
ttup@ttu.edu
http://www.ttup.ttu.edu

To the two enchanting ladies in my life—Jean, who in such matchless grace shared the early trials, and Nella Faye, who lent an immeasurable joy to my valedictory years.

Editor's Note

A few months ago a copy of Al Dewlen's *The Bone Pickers* in "like new condition" sold on the Internet for $1,300. A "very tattered" one sold for $300.

The book, considered one of the fifty best books of Texas by Texas literary critic A. C. Greene, is a remarkable study of human nature and unforgettable characters. Who can forget Spain Munger, whose mixed metaphors ("speak straight from the hip") grow more hilarious with each family crisis? Indeed, no reader could forget any of the Munger clan, including such in-laws as Richard Mooney, whose monumental struggle with self and his position in the Munger empire shatters the veneer of his postwar, middle-American comfort and success.

Although set in the Texas Panhandle in the 1950s, the story could take place in any part of the state. The Munger family, suddenly finding themselves very rich, are dealing with some difficult adjustments as they change from struggling cattle ranchers to oil-field multimillionaires. The related jealousies and vanities and the pressures of big-time money that figure in this tragicomic tale are universal. It is a good story, one that pokes a good bit of fun at—even ridicules—the actions of this fictional family. The ironies are numerous and surprising. The story is big, interesting, and cleverly written.

Al Dewlen was a journalist and short-story writer before trying his hand at novels. He grew up in Memphis, Texas, seat of Hall County in the eastern Panhandle. In the mid-1950s, when he was writing *The Bone Pickers,* he lived in Amarillo. Dewlen knows the region and its people well. It shows in his mastery of character and voice. Despite some deliberate and humorous exaggeration—as in the case of Spain's abuse of adages and platitudes—Dewlen's characters are grippingly real. Their speech, thoughts, and perceptions are unerringly true to their place and time, the Texas Panhandle of fifties, and unfortunately, also to the ethnocentricity of their era.

Consequently, *The Bone Pickers* contains words and phrases that are no longer acceptable. Yet in their inclusion, Dewlen is faithful to the first tenet of good literary fiction. His portrayals hold the mirror up to life; expose the complexity of his characters, in both their merits and their flaws. Were the same novel written today, it would need to be just as honest in its portrayal of its characters' cultural enlightenment, or rather lack thereof. Though we as readers today deplore cultural insensitivity in any form, it is such works as *The Bone Pickers* that compel—and have always compelled—us as a society toward introspection, self-examination, and enlightenment. Through them, we confront the worst and the best in ourselves, and perhaps thereby, grow better at nurturing the latter.

PAUL H. CARLSON

INTRODUCTION

With readers paying many times the original price for *The Bone Pickers*—when they are lucky enough to find a copy—then driving great distances to have this treasure signed by the author, the statement is made: *The Bone Pickers* is an enduring book. Readers will not let it be otherwise. This drama of human needs, hidden dreams, and battered aspirations occurs in characters of such depth they may well become the most vivid people you know.

Texans, especially, have taken the book to heart, in part because of portrayals and settings they readily recognize. The ambience and essence of matters uniquely Texan is a pervasive underscore to the gripping themes and raw, rending conflicts. Now, because of this new edition, new generations of readers are offered access to this uncommon world—to enjoy, to savor, to revel in; to share the pain and triumph, to laugh and weep at the same instant in every outwardly ridiculous, inwardly grim, situation. It may, too, cause one to think about his own private absurdities as candidly, perhaps, as he appraises those he has discovered in the lives of his friends. This novel could translate into any language, in any era, among any people, and find there an honored home.

To understand how *The Bone Pickers* and Al Dewlen's other widely heralded books were born, it may be helpful to consider a few certainties about the author. In anything he writes, he will not be concerned with the tawdry, the ephemeral, the fads of the moment. You know that his ideas will seize you, sting, and linger on. You can count on his people to be both real and immersed in reality. The whole will be a living creation of mood, atmosphere, a tactile sense of place, of color, of movement, and of life-affirmation. And he will compel you to read.

Al Dewlen grew up in Memphis, Texas, in a family that taught him to value the truth; played football at Baylor, a school that taught him to do his civic duty; joined the Marines in World War II. He served forty-five months, eighteen of them at Bougainville; in the Philippines, Okinawa, and North China. In later life he spent nine years in sub-Saharan Africa, researching apartheid in South Africa and development in Kenya. Each step seemed to reinforce his concepts of integrity and honor.

In journalism he steered by a sure inner compass, on the Memphis *Democrat,* the Amarillo *Daily News,* and the Amarillo *Times,* and later with the United Press in Dallas. He rose rapidly because of writing talent, intensity, and a passion for truth, factors soon prompting him to seek wider scope and a broader audience. He worked half-time for the United Press in Oklahoma City in order to take further writing study at the University of Oklahoma.

There he wrote fiction and articles for major national magazines and produced his first novel, *The Night of the Tiger,* a fresh, literary sort of western about love and honor. It became a book club selection and a movie.

His *Twilight of Honor,* winner of the McGraw-Hill Fiction Award, an international best-seller and major motion picture, had its genesis in the sensational Tex Thornton murder in Amarillo. As editor and writer, Dewlen covered the case. Years later he completed research on the legal system and the ethical dilemmas confronting lawyers and poured his findings into the novel. The very impressed American Association of Trial Lawyers engaged him to address their national convention in Chicago, having mistakenly assumed the author was an attorney.

In *Servants of Corruption,* the author examines the destruction wrought by religionists when they adopt a political creed as an element of their faith. The wrenching *Next of Kin* arose out of the heroic death of his son in Vietnam. Then came *The Session,* an exhaustive study of a state legislature, its functions, temptations, shames, and successes; a study in honor and integrity.

The Bone Pickers, also, is concerned with these values, but in subtle, different ways. Rich in texture, the book makes the reader aware every moment of the look, feel, touch of place, the breath and life of each character, and accomplishes this without blocks of impeding description. Deft touches are constantly woven into the flow of the story, always presented in motion and emotion:

> Cass Street, some said, caused a permanent curl of lip on those reared there. The air seemed visible, its power stretched the nostrils. As a boy, Moon breathed it shallowly. He had ghastly green visions of what might be happening to the flesh that wasn't renderable. But he never quite yielded to Cass Street's air. . . .

So much is said about Moon's background in these few flowing words.

And in this spare scene, of action and reaction, the reader gets a full, forceful picture of a family:

> She, the eldest, advanced on the casket and put her closed hand on the metal counter of it. They saw her bend down toward the swollen, bleached face.
>
> Texas said, "So there you are, Papa."
>
> The words hung hypnotically among them. Behind her, Bethel heard China sob; China would not yield to what the rest of them had no will to fight.
>
> In that moment, what sort of 'verts' were we?
>
> They stood in the room like a community of remorseless murderers. Behaving as if each had helped put Papa in his corner, as if each were an avenger. It was smug and cold. For an instant Bethel thought Papa hadn't died of the dog bite.

What living characters and scenes Al Dewlen creates in this novel!

Three characters are virtuosic creations. The sultry Teddy Birdsong, who goes to work for the camera shop operated by Moon and Frank, is experienced and pragmatic, controlled and controlling, quite aware of her effect on men. But, after a few drinks, very scary indeed. She proves to be a catalyst for both Moon and Frank. Brother, a mature man with the mind of a child as the result of an accident in his youth, is the one member of the Munger family who remains at the old home place ranch. He is kept away from public scrutiny and under constant rein by a cashiered cop, Remo, also a well drawn character with a full role to play. Because Brother is rash and unpredictable, frequent meetings of the family, as directors of an oil empire, occur to deal with his escapades.

And there is China, Frank's wife, an angelic beauty who charms all. All men love her, and she is idolized by Brother. But there is much, much more to China.

Every absorbing character is created with depth and understanding, especially Spain Munger, who presides over the estate and its board of directors, keeping a tight control over every action by the board, supplicating, persuasive, persistently driven by his past. He assigns each member of the family the part of town where they will live, the cars they will drive, and their civic memberships and duties. He has a need for both the success of estate ventures and respectful acceptance in the community. The two obsessions join as a compulsion.

Moon, as an in-law, strives for independence and control, but he is the one Spain can count on for clean-up after blunders. And in the end, for a great deal more.

The Bone Pickers is the story of Everyman, with a rich, full cast, all with baggage of the past, all with problems, hopes, and dreams, and a central struggle for integrity. It is a masterpiece, with unfolding layers one returns to, as to a fine painting.

W. U. MCCOY
2002

Author's Introduction to the 2002 Edition

The idea for *The Bone Pickers* came to me on a Saturday afternoon in 1956 as, in a snit and grumbling about it, I mowed the lawn. I had counted on a pleasant day of tennis. But, at the insistence of my wife, and under the chilly regard of my neighbors, I found myself cutting the ankle-deep grass. It rankled that instead of what I wanted to do I was seeking status in a neighborhood where, except for my part of it, all was trimmed and wetted and fertilized and debugged and almost never trod on. The annoyance set me to speculating on just how much one undertakes solely to court the good opinion of others.

"Image," the modern term for this hypocrisy, had not come into usage then. People did not speak in those days of prompting others to think of them as in fact they were not. But we were all busy at it. I had to ponder how much of life's time and talent was being squandered in so silly a pursuit. It struck me that if borne to extremes, this compelling quest for acceptance in other eyes could critically distort, and perhaps even destroy, a life. That evening I set down the notes that developed in *The Bone Pickers*.

I spent six months drawing the characters and orchestrating them, drafting the story structure, planning the pivotal scenes, settling on the viewpoints. The writing happened over four months of twelve-hour days, during which a number of secondary themes came boiling up out of the separate conflicts raging inside the story people. These created personalities became very real to me. I remember them, still, as souls in agony, displaying foibles that are as much mine as theirs. I am pleased that now a later generation of readers will meet them.

Fact is, I think I, too, can profit from meeting them again.

AL DEWLEN
2002

part one

. . . . . / . . . . .

/ *I*

I

On the Munger Estate's alphabetized payroll, which received its weekly run-through each Friday forenoon, the name John Remo appeared in emphatic black capitals. This extra weight went unexplained to Mr. Harlan Jacobson, the sorely ulcered chief auditor. It was a matter Mr. Jacobson speculated on each payday, usually during the eight-minute recess he took for his fourth glass of raw egg and warm milk.

The auditor was a narrow, dry little man, markedly warped if not altogether wopshot, as one of his underlings had once said. Since he preferred severe striped suits, Mr. Jacobson succeeded in seeming to be mostly knots and grain, like a sliver off a discarded old plank. He would sit alone on a stool in the Baldwin Building's small drugstore, sipping the dreadful drink that was not his health but his survival, and he would quiver occasionally with a delicious hatred for John Remo. They had never met.

It could be thought that the gossip about this Remo's special duties for the Munger family was not inaccurate. Or, that the annoying emphasis had begun as a simple stenographic error.

3

Between the two, Mr. Jacobson had been unable to choose. There remained, then, the discrepancy: Mr. Jacobson's name put down in ordinary overlookable type despite the value of his position, and this man Remo, a mere watchman, listed in a disproportion certain to offend any bookkeeping eye.

Recently, Amarillo had seen John Remo only rarely. So the townspeople kept speaking of him. Somewhat darkly, they spoke of him as a man of heavy textures, whatever that might mean.

The term had originated years ago with a fellow who combined a career in poetry with another in crime. At his trial, the poet complained of rough police handling, particularly by a "heavy-textured" officer who had visited his cell late one night to solicit a confession. Rightly or not, the phrase attached itself to John Remo.

It seemed to allude, nicely, to Remo's mismated blue eyes with their wrinkled, half-dozing lids, to the great wad of coarse red nose, to the ridge of keloid tissue sketched along one cheek by the quick switchblade of a forgotten Fourth Street wino. The expression summed up handily Remo's scant wardrobe of slick short-tailed blue serge suits, hand-tooled Western belt with enormous silver buckle, and lumpy high-topped shoes. It encompassed his ponderousness; it took note of the huge team of hands that could twist the neck off a Mason jar if its cap didn't yield and on the palms of which he could, when inclined to be astounding, strike the kitchen matches he used to enliven his pipe.

Anyway, a man of heavy textures, said the voices that quote poets. Remo himself had examined the words and found them only silly. Nevertheless, he enjoyed applying them to himself.

On this Saturday morning in February, Remo lay as he had slept. He was vaguely concerned with whatever had awakened him, and resentful of it. He had dreamed as bachelors do, but incompletely. There remained a wistful ache in his thighs, a ridiculous tension in his neck. He brushed his eyes shut with his hand and deliberately canvassed his thoughts for some fragment of self-approval or, in its stead, a good indifference.

These were his balms. Sometimes his mind could concoct them; other times it could not.

At the moment, he considered that his heavy textures were making him an ordeal for the noisy, old-fashioned springs of his bed. Brother June had stomped the springs half to hell a long time ago, the way he tore up everything else around the place. At once, Remo fell to imagining curses he might pound down on June Munger's fat pampered head, and his day was afoot as usual.

He wrestled over onto his back and looked down at his mound of belly. This was unfitness and advanced age, neither to be approved. He excused himself into apathy and lay back, sighing then at his weariness from last night's drive home from Dallas.

This morning, the trip seemed insane. Four hundred miles, wheeled off in five hours. The near misses, the screaming asphalt. Jesus, what a man will do to get a little peace. . . .

"Faster, Mister Remo, faster'n that! Can't we go faster, huh, Mister Remo? Make them telephone poles go by?"

"Shut up. We got no siren."

"Can't we get us one of them, Mister Remo?"

Remo almost wished they could. Sirens were his history; like howling dogs, they strayed about in his finest memories.

His full name was John Remolewski. But most of his fifty-one years, which seemed now to have limped past him as a dull procession of silent old men, he had been called John Remo. They put this on his police-department pay checks. The whole Remolewski hadn't been mentioned, even, during his one blaze of cruel publicity. Now, in his days of nursemaiding for the Mungers, he seemed to have become, with finality, just Remo.

He sort of favored the bobtailing. He had to smile at how his mother did not. She hated it with all the brittle privilege of her accumulated years. During her periodic spells of anti-Texas Polishness, she would stab him deep about disloyalty to origin.

To unhamper the great deal she had to say, Mother would

5

fetch out her ill-made teeth, which served, in fact, as nothing more than pacifiers to be sucked on. With her mouth roomier and more moist, she would tell him in sprays and whistles that Remolewski was a great name.

When kept intact the name was, she declared, the entire kit-and-kettle of what she and he might save of the Old Country for themselves. To her it mattered nothing that Remo had been knocked along to his manhood in North Amarillo, that he had never gotten nearer proud Poland than police headquarters at Cincinnati. Any Pole, Mother thought, owed the root country the preservation of its brand names. Even a Texas Pole.

"You say, John, why iss this? And I say, iss to pay back the gift of brave blood! All Polish peoples iss brave blood. Only to save a 'ski' straight where it wass born at, this iss a small little ting!"

The point, Remo thought, might best have been stowed away in Mother's old trunk among other musty things. But she never put it away. Finally, last October, he had sent her back to Pennsylvania to live among the old country friends she was convinced still knew and loved her, despite an interim of fifty years. She would find there, Remo guessed, a place of polite isolation. And while she was refusing to notice, loneliness would begin killing her. It appeared likely to Remo that he'd not see his mother again. The discomforting truth was that he very much cared.

He looked at his watch, just as the clock-radio clicked on. Music billowed in suddenly. He recognized Nat King Cole, at the middle of a record, sounding as though his throat needed a morning swabbing. Remo reached and trimmed down the volume. It was seven o'clock. The air of the house tasted a shabby gray. Outside there seemed to be a fuss among the chickens. He thought of fried eggs, and the coffee he liked best when it was creamless and bitter and stinging, and he started getting up.

What the Panhandle native sometimes pointed out to strangers as The Old Munger Place wasn't truly old. The big yellow sprawl of treeless Munger land, which had been let go to grass after the first year of the serious oil play, was as aged as any patch of ground, give or take an eon or two. But the house itself had barely turned thirty-six, so that by traditional measure, it lacked even maturity.

It stood a hundred yards east of an ordinary section-line road, an exact thirty-two miles out of Amarillo. The tall front door faced the west sun, for no purpose except that the main road lay that way.

Confusion of intent was a mark of the place. Never could the house have been credited with reflecting any definite personality. Like the Mungers themselves, it seemed, much of the time, to have no presence at all.

Old Cecil Munger had built the house with money he despised. It came from the painful sale, through a railroad's condemnation suit, of a strip of his precious pasture. The old man had fought the easement down to the last jury. To his strong mind, land was for acquiring, not for selling. When the courts forced him to settle, he looked upon the money as too unprincipled to hold in hand. A new house seemed the way to get rid of it hastily.

The construction received only a little of his attention. People said he drank a quart of rye the day it began; they said he and Melita and their flock had been moved in a week before he rallied enough to realize it. Thus the house turned out as scarcely more impressive than the wind-tilted, board-and-batten cluster of shacks it replaced. There was the high boxiness, the vain little gingerbreads so common to farm homes of the Plains. And at first sight, you could tell the Munger place would smell, inside, of singed feathers and dead geraniums and souring cream.

A yearly layer of white paint had been dobbed onto the shiplap siding, so that now it was encased in a thick flaky skin. You could see how crumbly and thick if you chanced to inspect the edges of the thousands of round holes Brother June kept boring in the walls with his brace and bit.

Across the front was a slanting, pillared porch, decorated at the roof with a jig-cut cornice. There were broad concrete steps and at either side, a lacy green latticework which hung like a petticoat from the floor level to the ground. There was a steep six-gabled roof sheeted over with dusty raw shingles and edged by tin troughs and tin pipes which merged hopefully at a tin downspout over the backyard cistern. Cresting each gable was a wrought-iron lightning rod, and recently bolted to the foremost rod was a multichannel television antenna.

Cecil Munger's nonunion contractor had quartered off the upper story into four vast cold bedrooms where, originally, there had been massive iron beds with lidded white chambers underneath. Downstairs consisted of a cluttered living room, an enormous kitchen, an arch-doored dining room, a hall like a bowling alley, and two more bedrooms. Canted off the rear wall and looking newer than the rest was a lean-to bathroom that opened into the kitchen.

The eleven-foot ceilings suggested that the scab contractor had estimated the Munger children would grow tall; taller, even, than in fact they had. He papered every ceiling with that standard silvery pattern which must look forever, to imaginative young ones, like a horrible and fascinating tangle of bloodless entrails. The paper had sagged for years with yellow, cloud-shaped water stains. These used to stir the Munger flock, when bedded down at sunset and staring upward, to whisper of mystery. They decided that somebody lived up in the attic, and whoever he was, whatever his business there, he was certainly a steady and prolific bed-wetter.

There were floral-print walls, wide woodwork of pine painted brown, uneven floors of groaning planking, heavy drapes dripping tassels and dust, long wires that dangled unfrosted light bulbs. It seemed a house in which to hang up dirty overalls, or to boil lye soap.

It did not look like the place where a hundred sixty million dollars lived.

A few strides to the southeast, at the end of a path that angled past the cistern, stood the outbuildings. Largest was an unpainted barn, with a vacant implement shed attached. Next

8

to it rested a Rooseveltian sanitary toilet in retirement, although still plumb and solid on its concrete base. Close by, facing away from the north winds, were an almost new chicken house and its padlocked feed bin. The high fence enclosed everything. It had been made by sinking used railroad ties as posts and spiking rough two-by-six runners around them.

From the county's caliche road, the Mungers drove onto their property across a pipe-and-concrete cattle guard. They could follow the gravel driveway to the front yard and park anywhere they wanted on a half-acre square that had been curbed and spread neatly with crushed rock. Or, they could continue on around north of the house, until they encountered the building that they themselves had trouble getting adjusted to.

This was the three-car garage, made of green cinder blocks. The doors, always left raised, were fancy overhead rollaways. In each exposed port stood a Cadillac sedan, nose outward. They were identical 1956 models, except no longer of equal worth.

The sedan in the northernmost stall showed a smashed-in face; it wore rusting scars along its black flanks. The center car remained spattered with red mud from an otherwise unrecalled rain, and if not crippled so obviously as the first, it did appear to sag low in front, as though its gentleman's spirit had been broken.

The third automobile glittered fitly, its showroom poise unruffled except for a few tan smudges put on the grill and windshield by suicidal insects. It seemed anything but tired, despite having thundered and honked and shot itself across Texas until last midnight.

The sedans belonged to Brother June. They were a part of the reason that in certain bitter moments the auditor, Mr. Jacobson, might remark guardedly, "Well, whatever the trouble about that Brother, he *is* the only Munger of the whole consarned bunch who gets any pleasure out of all that money."

Brother did find pleasure in many ways. He might have rooted out more, of an even gayer variety, except for the ob-

9

stacle he had to deal with. This was John Remo, the professional obstacle whose authority filled the other downstairs bedroom.

Remo scooted to the edge of the bed and slowly sacked up his feet in black cotton socks. Afterward, he twisted around to peer through the hole in the wall. He'd had to petition repeatedly before Spain Munger consented to cutting it there. The opening provided ready view of Brother's room. Remo frowned. At the foot of Brother's tall brass bed were heaped the bright red blankets and soiled sheets. Brother was up and gone.

Remo knew this to mean peril. By way of taking steps, he had wired a dozen dime-store Christmas bells to June Munger's bedsprings. These jangled brashly when the big man began jouncing and floundering from having slept enough. Remo listened for the bells, by the same habit that kept his ears sharp for the creak and groan of the old floors whenever Brother's two hundred forty pounds crossed them.

This morning he had heard neither. He swore. The guy must have wandered on outside.

Remo hacked his way through his morning fit of coughing and went about dressing. First the big soft shoes which, the last half of the way, laced with hooks rather than eyes. Then the pleatless trousers, worn at a slack halfmast, so that the engraved rectangular buckle hung beneath his paunch and helped truss it upward. Next, he took up yesterday's shirt, which gapped badly where it buttoned over his moneybelt.

The Munger family furnished the belt; they kept it heavy with Brother's allowance. Out of it John Remo spent, these days, as he'd never dreamed of spending. But he drew no fun from it. Occasionally the family fell to worrying about the fantastic, nondeductible amounts that ran through this depository, and their call for an accounting always brought Remo a critical moment.

He heard a sudden furor among the chickens, and nodded at himself in the mirror. Brother was located. Out at the lot, probably feeding Grape-Nuts Flakes to the flock. At twenty-seven cents a box.

He should talk to Spain Munger about that.

Since television, Remo had ordered the cereal, unwillingly, by the case. When a new case arrived, the happiest Munger sat down with it on the kitchen floor and sang excitedly while his fat hands ripped through every last package and dug out the little plastic motorboats. The house was strewn with red and green and yellow motorboats; each day Remo crushed a few underfoot.

"Oh, hell. Look here, June—"

"Them, Mister Remo? Oh, those ain't my boats, no sir!"

"Don't give me that."

"Shoot, Mister Remo, I don't want 'em no more. If they ain't mine, they must be some other body's boats, Mister Remo!"

Remo would wonder what nuisances they put in cereal boxes before plastic, anyway, and he would worry about the cereal, all heaped up loose in the packing carton until Brother could get around to delivering it to his Leghorns. After so many years of police pay, Remo saw it as a shattering waste.

But, stop seething about it, boy. It's the Mungers' money, and their own fat child.

From the dresser, Remo took up his stubby old pipe. Its lacquer had cooked loose and peeled; the bowl was partly burned away. He set it between his teeth, encouraging the friendly taste of it to drive back the smells of the house. Spain Munger hated any sight of the pipe; it was disreputable in a way that irked Spain thoroughly. Remo grinned around the deeply bitten old stem. The pipe made his job more bearable.

The chickens threshed, then quieted, then beat and clamored again. Remo winked an eye shut and listened. It sounded as if Brother were kicking some of the downy behinds, as he might at times when he thought the birds too greedy. Remo supposed he should get out there, but he wasn't in a mood to hurry.

He crossed to the south window, propped an elbow on the rotted frame, and looked out. The sky was high and clear. He blinked, and scowled toward Amarillo.

He had never been a clever policeman; he knew it. Nor an especially dedicated one. Certainly, never like all the new young cops joining the force these days to play *Dragnet*. But the thing was, he had carried an Amarillo badge for twenty-four years. Yet now, so many miles over there, the law and the patrol-car bull sessions and midnight waitress baitings and payday poker games were going on without him. Which wasn't fair.

He wiped his breath's fog off the glass, and he saw the haze of the city. The Plains, he conceded, was quite a country. More of it than some states, more of it than Mother's mighty Poland, very likely, and on a day such as this you could look across the flatness and know your eye spanned at least twenty miles. Presently he made out the upper half of the smokestack at the smelter. On the town's near side, the plant must be almost thirty miles from his window.

Zinc. His father had helped them make zinc, until the dust and grime and fire finally ground him down into his grave. Since the cloudlessness of the drouth, Remo could count on seeing the stack every day. It had become the part of his town he worried about. They used to whisper that the smelter cooked enough gold out of its Mexican ore to pay for the operation, so that the zinc came free. This Remo doubted, because his father had never confirmed it.

He watched a lean belt of gray smoke rise, climbing straight up, but hesitantly. Just like the prayer of a sinner, his father once said. Sometimes Remo suspected that if he should pray—even generously, as for Mother's back pains, or a good soaking rain—the words would travel upward like the smoke, slow and gray and much too thin. It wasn't worth the risking.

He swore, and bent to raise the window. A wash of cold funky air spilled in, and he shut the frame quickly. That chucklehead, he was ruining the ground out there, altogether ruining it. But to report it to Mr. Munger, Remo saw, would be stupid. Like asking how to housebreak a puppy. Remo turned away to the hall, back to the kitchen and through it to the back door.

The low red winter sun blazed directly at his eyes. He squinted until he could see Brother's calfgrain golf bag leaning against the lot fence. The big rube would be driving out of sight another forty dollars' worth of golf balls.

"He's, uh, like—like a child," Spain Munger had explained. "He sort of knows, and then he doesn't know, you see what I mean? Fifty per cent of the time, it's only play. . . ."

A child. But less a child than Spain Munger thought. Brother hit a golf ball three hundred yards, when he didn't miss it entirely. And on some of these harebrained trips, since he had learned that if he set up a squall, Remo would relent and hire him a woman. . . .

It was a pretty morning. Air bright and cold, and just the least bit unsatisfying, as if it needed salt. Remo yawned it in, deeply, against the logyness from last night's wild driving. He went back to his room and carelessly put on a red necktie that hardly showed its spot of Jay's shrimp sauce. He took the snouty little Colt Cobra revolver off the dresser and put it in his back pocket. It seemed, then, that he was dressed.

Remo could carry a gun and forget it, which was among his few lasting self-approvals. A weapon made most men swagger; it became an iron poultice that drew the buried hatreds to a sudden dangerous fester. Which was why, he had concluded, most policemen were obnoxious to Joe Citizen. Joe, after all, had to go at life bravely unarmed. It pleased Remo that his gun was merely a tool he needed, one the Munger family nodded upon as the logical companion to the moneybelt.

He returned to the kitchen, flicking his cropped-off gray hair against the grain as he walked. He switched on the electric range and started coffee. Once more he heard the chickens. Of a sudden, he understood that they cawed and battled for more than Grape-Nuts.

Remo stepped out onto the sagging back stoop. His gaze caught the chrome glimmer of a golf club. Its mahogany head raised above the fence in backswing, then hissed downward. Remo jumped to the path, running.

Above his immediately noisy breath, he heard Brother singing "Jesus Loves Me, This I Know." And why the devil, just why the devil, had China Munger bothered to teach it to him?

13

"...for the Bible tells me so!" It carried far in the new morning. Brother's voice held the gruff restraint he believed kept his contentments secret, thus making them the more savory. Remo puffed, and slowed to a trot.

The club cocked up again. Above the top fence runner, Brother's head came into sight. It gleamed. He was monk's-cap bald, above a rim of high-clipped hair that rested on him like a garland and shone there much too silvery for a man of thirty-nine.

Brother's was a plump fair face, babyish except for bushy copper eyebrows, which he would not allow to be trimmed, and fluid blue eyes, which could light with an occasional dance of shrewdness. Now his massive shoulders and soft jelly body were locked still at the peak of his backswing.

He wore big blue overalls, half unfastened; he had his blousy peppermint undershorts on the outside. His ragged tennis shoes were crimson with new blood; it had spattered his pants up to the knees.

"Hey!" Remo yelled, and he sprinted.

Grape-Nuts Flakes rustled about in a scatter on the ground. Brother stood at the center, his knobby feet broadly stanced. About him, Leghorns swarmed spur-deep in cereal. Brother waited in readiness until a reckless pullet darted out in front, pecked down, then stretched up a full neck to swallow. Easily, neatly, Brother shifted a foot and swung the driver. The pullet's head clicked off, arching away over the fence and carrying far beyond. The body went flopping back into the frantic flock, its stub of neck gushing.

Remo hit the fence. "Oh, Christ, June!"

June Munger looked up. Startled, but with a sort of wisdom alive in his eyes. Then the eyes pleaded.

Remo glared at him. Brother looked away toward the sky, then down at the chickens. "Nice chickie, chickie," he crooned, and one big hand poked the golf stick at them gently, playfully. His face turned slowly back to Remo. "Nice chickie," he said.

"Christ, what the hell now!"

"Hello, Mister Remo. Yu' seen Kittypoo? I can't find Kittypoo noplace, Mister Remo!"

"So what you think you're doing?"

"I hunted just about everywheres, Mister Remo."

Remo gazed around the lot. Blood puddled about, and was steaming. Some had splashed onto the fence. Headless chickens lay in twitching white heaps, their feet drawn into shocked, yellow fists. The pullet kept threshing, its breast cawing against this callous infraction of the ground rules.

Remo panted, and swore. Seven dead chickens. The survivors milled about and watched, blink-eyed and cautious, yet unpersuaded to abandon their Grape-Nuts.

"You done it now, dammit. You really done it!"

"Me, Mister Remo?"

"Goddamn you, can't I never get a minute's sleep, unless you —oh crap, you know what you done? Lookit them chickens! You know I got to phone your brother and sisters; you know I got to tell 'em? You know that? You know they're gonna chew my ass out from here to yonder?"

"'Scuse me, Mister Remo."

"I mean it; I ain't bluffing. I got to call 'em, tell them what you done."

Brother's round, unguilty face came up slowly. Beneath the big scar at the temple, it struggled against eagerness. The eyes were lit in that seldom, brief way that could make them infinite and beautiful. Softly, Brother said, "You reckon, Mister Remo, you reckon they'll come out here?"

"They'll come. They'll land on you with all ten feet."

"You—you aim to call 'em all, don't you aim to, Mister Remo? China and Bethel an' Laska an' Texas? And Spain and Mister Moon, too. The whole batch, Mister Remo?"

Remo blew out his breath.

"For Sunday dinner, Mister Remo? They all comin' to eat Sunday dinner at the house, you 'spect, Mister Remo?"

Remo's feet were on the bottom rail, his hands gripping hard on the highest one. His limbs still shook, but now, it seemed, mostly from the morning chill. He muttered another oath, and

15

spat into the lot, and stared down at Brother. The happiest Munger scrubbed a fawnish eye, artfully, with a hairy fist.

"Them Grape-Nuts sure makes a chicken bulge out, Mister Remo!"

The observation rebuilt Remo's rage. Teeing up live chickens —this was a first. Yet, beneath his anger, Remo sensed that only the mechanics of the caper were new. Reluctantly, he had come to understand the mischiefs. Brother, Remo knew, had discovered how shock could serve where pleading failed. Shock brought his family to him. One stunt, if bad enough, and the great ninny could gather his brother and sisters about him, to scold him lovingly through most of a day.

As the last Leghorn shuddered and gave up, Remo met Brother's waiting, hopefully lit eyes. In them, suddenly, Remo thought he glimpsed another truth. Brother realized, damn him, —and counted on the fact—that his "Mister Remo" had unmasked the real why of these things.

It was yield, and yield again. Surrender to a mushbrain, else worse would follow. Remo began again to swear.

"I'm gettin' kind of cold out here, Mister Remo."

Good, you fat bastard; why don't you freeze?

Sourly, Remo said, "Okay. Pick up them chickens and let's go to the house."

"You still chapped at me, Mister Remo?"

"Plenty."

"You gonna lick me, Mister Remo?"

"Hell."

"Huh, Mister Remo?"

"I ever whip you?"

"You ain't never, thank you, Mister Remo; only Spain said, he said you'd lick the stuffin' out, if I—"

"I will, too, dammit."

"Right now, Mister Remo?"

"Look. You go to your room, put them drawers on right. You keep messing around, I won't read you the funnies no more for a year."

"You fixin' to lick me after breakfast, Mister Remo?"

"No, goddammit."

"You're a real good sonofabitch, Mister Remo."

"Quit talking that way. You know it makes your folks climb my back."

"I got a heap of kinfolks, ain't I, Mister Remo?"

"Yeah, you sprung from a long line of kinfolks."

"China, she don't care none, Mister Remo."

"She don't care what?"

"My sister, she lets it be all right how I talk, Mister Remo. China, she says my drawers is pretty on the outside, if they ain't nobody much around. She likes me best, don't you reckon she does like me best, Mister Remo?"

"I reckon so."

China Munger Wallace, thought Remo, liked everyone the best, and everyone equally, yet each especially. It was a quality. At first, he had suspected that she realized, fully, what a tenderness she could lay out and set aglow with just the least smile or slightest glance, and he had imagined that, womanishly, she made practical use of it. But once a bit of her had beamed over him, he knew better. She wasn't aware. The thing, resembling kindness but in fact much greater, flowed naturally through her blood as if produced by a busy and magnificent extra gland. She was radiant; she was a sweet and easing drug you had to respond to. China laughed, and you turned giddy with warmth; you had to reveal to her whatever gentleness you had left in you, even if it were no more than the tattered leftovers from childhood.

Once Remo had caught himself on the verge of speaking baby talk to her, which would have been all wrong. Often he wished to touch her cheek; certainly her skin would have a strange and different feel. Whatever China's magic, it was too rare for naming. You identified it when you said her name. At times Remo thought that a woman like China Wallace could not be; there was something improbable about it. But when she was on the place, he believed. He sensed her enchantment like peace, like rest; maybe like God.

He recalled the last time they'd talked: Tell me, Mr. Remo, Brother *is* wonderfully inventive, don't you think? Yes ma'am, he had said. He hadn't dreamed of explaining how Brother saw a comic wearing exterior underwear in a Houston burlesque house; how he'd wanted golf clubs only after a Ben Hogan movie short they'd seen at Albuquerque; how even the blue language was in imitation. Instead, he had watched China's face and said, "Truly, ma'am, he's smart as a whip sometimes," and at once he had felt as kind as a Christian. . . .

"Does it hurt, Mister Remo?" Brother said.

"It hurts."

He sat now at the kitchen table, with Brother watching while he dug into his hand with his penknife. He gouged out, in pieces, the long splinter he'd snagged off the fence. The wound began to bleed.

"Oh, oh, oh," Brother moaned in fascinated sympathy.

"Get me the monkeyblood."

"Oh, I will, Mister Remo! Except, if I knowed—"

"In the bathroom."

Remo painted his wound, gasped, then blew the sting cool. Brother hung over him, absorbed; puckered but not blowing.

"Get off my shoulder, June. And see if that water is boiling yet."

" 'Scuse me, Mister Remo. I ain't gonna bother your shoulder none—"

"Water hot?"

"Boy, it's scalding hot already, Mister Remo. Plenty!"

"All right. Let's commence."

" 'Fore we eat us some breakfast, Mister Remo?"

"You killed 'em before breakfast, didn't you?"

They lifted the two hissing kettles off the range, spilled them into the wash tub that held the chickens. After a minute, Remo snatched one out. He handed it by the feet to Brother.

"All right, get to picking."

"You can shuck 'em if you want to, Mister Remo; I never did care for chicken pickin', not to speak of—"

"The hell you don't. Take it."

Remo bent to the tub for another. The water burned his hand, and he swore.

"Boy, Mister Remo; you want that ole monkeyblood some more? Me, I can—"

"Shut up."

Remo stripped his chicken nude, rapidly, in fury. "I want to know, how'd you get up this morning without me knowing?"

"I just got up, Mister Remo. I didn't aim nothin', I just taken my clubs—"

"What'd you do to them bells?"

Brother tugged a clumsy fistful of steaming feathers from his Leghorn, looked around the kitchen as if his brother Spain might be there, then poked the dank wad into the only pocket not closed off by his drawers. He hummed, as if hunting a key, before settling on a long nasal tone that tuned him for "Jesus Loves Me."

"What about them bells?"

"They was awful loud, Mister Remo. Awful loud, and I didn't care to bother you none, Mister Remo."

"So you yanked the clappers out."

"No sir! No sir, Mister Remo! I didn't hurt them cloppers none!"

"You been pulling more cotton out of that mattress? Stuffing them bells?"

"No sir, I didn't do that! It wasn't nothing but some old rags, Mister Remo!"

"Oh, hell. We get through here, you go in yonder and take them rags out. Hear me?"

"I hear you, Mister Remo."

"Don't forget it."

"Mister Remo, I don't know if I ain't sick or not." Brother opened his mouth wide. "See, that there moss on my tongue? Maybe, Mister Remo—"

"Dammit, June, I carried you down to Dallas, didn't I? Done what you wanted to in Dallas, didn't we? And quick as we get back, you go to tampering and screwing up."

"What was that we saw, now, down at Dallas, Mister Remo?

19

At that show, where I hadn't oughta belched like I done? I forget what that was, Mister Remo."

"Cinerama."

"Yeah, boy, Mister Remo! That railroad train on the hill, it was ballin' and a-whistlin', didn't it, Mister Remo?"

They picked the chickens. Remo slashed and drew them, then piled them in the sink. He sent Brother out with the tub. He heard a whang and a thump as Brother missed the barn nail the tub was supposed to hang on, but whatever followed was drowned under the roar of the morning's first airliner. The Old Place lay beneath the city terminal's flight pattern, so that noisy ins and the noisier outs rattled the Munger windows at all hours. Remo was growing accustomed to it while still believing he never could.

He poured coffee and drank it at the cabinet as he scraped pinfeathers. He tried to sort out the day's circumstances, to find in them an excuse that would do when he answered to Spain.

"Airplane!" Brother burst back inside. "Scairt Kittypoo, I bet, Mister Remo, only I ain't see Kittypoo noplace!"

The lean fierce-eyed old cat, shrunken too small for its mottled and short-napped gray coat, was seldom missing yet rarely seen.

"Well, what'd you think? Cat don't like being flailed around all the time. I'm liable to mention that to your folks, too."

"Oh," Brother said. Then, brightly, "You ain't called 'em up in Amarillo yet, Mister Remo!"

"Too early."

"You told me, Mister Remo! You said you'd call 'em up, and tell 'em what it was I done, Mister Remo!"

"I will, too, by God."

"This here telephone—"

"Just keep your britches on."

Brother leaned against the cabinet, his big face pale and strained over keeping his britches on. His hands snapped a fifty-cent cigar into five equal chunks, four of which went into the sodden pocket that bulged with white feathers. The other Brother put into his jaw.

"I done right, didn't I do right, Mister Remo?" His broad eyes deepened, became bluer, plainly thoughtful, and a little sad. "If all us Munger family is comin' out to Sunday dinner, Mister Remo, ain't it real keen I got busy and got these here chickens about ready?"

"Wouldn't be nobody coming, if you hadn't—aw, forget it."

"Well, chicken is about what they crave to eat, don't you reckon it is, Mister Remo? China, she likes chicken, she tole me. Huh, don't it look like we kilt about enough?"

"You killed enough."

"You're a good sonofabitch, all right, Mister Remo. Moon, he's a good 'un, too, if he tells about the war, Mister Remo. And China, boy, she's a good son—"

"Quit cussin'. And don't spit on the floor."

"Is they gonna be a meetin' after the dinner is et, Mister Remo?"

"You listen to me, June. I don't want you cuttin' up while they're out here. I don't want my tit in the wringer."

"You mad at me, Mister Remo?"

"What you think?"

"Me, I'll shut up, Mister Remo, only I never said I was gonna stick yore tit in no wringer."

Remo gathered the chickens between his hands. "Open the goddamn icebox!"

The Mungers would come scurrying to The Old Place. Grave-faced, almost furtive, but, safe from Amarillo's winking eyes, they'd eat, then be called by Spain Munger to "sit formally" in fruitless judgment of their weakling.

Sometimes, while out here, they dealt also with the odds and ends they spoke of as "the little business." The Mungers examined any problem protractedly; they beat it about, shook it, squeezed it until they had recast it, at last, into an answer they could adopt unanimously and in that strict sort of disorderly order they regarded as parliamentary. The procedure was the same, Remo supposed, in the family's downtown conferences, those held in the great chamber acquired soon after Old Cecil Munger's death.

Once, Remo had seen the place. A severe, paneled and polished room, a long, mirroring mahogany table, a dozen great swivel chairs with head-high backs and upholstery of fine red leather edged by imposing rows of brass tacks, the heads of which were shaped as diamonds. Under a muraled ceiling, the Mungers voted through the Estate's grand decisions. A few times, however, the family had dealt in millions while at The Old Place, doing so in modulated tones that scarcely carried beyond the dim stuffiness of the dining room.

Despite his brave Polish blood, Remo dreaded any day that brought them out from town. Each occasion assured him of at least one humiliating moment. But, truthfully, he found no Munger Sunday wholly bad. It brought him the air of China Wallace to breathe, and often before leaving, she would fix her mutating attention on him while wishing him fewer trials with her "Beloved." Remo had to be careful, always; letter-careful, lest his eyes go picking over her like hungry insects. And then there were the Mungers-in-law. Especially Richard Mooney.

Remo did not care about Frank Wallace or Sid Glass. But Moon was his friend. He wished not to lump him with the others; yet often he did.

Remo would watch the three of them, meandering about The Old Place, trying to look as though the dining room had not excluded them. They kicked clumps of grass, tested the wobble in the fence, made solemn scrutiny of each other's automobiles, all as if they missed the conference out of a preference for pure country air.

People said they were both necessary and useless to the Mungers. Even rich women must marry and try for offspring, it was said. Yet beyond this, the in-laws had been patiently and thoroughly dehorned. And this, Remo thought, made precise his own reasons for laughing at them; these men's horns had been cropped much shorter than his own.

He stacked the chickens in the refrigerator and washed his hands, noting the scratchy sound his palms struck from each other.

"Mister Remo?"

Brother stood at the end of the cabinet, a brown drop threatening to drip off his chin, a set of fat fingers agitating the telephone. His eyes looked bleak with uncertainty.

"You go make a stab at shaving," Remo said.

"Mister Remo, you ain't phoned China and all them; you said, Mister Remo—"

"After breakfast. Shave, and wash your face, too. And you're sure as hell taking a bath tonight."

"Account of China an' all them is comin', Mister Remo?"

"Yes."

Brother grinned. "A ole bath don't matter to me none, Mister Remo!"

Remo swore, and put bacon on to fry.

II

For the Panhandle, more modernly spoken of as "The Golden Spread," 1956 became the seventh straight year of drouth. Except for one savage blizzard, it had arrived ash dry, and it continued that way.

At the heart of the Spread, Amarillo sat thirty-six hundred feet high, smoking the inflated cigars of an incongruous record-breaking prosperity and boasting how it now had fifty-five known millionaires. Drouth could not touch oil and gas. Only a minority of credit-exhausted sodbusters actually suffered. These watched their fields chap and split as their seed blew away; they took blow torches to yellowing prickly pear, burning off the spears so the stock might survive a bit longer. To them, Amarillo's two-eighty-four-a-barrel boom looked like sin. But even in a reasoning set askew by desperation, they could not blame the city.

A few looked upon the seventh famine year as a woeful fulfillment of scriptural promise. Most, facing a spring when only the snakeweed would be green, regarded the dry skies as just another Eisenhower blunder.

It was these, the mortgaged and cropless, who set off the

talk of disaster. The fifty-five millionaires, who established public topic quite as easily as they chose traffic systems or school sites, went along. Out of charity, perhaps, or because they could, at least, smell the dust. Suddenly there were angry editorials and demanding speeches.

The Mr. Congressman made a public disclosure that he was sharing the disaster. He reported countless sleepless nights, fraught with compassionate tears and a thousand prayers for guidance. In one of these nights, wisdom came to him.

Then, loyal Panhandler that he was, he claimed the floor of the House on a day that it was empty and he shouted into the record which must soon reelect him that unless there were less of Mr. Benson, at once, and more of those perforated green symbols of Humanitarian Government, these to be issued immediately, then the whole GREAT Golden Spread of Texas might sizzle to a crisp, and perish: a calamity that might well occur before God and the Democratic National Committee had time to bring about some good gully-washing rains.

It was crisis and emergency.

But if the disaster, or the blanket of Federal pity that was descending over it soothingly, touched Richard Mooney, it was only in the smallest way. He had the dust to breathe, and maybe it was the dearth of growing things that made these February mornings less zestily sharp than they had been when he was a boy.

He lay in bed smoking. The family was oversleeping. On weekdays, his daughters—lovely Carol and strange, tall Hannah—needed to be off to school at eight-fifteen. But on Saturdays, it made no difference. Actually, on any day, what could be delayed or damaged because a Mooney overslept? At once, he condemned the thought as worthless. Of late, it seemed, he had grown too ready to draw small implications and to let them register hard with him. He must put a stop to it.

He looked across the gap between beds. Bethel lay thin and long and almost pretty. One pale cheek was crushing a bit of the short blond hair which seemed, unnaturally, to go through the nights unmussed. One thin white arm rested above the

25

covers, extending along her side. His wife appeared most frail, he thought, most vulnerable. Asleep, she seemed to need him. He felt an uncommon surge of yearning for her. To nourish it, he watched her a long while.

Gradually he began to smell the Mooney coffee, perked two hours before by the electric pot which Bethel primed and set at bedtime each evening. By now, the stuff would have simmered to an acid. Here was something spoiled because Richard Mooney overslept. The negative thought had slipped in again, and it drove him out of his bed.

Behind him, Bethel yawned. He twisted about to smile at her. Positively.

She appeared to have awakened, totally, in an instant. It was an ability to be admired. With Moon, setting aside a good sleep was slow business. Usually, he felt all scattered out and unwilling to gather himself together.

Bethel winked a wide eye at him. She said, "I should have been up hours ago. I'm becoming a very grubby wife." It meant, I love you again today, Richard; how is it with you?

He walked around the bed and kissed her throat.

"Thank you," she said. "I'll be along after a minute."

Moon went into the small hall, on through the tight cube of living room and into the kitchen. He took a stool at Bethel's pink Formica breakfast bar and drew a cup of the bitter coffee. He tasted it, winced, and looked at himself in the chrome shine of the urn.

At thirty-five, Moon looked better than in any season of his life. When so put to himself, this became an incidental matter involving no vanity. He stood an exact six feet, he weighed two hundred six, and he could go onto the tennis courts or into the club pool with confident ease. His were green-gray eyes, set above small firm puffs of flesh that suggested worldly excesses he'd certainly never had; he had the athlete's massively shelved brow, this only partially earned. His nose was short and blunted, his mouth wide with a heavy lower lip, his hair brown and butch-cut. A pleasant sort of ruggedness, Bethel called it. "Hormones, Daddy," Carol had once crooned at him.

Moon had found he attracted people easily. At Jaycees, in the Chest drive, at church, he encountered quick popularity. But there was a reservation in it. Something like prejudgment, because he was a Munger-in-law. In much of Amarillo, this meant at best a piddler; at worst, a façade, definitely not a man. Moon was accustomed to faces that took him for granted, eyes that appraised him as a handsome, vacant husk. Richard Mooney, a nice enough fellow, to be sure, but with little inside him except light sterile air.

He heard movement back in the house, and supposed Bethel had gotten up. He frowned at the coffee urn, for reflecting him in one of its distortions.

As he sat, he appeared extremely long-headed while his body had shortened to a lumpy stub. Slowly he put down his cup and leaned back on the stool, away from the image, and he watched himself stretch and draw and change. In the chrome he turned chesty as a frog; his arms grew fantastically muscular. But his face had widened at the jaw, and pinched in at the temples, and his skull became a weaving cone that pointed upward toward infinity, and he was a pinhead.

Forward, just a little. There; stop. No, back a little. Now. Well, maybe. His face had corrected itself. Only, his neck was gone, and his body streaked away downward to a legless nothing. He was a head atop a wisp, and when he withdrew, he became again a pinhead and ape.

Very well, sit still. Be an ape.

Moon had fenced with the coffeepot before in a grim sort of amusement or, occasionally, in exasperation. He had discovered he might select an Olympic body, if with it he would accept the head of an idiot. Or he might keep his own head, provided he'd settle for the grotesque torso of a monster.

Wait a minute. If he were to get off the stool, stand at something of an angle, head inclined toward the pot, and body hunched in an arc? Well—

Once Carol and Hannah had surprised him at the game. His daughters adopted it happily. He remembered how absurdly irked he had been because they played it gaily. Like dancers they spun up to the pot, then away from it. They swirled their crackly ballerina petticoats, they curtsied and posed and tumbled their hair, they put their cheeks together and entwined their arms and screamed laughter at the macabre reflection which merged them into one fat two-headed child.

He shouldn't have exploded at them. But it had happened on a morning after he advanced an idea to the Mungers, then watched it wither on the table. He was thinking that the pot might know the truth of him; that he was, indeed, a curious specie, one of magnificent fragments coupled onto a malformed remainder.

Moon pushed the percolator away from him. "Bethel," he called, "what're you doing?"

"Coming," she answered from the bathroom.

He laid his left hand out, palm up and open, and scratched hard. He'd brought the mature old fungus home from the Pacific. The hand was rough and dry, it scaled off skin in dead flakes, it itched blood deep and always beyond reach. If you got the fungus in the Caribbean, its name was spic itch, and if you got it in the Pacific, it was jungle rot. Either way it was a nuisance, apt to recur for life. Any more, Moon didn't really mind. The fungus had come to him when he led a tough platoon, when manhood felt sure and rich and glorious because he never doubted it was there. Now, to itch and to scratch—it was somehow nostalgic, like the pleasant fondling of a souvenir.

John Remo rummaged out of a cabinet drawer his list of telephone numbers. He sat down at the table with it. During his months with June Munger—Jesus, they ran to nearly two years now—he had developed an order for contacting the Munger family. Heading his list, in the neatest script he could manage, was the name of Mrs. China Wallace. Still, Remo never began his calls with her. China, he thought, deserved good news the earliest and bad news the latest. If her heart must ache, then he intended it to ache the shortest possible time.

Originally, when the job was new, Remo had kept Spain

Munger's number at the top of the list. Then Remo met China, and Spain seemed to sink automatically to second place. Whenever Remo looked at the list, he felt a trifle disloyal. It was Spain who had hired him, back when even the lamp posts seemed to shrink from him; Spain who summoned him, quickly and courteously and before the Amarillo Police Department could finish wiping its chin from having spat him out.

That summer had been hot and gritty, so that the clean cool Estate offices struck Remo as a haven the moment he entered them. Remo had been heavily conscious of the stigma still so fresh upon him; he was just beginning to learn the skills of wearing it. At any rate, he had been prepared to tell the rich Mr. Munger his side of things, and to argue if need be. At least, he'd had time enough to identify his errors.

To begin with, Remo realized he had invited the cave-in of his career when, for no sensible reason, he offended that young news reporter. It was generally known that this sassy-eyed cub had nominated himself as the City Hall conscience, a matter Remo shouldn't have ignored. Further, after so many years in the public servant's glass house, Remo knew newspapers well enough; he knew how the prime mission of a paper becomes reprisal, once any tender ego on its staff has been wounded. But who would have guessed that a boy so green would be so well up on the code?

The vengeance broke swiftly. Remo spent a numbing hour with the chief. "Let's not be formal," the chief said, and as implement to this, he raised the long legs of the law and propped them on his desk, and from between his feet he said, "I'm sorry, John; damned sorry." Then the paper itself overtook Remo at his bus stop before he could get home. "Detective John Remo admitted to Chief Harold A. Ritchey today that for several years he has been taking various unclaimed articles from the police department's lost-and-found bin."

The mailed dismissal notice called it theft. Remo longed to tell Mr. Munger how the cataloguing and custody of things found had been his unpaid extra duty for a decade. Seldom was anything claimed, and to use what was useful was scarcely more than frugality. But "thief," they said. It put his mother sick. Erased, without any recounting, were his knife wounds and all the plodding years.

Spain Munger had waved the story away, unheard. Whether considerately or accidentally, Mr. Munger may have been wise. Remo realized that with no one to tell his tale to, the bite was draining out. Lately, he could think of Amarillo as just where home used to be.

He looked at his watch. It was almost nine, when TV would bring along Miss Frances and her *Ding-Dong* bell—no, this was Saturday and *Super Circus*. Either one could settle the happiest Munger for a while.

At the outset Remo had believed he might be a watchman, as titled. Spain directed him to tour the hundred-odd Munger sections "once in a while, please"; to make certain, Remo could only assume, that the land remained there unstolen. It confused him as to what banditry the family might fear among their oil wells. The derricks were gone. Mesh steel fences locked in the nodding gray pumping beams and the orange diesel engines that cranked them. On the Munger land, rabbits ran, the sky stayed high, and if the ground bleached out and cracked, well, the engines smoked and purred and kept jacking forty-gravity crude up from the deep brown dolomite, or gray lime, or the gray dolomite and granite washes of the buried Amarillo Mountains, and the Mungers got richer, and, it seemed to Remo, nothing else was happening.

A few times, Remo did tour the property. He used Brother's Cadillac, and had to cart Brother along. Shortly, Remo understood that a watchman's salary deducts as readily as a nurse's, and reveals much less.

With this, the job shook down. Keep Brother in hand. Guard him from notice. Be his friend, his cook, and treasurer. Be his valet, guide, and disciplinarian.

None of this had Spain ever spelled out. But once, the Munger chairman almost described a more serious facet of the assignment. It occurred on a summer Sunday, when China kissed her Beloved good-by, and he begged her to kiss him again and again while presenting his lips instead of his cheek.

Spain had watched, embarrassed and scowling.

"Uh, Mr. Remo, I think you, uh, grasp the symbols. I dislike to . . . well, you realize my brother is, uh, fully developed, physically speaking. There's, uh, impulse there, which is only natural. That's why, when Brother feels a little destructive, we must bear in mind his need of release. We mustn't let anything get out of hand, certainly. But I think if we allow a few, uh, outlets, then we'll be ninety per cent on the safe side. You must watch carefully, and never delay about calling us. . . ."

Remo smiled to himself. What would they think, if he told them of the "outlet" he had allowed Brother on some of the trips? There would be the day.

The TV boomed on deafeningly. World's greatest baby sitter, Bethel Mooney called it.

Remo got up and crossed to the telephone. He worked the tiny key in the cylindrical lock Spain had bought for the instrument. He gave the operator the number for the Mooney house.

Old Moon. Remo would be glad to see him.

Moon took the call on the kitchen extension. "Oh, hello, Remo. How was Dallas?"

"You know Dallas. Still a hoity-toity old woman."

"I didn't imagine you were back," Moon said. "The trip didn't last long."

"No. June changed his mind. Him and me seen the Cinerama, went and ate some fish at Jay's, and all of a sudden he decided that was a-plenty. We came on in last night."

"How's the new Cadillac?"

"Good. Runs good," Remo said. "Just like them others, before they was gutted. I swear it, Moon, I ain't letting him rip this one apart, I don't care how loud he howls."

Moon laughed.

"Say, Moon, have you seen *her* lately?"

"China? Sure."

Remo fumbled at it, then said, "Well, I was wondering. She wasn't feeling good, last time she was out here."

"She's all right. Want me to give her a message?"

"Go to hell, Moon. What I called for is your brother-in-law."

"Have you lost him?"

"No. Can't you hear that damned TV? He just got us into a little mess this morning. He got out early and kilt some chickens."

"That's nothing."

"He batted their heads off with his golf stick. I guess Spain'll call it a regular bloody orgy."

"Have you talked to Spain yet?"

"You're the first. Reckon there'll be a session?"

"What else?" Moon said. "I'd planned to play tennis tomorrow."

"I'm sorry, Moon, really am. But if you're coming out, how about bringing me a little something?"

Good old Remo. Moon said, "I didn't know Dallas had gone dry."

"It ain't; I just didn't figure the big slob was gonna want to leave so quick. I ain't got a drop on the place."

Bethel was there when he hung up. She had heard at least part. Her cheeks had already lost their color, which was almost no color at all. Like her sisters, Bethel had cheeks only slightly less pale than the rest of her.

"That—that was Mr. Remo on the phone, wasn't it?"

"Yes," Moon said. Suddenly he was uneasy about being undressed. "Don't get upset—"

"It's Brother!" She said it in belated fright.

"He isn't hurt or anything. He killed some chickens with his golf clubs, that's all."

Bethel turned away, so she might lean her hips against the cabinet, and she was visibly trembling. "He—he killed them all?"

"Just a few, I think."

Now her tears appeared, fading her eyes so that for an instant, he thought her almost deathly. She said, "Oh, that John Remo; he was supposed to get him away on a trip."

"They went, and they're back. Please, Beth, you're taking June too seriously."

She straightened, and he saw her delicate little knob of chin hardening. Thank God, there was nothing theatrical about his wife. The tears, the compassion, were painfully forthright. As he returned to his coffee, she frowned at him. "I wish you'd not say that to me again. Because someone is like Brother, you don't love them any less."

"Of course. I'm sorry. Are the kids awake?"

"No. All that late television. Is—is Mr. Remo phoning the others?"

"Said he was."

Her shoulders rose thinly, then dropped. Not to shed this new anguish, he thought, but more as if to stack it neatly atop all its predecessors. He wished he might help her.

"It's a small thing, Bethel—"

"Unless you hurry, Richard, you'll be very late at the store."

He grunted, surprised at this crashing curtain that fell so abruptly over another Munger crisis. Usually, she shut him away more gently. It seemed a clue. As she took down a cup for herself, he glanced aside at the shelf above the sink. It was there that Bethel, when a Mean Week lay upon her, kept her "mean pills." Out in plain sight, as if in fair warning to the household. Moon had come to watch for the white-capped brown bottle as if it were a tornado flag. It wasn't in place.

"I'm sure we should all go out tomorrow," she said.

"That will be fine," he tried to be sincere. "Carol loves it."

"Hannah, too," she said tightly.

Do not divide the children, she was saying. But if you must, you've already chosen Carol. Then, Hannah is mine. It struck him as senseless. He wished they might talk about it.

The silence, he thought, had magnified this thing about the girls. To him, it was simply that the kids were different people. Hannah, the eldest. Unique and strange, being her own guy. She let you take her or leave her, and if her way of it lacked pertness or charm, you learned to admire her for bearing plainness with a strength. This way, you loved her.

But Carol you loved undeviously. Carol was a sweet, coming replica of her Aunt China. People commented on this, almost from the day she was born. It was noticed, first, by China herself. China had come across town after the birth, staying with them a week to help out. At her every glimpse of the baby, China had clapped her hands in delight. That week, Moon and Bethel had laughed a lot; Bethel until it prolonged her soreness. It was wonderful, until China moved back home.

Moon wondered if Bethel had ever noticed how many stresses of their marriage dated from those days. Until Carol, if Moon's memory was dependable, there'd been no such thing as Mean Week. . . .

"We shouldn't be so lazy," Bethel said. "Didn't you intend hiring a stenographer or something today?"

"There's a woman coming in at noon."

"Richard—you will be sure and get in touch with Spain, won't you? I mean, before you do anything definite?"

"I'll get in touch with Spain."

Bethel looked at him directly, her eyes slightly reddened now from the tears. "Dear," she said gently, "I hope I haven't put you off-temper this morning."

Moon braced his head with his hands and looked down into his cold cup. "No," he said.

Bethel began breakfast in her deft, wasteless way. He watched her lay an electric skillet with bacon. She loaded the toaster, put butter to melting, started a fresh pot of coffee, cleared the bar of his full ashtray and spilled ashes, set their places with the glossless, costly black crockery which she determinedly believed gave tone to her home's otherwise austere habits, and she seemed to perform it all simultaneously and in a tall blond efficiency that permitted nothing to rattle or clang or spatter.

"You might go get dressed," she said. "If the girls get up, they needn't catch you at breakfast half-naked."

Moon tasted his sour coffee. Before Remo called, he thought

he heard the dainty gnashings of her Lady Sunbeam. It made him watch her, now, with a curiosity he was ashamed of.

The latest luncheon was responsible. One of those silly downtown meals he had with Frank Wallace and Sid Glass once in a while. Munger-in-law meals, they called them, for Munger-in-law talk. It was Frank—yes, naturally Frank—who said the thing about Texas Munger. Moon had not forgotten it.

There was a secret about their wives' eldest sister, Frank said. Of course, Texas was no freemartin; she wasn't committed to hypos of B-12; her wardrobe wasn't running to slacks; nor was she winking at other women. Nothing like that, said Frank. It was simply that Texas needed, as he understood it, to shave her upper lip occasionally. A little shave every few weeks, boy.

Moon and Sid had stared at each other.

Frank said, "Makes me wonder about my own Mrs. Wallace," and he laughed hollowly. Then, embarrassed with himself, he had raised his beer, exaggeratedly, and finished: "To all the sisters Munger!"

Moon had been too outraged to argue. He had gotten up and left. He did not believe Frank, of course. But it amazed him that he could clearly visualize it with Texas. She the eldest, the loneliest. Almost as quickly, Moon could imagine it, even, for the brash-voiced Laska Glass. But never, never for China; no matter if Frank should know her the best. And never for Bethel.

He wished the ugly thing wouldn't keep coming to his mind.

His wife was moving about the kitchen, the worry of Brother oddly soft on her face. She looked, suddenly, quite pretty.

Bethel's Munger-light hair lay waved in perfect place; her skin shone clear and fair, no longer dusted by the freckles he had seen at their wedding. She had made her face with the thinnest lipstick, the least powder, so that she looked free and natural. There had been a few closer times when he could tease her about this, could accuse her of being a "holy-roller" at heart.

To Moon's eye, most exceptionally tall women looked awkward. But beneath the pink satin wrapper, Bethel's long strides impressed him as a curious grace. True, his wife's breast line had lowered; her stomach had arched out slightly through the years since Carol. Yet, in general, he thought this less flaw than improvement.

"Richard, I do wish you'd stop scratching your hand."

"Itches," he said.

"If you'd go to that new skin doctor—you know, the one who helped Laska's allergy."

"It's no allergy. Jungle rot is a minor leprosy, I think."

"Oh, sweetie," she shook her head and smiled.

She served the black plates, put new coffee in fresh cups, and sat down opposite him. Moon was grateful that the children still slept. The way Hannah chewed, with her lips wide apart— the sound of it could, on tedious mornings, grind him to the bone, a reaction he was ashamed of. Besides, he wished to talk.

"Since we'll be going to The Old Place—" he began.

"Let's don't discuss Brother now."

"That wasn't it. I was thinking of the idea for doing something with The Camera House. The board will be together. Do you want to hear about it?"

She nodded; she folded her hands beneath her chin in the manner of her brother Spain, and she listened intently, so that as he spoke he grew excited.

Moon operated the camera shop with China's husband. Or rather, with Frank Wallace (he must stop thinking of Frank as having no name of his own, or of Sid Glass as just "Laska's husband": too often, Moon himself had been only the man who married Bethel Munger). The little business, now more than a year old, was the fifth for Frank since the war, and the third try for Moon. Until recently, Moon had allowed it to bore him.

They stocked cameras and projectors, film and flash bulbs; light meters, enlargers, Strobes, carrying cases, tripods—all the costly, slow-moving gadgets that disposed toward a deficit business, which The Camera House was. Moon and Frank could lock up at noon, treat themselves to a two-hour lunch at the Downtown Club, and be reasonably sure they'd not lost a sale.

36

Like all Munger ventures, The Camera House was incorporated. Its stock was held in equal portion by the Munger heirs, Brother June included. The result was a board in common with such giants as Panhandle Green Petroleum, Big Plains Investment, and Grassland Enterprises. Just as with Sid Glass's immaculate little dog clinic, The Camera House met its considerations in the Munger conference chamber, solemnly, formally, off an agenda that strewed the small affairs among the million-dollar decisions. People could speak wittily of this, Moon knew; his retail neighbors enjoyed chuckling over it.

Despite everything, Moon did not believe that the shop had to be futile. In disregard of Frank, he had set out to prove it. Now, for more than a month, he had worked every day and most evenings. He lost weight, he retired his "pandemonium" sports jackets for the most reserved of his suits, he felt good. He put in bids on equipment for the schools, he dropped in on camera clubs. He took cautious amounts of newspaper space and laboriously composed appealing copy.

Thus far, The Camera House had not rallied. But he had his idea.

"Have you mentioned it to Spain?" Bethel said.

"I haven't been ready, until now. You know we have all that unused space in the back of the building. I want to put in darkrooms and processing equipment. Duplicators and printers and an editing machine, for movies."

Moon gave her an interval; he watched her dip a piece of toast in her coffee, a habit she sometimes laughed about as "pre-oil."

"With the equipment," he said, "we could process these business documentaries, the game films for football coaches, the home movies. People send all that to Dallas now. I've checked around, Beth. I know we can get some of that business. For about thirty thousand, besides the salary of a technician—"

Bethel whistled, as if involuntarily.

"It isn't so much money," he was hurrying now, "and the return will be fast. If you could get the board to do something, I'd meet with the school trustees Monday night. They're about to renew their football film contract at Dallas. I could get that, I think, as a starter."

She said nothing; she looked at him with a look that was surprise, affection, and fear. He had seen it often, and it always made him desperate; it transformed them, somehow, into a set of wary duelists.

"Will you tell them about it?" he said.

"Of course, Richard. But it is such short notice, and since you've said nothing at all to Spain. . . ."

Moon watched her lift her cup, and he wished to get wildly angry. It seemed a time to fight and win, for the brown bottle wasn't out.

If Moon had learned slowly, he had learned his wife well. Bethel was a chemistry set. Self-cycled, self-catalyzing. Since Carol, there were times with her, and then there were other times. Whatever he did nowise altered it.

Through twenty days of a month, Bethel was agreeable to live with. She loved him with an eagerness, almost like a starvation, and she let him know it. She lived the good days actively and seriously. She indulged the children. Watching her arrange their hair, or fit their beanpole figures into starchy new dresses, Moon could feel sudden flashes of attraction to her and relax in them. But always there had to follow the other days.

Bethel herself had given this time its name. She seemed to have despaired of coping with its terrors. She did still take, unsecretively, the pink capsules the doctor had provided. At least she had developed no hypocrisy. Bethel confessed readily that hers was an extreme delicacy.

She would awaken one morning with the lines deepened in her forehead, her pale brows pinched together, her nails bitten. She'd neglect her grooming. Tolerance, reason, even pride would have fled during sleep. Instead, there was slovenliness and a depression which could become an incredible wrath. In Mean Week, the mere act of speaking to Bethel might be accepted as an attack. She construed everything, immediately, as criticism of her talents as wife or mother or housekeeper.

38

Carol might report, "Mother, there's a hole coming in my school shoes," and Bethel would snap back with bewildering vehemence, "Well, I can't get you new ones tonight; my Lord, you know the stores aren't open at this hour!" Or Moon might suggest, "If you don't feel well, let's stay home this evening." And she would counter, "That suits me, Richard; I hope you don't think I'm heartbroken because you detest being seen with me!"

If China and Frank or anyone else dropped in, Bethel would turn surprisingly bright and talkative, only to lapse into a raw silence the instant they were gone. At first, Moon thought this vicious. It seemed inconceivable that he should be the last person she could be civil to. But once, when he put this to her, she shouted that if she couldn't abandon pretense with her own husband, then she couldn't do so with anyone; that she was sick and tired of making a lifetime act of joy and singing. Although Moon couldn't quite understand, it did humble him. He accepted Mean Week more generously, for a while.

When Bethel first began her pills, Moon thought her gloomy persecution lessened. But recently the drug seemed useless. In his discouragement, Moon let his temper strike a crescendo like her own. Sometimes he felt just that his wife needed to be grabbed and choked until the helling was out of her. The notion left him feeble with regret.

When a Mean Week was past, they went at the cautious diplomacy of making up. It occurred as regularly as the gas bill. Ultimately, Bethel would cry, she would beg his pardon, she would try to describe how helpless she had been. "I know, and it's all right," he would say. Just chemistry, they both knew. But the knowledge got pushed away when the next siege was on; it diminished none of the tension Bethel laid over the house, it helped neither of them at enduring.

Moon had learned to forecast this wretchedness by the calendar; yet he couldn't teach himself to expect it. Each time was the first. During the good days, it seemed all Mean Weeks had gone permanently into the past. Then the cycle would catch them uninsulated, and he would sink beside her in the morass, and blame himself for it all. Even thinking about it— and he shouldn't be, not now.

Bethel leaned across the table to light the cigarette he'd been holding. "Forgive me, Richard. These things about Brother are always such a shock."

"It's all right." He looked at her in a way he hoped wasn't pleading. "Will you go to bat for me, Beth?"

"You know I will." She smiled. "Spain will be startled, I think. He hates sudden things."

Moon looked at his watch and got up. It struck him he had achieved something. He felt almost humble, and he wished he'd not sat so long in just his underwear. He started for the bedroom.

"Richard—"

He turned. Swiftly, poppingly, Bethel kissed his mouth. She had come up to him without rising on tiptoe, or even stretching. He responded a little clumsily, confused at how abruptly they felt close.

He left to get dressed. It irritated him that he never had the words to magnify a tender moment.

III

On her cheerier days, The Old Girl, as she was called, might think of herself as Key Personnel of the Munger Estate. She the hub, the anchor, home plate. But unassumingly.

There were others, she conceded, perhaps claiming as much for themselves. Offhand: Mr. Williams-the-lawyer, whose firm was so absorbed by the Munger affairs that he had moved his offices into the Munger suite. And Mr. Williams-the-consulting-engineer who, with his staff of brisk young men, had been installed in Estate offices also. Or the unhealthy Mr. Jacobson who passed out the salary checks benignly, and usually with a reminder that Mr. Munger had entrusted him as "a sort of a watchdog of the whole."

They amused The Old Girl with their need. For herself, she was secure.

Some in the office could see that she had attained safety through simple country virtues. She was loyal; fiercely so. And she possessed real common sense. These were qualities that Mr. Spain Munger appreciated.

Her name was Corinne Northington, said the sign on her giant steel desk. The desk stood in domination of the reception room, like a battlement before the restricted inner offices. Aside from shuttling callers in and out according to an inviolable appointment calendar, The Old Girl carried off a staggering mass of secondary chores.

She managed the small PBX board. She typed a letter, a pipeline or crude-sale contract, a prospectus on secondary-recovery, a production report, or a petition to the stubborn Railroad Commission of Texas whenever it threatened a cutback in the production allowable, and each she did flawlessly.

She operated the aluminum blinds on the west windows, regulating the vanes six times daily at almanac intervals, thus defeating the sunglare which otherwise might have reached into the third floor of the Baldwin Building to stare all the rich green color out of the Munger carpet. She licked postage stamps, she bit her lip at file clerks whose talk got too gay. She saw to it that not one of the expensive IBMs went uncovered overnight, although this should have been Mr. Jacobson's responsibility.

Often, The Old Girl carried in Mr. Munger's noontime sandwich and vanilla malted.

She was short and haplessly dumpy. Sensibly, she knew it. This released her to choose styles planned especially for dumpy women. If never attractive, she looked forever neat. She had arrived at forty quite gray; calm, and aside from the Munger Estate, unattached. She regretted almost nothing. Her job was enough.

As the first employee selected after the reorganization by the heirs, The Old Girl held indisputable seniority. In lieu of any pay advantage, this gratified her career instincts. It meant she could walk into Mr. Munger's presence whenever there was any need. She glowed from the intimacy.

Some days, when lunch was "in" instead of "out," she got an invitation to have pimento cheese with the chairman and president at his desk. Then there was nothing difficult about being homely.

Once—and she'd not forgotten it—she had heard China's husband, that Frank, make a crude joke about her. "Hell," he said, "she doesn't go to the beauty shop; she sees her embalmer."

Her reaction had been only a half-related thought that avenged her very satisfactorily. She thought, I know more about Estate business than he ever will; he's a fool who knows nothing at all, and indeed, if it came to it, I could run the thing, and he could not, nor could any of those sidelined, puttery appendages—yes, not even Mr. Mooney, however handsome he is.

Being sensible, The Old Girl did not allow her competence to become an excuse for pretensions. Country bred, country reared, and just "down-to-earth countrified," as she freely admitted, she meant to stay that way. These were proud factors. They had become so years ago, when Mr. Munger lauded her to a visitor as "a sort of real good old country girl."

It gave her only a small shock. She saw how accurately the appraisal tagged her, because it was by Mr. Munger, because she had her common sense. It welded the essence of her appearance to the best of her character. Thus thought of, it was complimentary. A shortened version of Mr. Munger's reference stuck, since she allowed it to. If it was a nickname, she wore it as a title. Except for an instance or two when she still regarded bachelor men a bit predatorily, she had never resented it.

Presently, Mr. Munger rang for her. She was at work on a hangnail. She sprang from her chair, sweeping up a note pad and a pair of the stubby pencils which testified to her thrift on behalf of the Estate, and she hurried down the corridor. Behind her the buzzer continued insistently. She had a premonition. She walked faster. She patted her big bun of hair before she opened his door.

Spain Munger's fleshless elbows were propped; he had his white bony hands interlaced beneath his chin with his head's weight upon them. The unfortunate pale blue eyes, which had deprived him of service during the war and nowadays restricted his driver's license, squinted out through thick gold-rimmed glasses. She noted how his mouth set straight and thin, how his large jawbones had spread angularly.

"Sit down, Miss Northington."

She snatched the remnants of his early "in" lunch from his desk, dropped them in the trash. She felt at once a coldness, and she began to tremble.

"Uh, Miss Northington. . . ."

She sat down quickly, stabbed one short pencil into her hair, poised the other over her pad, and leaned ahead to listen. There were situations in which Mr. Munger's speech, while remaining precise in detail, grew structurally unclear, and she despised ever troubling him for repeats. He wore one of his loose, double-breasted suits. The shoulders overhung him like eaves, failing, nevertheless, to give him quite enough width. The thin blond hair was ruffled. His gaze, pitiably faded, she thought, and but dimly interpretable behind the dense lenses, was aiming past her at the door as if to seal it more tightly.

She said, "Yes, sir?"

"Uh, you won't need to make notes. If you've time, I thought we might just visit for a moment."

Her mind sorted quickly through the morning's calls, until it laid finger on the one which must have disturbed him. That gruff Mr. Remo, calling from The Old Place—what could have happened out there?

"Uh, one thing," Mr. Munger was saying, "the directors will meet out in the country tomorrow. Would you prepare an agenda—you can discuss it with Mr. Williams-the-lawyer—in case the board wants a full day's work?"

"Yes sir. I'd be glad to keep the minutes, if—"

"No, thank you. My sister Laska will, uh, take down whatever is necessary."

The Old Girl was thinking of Brother June. She knew only enough to pity him, or at times to hate him for the hurt he caused Mr. Munger. She had always thought a nice private institution. . . .

Mr. Munger cleared his throat.

The Old Girl swallowed. Here it comes, she thought, and all day I've known it was building.

"Uh, you get out and about, don't you?"

"Well, yes sir. Some, of course."

"—I mean, among the town people, and all. Since you work —well, since you are with us, Miss Northington, and let's see, you have been, more than fifty per cent of your professional life, isn't that about on the nose? Uh, now, I'd like you to be perfectly frank with me."

Miss Northington moistened her lips. God willing, she'd do better than last time.

"Surely you, uh, hear things," Mr. Munger went on, tortured by this necessity. His pale narrow look held on the door. "There's a certain amount of idle talk about everyone and I think you understand, Miss Northington, how it's, uh, practical in business to be cognizant of public opinion, don't you agree?"

She blinked. "Oh, yes, Mr. Munger."

"Well, uh, as I said, I've very little on my mind. I simply thought we might visit. Uh, first though, I wanted to ask: is anything disturbing you? I mean, are things going ship-shape?"

"Everything is fine, thank you, sir."

If only he'd not get so white.

"I am obligated to stay in touch, of course. On whatever people may be saying about my—about the directors. Anything that has crystallized, I mean. Uh, you know I like to think of our people as reliable sounding boards of other circles. Of course, if nothing has come to you . . . ?"

The Old Girl ached with loyalty, with the sorrowed pang of heart she felt when Mr. Munger suffered. She looked down at her folded hands, knowing it ridiculous to expect she'd find an answer written on them.

She hadn't heard anything, not this quickly, about this new problem. But she did hear things. Ugly, envious things. "Trouble is, those Mungers try too hard; try to buy without spending . . . odd ducks, you know, hiding that idiot out on the farm, and say, if he ain't a character . . . dumped it all in their laps, that drunken old man did; bet they'd never have made a dime on their own, and say, did you hear how that Spain hap-

pened to go to college? They tell me the old man noticed one
day that he had ten million in the bank, so he told his wife to
pick out the brightest one and send him off to school. . . ."

The Old Girl shuddered. Her weekend visits down home,
even, could be awful. People came around to pick at her
bluntly, expecting her to tell them a tale.

"Is it true that they live in plain little FHA houses, for God's
sake? Which is maybe all right; I remember when that bunch
of dirty kids went around with boils all over them and rats in
their hair. And my cousin, she used to share her lunch with a
couple of them girls at school. Bet they forgot that, the day they
got rich. And those in-laws, they give me a kick. Like a bunch
of baby kittens trying to nurse off a lion. . . ."

"Uh, naturally," said Mr. Munger, "if there's nothing—"

"Oh, no. I mean yes. I was only remembering. Actually, I
don't hear a great deal. I stay home a lot; I have some parakeets
to tend. I think I've mentioned them."

"Yes."

"But what I have heard, I'd say, is just fine."

"Fine?"

"Yes sir. Nice, you know."

"You don't think of anything in particular? Specifics, Miss
Northington; there's your gizmo here."

He hadn't unfastened his gaze; it seemed he'd not moved a
muscle since she entered.

"It's hard to—well, I'm afraid I don't really listen much to
talk. But I get the impression people think highly of all our
directors. Just from little things, really."

At last he had turned his eyes from the door and was looking
at her. The pale light of him thanked her, but reproachfully.
She felt ill over the lie now suspended between them.

As though to signal the end, Mr. Munger brought his long
hands down. One thin white thumb riffled the pages of the
new *Business Week*. The Old Girl was devastated. She yearned
to run, to hide in the file room and cry.

"Thank you, Miss Northington," he said. "I, uh, hope I've

not pooped up too much of your time. By the bye—we'll have some dictation a bit later."

"You just ring!"

If it will help, Mr. Munger, I'll die dead for you. This minute. Flat on this floor.

She paused just outside, holding his door lingeringly ajar. She pondered returning. On any pretext. To repair it for him. Except, where were the means? She drew the door toward her, gradually, reluctant to shut him off alone. Through the last crack, she heard his voice.

It whispered, distinguishably. The Old Girl was startled. It sounded as if Mr. Munger, who never swore, had sworn; as if he had said, "Oh damn, a mattock is like a hoe."

The Old Girl realized she was straying dangerously from her forte of common sense. She had hurried back to her desk without poise; she sat down trembling. She had used her handkerchief, almost before Mr. Jacobson's prying eyes shifted back to his journals. She would be miserable for days.

The switchboard purred.

She let it call a second time. Then The Old Girl was picking up Mr. Munger's plug, tenderly; pushing it into the jack, compassionately, her sturdy fingers touching the bell key lightly; and she rang him three times, softly, and she hoped, oh she hoped, that in the gentle bell he could hear the mighty pulse-throb of devotion as it rumbled about in her breast.

IV

Moon crept his exhausty, three-year-old Chevvy into Polk
Street, "the world's best lighted," according to the city's new
traffic engineer. Then he turned left, against a No-Left-Turn
sign, and The Camera Shop came into view.

High up, blazed across the dingy, sixty-foot white-stucco
front, a red sign declared the establishment. The building, a
half-block off Polk Street and owned by the Mungers, was
cleanly faced but otherwise decrepit. Since the sudden flight of
retail business to the new suburban centers, the Estate found
it unrentable. Thus it had been available as quarters, as the
arena, for each of the ventures Moon and Frank Wallace undertook jointly.

Each successive attempt, Moon had to concede, had col-
lapsed more readily than its predecessor. It hurt, and he cared.
Yet Frank seemed not to give a damn. Often, Moon believed his
partner was disappointed that The Camera House hadn't closed
overnight. Frank said nearly as much.

"Good Lord, Moon, get this through your head, and ask Sid,
if you think it's just me. Ask him; he'll tell you we're intended
to mess up. The primary function of The Camera House is to

keep us boys out of mischief. Hell, it's a nursery! The only contribution Spain expects from us is some convenient losses. You might as well wake up. We're in the Munger Estate tax department, boy, and that's it."

If drinking, Frank projected his theory even further. Not the Mungers-in-law, but the blood Mungers to do and to be. Moon, Sid, and himself to be boxed off in make-believe careers, to dangle in harmless storage and there, perhaps, to exalt the true Mungers by comparison. Most of the time, Moon couldn't disagree. But unlike Frank, he meant to do one thing well in spite of them. He had told Spain as much at the close of The Camera House's first fiscal year.

He and Frank had sat together at the foot of the glistening conference table, aware of the lawn-colored carpet, the leather chairs that squeaked like saddles, watching Spain Munger read through their report. When Spain looked up, Frank said, "Bad, ain't it?"

Spain hadn't been in the frame of mind to regard anything lightly, yet he had begun elaborately to excuse them. He recited the percentages of new-business failures, he thought The Camera House still had a place in "the big picture," he wasn't so startled by the overhead, although overhead was plainly the giz, he could see. "Uh, if the board agrees, we won't call it a flopper for a while yet—"

It had set Moon into an argument for freedom, one that became a tirade, so that Bethel cried with humiliation when he drove her home. Then, as if in peace offering, Spain had suggested they hire a helper. Someone "all-around," he said; typist, dictationist, bookkeeper, and clerk.

Moon and Frank hadn't tried to convince each other they needed assistance in their daily inactivity. They had agreed, however, if for different reasons. Frank thought having a third person around might make the idle days more tolerable, might keep Moon and himself from driving each other nuts. Moon thought someone would be needed, later, if his idea survived the board.

They would consider it tomorrow. Immediately, he dreaded

the decision. Except, maybe this time Bethel sensed how badly he needed a project, how miserable it was to make a career of drinking coffee.

Moon swung the car into a one-way alley, shocked it across an iron manhole, cut the wheels hard and screeched into his parking stall behind the store. He left the Chevvy quickly, as if to elude his mood, and admitted himself through the barnlike alley door.

His heels clicked hollowly in the empty semigloom of the building. He walked on toward the lights up front. A thin partition sliced off the shop from the dusty space behind, and on his hook there, he hung topcoat and hat.

"Eeyo," Frank Wallace greeted him.

Frank leaned in the doorway of his plyboard office, identical and adjacent to Moon's, and he held a can of beer at waist level.

"You're going to get caught with that stuff," Moon said. "We people are United Drys."

Frank laughed as he led Moon back into his office. "*I* people am a practicing wet," he said. "And in a pinch, I can plead bad influences. You're late."

"I guess you've unlocked the doors?"

Frank sat down behind his gray steel desk, a replica of all others the Mungers had purchased. The soft black top of it was clean, aside from pen set and calendar, flex-necked pod lamp, a pack of Pall Malls, copies of *Male* and *Stag*, and a recently begun jigsaw puzzle. "I've even had a customer. Two rolls of one-twenty. Gad, man, we're made!"

"I don't feel funny today, Frank. Give me some coffee."

Wallace swiveled about, toward the tiny corner shelf and its hotplate and pot. "What is it, hell week at the Mooneys'?"

Moon smarted. Ill-consideredly he had talked to Frank one day about Bethel. It seemed it might help if he could discover that all women—no, not all women (hadn't he been thinking specifically of pretty China?)—suffered such critical cycles. He had probed, in faith there'd be a negative answer. A Mean Week by China was less likely than sunrise in the west. But Frank hadn't said. Rather, he had merely adopted Bethel's chronics as a fair piece for conversation. Trigometrics, Frank thought fun to call it. Moon had vowed never to tell Wallace anything again.

Scooting down in the extra chair, he held in both hands the hot mug Frank had passed him. The office indicated his partner was feeling individual today. Besides the defiant beer, Frank had his interior decorations in place.

Mounted on a maple plaque and hooked on the rear wall was the double-barreled shotgun. Stock, barrels, receiver, the whole weapon gleamed an enameled ivory-white. The gilt lettering read, "Custom Shotgun, for Formal Weddings."

To Frank it was a thigh-beater. He managed to have it hung when any salesman was due in. But by various guises which Moon could recognize, Frank made certain none of the Mungers saw it. The gun vanished if one of them, even China, threatened a call.

Without turning to see, Moon knew that Frank's supreme joke would be on the wall behind him. Like the shotgun, this went up and came down according to who was expected. Frank hung it just inside his door, so that a stranger might be preparing to leave before being staggered by it. There was an ornate Italian frame, and in it a large color print of Walter Sallman's "Head of Christ." The perfect face, the upraised blue eyes, looked away left and upward, as if to avoid knowledge of the inscription in the lower right corner. Scrawled there in brash red ink were the words, "To Frank, with love, J. C."

Moon couldn't bear a direct look at the picture. It caused his neck to crawl. Initially, he'd thought this a part of the Presbyterianism he had absorbed, on the Munger impetus, since the war. Partly, this was true. But underneath his horror at the blasphemy, Moon resented the thing as a too intimate exposure. The picture offered open view of Frank's soul, displaying indecently the only secret of one man that other men ought never see.

His brother-in-law was idling, now, with the one-thousand-piece puzzle. China's husband was short, gray, partly bald, addicted to pills and diets from having treated his stomach like a garbage pail. He wore rimless, pink-tinted glasses and double-breasted suits disguising the slump of his middle. His face was a mesh of broken red veins. Except for his careful grooming, Moon thought, Frank would have looked an outright reprobate.

Frank had begun as a pharmacist. For twenty years he ran, with good conventionality, a sidestreet drugstore. The dingy cubbyhole with its fly-specked tin lining and crowded shelves and wobbly overhead fans had accounted for Frank's life into his middle years, the important moments of which were checked off methodically on the soiled pages of a big Cardui calendar.

At Wallace's there was a liquor counter, and you could charge it, which was why Old Cecil Munger, back before the oil, always went there. It was how, too, Frank Wallace got the chance to give an occasional ice-cream cone to the angelic little girl named China, for sometimes the old man had her in tow.

Amid the smells of Lysol and dust and fresh ink on the one-cent-sale streamers, smells that never quite strangled the place but always threatened to, Frank did well. He dispensed wan Cokes from a sputtering old fountain, he issued Doan's and Sheiks and Carter's Little Livers to customers who liked him. He sent in his Chamber dues each January 2d, he tacked up gaudy flags at Tri-State Fair time, he exhibited good-quality trusses and knee braces and hot-water bottles in his windows. He could shoot high scores on his pinball machines. One year, he fought, victoriously, the clique of doctors who demanded prescription kickbacks. One winter night, he took a cold-blooded beating rather than surrender laudanum tablets to a brace of young thugs.

Inspectors always found Frank's narcotics records in order, despite the marginal character of his neighborhood. Frank himself was usually in order. After closing each night, he drank one beer. He talked of eventual retirement to the New Mexico trout streams, even though he didn't own a pole. And if he talked a good deal about women, it was no more than expected from an aging single man. Talk was as far as it went, until China finished high school.

Among his daughters, Cecil Munger intended only China to marry. The others grew tall and large-boned; in their father's own view, just "hicky as hell." Anyone playing sweet with them would be prospecting for oil. But lovely China—for her, the sooner the better, he thought. He wished for his jewel someone dully safe, even fatherly; somebody set up on his own legs. Frank Wallace fitted, but no one imagined he could win her. He was twice China's age. Inexplicably, the girl wanted to marry him.

Frank stretched and beamed across Moon at the Christ's head. Poor ass, Moon thought. He thinks the gun and the picture express him. Inside the pickets of his own private void, they make him feel creative, not quite reduced by the Mungers. But they aren't really his doing. He swiped the gun idea from a sporting-goods store across town, and knows he did. He remembers, surely, that he first saw the autographed Christ in a YMCA dormitory. Moon shrugged. He thought the irreverent gags less strange than the fact that although Frank had China, he frequently would pause at department-store windows to watch the mannequins being dressed.

Frank sniffed. "Hey, Moon. Got me some new films this morning."

"You pig."

Frank grinned. "Care to see 'em? I haven't run them yet myself."

"You don't enjoy looking at those things, Frank."

"No. Hell, they nearly make me sick."

"Suppose they are traced to you?"

Frank stirred the coffee he would try atop his beer. "Who you worried about? Me, or Mrs. Wallace?"

"You aren't easy to get along with, Frank."

Wallace grinned. "How about the films? These are the ones they showed at the VFW stag the other night. I got them for a week. I hear they aren't so damned ancient as most; you can tell the new ones by the hair-do's."

Moon blew across the lip of his cup, watching the steam drift toward his partner and vanish.

"Not interested?"

"No."

Frank took off his glasses and rubbed the dents they had dug in his nose. "Well, if you'll look out for the front, I'll try them after a while. Hey, how about your plans for the back room?"

"Talked to Bethel, that's all."

"What'd she say?"

"Nothing."

"You'll lose this deal, Moon. We lose them all, until the trust period is up—and maybe then."

"We'll see."

Frank sat in thought, as if burrowing back into his seniority. Then he grinned, more daringly than his years, which were fifty-three, and he said, "I'll bet you twenty."

"I won't have twenty until next week."

"Ought to save your money, boy. Put something aside each week."

They sat drinking, raising their cups together, lowering them together. Like shadows of each other, Moon noted, and neither of them pleased by it.

"You heard about Brother?"

Frank nodded. "China phoned. Tomorrow it's dinner on the ground and all-day singing. That's how it goes, huh?"

Moon put down his cup and looked at his watch. "Wonder why our girl hasn't shown up?"

"Oh, her. She called, she'll be a little late. Which reminds me; you want to talk to her, Moon? I don't. I get no kick out of offering somebody forty-five lousy bucks a week."

"I'll talk to her. What does she sound like?"

"Like a stenographer, I guess. And kind of loud; maybe she'll weigh two hundred pounds." Frank stood up. "Come on. Let's lock the door and see some of the pictures. Joe Hontz saw them at the VFW; he says there's one deal with six of 'em, three men and three girls—"

54

"You make me sick, Frank."

Wallace shrugged and bent to unlock the desk drawer. He took out two battered reel cans, then put one of them back. "I'll thread this one up. You come on back when you're ready."

Moon sat on alone.

China's husband kept a projector, out of store stock, in the rear. He would set it up on a packing case, projecting his 35-mm. "medicals" onto a patch of wall that he had scrubbed clean with Bon-Ami. He conceded that the surrounding frame of grime made his spot look tellingly like what it was. He had pledged himself to cleaning the rest of the wall, but hadn't gotten to it, and probably never would.

Dozens of times, Moon had seen him sitting beside the crate in his cheap cane chair, hunching intently forward, a hand on the machine so he might reverse it to rerun the "good parts." Often his lips would move, as though he talked to himself, and now and then he wheezed through his nose like a crotchety old man.

Moon heard the switches click and the projector began whirring. He got up, left the office without a glance at the Christ's head, walked past his own cubicle and through the partition. He made a turn around the shop, standing for a time at the front, watching the busy people hustle by.

"Hey, Moon," Frank yelled. "Lookit this!"

Moon lounged against a counter, scratching his palm with the view-finder on a Czech miniature camera they should never have stocked. I'll count to ten, he thought, slowly, and before I finish, someone will come in. Customer, tax collector, loafer. Anybody.

Frank called again. His voice may have carried out into the street. Moon swore. He folded the bell arm down over the door and tensely, dreadfully, he walked back toward Frank's wedge of smutty light.

The woman came in as if The Camera House were a place to hide; as though without turning her head, she kept a watch back over her shoulder. She forced Moon's attention instantly;

he watched hard as she put both hands behind her to close the door. She met his gaze matter of factly, then came directly toward him. She did not weigh hundreds of pounds.

She moved choppily on the precarious balance of remarkably high heels, her short quick strides handicapped in a skirt scarcely more full than a sleeve. A gray fox fur hugged her neck tightly. The day was mild, but the fur was not enough wrap. It seemed to be trying to garrote her with luxury while, most probably, she was freezing.

"Mr. Mooney?" she said.

He thought her familiar, yet knew he'd never seen her before. He would not have forgotten the amazing figure, the Indianish face.

"Yes. You must be Mrs.—let's see, Mrs. Byrd, isn't it?"

She smiled. "That's the usual approximation. It's Birdsong."

"I'm sorry."

"Oh, I should apologize. For being late. It's not a good way to start," she smiled. "But so far, I've had a hell-acious day."

She had paused a few feet short of him, so that he had full view of her. She unclamped the fox teeth, letting the stole skid to her shoulders and off them, and she caught it at the last instant with her elbows. With the oath, or maybe it was just a half-oath, the gesture became a demonstration. Her eyes seemed plainly inviting him to inspect her, yet she appeared almost sorrowful.

She wore the dull black skirt new-look long and so close he could see the seams of a girdle where it crossed the highest rise of her thighs. Above, a crew-necked jersey blouse, also black, and stretched to semitransparency over incredibly large breasts. Blatant, wenchy, he thought; aware of her assets. He discovered then that her eyes had been waiting on him; their brittle light confirming that he had behaved just as she intended.

He disliked her.

"I could come another time, Mr. Mooney."

"Oh, of course not. Let's go back to the office." He signaled her through the partition.

Ahead of him, her heels clicked crisply on the asphalt tile, the ankles wavering gracefully as each springolator touched down. The resulting small shocks put a motion in her breasts, and it struck Moon that he must have thought, until now, that they were unreal.

"Where?"

"Through the door, and turn right."

Even on such heels, she was many inches shorter than Bethel. He could look down on the jet hair; dyed hair, worn bushy and too long like a showgirl's and, together with the weight of her bosom, giving him the idea that soon she must topple over.

"Here?" she asked over her shoulder.

"This is all right. Mine is the other office. But my partner is out, and we keep the coffee in here." He held the chair for her. It pleased Moon, then, to begin knocking her down.

The eyes were set too close, under brows plucked into an entirely fraudulent arch. Her lips might have been a boy's, but had been painted on much wider. She was masked under pancake make-up so thick that he supposed she might peel it off like tape. Even so, at her nose, a hint of oiliness showed through. Her cheekbones were high and too large. Despite the rouge's careful distraction from them, they stood out like a squaw's.

Not a beautiful woman, then, he concluded. Not even pretty. Just an astounding body, with a tough or vicious or frightened somebody snared uneasily inside.

She crossed her legs. Her perfume smelled strong but unsweet. Trouble with this woman, he thought, she's aware of her own details; she might have appraised herself in some odd-shaped coffeepot.

"Coffee?" he said. "I'm afraid it's getting stale."

She shook her head.

"Well, we're interested in a sort of all-around person, Mrs. Birdsong. Someone who can type, take a little dictation, do what bookkeeping we have."

"I understood that, from the agency."

"There'll be some time up front, too. We don't have a large

business. Just cameras and film and stuff, as you see. I know, a lot of stenographers object to being shunted around."

"I clerked several years, once. I don't mind."

He still disliked her. Perhaps, for a job of doing nothing, you should hire someone unappealing. "Good," he said. "If you'll excuse me a minute."

He went to his own office and got the four-page application form which Spain and his board had made standard throughout the Munger companies. When he returned, she was staring up at Frank's shotgun.

Frank would have been disappointed. The woman appeared neither offended nor amused.

"Your full name, if you don't mind," Moon said.

"You'll not believe it."

"I'll believe it."

"Billie Ted Birdsong. Maiden name, Ingalls." As he printed it on the form, she said, "You'd think my parents wanted a boy, wouldn't you? The fact is, Billie was for my grandmother, and Ted for my father. It's so silly I don't mind it."

"Age, it says here."

"I'm thirty-two."

Moon had anticipated a lie; she looked much younger. "And, you're presently married?"

"I'm a widow, 1944 model."

Frank Wallace, returned from his midday beer, paused at the door, watching the woman a moment, then, looking almost grim, he turned away as Moon prepared to introduce him. The form went on: she had no children, she had learned stenographic skills at Draughn's, she could furnish local references, and as they arrived at that, she put a long cigarette in her mouth and dug about in a black-patent bag equipped with thin shoulder strap and rhinestone clasp. "By God," she said loudly, "I'm always losing my matches."

Moon started, then tried to smile. The oath affronted him. When a woman swears, it's too deliberate, too exaggerated; she is showing a man the estimate she's made of him, and it's

58

never so high as he might wish. Spain Munger, he thought, would now be dismissing her.

He leaned across and lit her cigarette. "This form runs on and on," he said. "Why not take it with you, fill it in later?"

"We've not mentioned the salary."

"I'm sorry. The salary can't be very much. Truth is, this is a struggling business. My partner and I don't really need help, except that we want to get loose for other things once in a while."

She blew out smoke, and smiled. Her teeth were even; they lacked the brown-stain mottle so ordinary among people reared on the High Plains and its water. He should have found out if she was native; he wasn't being businesslike at all.

He faltered. "I haven't any idea what salary you are accustomed to. But I think—well, how much do you feel is necessary?"

Spoken like a Munger-in-law. He felt idiotic. When the Mungers hired they asked, "Uh, what are your circumstances?" and they meant, "What's the least we can get you for?"

The woman's false lips stretched in a grin. "I'd imagined the job was set at a particular amount. Usually, that's the way, and you take it or leave it."

"This is a new position; you aren't replacing anyone. My partner, Frank Wallace, and I had in mind—there's so little work around here—"

"I think you said there is very little work." She was entertained, damn her.

"We expected to make out for about forty-five a week."

"Oh."

"And that's for six days, too, I'm afraid."

"Six days, of course," she said.

"If it seems too low, I'm sorry."

She said, "My apartment costs a hundred twenty-five a month."

Moon shrugged. Not for a minute had she looked like a Munger salary. But then, who did? He peered at her across their stalemate, uninterested now in playing the game on through. The typical Polk Streeter would, at this juncture, agree but differ. Something like, "Yes, living is awfully high. But we can't justify a large salary. We're just *little folks* here." It wasn't worth the breath.

She began threading her shoulder through the purse strap, but did not rise. "You see, Mr. Mooney, I'm getting eighty a week now. I couldn't consider any less. It's salary that has me thinking of a change."

"You needn't explain."

He leaned back, finished, promising himself he'd get out of here for the rest of the day. But she remained in her chair, waiting for something more. Her expression was not quite good to look at. A bitter-sad-hardness; or something, at least, that defined itself as vaguely.

"I'm disappointed," she said, and she slid a forefinger inside the band of her skirt, poking down her blouse. It was nothing, yet his face heated.

"But, if that's the limit," she sighed, "I—"

"Wait." Moon got up, strode around her and out the door. In the dark rear he could see Frank sitting with an elbow on the projector he had run most of the morning, between trips to the street.

"Shut that thing off," Moon said.

"It is off."

"Have you heard any of this?"

Wallace nodded. "She's not the way to build a business."

"Not so loud. What do you think of her, really?"

"We don't need that one around here. If I were you, Moon, I'd find out whether those tits are real, then I'd get rid of her."

Moon said sourly, "She does make those flat floosies in your pictures look like a bunch of old tubs."

"Hold on, Moon." Wallace took off his glasses and wiped them. "We've got nothing to hassle over. I mean to help. Now, you want me to tell you to go ahead, she'll be fine—all right, go ahead, she'll be fine. But she won't. Me, I saw her and I heard

60

her. She's bad judgment—but that doesn't matter, anyway. She'd go bouncing out of here the first time she jiggled herself at Spain. Or in front of your wife, or mine. Besides, you heard what she said. You can't get her for the pay. So what's there to argue about?"

Moon took the matches Frank offered up. He lit the cigarette he'd been holding. He wished China's husband wouldn't think himself so fatherly. Wallace advised too much; he treated Moon as someone in need of a guardian. Yet whenever Moon snapped back, he regretted it. Under his crudity, Frank was trying to be generous. And the issue did bear, most often, on the one link between them, their comradeship in probation.

"I am going to try to hire her, Frank."

"Why her? Why not another one?"

Moon didn't know. Perhaps to give this woman their job would be pretty much like slapping her for swearing; maybe that was what he wanted. "She would do," he said.

Wallace shook his head. "Stop pawing the ground. You don't have to hire her if you want to lay her."

"You never think of anything else, do you?"

"Not often."

Frank reached up a red hand and prowled a cigarette out of Moon's pocket. He lit it, and they were silent while they exhaled smoke together.

"I didn't mean to get hot," Moon said.

"Forget it. Maybe I sound off too much."

Moon said nothing.

Frank's eyes came up, his lips foraged for words before finding them. "Look, Moon, this is the year. In May, the trust period is up, and it's no time to horse around. Me, I've shot my wad already. But not you. You can wait them out, be smart. If you bring that conference room down on your head, then make it happen over something you really want. It ain't worth it, not just to have that sweater to look at."

"I don't see how you can label her. You've barely seen her."

"Lord, Moon, you forget. I'm the authority."

"She's waiting," Moon said. "Listen. I'm thinking of going ahead. I'll phone Spain about a better salary, anyway. What do you say?"

Frank drew on his cigarette, issuing a sigh which expelled none of the smoke. His hands brushed his lap clean of nonexistent dust. "I say, why did you bother to ask me?"

"Just courtesy, I guess," Moon said, and he thought, because you are China's husband.

He went to his own office to make the call. The Old Girl kept him waiting two minutes. Moon stood with his foot in his chair, he kept his voice low.

"Uh, what girl is that?" Spain said.

"For the shop, remember?"

"Oh, yes. You had me by the hair stubs for a minute there; I've had a real buzzing morning.... A widow? Well, if she suits you, then she's hunky with me; you know that."

"I wondered what you had in mind about salary," Moon said.

"Didn't we establish something on that? Anyhow, I believe something along about the level of the others. Forty–fifty a week, if that's about your thinking."

Moon set his teeth. "She's at Horvath's now. They pay her eighty, and she's probably worth it."

The line was silent. Then: "Uh, I see. Do you think, Moon, that she may be overqualified for our job? Someone else will come along—"

"I doubt it. We're requiring so many skills."

"I've just been reading where seventy-three per cent of your white-collar girls draw fifty dollars or less."

"That's too little." Moon said it almost fiercely.

"Uh, we don't disagree there. But you have to keep your larger picture in sight. You'll discover how it's the exceptions you make that do you harm later on. We'd not be wise to be the first to alter the standards, don't you see."

There it was. Munger policy and dictum.

If a rider on one of the Munger ranches suffered from his thirty-five per month and chuck, he could pack himself off and forget it. Grassland Enterprises could hire another hand

62

the same day, to sleep in the same bunk and draw the same pay, and no fence went unmended, no animal was left stranded in a sinkhole. "A cowboy is a cowboy," Old Cecil Munger was supposed to have said. One man the same as every other. Moon knew the tale of the young accountant who once asked a hundred a week as a start, then suddenly was seen in flight with Old Cecil shouting at his heels, "No sonofabitch that eats an' farts is worth a hundred a week to me!" Spain, as far as Moon knew, had never acknowledged the policy. But consciously or not, he made it work.

"You still there, Moon?"

"I'm here." Abruptly, he chose a bolder direction. "I'll offer her fifty. She won't take it. She'll go on back to Horvath's telling them we're cheap."

It touched a nerve. "Uh, wait now a minute," Spain said. "I, uh, never like to be unreasonable. You want this woman badly, didn't you say?"

"She's qualified."

Spain did not muse; he fretted. "We have a queer age, Moon. Drouth making everyone poor, but your plumber carries caviar in his lunch pail. Well, as a special favor to you—let's say, as a kind of a trial balloon—we might offer this woman up to seventy dollars. You realize that we'll have to get a reapproval by the board. Or—"

"I'll try seventy," Moon said quickly.

Spain coughed. "Uh, yes. Another minute, Moon. I wanted to ask if Mr. Remo had got in touch with Bethel this morning."

"Yes, he called. And you might be interested to know that he called me, not Bethel."

"A serious matter for all of us. I thought if we could all take dinner out there tomorrow—I hope that won't horn up any plans . . . ?"

The woman was standing, the fox fur restored to its snug hold about her throat, and she gazed at the blasphemous picture.

"Your partner's?" she said as Moon came in.

"Yes. Frank doesn't mean anything by it, but I am sorry you saw the thing."

"I guess Christ can take a joke," she said.

Moon shuddered; Mrs. Birdsong appeared unnaturally serene. The painting had not troubled her. Maybe Frank's opinion was right.

"Is there any need for me to sit down again, Mr. Mooney?"

Because she obviously thought not, he said "Please do." He got into Wallace's chair. "I'd like you to come with us. The salary can be improved a little."

"Good," she spoke before he could continue, "I've been thinking. You did ask what I must have. I do enjoy a few lumps in my soup," she smiled, "and I believe I should earn a hundred a week."

He blinked. Intuitively she had pounced ahead of him. Now she watched him with an infuriating aplomb, as if she understood people controlled by the Mungers; as if she'd meant all along to dangle herself just beyond his reach. He heard himself saying, coldly, "When can you start?"

It sounded brisk, businesslike; the sound of the free agent. At once he felt he should retract. Now, or later, perhaps, in a reversal that could be blamed, gracefully, on the Munger board. It startled him that he had no such intention. He was grinning at having tripped this woman, at the decision that had lighted in him; he needed to let it go soaring.

Mrs. Birdsong sat down.

Again he said, "When can you start?"

"Why, Monday, I think. I've had Mr. Horvath on notice for a good while."

Moon nodded. A good hot lightning played inside him, and unguardedly he stared at the almost-revealed tips of her breasts. "Are you free today?"

"Yes; I only work until noon."

"Then let's have lunch." Until now, he'd not been hungry. "I can explain what you should know—which isn't much."

It had caused a litter of ideas; they scampered and frolicked. To disregard the board chairman seemed to put him extraordinarily alive. She was standing, saying "Of course"; he was getting coat and hat. One hand under her elbow, he steered her toward the front.

Frank Wallace was in the shop. He had climbed a box, and scowling, grunting, was lifting his projector back to its shelf. When his arms came down, he was panting.

"This is Mrs. Birdsong, Frank," Moon said.

"We've met," she said.

"Just briefly," Wallace grinned. "We exchanged bad impressions."

She clicked on out to the street. Moon caught her arm and jaywalked her across toward the slatternly restaurant called Georgie's where he sometimes bought dry sandwiches and half-chilled milk.

"I didn't know you'd talked to Frank."

"I didn't," she said. "Except barely. I think he meant to scare me away. Or is he just an out-and-out bastard?"

This time her profanity seemed less strained, it annoyed him less. He said, "Have you known Frank before?"

"No."

"He said something to you?"

"I'm used to it. A lot of men want to know if I'm Indian, and if my figure is real." Her voice was calm, yet lined with anger. "If you mean to ask, the answers are no and yes."

They took Georgie's only vacant booth, one whose plastic was knife-slashed so that dirty cotton stuffing bloomed out. Between them lay the debris of a Burger-and-Fries. A silent waitress appeared and put soggy rag to it.

"You'll have to learn how to take Frank," Moon said. "Actually, he's a good man and ashamed of it. He's my brother-in-law."

"I knew that," she said. "And the store—it belongs to the Munger Estate, doesn't it?"

Moon opened a greasy menu.

"Am I nosy?" she said.

"Sauerkraut," he said. "They've served it every day here for thirty years. About the work—"

"No," she cut in. "About the salary, first."

He looked at her sharply. "I thought we agreed on that."

"I'm a grown girl, Mr. Mooney. I don't see how you can pay a hundred a week. Wait, don't unwind. Your offices are very flimsy, that's all. I had to hear."

"You'll have your salary," he said. "Maybe you'd like it in advance?"

"Ouch," she smiled. "But I did hear, and I have an untrusting mind."

It would be almost pleasant to fire her, he thought. But she'd not yet begun.

Besides the check sent out each week from Estate offices he must hand her an additional thirty out of the weekly hundred-fifty he drew as co-manager with Frank but which was, in fact, an allowance, for he had drawn it between enterprises.

"While we're inquiring," he said, "tell me why you are leaving Horvath's. It isn't the money, is it?"

"No. If you're acquainted with Mr. Horvath, it won't take much explaining. He wanted to pay my rent." She smiled. "You are about to ask if I minded. Yes. And Mrs. Horvath minded."

"Then," he said bluntly, "you are being fired."

"That's what Mrs. Horvath wanted. He refused. I think he's after a divorce, so I'm leaving in advance. God, I think his wife deserves him. He smells like garlic half the time."

Moon said lamely, "You're frank enough."

"Not frank; just cold-blooded. I'm of the materialist school. A modern."

He stared, appalled at this woman who offered no "ifs" and "buts"; suspecting her of having effortlessly made a tool of him, yet disbelieving it. Her paint lips stirred with the words as she read the menu, her thumb slid downward along the price column. She might have been an overdressed, top-heavy, studious child.

Abruptly, she glanced up laughing. "Another thing, Mr. Mooney, Horvath just pays me part of my eighty a week. The rest is my husband's GI insurance. And the rent on my apartment is actually just seventy-five. I often lie to strangers."

Moon flushed.

"It wasn't fair, was it?" she said in a way that meant all is fair.

"Why are you telling me now?"

The thick make-up cracked at her eye corners into wrinkles he'd not known were there. "I don't know. I could have rationalized my lies and forgotten them, couldn't I?"

"Oh," Moon said bitterly, "you are morally opposed to rationalization, I take it."

"Of course not, and I hope you're not really peeved. I think rationalization is the most dependable thing in the world. Mine works like a thermostat; cuts in and cuts out, to keep the balance. Keeps me from going crazy. Doesn't yours?"

"I have no idea what you're talking about."

"Then you need practice. Get the trick, and you have it all. Conscious rationalization is better than the other kind. Makes the age you're at the best age there is; makes whatever you do sweet and honorable. Lets you go after whatever you damn well want. See, I lied to get your job, but it's all right, because I'm a hard worker. I've done you a favor."

She smiled as she spoke. She looked squawishly dark and, in some peculiar way, quite terrible. He suddenly wanted to be finished and away.

The soiled waitress found them. At Georgie's, waitresses always leaned smeared aprons against the tables, they held green pads at port arms, they disguised none of the harried monotony on their faces. They were part of a seaminess Moon suddenly found depressing, now that the hot lightning was gone.

He ordered them the Merchant's and coffee. He looked across at the big cheekbones, the flat lips, the wild long hair. The deception he had elected upon loomed large and bleak and unexciting, now, and he wondered if he could explain it to Bethel.

"Do you eat here often?" Teddy Birdsong said.

"It's handy," he nodded. "But it's a crumby place."

"I do that," she said. "Pick out dirty places. You can feel so clean when you get back outside."

Moon had had a gorge of her. "I come, I said, because it's just across the street."

Through her smoke, she beamed him an extended brown look, like a speculation that applied to them both. Behind it he saw her oddity once more. If sadness were molten, he thought, and you cast it like iron, the very hardest iron, and you had the shell of a woman to pour it in, this was what you'd get.

Their food came, and she sighed as she crushed out her cigarette. "All this wading about in the shining blue truth," she said, "has worn me out. I wonder if we aren't getting acquainted just a lot too rapidly?"

V

"Yes, Jesus loves me, yes, Jesus loves me. Er, yes, Jesus—"

"Whyn't you dry up?" said John Remo.

Brother dried up, but his lips sang on, pursing fatly over the cherished words that to him were China's song.

Remo stretched. On Sunday, a man ought to be let sleep late. But at least the gruff voice that could rattle windows had lifted him out of an intolerable dream. He'd seen his mother being shoved into the jail's big tank for women; he had watched her being pushed back, deeper and deeper, in a Saturday night's horde of screaming sluts and vagrants, and it seemed her teeth were out, and maybe held tight in her hands: how had he dreamt such a thing?

"'Scuse me, Mister Remo?"

Remo raised up and looked through the hole in the wall. Brother stood beside his bed, which he had turned into a wallow. He was naked, except for tennis shoes, and he grinned with fat pink excitement. "Sunday, Mister Remo! Ain't I got to put me on some clean britches, huh, Mister Remo, if China an' Moon an' all them is eatin' Sunday dinner?"

"Do I have to tell you everything?" Remo said. "And put your drawers on first."

"Boy, they're truly comin' out, ain't they, Mister Remo?"

"You saw to it."

Brother snapped his shorts fast, below a great balloon of white stomach.

"No cussing today," Remo said. "Hear?"

"No siree, Mister Remo, I sure ain't gonna cuss. I sure am gonna watch out for your tits today, Mister Remo!"

Remo got up.

"These here is new drawers, Mister Remo, an' China, she ain't seen these ones never, an' I bet if I was to—"

"No, dammit!"

"Boy, Mister Remo, ain't it keen I kilt us up a mess of chickens, all right? China an' them, she'll be glad; they wouldn't crave no goddam tuna sanwiches for Sunday—"

"No cussing, I said!"

"'Scuse me, Mister Remo." He padded over to stick his round baby face into the hole. "When all them comes, we ain't gonna talk none about them chickens, are we none, Mister Remo? I mean, ain't nothin' to a bunch of ole chickens fit to talk about, is they, Mister Remo?"

"You wear your socks today," Remo said. "Get the good ones out of the drawer. White shirt, too. And button it straight."

"I'm fixing to, all right, Mister Remo, and after that, I guess I'll just taken my bore-holer; Spain, he don't care none about holes, 'cause he don't care for this ole house noway—"

"The hell you will. First thing, feed the chickens. Then— you listening to me?—then you hook up the water hose and get out there under these windows and wash down the ground. Flush it off good."

"Well, me, Mister Remo, I got to wash up, you told me, and I got to see where Kittypoo is at, an'—"

"You heard me," Remo said. "You wash off the yard. How'd you like for China to know what you done out there?"

Brother pulled a denim suspender of the clean, unpressed

70

overalls over his shoulder, and on second try he hooked the metal clasp.

"China, boy!" Brother's blue eyes sparkled. "Lots of times China says to me, 'Hi there, Beloved,' don't she, Mister Remo? China sure thinks a heap of me!"

Remo swore and drove doggedly on toward his point. "How come you can't go to the bathroom at night; it's closer than getting out under my windows."

"Well, what about my pennies, huh, Mister Remo?"

June Munger collected stray pennies and dropped them in the biffy. Remo had thought to put a stop to it, but was convinced now that he never could. Once he had mentioned it to Moon, who knew the story. The children were small, Old Cecil Munger was gloriously drunk. He had called his youngsters, and as they watched, he threw a handful of coins into the bowl. "Your'n," he said, "if yu'll grab for 'em." And when Melita protested for her children, Cecil told her to mind her own goddamn doings, for this was how kids learned that money wasn't easy come by, and if you wanted it, you had to scrounge and get a little dirty and pay off the fiddler.

Remo glared through the wall at Brother. "You were outside again last night, wasn't you?"

Brother struggled, got the other suspender hooked, but with a twist in it.

"Well, wasn't you?"

"If it's all the same to you, Mister Remo, you can pee in the snow, and you can write your name, kind of, in the snow, if you ain't running too short of pee, and boy, the smoke comes up—"

"Hell, there ain't any snow."

"But they was some snow, Mister Remo! Remember the snow, 'fore we went to Dallas, huh, Mister Remo? I bet it was a foot deep; I bet it come up clean to my knees, Mister Remo!"

"You finished dressing?"

"Don't you recollect the snow none, Mister Remo?"

"Git, now. Feed the chickens, like I told you. Then hook up the hose, and I want you to wash down the wall some, too. Christ, when the sun hits it . . . !"

There would be a lot of sun.

Already the morning stood handsome over The Old Munger Place. The sky was without a cloud, so that it went up high and blue and dry. The air tasted dustless and young, and very near the house a clan of sparrows chattered as if beguiled of spring. Remo had seen a few blues-singing mourning doves yesterday, and the mail carrier had told him a few rattlers were out, which perhaps was early enough to be a record. Pretty soon, he supposed, there'd be red ants and walking sticks and centipedes for the tortoises to snap at. Drouth did queer things to a land.

He heard the Leghorns reveling in their Grape-Nuts, and Brother June's voice, wheedling impatiently, "Hey, goddam now, ole Kittypoo; where you at?"

Remo smoked a leisurely half a pipe. He plunged gingerly for Brother's pennies, and then examined the room's enameled walls for the pungent jingles the ox sometimes copied during his travels and reposted there. At nine o'clock the servants arrived.

The sparrows flurried up and away as the rusted old pickup burst around the house. Dry bearings moaned, and the uncapped radiator bubbled as if with rage. The truck had a rigor before the back stoop and died there. Harry, who told the other dark people of The Flats that he was "the Munger Estate's only nigger," grinned at Remo and jumped out. His wife, named Carrie, pounded her way out the dented other side. They lifted cardboard boxes of food from the bed and came staggering inside.

"We're here," Harry grinned. He was wiry and tall and bald and wine-eyed, and his hands were purple. He had borrowed a thousand library books, and Remo knew him to be more knowledgeable than he chose to let on.

Carrie only smiled. Never had Remo jailed or seen a colored girl half so pretty. Light-skinned, slender, clear-eyed, her hands and feet exceptionally small, her movement easy. The black silk dress became her. Over it she tied a stiff gauze apron, and she pinned a starched, pleated little fan of hat to her shining hair.

"Chickens are in the icebox," Remo said. "Seven of them. That enough?"

"Yes sir!" Harry said. "Only, I was wondering—what went with the heads? Mr. Spain, he favors to have the chicken heads cooked, so's he can crack 'em and eat the brains."

"No heads," Remo said. "Brother batted 'em every which way."

Harry put his long purple hands away in his armpits, to consider. "Yes sir. Well, I'd be much obliged, Mr. Remo, if Mr. Spain knowed that, pretty clear, before he commences looking for them heads on the platter."

Remo grinned. Harry was quick, and surprising. With his wife he comprised the whole servant staff of all the Mungers. As such, he was the servant pool, he was central supply. He was checked out and in, unwarned, by whichever Munger needed him most.

In general, Carrie had the comfort of an established assignment each day. She cleaned and waxed each Munger house once weekly. But Harry could never be sure which kitchen he'd be hanging his set of "personal" knives in. It hinged always on what wife felt ill, or was entertaining, or needed him to tinker with a troublesome appliance. He blazed the tattery family truck to and fro between households, shattering traffic codes and all calm, aside from his own, and he grinned brilliantly, as if each upheaval of plan delighted him.

"Harry," Remo said, "your job would drive me crazy."

"I got a good job, Mr. Remo."

Remo had dressed dandily, taming his heavy textures as best they would tame. With distaste he'd even patted a layer of talcum over the scar. Under a stiff shirt he had hidden the money belt; still it kept chaffing at his mind. He had no chance of balancing his cash against his stack of receipts. Even though, this time, he had kept almost every bill and sales slip. He couldn't be sure, yet, what had come over him. Mother had enough; didn't he send her thirty dollars every payday? But there was something, in Dallas, about seeing the Western Union sign. Suggestion and impulse, it seemed.

A burst of water struck his windows. He looked out. June Munger squatted on his heels, one thick hand loosely aiming the hose, the other clamped about a banana.

"The ground!" Remo yelled. "Wash it across the ground!" Brother grinned at him.

The slob. Glory was on him; his thoughts were singing, "China and all them, they're coming."

"Gets hisself sort of tizzied up, don't he?" Harry said after the breakfast of hot cakes he'd cooked for them.

Remo grunted. "He's glad, and he's scared to death."

Harry assaulted the kitchen, Carrie the accumulation of dust and disorder. It drove Remo outside. He gathered tin cans and cereal boxes out of the yard. Then, keeping a watch on Brother, he took sponge and water to the bugs on the newest Cadillac.

June's fresh overalls looked neat, except that the side plackets were unfastened and flapping open over rolls of bare flank. His shoes were wet, but his shirt—French-cuffed, because China had given it to him—gleamed sunny white. He wandered about in front of the house, pretending not to watch the road. Now and then he bent, teed up a piece of gravel and drove it whanging southward with his eight-iron. Once or twice he moved around north of the house to watch Remo, while thoughtfully he stuffed fat fingers into the holes he had drilled in the siding.

Near ten o'clock, they heard the first car. Remo left the garage immediately, trying to avoid sudden movement. He walked cautiously toward the front yard.

Brother stood in the parking area, his golf stick held in both big hands. His knees sunk slowly, and he hunched into a crouch.

Remo spoke quietly. "Take it easy, now."

Brother looked around as if caught in a searchlight. He stared at Remo, and dropped the club.

"I tell you," Remo said evenly, "let's go hunt that cat."

Brother looked back at the road. He let out a little yelp, and he went pounding for the porch.

"Hold on!" Remo shouted. "Don't do that!"

Brother's mouth hung open. His big feet pumped up high, jarred down flat. His paunch bounced as he ran; one suspender came free and streamed out behind him.

Remo was running to cut him off. "Wait, lemme talk to you!"

Brother dived to the ground, suddenly giggling. He scooted through the manhole in the porch's green lattice, disappearing beneath the house.

Remo came to the opening, and kicked it. He gasped for breath. "Come out of there!" he yelled. "Or I'll bust your fat tail!"

He heard Brother floundering. Making himself small and still.

"Oh, hell." Remo bent to speak through the lattice. "Look here; come out of there! You told me you didn't aim to stick me in the wringer!"

Brother was silent.

"Goddamn; you'll get filthy under there!"

From under the porch, a booming whisper: "If I ain't under this here house, Mister Remo, whyn't you go find me out at the barn?"

Remo swore. He took out his handkerchief and wiped his face.

The ox. He'd lie on stomach and elbows, withdrawn into the dark, but close enough front that he might watch as his family arrived. He'd scratch his bald top noisily as cobwebs tickled it; he'd spit from the wad of cigar in his jaw, and he'd think himself quiet as a mouse. He'd wait, until in the diamonds of light framed by the lattice, he could sight China's slim, pedicured little feet.

Remo cursed himself.

"All right," he bellowed, "I'm glad you ain't under there. Because that was a plenty big rattlesnake I chased under yonder a while ago."

He heard Brother's breath shut off like a sob.

"There, by damn," Remo muttered. "When he comes out, I'll slap him cross-eyed."

Remo waited.

Seconds went, and he heard nothing. He thought of Spain's thin eyes condemning all this through gloomy glasses. Then: what the devil. It was done.

Loudly Remo said, "Come to think of it, that snake did go right on out the other side, headin' for the pasture."

Breath resumed under the porch. Presently he heard panting and scratching and spitting.

Remo grinned in his misery. The blond tall women would complain that June was dirty. Spain would scowl, and regret insinuatingly that, a full fifty per cent of the time, this was the indecent and pitiful spectacle that greeted their arrival.

Remo squinted at a sunflash down the road. Moon's Chevvy, it looked to be, and Remo felt himself loosening a trifle. He brushed off his trousers cuffs, shined the big soft shoes on the backs of his calves, and sat down on the edge of the porch.

The floor remained damp and chilly from the scrubbing Carrie had given it. Underneath, Brother threshed about. Remo understood that his legs had blocked June's view.

Good, he thought. Partly, anyway, he was getting even.

Moon had been aroused early by the telephone. He did not recognize the voice on the line. "Who?" he said.

"Teddy Birdsong," she laughed. "Remember?"

"Of course."

"I'm sorry to disturb you at home. But I'm afraid I have to renege about starting work tomorrow. I've talked with Mr. Horvath—"

The whole night through, Moon thought probable.

"—and he got pretty hot. So I told him I'd stay on another week, provided you'll hold the job open."

"That's too bad."

"No," she said lightly, "it gives you a tidy way out, if you've changed your mind."

She needn't have stated it. He could, in a word, retire from his deception, plunge back into his mold. He should have expected the opportunity. Always when he seized upon real decision, something occurred to force a redecision; always, too, there was the inclination to undo and be safe.

"Well, Mr. Mooney?" she said, and she crooned the *o*'s gaily. "Before you decide—I've re—let's see, rethunk it. From you, just eighty a week will be enough. Later I'll hate myself, but this morning, I've had a few drinks. It's Sunday, and nice and sunny."

"We'll expect you Monday week, then," Moon said. "At the salary we first agreed on."

"Thank you." She spoke quietly now. "I didn't mean to be smarty. The truth is, I don't often drink."

He held the phone a moment after the call was done. Strange, he had liked her better. For once, no real hardness in the voice. But then he pictured her; not the figure, but the face, and he felt he must have listened very generously.

Bethel began the day with the burden of Brother gray on her face. But she had made up a trace more becomingly than usual. He said, "You look nice this morning. More make-up, isn't it?"

"Yes," she smiled. "I thought you might want to kiss me."

He kissed her, gently. It was rare that she had enough lipstick to taste. She turned to the cabinet, and he could see she'd not found remedy in his touch.

"It'll be a pretty day," he told her.

He stood at the back door. Hands in his pockets, clenched as if on their leisure. By now, on another Sunday, his family would have been in its Bible School crush. A lick and promise at breakfast, a speedy scan-through of the lesson, a flurry of starched clothes in the bedlam of four persons dressing all over the house simultaneously, a dozen panicky check-ups on the time—all to be climaxed with their arrival at church far too early. Moon just sort of enjoyed it.

Since the war, the Mungers had leaped into Protestantism with a vigor, albeit a vigor that was organized and calculated.

If it hinted at an about-face from their rearing, then at least, Moon thought, it was typically schematic. Equivalent to any Munger investment program, certainly.

China and Frank had presented themselves to the Baptists, selecting the church of Old Cecil Munger's funeral. Laska and Sid Glass were edging toward an amen corner among the Methodists. Aunt Texas, having enough time for the preconfirmation schooling, had become Lutheran, although she could be suspected of lacking enthusiasm about it. And practically by allotment, Bethel and Moon had joined South Terrace Presbyterian. He had understood that he was expected to rise there. Despite the initial resentment, Moon had risen.

The past few months, he had manned the high arched entrance to the sanctuary during morning service. In sternest black suit, he planted himself before the towering oak doors, opening them for late-comers at the propitious intervals marked for him by rows of asterisks on the Order of Worship. In between, he defended the doors stoutly, preventing entries while prayer or special music or The Moment of Meditation were in sway.

Traditionally, the sanctuary's two smaller flanking doors were kept bolted. This was ostensibly a heating-cooling economy. But more accurately, Moon gathered, the practice thwarted tardy members who hoped to sneak in anonymously along the side aisles. Otherwise, these might have used the camouflage provided by the leak-stained limestone walls, might have gotten seats unnoticed and uncommented upon by their fellows, some of whom claimed the right to shake their heads and stare openly their doubts on the sincerity of certain salvations.

At any rate, Moon held a sort of absolute St. Petership before the South Terrace gates. He spent his hour smiling, greeting, whispering, and shushing, and he forgot himself. He would come away rested. It was good, unexpectedly so.

"If you don't mind," Bethel said, "we'll have a light breakfast. Harry will make us a feast, out home."

Moon nodded.

"All right?" she said. "Just coffee and rolls?"

"Fine."

Through the screen he looked at his neighborhood. More than anything, he thought, it was a sameness. Curved black-top streets, rimmed uniformly with parkways and the FHA's monotonous postwar boxes. Each house artless and moodless, indistinct from all the others, as human tastes never are. A sameness of TV antennas up on long stalks, and of cramped front footages, pampered bluegrass, play-yard Gym Dandy sets. Every garbage barrel an oil drum painted silver. Everywhere, barbecue piles and young Chinese elms, each trunk guyed with wire against the southwest wind. Steel clothesline masts, false window shutters, concrete driveways used by unpaid-for automobiles, picture windows exhibiting garish lamps, boisterous children, and combative dogs. Over it all hung the cloying Jonesiness of thirty-year mortgages, the feel of conforming, spiritless security.

"Solid, middle-class neighborhood," Spain said in recommending it. Without doubt, the development was a masterwork of municipal zoning, Moon thought, but it wasn't a neighborhood. More correctly, it was a compound.

The city's wealth had retreated to the south and west, congregating in stretched ranch styles or French Provincials or hybrid Colonials, the copies of copies finished off with multiple garages and acres of steep shingle roof. If equally monotonous, it was the monotony of plenty. Here, people did live nearer their inclinations, and their money was showing. Moon had never desired a house among them, yet it seemed dishonest that the Mungers were not there. A hundred-sixty, or hundred-eighty, or hundred-something million dollars, it said in Dun & Bradstreet. Yet the Mungers made themselves a cross-section, the Mooney part of which was this GI district. Six boothlike little rooms, complete with GI installments—cheaper than rent, of course.

He shook his head. He must grant that Spain Munger, good general, posted no order not first applied to himself. Spain had three children, but kept them and "Mom" in a plain brick cottage no larger than the Mooneys'. China and Frank likewise lived small. They were south, in a place of the redwood-and-rubber plant ilk, and shoddy from the day it was built.

Sometimes, Moon regarded Texas as the luckiest. Her home was a hotel apartment. If it overstepped her needs, well, the board agreed that aloneness deserved compensations; perhaps they saw that Texas's spinsterhood was at times heavily borne. Her rooms were furnished tastefully, kept tidily. Seven floors up, the apartment gave a penthouse illusion that Moon liked.

By plan, it was Laska and Sid who'd fared best. Their big split-level house leaned against an exclusive West Amarillo hillside and confessed the Munger riches.

Homogeneity, that was it.

Moon remembered a meeting at Estate offices in early summer, 1952. Everyone seated formally, almost stiffly, around the long table. The in-laws unusually present because Spain wished to make a short speech. When finished, he passed out the checks each must sign, then the campaign buttons. "Gladly for Adlai" pins for Moon, Frank, and Sid. "I Like Ike" for himself and his sisters. Moon sat transfixed, aghast at the spectacle of politics-by-issue.

Spain expected no protest, least of all from Sid Glass. Sid had his animal clinic; he had his hobby, which was carnivals, so perfected that his garage was lined with kewpie dolls. Always Spain had found him pliable. But this time, Sid tossed his Adlai button back with the easy motion that put pennies in saucers, and he said, "I'm for Ike."

Spain squinted up palely, then looked aside at a reddening Laska, who ducked away from this impropriety by her man and was thus disassociated with it.

"Uh, I admire you, Sidney," Spain said. It sounded like one of his difficult days. "Coming out, right under the muzzles, and that's just fine. On behalf of the directors, I should have, uh, made myself more clear. Now, you take your newspaper polls. No question, the Panhandle will go for Ike, close to fifty-four per cent. But let's think, here, in terms of the big picture. After November, we'll go on being ninety per cent Democratic, and there's your nub of it to deal with. Uh, as a family, you can see—well, in political things, your hay is to win a little and lose a little, on the long haul. And I hope that gets your details clearer to your mind."

Sid, his unimpressive little frame held rigid, stood fast. His voice barely trembled. "I cannot support a Harvard smart-aleck for President."

Spain stared a moment, chin trussed up by the backs of his laced hands.

"Uh, I see. Well, there's no lock of the horns here." He picked up Sid's Adlai button and stuck it on his own lapel. He started his Ike button passing from hand to hand, down to Sid. In a minute, he had reshuffled the pile of checks, so the donation bearing Sid's name would go to Republican headquarters.

By a few quick gestures, politics were realigned; the Mungers stood in balance.

That was it, Moon thought. Within their collectivism, a balance. The analysis fit the nicely distributed church and club memberships, the impartiality of rotative shopping and banking, the careful, flexless diversity. It was what Frank Wallace seemed to know but what Moon, although he could see where Frank pointed, couldn't quite believe. If it were a means, where was the end?

Moon sneezed at the sun.

"Breakfast is ready," Bethel said.

The children came sleepily, then perked up to chatter as they ate. Through milk mustaches, they spoke of the windmill, the cistern that smelled funny and would holler back if you shouted into it; of the great big huge just-enormous Mr. Remo, who kept a real gun in his pocket. Moon watched them.

At eleven, Carol's voice was becoming something like China's, he thought. She talked with quick tosses of her head, with humor, even talent. Beside her, Hannah sat tall and straight, a whole year older. Hers was a reserved excitement that could be concealed by stoic gravity. It was hard to recall that Hannah had been a chubby, smiling baby.

Bethel had excused herself. Now, from the bedroom, she called, "You kids hurry, so we can get dressed."

"Well'um," said Carol.

"Don't you want to go out early, so you'll have time to play?"

"Yes'um."

"Carol, is 'yessum' and 'nome' all you can say?"

"No'um," she answered, and she winked at Moon.

When the girls were dressed, they scampered in to curtsy and spread bright print skirts for his endorsement. "Very pretty," he said, "both of you." Hannah nodded solemnly, and fled.

Carol kissed his cheek, sighed, and went swirling across the living room. She hissed, waved her arms, then oscillated in what he suspected was one of those curious dances taught at Junior Y.

"What am I, Daddy?"

"A female."

"That's wrong; I'm a tree!" She spread her skinny boughs and rustled her nylon leaves; her palms raised to support robins, or to drink in rain. "I'm a willow, I think—or maybe I'm a mulberry."

"I see."

"Daddy, I think mother was crying, in the bedroom. It's Uncle June, isn't it?"

"Yes. Go easy with her, huh?"

Bethel was dressed in green linen and short white coat, new from her shopping for spring. Moon noted, gratefully, the low-heeled sandals. These, which Carol spoke of babyishly as "Mama's Jesus shoes," surrendered Moon his scant inches of superior height. Bethel must have suspected how, today, he needed them.

As they started out the door, Carol wished to know if he didn't just love a good tree, and he said yes, especially a mulberry, and she screwed up her pretty face to remark that mulberries often creep with worms, and as she darted ahead of him, he lightly swatted her bottom.

"Richard!"

Bethel paused until the children were outside. "Dear, I don't think you should be rowdy with Carol; she isn't exactly a baby any more. . . ."

They took Moon's declining old Chevvy in preference to Bethel's new sedan because the children insisted. The car was so tattered the girls regarded it, affectionately, as ancient; Carol, when in it and headed for the country, liked to imagine she was Randolph Scott and riding shotgun. They drove through abandoned Sunday streets to Texas Munger's hotel.

The eldest of the heirs stood at the curb, craning for sight of them. Her trim gray suit diminished remarkably the great bones of her hips. Standing so straight, her feet together almost militarily, she looked seven feet tall. Texas's hair, not gray and always the fairest of all the Mungers', lay smooth and almost white beneath a saucery black hat. Certain days, Moon thought, Texas looked younger than her sisters, except China. Maybe there was something in the solitary existence that staved off time.

"Hey, Auntie Tex!" the children shouted, before Moon had quite stopped the car. Auntie Tex. She had become the curator of the family's few wanted mementos; she represented them on the Symphony board, at Little Theater, among the Federated Women. She reviewed novels; most perceptively, Moon had been told. And she had schooled herself to be the Estate authority on stocks and bonds.

Carol and Hannah climbed all over Aunt Texas as she squeezed herself into the rear club seat, where she had to sit with knees angled sideways. The girls looked at her big purse speculatively. Often, Auntie Tex carried the cleverest gifts. She kissed them, and warned, "Watch out for my skirt."

"Hannah, if you'd come up here with Daddy and me," Bethel said, but it was Carol who came climbing over the seat.

Pale blue tears stood unformed in Texas's eyes. "It's—too bad, about Brother," she said.

"Why does everybody always cry about Uncle June?"

"Hush, Carol. And sit still."

"But I don't see why you always—"

Moon looked at his daughter. "Please."

"Well, I'm thinking, Daddy."

He worked the clutch, allowing his tiny China to shift the gears grindingly.

"I dropped by Spain and Selma's last night," Texas said. "He's terribly concerned. As he says—" She patted Hannah's cheek. "I shouldn't talk in front of little Big Ears. But we've got to keep in mind, June does have—all the glands. Spain thinks if Mr. Remo goes on loafing on the job—"

"Spain shouldn't have read Freud," Bethel said.

Carol looked up at Moon. "Who's Freud?"

"If," continued Auntie Tex, "if Mr. Remo could set a better example, perhaps. Poor Brother, he is such an imitator. All those vulgarities, like on the wall. I—"

" 'Don't throw cigarette butts in the urinals,' " Carol quoted, " 'as it makes them soggy and hard to light!' Is that Freud?"

"Carol!"

Moon turned his grin away from them. Bethel had flushed marvelously.

"Where did you hear such trash?"

"Uncle June wrote it in the biffy. I thought you were talking about—"

"Don't let me hear anything of that sort again!"

"Yes'um."

Moon drove the short route through town, along an avenue brick-paved and choppy with shocking dips, then cut east on the highway fringed by gas stations and beer halls now closed and resting from the long Saturday night. Presently he turned onto the Mungers' rough caliche road. The car rattled.

"Richard, you're making an awful racket."

Carol smiled up at him. "Take it easy, greasy—"

"This road is getting horrible," Aunt Texas said. "Doesn't the county pave, any more?"

Deep cut, glaringly white between the drouth-stripped pastures and four-wire fences, the road strung away north like a very straight scar. Here and there the carcass of a coyote hung, head down and with hind feet bound together, on a fence post. Along the west side ran a row of gaunt utility poles, each

84

crossbarred six feet from the top, as if prepared for a thousand future crucifixions. Even in sunshine, Moon thought, the drive could be depressing.

Out here the earth had never been plowed. Aside from the wells, the Munger land remained as first found, and it did not blow itself away. Those who had broken the land raised, in rainy years, twenty-bushel wheat crops. Or below the caprock where the soil was red, cotton at a half-bale to the acre. But much of the wheat was so poor it wouldn't mill into white bread; the cotton harvested so dirty and short-stapled it served mostly to stuff mattresses. In the Panhandle, farmers had to be great kidders, else they couldn't keep pointing to themselves as the backbone of the nation. Old Cecil had lacked any yen for the game it became. Seeing his land, Moon could imagine earlier years; he could think he saw the land and its meaning as Old Cecil had.

Carol pointed across Moon, at a pair of Holsteins looking sad-eyed and unmilked, their heads hung over barbed wire to survey the road. "Look, Daddy."

Because she expected it, he tipped his hat to the cows and said, "Good morning, ladies," and she shrieked and hugged him.

"Carol," Bethel said, "can't you be quiet now? Your aunt and I are trying to talk." Moon scratched his hand brutally.

As The Old Place rose in sight, he saw John Remo, a blue-serge hulk even at such range, sitting on the porch. The big Pole watched them in, getting up hastily as they rumbled over the cattle guard. He was beside the car when Moon parked it in one of the rocking stops Carol delighted in, and he offered a heavy hand to assist Bethel out.

"Good morning, Mr. Remo. How is June?"

"He's just fine, ma'am. I reckon I oughtn't to of called, about them chickens."

"You were exactly right," Texas said. She was drawing her long frame awkwardly over the folded front seat. "Mercy, there went my hose."

Bethel said, "Where—is he up at the house?"

"Well, you see—"

"Not again!"

"Yes, ma'am."

Carol said, "Mr. Remo, let's see your pistol."

They stood together a moment. Then Bethel took Texas's hand, and they set slowly for the house, bent forward as they walked, as if climbing contrary to a wind. Remo looked after them with his miserable, droop-lidded eyes.

"What's up?" Moon said. "Where is he?"

"Goddammit, he's yonder, under the porch. I'll ketch hell, Moon."

"Maybe we can get him out."

Remo wagged his big head. "Not before *she* comes, we can't."

When Moon and John Remo talked, *she* had but one meaning, and it was specific enough.

John Remo threshed about no bushes with Moon; he fetched up none of the stumbling courtesy necessary around the other Estate people. It allowed Moon an equivalent candor. A talk with the red-nosed old giant wasn't stimulating, but somehow, Moon found it restful.

The old cop pointed. Moon looked at two automobiles on the road, the first pitching up white dust into the brows of the second.

"The millionaires cometh," Moon said.

"Them oughta been my words," said Remo. "You're a millionaire, ain't you?"

Moon grinned at him. "I stay broke all the time."

"Hell," Remo spat on the ground, "I ain't played with my toes in a long time; can't reach 'em any more. But that don't mean I ain't still got 'em."

"Are you making a point?"

"Well, you don't have to worry none about your old age."

Moon laughed. "Sounds like you're sweating yours out."

"Hell no. I sweat out this goddamn job."

Dr. Sidney Glass's Plymouth appeared through the last deep cut in the road. From the dust and roar, Moon estimated: "Laska is driving."

No matter how Spain lectured her, Laska liked driving about at ninety miles per hour. With shoulders broad and corded like a man's, and height an inch greater than Bethel's, she handled an automobile flamboyantly. Although forty, Mrs. Glass wore bluejeans around home, so she might sprawl unrestrictedly. She smoked long cigarettes of foreign make, and if her hands were occupied, she let the bitter brown things dangle from her lips a little whorishly, this to the horror of her sisters who declined to smoke at all. Spain frowned palely on Laska's evils; he condoned only a few small vices and reserved these for men only.

Laska's voice was forceful, growing rapid and coarse when she felt deeply. It was she who balked, at times, at all the Munger pussyfooting with Brother. Her toughness, magnified by the soft tolerance of June by the others, could protrude like a mellowed old grudge. Laska did not hedge. Moon thought this attractive, and he liked how she was always, always gentle with Sid.

She had married the little veterinarian when she was twenty-three and the Munger family still lived intact at The Old Place. Old Cecil had been away at God knew what, Spain was abed with his feet propped high because of a belated case of mumps, and Laska had volunteered to help Sid guide a Jersey through the breech birth of a calf.

Sid said his meeting with his wife, in the barn, was under the tenderest of circumstances, and he meant it. He liked his profession. As a young man, Sid had been dapper and full of breezy conversation; glib enough so that Laska was won before they had finished washing the new calf. But since Moon had known him, Sid had spoken seldom and very quietly.

Physically, Sid's wife dwarfed him. Middle life had made her larger while Sid had shrunk comfortably into sags and folds like a friendly old chair. If you no more than glanced, you might think him a small, tired, and harried man.

Remo nodded toward the Plymouth with a wink that meant the odd tale about the Glasses had come to his mind. Moon said nothing. The tale was true. For years, in the prime of their marriage, Laska had sought pregnancy and failed. Both she and Sid had examinations, read delicate books, and heard advice. Ultimately, the Mungers called a special meeting and there formed one of Spain's solid fronts for attack on the problem. Sid did not attend, and the directors looked at once to his psychology.

As Laska confided to her sisters, Sid seemed so concerned with the sporadic nature of his practice and his many hours of idleness that he approached her less than enterprisingly. The board voted, therefore, to buy a vacant quarter-block at the edge of town, and on it they built, to Sid's specifications, a bright and roomy animal clinic. They sent to Texas A&M for a pair of young vets to assist. The place succeeded immediately. Although Sid appeared well content, Laska still did not bloom as expected. In a second meeting, the directors voted her into the hands of some Dallas specialists, and she stayed downstate almost a month.

The doctors investigated her whole life, with particular emphasis on such childhood events as the severe electric shock she'd once had and which was remembered as "Laska's electrocution." Later, they discovered that her normal body temperature was several degrees too high.

Then it was that Sid's ordeal began. When ice packs availed nothing, Laska took to sitting in whole bathtubs of crushed ice. Groaning, forcing aspirin through chattering teeth, she watched her thermometer. When it fell, she leaped to the telephone and called the animal clinic. Chilled so blue she could not make an S, she would cry, "Didney, come home!"

"I'm busy, Laska—"

"Come home! Oh God, hurry; I'm freezing to death!"

These facts became common knowledge, and Sid knew it. One of his young veterinarians let slip premature congratulations and did so, whether coincidentally or clairvoyantly, on the very day the effort succeeded. Moon pitied Sid while enduring the humiliation with him. But out of it, Sid hit upon something good. Out of the hang-dog days of sudden summonses to midday copulation, Sid derived a new tranquility. He lived it like an art. Perhaps the exposure of his dearest secret shot him high above those who snickered, raised him to a plane of freedom where he needed pretense no longer. Moon could imagine no more grisly forge, but when he was with Sid, he thought the product fine.

Laska parked the car smoothly. Sid Junior got out first. Soon to be twelve and dead set against a party celebrating it, the boy might in some views have been conceived a few tenths degrees too coolly. Laska worried that he was a loner. He was handsome-faced, smooth-skinned, quiet as his father. The Mungers liked to believe he would become either painter or writer.

The Glasses left the car, Laska waving toward the house and waiting as Spain, his small sedan coated with her dust, parked precisely beside her.

Moon and Remo watched Spain bend his six-feet-four to Laska's kiss and hold out his hand to Sid. There seemed little wind, but as Spain led them upslope, his hatless blond hair lifted and whipped. At sight of Moon and Remo, Spain's white brow furrowed; in the sunlight, his face looked entirely bleached. "Uncle Spain," Carol had said, "is real pure looking, isn't he?," which capsuled the matter nicely.

Beneath the porch Brother drew a long rasping breath.

Spain greeted them, his gaze on Remo. "Uh, I don't see Bro— I don't see Mr. Munger."

Remo's heels closed together, the big feet pointing outward. "He's a jack rabbit, sir, once he gets to running."

"Under the house?"

"Yes sir, he is. I couldn't head 'im off."

Spain's jaw tightened. "Uh, you've not been under there after him?"

Moon said, "No need to try. You know how this goes."

Spain folded his arms and stood a moment kicking up a small mound of earth with his toe. When again he spoke, his voice was forced and low. "This terrible slaughter, Mr. Remo. It's not the chickens. Uh, I'm not spilling any beans you don't already know when I say what really counts is his behavior. There are your implications to be faced when you have a revelry in blood, with a man of his, uh, mature appetites—?"

"He wasn't reveling, no sir."

"Well," Spain said, "we can thank heaven for little apples."

Moon felt guiltily amused at the fencing match; at Spain unable to say the Munger nightmare was that Brother might one day assault a girl, at Remo refusing to offer his simple belief that June wanted nothing more than a visit from his family. The old cop had fished out his stubby pipe. He snapped worn teeth on the grooved stem, and the click of it caused Spain to grimace.

"Uh, Moon, do the children know where their uncle is? Seems to me, the way your little tidbits get retold at school, we might be wise to keep them away until we get him out. . . ."

Spain's head turned, almost in alarm, at the sound of the door; he smiled palely as Bethel came out. She leaned from the porch, so her brother might kiss her.

"Won't you come inside a minute?" she said. "Harry has a conflict for Tuesday. I counted on him for club, and Laska needs him at almost the same time."

Spain stepped up to the porch, one shanky leg putting his weight up jerkily, like a jack. At the door, he turned back to Remo. "I'd appreciate it if you'd supervise Mr. Munger closely today. I'd think he needn't play with the children. Moon, wouldn't you agree a hundred per cent with that?" He went on into the house, his long arms folded across his back.

Under the floor, Brother's stomach growled.

She arrived.

They got up, Remo dusting himself, as Frank Wallace angled his faded green Ford into place. Frank drove with fuddy-duddy care; "Sunday driver!" Remo muttered critically, and

Moon understood and laughed. The last family Sunday, China had driven out alone since Frank was in an uproar with his rebellious digestion, and she had stayed late to finish a cake Brother begged of her. It had been after sundown when Moon and Remo walked her to her car, Remo fumbling at telling her how sorry he was about the trailer that Brother had set fire to.

"Don't you worry; please don't," China smiled. "We think you do wonderfully with June." She'd gotten Remo's hand, holding it an instant as they stood at the car. Moon recalled how Remo's excited jowls reddened and quivered before he blurted, "Mrs. Wallace, I hope Frank is treatin' you right!"

Remo was at once abashed, as amazed at himself as they were. Until China erased the error, easily, as if by a flick of her wand. "Oh, how very kind of you, Mr. Remo! Thank you, we are both just fine!"

The loveliest Munger alighted neatly. No gawky immodesty; none of the strain of her sisters. She waved and Moon wagged his hand at her. The beautiful Munger. Today in a pleatless navy suit, markedly unornamented, yet on China as feminine as lace. Hair almost ash, glistening in the sun; sissy little feet, a waist Moon could have closed his two hands around. She stood on tiptoe and called across the roof of the car to Selma Munger.

Spain's wife had remained in their car; Moon realized he hadn't noticed her until now. Mom, Spain called her, and had called her since the arrival of their first child. Her three small ones were in the car also, apparently drawing instructions for the day.

Selma seemed more a Munger than an in-law. She might have married a dirt farmer and lived no differently. She catered to her brood, kept her house bare-handedly, accumulated bric-a-brac for ugly what-not shelves. She had grayed at the edges and was becoming quite fat. Selma escaped all Munger issues. When Moon saw her at all, he was apt to regard her as a nil, a zero—then feel immediately that he was mistaken.

China kissed her, and they came forward together. Frank

hurried ahead. "Eeyo," he greeted Remo, and to Moon he whispered, "Isn't this the year?" before he sped on inside to swallow a dose of soda.

China kissed Moon's cheek, then touched Remo's hand. "Beautiful day, isn't it? Where is Brother?"

Remo cleared his throat. "I'm sorry, Mrs. Wallace. He got under the house again."

"Shoot," China smiled, "you couldn't help that. Where? Here under the porch?"

Selma said, "Wait, I'll get the childen inside."

Moon lit a cigarette and retreated to sit on the steps. "I'm going to watch, this time," he said. "Maybe I can catch the secret."

China laughed. "No secret."

She folded her skirt behind her, squatted on her heels, balanced there with one white-gloved hand on the lattice. "Hello, Beloved! Where are you?"

A puff of dust came rolling out through the lath. Her eyes twinkled.

"Now Brother, no games! Why, I've not seen you in weeks and weeks. I've missed you."

They heard Brother's head thump against a floor joist, and he said, "Woops, goddam!"

"He must be someplace," China said. "I'll go—"

Brother shouted. "I ain't someplace, China; under here is where I'm at!"

"My!" China laughed deeply. "Why don't you come out? I can't come under there!"

"Comin' out, China, quick as I can, that's what I'm doin'!"

"Whatever got you under there?"

"Me, China, I was huntin' Kittypoo, that's all; can't find Kittypoo to save my hide, seems like!"

Brother grunted and floundered near the opening. The bald head burst through, shining with excited sweat. "Here I am!"

Moon looked at Remo and snapped his fingers. The happiest Munger wheezed to his feet. He grinned as China reached up to brush dust out of his thick copper eyebrows.

92

"Oh, Beloved, your clothes are ruined. Let's go wash up some, huh?"

"A washing-up don't bother me none, China!"

"Good for you." She took his hand in both hers and led him around the house.

Remo grunted and shook his sloven bulge of shoulders. He swore a chain of soft oaths. "You ever see the beat of that?"

"Hardly."

"That damned clod. To tell the truth, it bothers me, kind of. Seein' her patty-cake him that way. It ain't how I handle him."

Moon grinned. "You didn't get him out from under the house."

They sat a while with the yard to themselves, absorbing the sun, being easily silent as men can when they know and trust each other, until Remo fell to staring at Moon's car. Moon put him off, then nudged him, and they got up to walk across gravel. Abruptly, Remo said, "What is that Frank always says, about this being the year?"

Moon didn't like talking about it. Almost curtly he said, "The Estate's trust period is up this May."

Old Cecil Munger's will left the basic properties in thirteen-year trust, under terms that blocked their division or the disposal of one foot of land. The trust allowed the heirs a free hand with earnings, reinvestment, and management, so that in effect, the old man himself had established the family corporation.

Now, in just a dozen weeks, the strings could come off, or tighten; the Mungers could divide their holdings, or reorganize to continue jointly. The choice, as far as Moon knew, had never been indicated. But Frank was strangely confident of a split, he thought ahead to it constantly and pleasurably in a way that had Moon almost hoping.

To Moon, the approaching date had become an enormous urgency. After so many insignificant years, he was suddenly compelled to hurry. Do something, even something stupid, if it could be hard-headedly his own. Moon had realized, very lately, that to wait out the trust, to achieve his self-determination as a mere fact of the calendar, would eclipse him finally. If there was to be victory for himself, it mustn't occur as a gift, not because they changed the rules. The knowledge somehow made his plan for The Camera House into a crisis.

Remo said, "Reckon they'll divvy things up?"

"Frank thinks so. I don't know; it might be rugged from the standpoint of taxes."

Standing now by Moon's car, Remo twisted to look back. "Relax," Moon told him, "she'll keep track of him." He opened the trunk lid and unwound the fifth of Old Forester from the spare innertube which had protected its journey. They sat down with it on the trunk deck, where the raised lid screened them from the house. Moon broke the seal, and Remo drank first. The whole ritual reminded Moon of boys smoking corn-silk behind a barn.

"I hear Spain ain't bothered much by taxes."

"With the Depletion Allowance," Moon said, "he manages."

While Moon held the whisky, observing the colors the sun shot through it, Remo fell into a recital of the latest Munger story, one Moon hadn't heard. A gasoline attendant had declared the Munger family was on relief. "My God, Moon," Remo said in a voice cut lower by the liquor, "is there anything to that?"

Moon supposed the gossip welled up out of the government's emergency-feed program for drouth relief. The Munger ranches, particularly Martin's place in New Mexico, were indeed in the red, and Grassland Enterprises had put in for all the free feed they could get. Spain believed in getting back as much of his tax money as he could. On one dry year, it was said, a herd of registered animals was starved deliberately on the New Mexico range because the tax-relief picture required it. However astounding, Moon had learned, such could be shrewd business, not fraud, if brought off by big men.

Remo shook himself, lifted the bottle. "To brave blood," he groaned, and he drank hard, rubbing the whisky down-

94

ward along its course with the heel of a big hand. "Hey, Moon, what if you do get you a few million to take care of; what'll you do?"

"I'll see that you get a suit that fits you."

"Hell," Remo grumbled, "trouble with you, you ain't got no idea what you want. That's what puts the hitch in your get-along. Now, was it me in your shoes, I'd be out for something."

Moon took back the bottle and grinned at him.

"Here, gimme the jug. It ain't my business, Moon, but you could get you something right now; you could if you'd stop kissin' asses and start biting 'em."

"A drink thaws you fast, Remo."

The old cop twisted left and downward, peered around the fender at the house, and spat. "Naw. Naw, it don't. I got a loud trap, that's all."

Moon looked at Remo with an appreciation that surprised him. If grizzly bears modeled blue serge, he thought, this is how the biggest and clumsiest would look.

"Say, Moon. Reckon we oughta ask Sid Glass out here? No flies on that little man."

"He wouldn't drink. We might twist Frank's arm, though."

Remo shook his head. "Not that bastard."

Moon capped the bottle, rolled it in the innertube, tucked it away behind the spare wheel. Remo observed the event sadly; he said, "I got some Chlorets we can chew. Works pretty fair, if you don't belch." Then he gazed off toward Amarillo, his great droopy lids almost shut, and he mused, "Damn, I hope she's still got my slob in tow."

They sat farther back in the trunk, warm from the whisky, the sun, the mild air, if not from each other. They could hear the romp of the children, out near the barn now, it seemed, and occasionally they caught the ring of chinaware in the house. Once they started at a cry from Brother, "You're a good sonofabitch, China!" and behind it, even at such a distance, they could sense the sudden descent of a tense and pallid silence among those Mungers who felt themselves no sons of bitches at all, not even good ones, and after that, Moon let the glow of the liquor and talk go slipping away, so that soon it was another hollow Sunday, and when Harry appeared, smiling wisely, to recruit them for the dining room, Moon could hardly hear. He was chewing his gum too desperately.

VI

Harry made meals at The Old Place his masterwork. His shrewd wine eyes, brightly proud of the food Mr. Spain Munger would praise, inevitably, as "real country vittles," looked to the serving with a craftsmanlike, anticipative confidence which was itself a kind of grandeur.

His purple fingers punched unseen buttons in the air, and his wife reacted as though impulsed along invisible wires. Carrie worked in awe. She looked prettier because of it, she kept silent, and she spilled nothing. If Harry spoke to her at all, this occurred in the kitchen and no one was aware of it.

They presented steamy rolls, prebuttered as Laska preferred them; asparagus floated in cream sauce created from Miss Texas Munger's own recipe, and a thin rich gravy, heavily peppered, as Mrs. Bethel Mooney favored it. There was the chilled green salad that Mrs. Wallace liked to pick at, and for her husband, a chicken-and-rice broth left unseasoned in deference to his sensitive stomach. For Mr. Spain, Harry had fried the chicken to a crust, which made amends for the lost heads. And for Mr. June Munger, there were the ribbed molds of nervous red Jello. Mr. June enjoyed agitating them with his spoon: "See, China; Jello don't like to be looked at!"

The children ate separately, at two card tables put up in the living room. Their special child's society, it appeared to Moon, prospered under Carol's charge. She teased and chattered, her laughter ringing with an allure that was unmistakably China's. Beside her, Hannah sat listlessly; across from them was Sid Junior.

The boy looked strong-jawed, fair, and nearly beautiful. It remained Laska's pride that at two he had won a neighborhood beauty contest. He sat erect, and unlike the others, he did not bob toward his plate. At the other table, well-bibbed and with overhand grips on their spoons, were Spain's small girls. All three kept admiring blue eyes on Carol, except for small glances at Selma who, through the archway, still monitored their manners. The tables had been drawn up to the leather divan where Cecil Munger used to nap. The quilted leather excited them as a shrine of the grandfather about whom they had heard only a few, but most delicious, things.

"The divan smells like grandfather, Daddy; honest," Carol said.

"And how is that?"

"Well—strong, kind of. And not very nice."

The dining room's oval post-legged table had been elongated by the insertion of spare leaves. Its ancient scars from tin plates of the old days were hidden beneath lustrous white damask. Harry had known who would take coffee in place of tea or milk. Cups and crystal were correctly laid beforehand because he knew, also, where each one must sit. Moon almost resented Harry for it.

Spain sat at the head, Laska at his right, Texas on his left. Brother hunched next to Texas and beside him, of course, China. Across from them were Bethel and Selma. Around the table's kitchen end were Frank, who looked oddly old-mannish as he ate, and Sid, who shared a curve of the table with Moon. Remo ate in the kitchen, alone.

98

Most of them watched Brother. Their faces kept turning toward him, then quickly away. All the pale blue eyes pitied, regretted. Except for China, they showed the hurt. Moon felt sorry for them.

June smacked and smeared. He pattered unbrokenly to China, who did not shrink from the greasy paw on her shoulder, or from the taste offered from his spoon.

She marveled at the news of Kittypoo, she gasped genuinely at Cinerama. Moon saw her enter Brother's world, romp with him there, yet could sense that she'd never left her own. Here was her special quality. He realized he was thinking, much like Remo, that China was angelic.

He found Bethel's questioning gaze upon him; he wished to shake his head at her. No, Beth, no, this isn't it; this is nothing to do with you and me. In some other destiny I could have loved your sister. God, how deeply—but I don't. It's only that there's a quirk in a man. If you know a woman like China, you have to imagine her as someone you lost. To a man, every beautiful thing he's missed the chance to take or reject is a vital thing, one he should have owned. That's why I watch her, Bethel. What your eyes say is wrong. With us, it's something more. If today you'd fight them for me, with me. . . .

Laska pushed back and lit a flattened brown cigarette. Other chairs scraped. Selma got up to hustle the children outside. Spain asked his sisters' leave to smoke. Elbows on the table, he held his cigarette in both hands, inhaling from it thoughtfully while Harry cleared the table. The Munger women sat patting their lips with napkins, and even June fell quiet.

Moon wished to rise and walk out now, but he couldn't. He watched Spain accept a half-cup of coffee from Harry, heard him tell the Negro the meal was "certainly fit to eat." Still he sat.

Spain drank his coffee, then smiled at all of them. "Uh, I hate to be the one," he bent to bring a worn briefcase up to his lap, "but there are a few bones that ought to be picked. I thought we might sit formally, just for a jiffy—"

Moon, Frank, and Sid got up as marionettes on one string. Remo had appeared in the kitchen door. Brother stared about frantically.

"China, you aim to have one of them star chamb—"

"Mr. Munger," Remo said, "you can come with me now."

Spain squinted palely across bridged hands. "Uh, yes, June, if you please."

"But China, ain't you comin' out? We got to get holt of that Kittypoo; you said it, China—"

She patted his hand. "Later, Beloved. You run, and I'll come after a while."

"Well goddam, me and you—"

"You mustn't talk that way. And I promise, I'll come soon."

Remo had a grip on one fat arm.

"Uh, Mr. Remo, if you don't mind, could you stay on a few minutes. Go with Sid, June—"

Already, Moon was leading the way out. Through the kitchen, away from Munger single-mindedness, from wariness, from business intolerant of in-laws, from affairs cold and blood-less as actuaries. From humiliation. If you were young, you should be able to outwalk humiliation.

Brother followed.

"You gonna tell me about the war, Moon?"

"I've told you, a lot of times."

"Boy, you sure have, thank you. An' I ain't glad none, either, about you doin' without no Cadillac."

"Why do you say that?"

"Me, I got three Cadillacs, an' you can take whichever one, if you crave to take one, Moon. You want it, me and Mister Remo, we just as leave."

Moon leaned against the lot fence. He watched the sun glinting off Brother's chrome-plated brace. Now and then, his spine crept as the dry wall of the house struck a screech from the overheated bit. A few yards away, the children marveled hushedly at this happy destruction their uncle could carry on in impunity.

June's was a labor of love, Remo had said. The curls of clean wood fascinated him; he loved to muse on how the bit seemed to plunge into the wall, yet grew no shorter. He sang, or cursed, and drilled intently.

Nearer, in the afternoon shade of the house, Frank and Sid tossed lazy horseshoes at truck axles driven into the ground. Moon had refused to join them, he was in no mood to parry Frank's jokes, or to covet Sid's composure.

John Remo stepped out on the back stoop. He spat, then came tromping across the yard. He appeared sweaty, angry but subdued. His shirttail hung partly out in front; he'd left his coat behind.

"Disheveled," Moon said. "You look disheveled."

"Crap, Moon; no jokes."

"Was it that bad?"

"Spain gimme high hell, goddammit. In a nice sympathizing way. I ain't supposed to get no sleep; I'm supposed to keep my finger hooked into that fat bastard's ear all day long, and sit guard on them chickens all night!"

"Bitter," Moon said.

"You damn bet."

Unreasonably, Moon was delighted. He said, "We only expect every man to do his duty."

"I got a notion to get me some redbirds. Knock him out cold every night; that'd hold him."

"You didn't put that good idea to Spain, did you?"

"Hell no, I didn't put nothing. He did the puttin'. But I'm sick of gettin' chewed on, Moon, just on account of taking a minute's rest. Spain knows they ain't any other jobs waiting on me; he's got me by the ying-yang. I got my mother to look after. And I don't even know why I mess with that, because hell, one time she boiled my pipes in soda water; my own mother did that!"

"What brought that up?"

"About my old lady? I dunno. Spain makes me sore at everybody."

Remo set his great back against the fence, creaking the lumber, and he got out his pipe to suck through. "They talked and talked and talked, and after a while, Spain decided they were making me think they got no sight of my problems. That's what he said, and by Christ, he put 'em to a vote, where they all held up their hands to show me they was 'in-general by-and-large on-the-whole satisfied!' "

Moon looked back and forth at the mismated eyes.

"That's the truth, Moon, that's what they did."

"Congratulations. You got a vote of confidence."

"Yeah."

For a minute, Moon thought about it. "I'm sorry," he said.

"Well, it did give me a chance to tell 'em about the new trips. The ox, he's been after me to go to New York—for that *Li'l Abner* stage show, on account of 'Li'l Abner' in the funnies. Besides that, he's blisterin' to go to Los Angeles. Wants to see that program on TV, where all those women get up and swap their miseries for free washin' machines."

"Are you going?"

"Maybe. They give me a real polite gig, for lettin' him get the urge, but they shelled out the money. I got three thousand dollars on me. Spain had it, just like he knowed this was coming up."

"A lot of money," Moon said.

Remo shifted to rub a knee that was cramping. "A lot of trouble. I'm in dutch, right now, over that Dallas deal. My balance is way off. And Spain didn't exactly get hot; be better if he did. He just looked at me, through them big window lights of his—"

"Well," Moon smiled, "you really oughtn't to steal from us."

Remo's big face jerked up. He looked amazed, then relieved and somehow, less ugly. He said, "I wish I hadn't."

Moon stared at him. "I was kidding, Remo."

"I ain't. This family could send me up for a few seasons with Uncle Bud, if they're a-mind to."

"Don't tell me, John."

"Hell, I ought to. I aim to put it back, next payday. But I still got to own up. At Dallas, I took a hundred. Sent it off to my mother, telegraph. She don't need it; I don't know how come I done it. Maybe it was because people treated me like a thief when I wasn't. I don't know."

They sat down on their heels, silenced and ashamed of this intimacy. After a minute Moon said, "I hope your mother is getting on all right."

"Guess so." Remo rubbed his neck. "What do you think, Moon? A man swipes a little something once or twice in his life, and the rest of the time he's straight as a die—what do you think? He an honest man, or a crook?"

Moon looked up, at the airliner passing over, low, with landing gear down. "I don't know. I guess he's neither one. I guess he's just human."

Remo marked a herringbone track on the ground with a stick.

Moon gazed at the house. "June's drilling away."

"Yeah," Remo said. "Sounds twice't as loud, inside. Jesus, he's wrecking the place. Wind whistles through them holes —I guess if I go to New York, I'll get me a night's sleep in a warm bed."

Moon grinned. "I'd trade places with you. For a couple of your trips."

"Hell, you're welcome."

"Truth is, Beth and I never had a real trip." The Mooneys took only "normal" vacations. Every summer they went to New Mexico and took a cabin in the Sangre de Cristo's. The kids gathered pine cones, Bethel suffered from the altitude, and Moon read a few books. "Sometime, I'd like to get on a plane —hey, are you and Brother going to fly?"

"To New York, I guess. We'll drive to Los Angeles; that is if we go. I'm supposed to talk him out of going, if I can. Spain says get 'im busy around the place. They want me to get him to chopping weeds, paintin' the barn. Stuff like that."

"No chance, is there?"

Remo blew out his breath. "You oughta hear them excuses. The garden last year, that was the most he ever done. He wouldn't plant nothing but squash, and when the goddamn stuff made, he flailed it every which way with them golf sticks. Said China didn't care none for squash."

Moon stamped tiring feet and climbed to a seat on the fence rail. Across the yard, a stake clanged as a horseshoe glanced off it and went rolling.

"Wallace throws like an old maid," Remo growled.

They watched Sid Glass step up and toss smoothly. He laid on a ringer, then settled another on top of it. "Good," Remo slapped a great thigh, "I hope they're bettin'. Doc Glass will pick him clean. . . ."

Moon closed his eyes. In a grim sort of make-believe, he beamed his thoughts out toward the house; he seemed to feel them passing through his forehead. He pushed his mind at Bethel's, to tell her that for him, she must resist this once the family's strange oneness against all outsiders. The effort, the sun, or the whisky caused his head to ache. Shortly, his palm began to itch insistently, and he scratched it until the blood came.

The family sat in the places of the noon meal, except that they had drawn their chairs closer together. Spain liked the nearness of the women; it touched him as expressive of the single-mindedness so essential to the harmonious operation of your family corporation. He thought his sisters handsome. He approved their reserved dress, their very faint perfumes, their alert and ready manner.

The board understood how much was to be done; it was dedicated and earnest. Spain was grateful, for he realized how easily matters might have been otherwise. He knew oil families who lived, at best, as idlers. This hadn't happened to the Mungers, because from the first, Spain had seen the danger.

As he once explained in a candid speech before his board, certain large oil fortunes tend to choose their own direction. He was speaking of wealth taken from a mature field, where all the heat and plunging of original exploration and development are past. The Munger holdings were of this nature. Their crude needed only to be pumped and sold; thus the management of the properties was scarcely more than a job of maintenance, bookkeeping, investment of earnings, and the exercise of good tax judgment. Spain had identified these facts for himself, out of a careful and objective study of Panhandle oil history.

He conceded that to a large extent, the tough, brilliant-or-lucky pioneers who found the oil developed the industry so rapidly they left nothing basic for their heirs to worry about. The mammoth black ocean remains on safe deposit below the prairie; production from it is prorated by monthly order from the Texas Railroad Commission, relieving the inheritors, even, of deciding how many days per month their wells should be pumped. The state matches supply to demand in the name of conservation, but with the more tangible benefit of price-fixing. Under this regulated allowable, arrived at through the system of advance purchaser nominations and in light of such known factors as pipeline, transport, storage, and refinery capacities, the oil market has become a constant. Price is whatever the industry wishes it to be.

The aggressive old-timers saw, as well, to oil's tax questions. They drilled the exemption called Depletion Allowance deep into expedient politics, charging their heirs only with keeping public attention diverted from it. In the jolly petroleum society of active 27½-percenters, only the impolite ever mention this windfall above a whisper; in the oilless lower echelons of Texas, only the vulgar newcomer or perhaps a testy visiting Yankee Senator brings the DA into discussion, and they are ignored the way uncouth people should be ignored by the well-bred.

Spain's analysis told him that investment of earnings was the most delicate of the heirs' responsibilities. A pattern clearly indicated itself. Why not buy more grassland where oil might someday be found and which, in the meantime, could prosper on Agriculture Department subsidies? Why not accumulate municipal and school bonds, these almost riskless and with tax-exempt yields? Gradually it had become apparent to the Munger chairman that the greatest concern of the oil heir is how to spend his time.

Some of the young scions of Spain's acquaintance had taken hold of charity to squeeze it of every last sweet drop. Some, convinced that culture is the true obligation of second-generation wealth, went chasing after the arts with checkbooks flying and, to Spain, looked quite foolish at it. Others had put on white Stetsons and custom-made boots and traveled about in the role of all the absurd Texas jokes; Spain supposed these were experimenting to discover if there can be, actually, a total leisure.

Well, Spain thanked his stars, his family had never debated such questions. They took the business facts for granted, and they knew what to do with their time. Without need for words, they agreed on their goal; each of them had seemed to understand it from the moment Cecil Munger died. To Spain, it was a rainbow. He hungered for it, his mind envisioned the course; his sisters linked hands with him and they drove ahead together.

In almost thirteen years, the minutes of the Munger board were yet to show a dissenting vote. Your outfits like your New York Central and your Montgomery Ward, Spain thought, might well pay heed, take a lesson. . . .

He frowned at how Laska's smoke lay stale and trapped beneath the ceiling; at how, in this lull, his sisters listened to the gnawing of Brother's bit as it bored into the wall, then exchanged the looks of sorrow that were also of love.

The dining room was hot.

"Uh, to get on," Spain said, "about your road deal. It's true, as Texas points out, that our road is rough and it's one of the few in the county still not paved. I seem to have read where ninety per cent of the county has your blacktopping under your farm-to-market program—"

"There are so many dreadful holes," Texas said, "and if we have any standing at all—doesn't the Commissioners Court see to such things?"

106

"Uh, if you're proposing we send a delegate before the commissioners—"

Laska tapped her pencil against her teeth. "Excuse me, but
what are we now, Spain? For the minutes, I mean. We can't
discuss a road as the board of Panhandle Green Petroleum,
can we?"

"Uh, I doubt we need minutes on this. Now, your board
should be alert to how such public matters as paving can put
the petitioner on public trial, so to speak. At first flash, I do
think the fact we are, uh, substantial taxpayers will carry some
weight with the commissioners. But from the standpoint of
the test involved—"

Laska blew a tree of smoke. "I guess this can come under
Estate, or maybe Trust Administrators. Only, since the road
is the back way to the wells, this might be Panhandle Green's
business after all, don't you think?"

"Uh, very well, PGP will do. Now, if the question is whether
to send a delegate before the court, then I'd say we shouldn't
act off the tops of our heads, and I think you all agree to
that."

"Take that gun club," said Texas, "didn't the county pave
their road?"

"Yes, but to speak straight from the hip—"

"I'll just put the notes under Estate," Laska said. "If that's
wrong, Miss Northington or Mr. Williams-the-lawyer can
straighten them out."

"As you wish. Uh, as I was about to say—"

"If I spoil the minutes, I'm sorry."

China was smiling. "You handle them perfectly." She paused
while an airliner went over. "I don't want to sound contrary,"
she said, "but the road does dead-end at the river, and hardly
anyone uses it except us."

"There," said Spain, "you've put your finger on the point
that could be, uh, embarrassing; that is, if we should set off
any sort of public hearing about the project. Still, if it's the
temper and consensus of the board—"

"Why," Bethel demanded, "must they fly those things right

over us when the airport is miles away? Mightn't we petition about that, too?"

Spain looked at his watch. "To get on, who would like to step out of ranks and carry the ball for us before the commission, so to speak?"

"There aren't any female commissioners," Laska said.

"Uh, true. Perhaps I better tap myself on the head. But the board hasn't expressed itself—shall we vote? Very well, thank you. I'll report to you, just as soon as—uh, by the way, I think the friendliest approach might be to ask the commissioners to lunch with me, unofficially. This is your pork-barrel breed of thing, and the expense wouldn't be great; I can take care of it out of my own pocket."

"Certainly not," Texas said, "that wouldn't be fair. Surely we can charge it to Estate."

Laska shook her head. "Offhand, I doubt that. I'm under the impression we have acted as the board of PGP."

"Then, why couldn't we make up a little pot?"

"A pot would be fine," China said.

"Uh, I appreciate the thought. But to be businesslike, if you'll not allow me the honor, we might go ahead and charge this to Estate, and Miss Northington will know which way to route it. Let's consider this child's face washed, and move along—"

"China," Bethel said suddenly, "are you ill?"

All the blond heads turned to the pretty one; she had leaned forward to rest her face in her hands. Someone said "Oh!" and chairs scraped and the directors were up and gathering about her. China looked up, shaking her head and smiling at them, and she said, "It's only a little nausea."

They offered her water, they drew off her coat, Texas rubbed her wrists while she told them again she was all right. There was always this protective, quick anxiety about China. Spain felt it, yet objectively recognized it as an asset; perhaps, even, it was the Munger cornerstone. He returned to his chair without taking his gaze off his baby sister's lovely face.

For years it had disturbed them all how, for no identifiable cause, China suffered from an occasional, curious "salt attack."

The sensation, she said, was as if a lump of salt formed inside the tip of the tongue, so that she must taste it sickeningly. Her doctor had never explained, leading to the assumption that he could not. The attacks never lasted very long. Somehow, they made Spain angry. However illogical it was, he always suspected the malady was in some way related to Frank.

"No, it isn't the salt," China laughed. "I'm over that; I haven't tasted it for at least two months." Her eyes glistened with beautiful, puzzling, childish joy. "I suppose I got too warm."

Spain was reminded how much he counted on her. Naturally, easily, China could bring the board back from troublesome tangents. She could rally them, merge them, by the simple sweet force of her love. It was no mean way to manage, Spain thought. As his sisters returned to their places, he told her, "If you'd like a short recess—?"

"No, thank you, darlings," China said. "But there's something I can't keep any longer. I'm going to have a baby."

For an instant, they were stunned. Then the tall women raced again to her, noisily, bending to kiss her suddenly flushed cheeks, chattering wildly over her fair head as she hugged them back and laughed. She amazed them that she'd known for two months without telling anyone; she upset them by confessing she'd seen no doctor because there was plenty of time and she felt so good; she delighted them by having kept the news from Frank, whose surprise they might now look forward to observing and enjoying.

Spain stared palely at her. This was outside the realm of his planning. China had been married seventeen years. Spain, all of them, had thought it reasonably settled that she would have no child. It had been an easy conclusion, for Frank wasn't young, and China herself was, to her family, as much the baby as she'd always been. China the tiny one, sitting just chin-high at this same table not so long ago and passing dainty judgments on the food; she who, even as a tot, had owned such wise grown-up eyes, magnificently expressive eyes that could doubt or reproach or approve in sweet glances that warmed you and became unforgettable.

Spain shuddered. That Frank Wallace, so unhealthy, so near

retirement years, should have made China pregnant seemed almost disgusting. But Spain put the idea away from him. His sister was lit with her happiness. It behooved him to be glad, to fit the event into the big picture. Surprisingly, it fitted promisingly. With a child of her own, perhaps she'd not coddle Brother so generously, not stir him so with the intimacy. . . .

When at last the dining room quieted, Spain cleared his throat. "Uh, to get on, despite the happiness we all feel about this development—on this road deal, I want to say we mustn't expect too much. I think that right from the gun, we ought to realize we may get the paving, or we may not get the paving. Uh, if your public opinion is your controlling factor, then I'd say we're pretty well situated, for I do keep my ear to the ground. Still, on the skin of it, I'd say there are other niggers in your woodpile, and we mustn't give ourselves more than a fifty-fifty chance, and I hope that gets us all clear on that."

They smiled at the speech, at how China's announcement seemed to have staggered him.

"Please see the doctor," Bethel said, and China promised, "Of course I will, when there's any need," and then she told them how wonderful it was to expect a baby when it was spring, when the grass was coming green and the trees ready to bud and the whole world starting to come alive so that even the animals were having a ball—"which reminds me; why don't we give a party?"

"Uh, party, you said?"

"Sure," China laughed. "We've never had a party, not a really big one. Couldn't we just invite everybody?"

Bethel said, "Richard and I do owe a thousand social dates. Maybe we should—"

"If you'll pardon me," Spain rattled The Old Girl's onion-skin agenda in his hand, "we have other matters to put the spotlight on. If we might postpone this party matter, since we have just launched one rocket of an adventurous nature—"

"It was thoughtless of me to bring it up on such a busy day," China said. "I'm sorry."

"Not at all, and, uh, please don't think I'm throwing on the

110

wet blanket; I hope that's clear to everyone. But since we have no, uh, precedent already lying in the manger to guide us, and time is so pinched, it seems best to my mind if we just keep the idea for a social out on the horizon for the time being."

"It would have to be at my house," Laska said.

"Uh, what's that?"

"The party."

"I suppose, yes. Now, on your agenda, we have your contract item with Parsons & Cole. It shouldn't take more than a quick jiffy, and as Mr. Williams-the-lawyer pointed out, this is rather pressing."

Spain reviewed the agreement. Parsons & Cole was building them a new thirty-five-mile, ten-inch transport line under terms that required payment on a completion-percentage basis. "Your ditch is cut eighteen miles now, and that's roughly fifty per cent of your mileage, and the pipe is distributed along the site. The contractor estimates this to be a completion of twenty per cent of the whole kaboodle—"

"China, loosen your blouse; you look to be perspiring."

"Thank you, dear; I'm fine. I've been sick in the early morning, but that's common, isn't it?"

"Uh, if I may have your attention—I drove out to the job this past week, with Mr. DeMarco and Mr. Williams-the-engineer, and we agreed—"

Laska said, "That name always reminds me of Moose."

"Who?"

"Mr. Williams's son—the lawyer's. He's the big husky one so good at football and everything. Mr. Williams is awfully proud of Moose—isn't the boy's name Cicero, actually?"

"Uh, as I was saying, we agreed with the Parsons & Cole estimate. Now, I'd like to ask the board to authorize a twenty per cent payment of the contract price. Of course, I brought some photographs of your progress, if you'd like to confirm the headway to your own eyes—"

Texas was laughing; she told them it was mean of her but she could not help it, for she was thinking of what Carol said about Mr. Williams: Carol said the attorney was like one of Uncle Sid's old dogs, in that as he grew older, his gums turned more black. Texas added, to Bethel, that Carol was growing like a weed, wasn't she?

"Uh, if you'll pass your photographs around, you'll see in View Number One, all the pipe strung along the ditch—"

China said, "Let's just vote."

"Fine, and I assure everyone this project is in jim-dandy order."

"How much is it?" Laska said.

"Well, twenty per cent of two million one hundred thousand, that knocks down to four hundred twenty thousand. The draft should be on the Republic National account, so that your Bank & Trust accounts won't require any transfer."

Laska sighed. "Here we sit as Panhandle Green. But didn't we decide last month that Big Plains Investment would build the pipeline and lease it to PGP? Lordy, we can't sit as PGP and spend the funds of Big Plains."

"Uh, I appreciate your being alert there, but if I may refresh your mind—we reversed ourselves on the lease plan, and your Big Plains is lending the money to Panhandle Green, which is the giz that confused you. As a matter of fact, we must settle soon on an advance payment of interest by Panhandle Green to Big Plains, since the tax quarter is breathing down our throats. But that can wait, it's a bird on another bush. So, if everyone is agreeable to paying Parsons & Cole under Clause C of the contract, I would entertain a motion—"

"I move it."

"Second."

"Uh, thank you. All approving will say 'aye.' "

"Aye."

"Good, we're a hundred per cent on that. Now, Miss Treasurer, if you'll drop down about noon tomorrow to countersign the draft—uh, Texas, can you hear me?"

"Oh. Yes, I'll come down."

Spain wiped his forehead and bent to check off the item on his now rumpled, soiled agenda.

"My objection," Bethel was saying, "is that he swears so much."

"Who? Oh, Mr. Remo."

"Well, I was speaking of poor Brother."

"It's all the same," Texas said. "He hears it from Mr. Remo, I'd wager. An ex-policeman, and all that, and he looks like a man who might curse frightfully."

Softly China said, "Brother used bad language before we got Mr. Remo. I hope we aren't being unfair."

"Uh, if we might churn right along—"

"China, I don't see how you bear it, when he calls you—calls you that name."

"Oh, it's sweet of him, really!" Her voice wavered. "Poor Beloved, he's only saying he loves me."

Spain said loudly, "We do have a couple more chestnuts in the fire. Now, spring isn't far off, and you'll remember the lawn problem of last year, and I think we learnt our lesson good and solid. I'm afraid that sixty per cent of the time, our lawns looked pretty sad-sack alongside our neighbors'. The joker was, that hand mower doesn't allow Harry the time to get around often enough. I'd like to hear your thoughts, and my own suggestion will be that we take a cold look at buying a gasoline mower."

"Would this enter as Big Plains Investment?"

"If we can shake this around just as a family, in a purely exploratory way—I contacted several hardware stores, and the best bid on your twenty-inch power model came to seventy-nine fifty. That's your good quality machine, and I'm told the price is ten dollars below list. There is one sleeper—uh, your grass-catcher will come extra."

Texas said, "We should try to avoid the—the complaints that were made against us last year."

"Exactly. Now, with your good fast mower, and a correct schedule for Harry, I'd think he could keep all the lawns trimmed passably well. Uh, in event any of you aren't aware of what a blot this grass business put on the big picture—and we're all in the same canoe—let me say—"

"Excuse me, Spain," Laska said. "But did you know Brother has been discussing this very thing?"

"Uh, no."

China laughed. "That's my fault; I talked with him about it. Bless his heart, he wondered why each of us didn't get our own mower. He offered to come to town and run mine for me."

"We shouldn't involve him in such things," Laska said.

Spain looked narrowly about the table. "That's true, and I don't wish to throw any stone. Uh, I dislike touching on the subject again, the way we've been through it today. But we must all watch our Q's in his hearing, the way he picks up ideas. And believe me, I wish I didn't feel compelled to point that out."

China smiled at them. "You're right, of course. But, love him, he does want to be included."

Spain nodded. "Well, to lash right out, what's the pleasure of the board on the mower deal?"

"I'm for it," Texas said, "even if I have no lawn."

"Then, if we're a hundred per cent, I'll go ahead about making the purchase. And, as far as I can see, that brings us around to adjournment."

Bethel sat up straight in her chair. "If I may, I'd like to get everyone's opinion on a couple of things. If—"

Laska said wearily, "How do we pay for the mower? Certainly it can't be PGP."

"Uh, we did leave that hanging, didn't we? Well, I'd suggest we carry this through just as family. We might each put sixteen dollars into a kitty, and that would get the wheels to grinding."

Laska put down her pencil and stretched. To China she said, "Let's you and I go shopping tomorrow and buy you some maternity dresses."

"Oh, have I really begun to show?"

Bethel said, "There's something I hoped we could talk about today; it won't take long."

Spain frowned. "Well, we do have to ask Moon in, about his new clerk and for the, uh, presentation."

"It's Richard I want to talk about," Bethel said. She sounded tensely earnest. "Two things. First, I do think Richard might have a new car. He hasn't suggested this. But we drove out in his car today, and it smokes awfully. He did say it blows all the oil out the hind end, or something."

"Uh, that's a Chevrolet, isn't it? Well, let's remember to look at it before we shut down shop and get away."

Bethel rushed on. "The important thing," she said, "is about The Camera House. Richard has an idea about movie films, and I want to urge we consider it fully. It would cost a great deal of money, but he believes in it, and I think it's wonderful. . . ."

She told them; they listened without interruption. As she finished, Spain made his hands into a frail bridge for his chin and he stared, in thought, at the wall. "Well," he said, "let's ask Moon to come in, if he will."

"Movies," Texas said. "What a novel idea."

Bethel waited miserably for her husband to appear; she suddenly felt like his betrayer and at the same time, she seemed cut off from Spain and her sisters in some curious, uncomfortable way. It was good to have thought about his car. But on Richard's plan, she felt a guilty dissatisfaction, as if her endorsement of it had been unfair to all of them.

Her sisters were chatting, about a shopping tour for China that was developing into a family outing; about the doctor to be chosen. China glowed, her beauty now more striking than Bethel could remember it. Then abruptly, sweetly, China changed the topic.

"Have any of you seen Reverend McLean recently? He's growing long sideburns; there's just the nicest touch of gray in them."

"Lordy," Laska said, "are they Van Buren's, or the rock-and-roll kind?"

"Oh, neither. Just sort of Western, and very handsome. They take away from that—that discoloration on his face."

Bethel understood, then, that China hadn't really changed the subject at all. "Surely you remember," she was saying, "when he preached Papa's service. He has a birthmark, I suppose it is, and it looks inflamed most of the time. But with the sideburns, you hardly notice it."

Bethel recognized in her sister the ancient fear of all pregnant women: will the baby have a perfect body, will he be all right in his mind, will he be born without ugly marks—

Laska said, "Won't the deacons shave him?"

"I hope not," China smiled. "Poor fellow, he's been very self-conscious."

Bethel heard Richard's tread on the back stoop, and suddenly she identified her sense of separation from him and from her family. The truth was that, even while she described it to the board, her husband's idea sounded to her own ears quite absurd. She might have been saying, this is silly, but I love my husband, and won't you please help me make him happy? She had asked them to vote not their business sense, but her heart, and it wasn't fair to any of them, least of all Richard.

At the door, Moon hesitated. After the sun, the room looked dark, and the people were strangers. As his eyes adjusted, he picked them out. Separately, he knew them. But together, he did not. For a moment he stared at Laska, and she seemed to be Bethel; he had gazed at Bethel, and thought her China. About this table, or the one downtown, it seemed the beautiful Munger grew less so and the unattractive ones appeared more handsome. He had seen the mutation before; he knew it to be no trick of light or of his mood. All the blond heads, the tall bodies, the lean cheeks, the identical sets of wan blue eyes. Seen this way, they were duplicates and inseparates, each one unknown to him.

"Uh, Moon, come in, come in!"

He took the chair he'd used at noon. He searched about for some sign that Bethel had spoken to them. His wife's face looked withdrawn, a unit of the massed opposition. He wished she'd come sit beside him. Or couldn't she hold out her hand, or maybe, just show him a smile?

"Well, about your new employee at the store—"

"Shouldn't Frank be here too?" Moon said.

"Uh, he said you'd speak for both of you. Have you brought along this woman's application?"

"No," Moon said, "I didn't rush that, pending approval of the extraordinary salary."

Spain's pencil neck may have colored, but the pale eyes did not alter. The chairman told his sisters, in detail, that he had approved, tentatively, a "premium salary" for the new woman at The Camera House.

"What is the salary, Richard?" China said.

"Seventy a week." Moon lied to them easily now, and it frightened him. A lie should come hard.

"Good gracious," said Texas, "is she AF of L or something? That's twenty-four barrels."

Plus, Moon thought, a dozen barrels on the side.

"Uh, if I may stick an oar into the pie on Moon's behalf," Spain said, "I did feel seventy might be commensurate, considering we are asking this woman for several skills. I think I know what concerns all of us. But in that regard, let me say I doubt a single instance of this sort will force us to any, uh, reevaluation of personnel policies. In fact, a little drift off course in these inflationary times, as I told Moon, may be necessary to fill this job at all."

"Then let's approve," China said. "It's getting late, and I'm sure the children are tired."

"Well, I'd hate to shut off discussion, if you think this does snipe at basic policy—by the bye, Moon, what was her name?"

"Billie Ted Birdsong."

"That's—odd," Texas said.

"It's fascinating," China smiled. "I vote yes."

As they approved Teddy Birdsong unanimously, Moon tried to catch Bethel's eye. She did not look up; she appeared to be sketching tiny squares on the margin of her agenda.

"Now," Spain said a trifle loudly, "while we're convened as The Camera House board, we understand you've a major bone to pick."

Moon's hand shook as he felt inside his coat for his notes. As he brought them out, Spain said quickly, "Bethel has gone over the idea with us, and I know I speak for the entire board when I say you are to be, uh, commended on blasting right out with such a progressive thought. However—"

From there it went quickly. Moon held his notes but half unfolded in his hands. For a while, he listened; he heard all the familiar echoes. Your Estate had to keep an eye on your big picture, first and foremost; each limb to be encouraged or pruned in light of all the others, this being the soundest of your principles in management of your diversified corporation, and this didn't imply that the idea was bad; indeed, the first impression was of its great merits. But then, ninety-nine per cent of the time, your conservative thought was your brilliant thought, "and it's not often prudent, Moon, to expand a business that's, uh, losing money, which is the hitch we have to face. . . ."

It continued. The cold logic, the almost paternal annihilation of the dream. Moon saw Bethel dimly. Her eyes pleaded; for what, he did not know or care. He was aware that the other faces watched him; they did not judge, they offered friendly mercy. He dug at his hand; he wanted to yell.

He realized Spain had asked him something and was repeating it. "Isn't there something more?"

"That's all," Moon said and got up.

"Well, if you would gab with us a moment more—Bethel tells us you are interested in a new automobile."

He turned back to face them, to glare anger at his wife. "No," he said flatly, and Bethel flushed as if the two of them were now to exhibit a private fight.

"Well," Spain was saying, "if you are having trouble with your car, perhaps you should trade. It has occurred to me, that if you'd not mind a sign on the door of your next one, then we might buy it as The Camera House board and depreciate it for taxes, though of course you'd have to use commercial license tags."

Moon reeled. One blow following another in stinging combinations, and they didn't even realize it.

Then he fought them back with the first thought he had,

118

the recollection that two hours ago, Brother June had offered him a Cadillac. He said, "I want a Cadillac."

Spain started, his chin sank to the bony support of his hands, and he tried to smile. "Uh, it pleases me, Moon, that we can be plain spoken on matters where you are concerned, and, to be frank and lay our cards above-board, let me say the Estate has a certain, uh, delicacy to deal with on public relations, if that's the term. With three Cadillacs in the family already—well, you see the position, I know. Now, let me make clear you needn't put up with shabby transportation, not for a minute, as far as this board is concerned. The fact is, I'd like to be the one to propose we make a sort of stand-by approval for another Chevrolet, just in case of your breakdown. There's no bother I know of like your car you can't depend on in the clutches. So, I move—"

"Forget it," Moon said. He turned toward the door.

"Are we still The Camera House?" Laska said.

"Wait, Richard!"

Moon stopped, looking back at his wife.

"Please, dear," she said. "I—I want you to have a new car."

"A Cadillac?"

"Oh, please—"

Spain came to his feet, a strained smile shaping his mouth unnaturally, and he said, "Uh, we're all tired, and perhaps we should leave this under advisement, for the time being. Besides, while Moon is with us—and if I may have your attention, because this news will warm the roots of your hearts—I have an announcement, and a ritual that will be pleasant to perform."

Moon stood waiting; it was all too incredible to walk out on.

"Uh, to get to the brass tacks, your Mr. Giddings telephoned and spoke in, uh, lavish terms of our Richard Mooney's job in the United Fund drive. This board should understand how favorably impressed Mr. Giddings was with our, uh, flag bearer, and he made it clear he wants Moon back for the next campaign."

"How wonderful," China said.

"Indeed; an achievement of enormous value, Moon, and we all take our hats off." Spain's long body bent to his briefcase. He drew out a silk-upholstered black box and came lankily around the table with it. He raised the spring lid before putting the box in Moon's hand. "To express our appreciation, in just a small way. . . ."

Moon stared down at a set of triangular cuff links set with diamonds. Spain droned, "Speaking for these directors and all the companies, let me congratulate you, and I want us all to give our hustler here a big hand!"

Moon looked about him, rattled, angry, indecisive in the presence of this enormous new absurdity. The Mungers, augustly assembled, blessed him in five identical smiles; they pounded their hands together with the vigor of sincerity. He saw Bethel come to her feet as if lifted by the pride, the love, the ownership dominating her face like a fever. He shook his head at them, and he groaned. At once the Munger faces were amused and sympathetic: God, they thought him overwhelmed!

He strode out through the kitchen, letting the rickety screen slam hard. Behind him hushed, delighted utterances filled the dining room, and one of them continued applauding. He plunged on toward the barn; he had stepped on Remo's squat shadow before seeing the man. He stabbed the jewel box into his pocket, to get it out of sight, to conceal his shame. At his elbow, Remo chuckled. The big Pole had heard the cheering.

"That's how she goes, boy."

Moon swore. "And I don't really give a damn."

"Now who's bitter?" Remo grinned. "Makes me think of a nigger I used to stick in jail just about every Saturday night. A good nigger. He told me once't his wife fixed greens, mostly collards with bacon, every day of this world. At first, he beat her up. But he quit that after a while. He told me if you eat greens long enough, the bitterness gets to taste sweet to a man."

To Moon the talk seemed distant; he heard himself speak,

but he wasn't participating. "All right," he said, "what's the philosophy?"

"Hell, I don't know," Remo said. "I just happened to think of it."

"Collards?" Moon said.

"Yeah."

Moon attended, slowly, to his hand. For no reason, he thought of those Red Cross boxes he saw once in a Navy hospital. Filled with toothpaste and razor blades and candy bars and paper-back books. "Comfort Boxes," they were labeled. You just reached in and took what you wanted. Moon, through two weeks as an ambulatory patient, had tried to use them. He'd never done so; he couldn't make himself dip into such benevolence.

"None of my business," Remo was saying, "but it ain't your speed to get all pitiful."

"I'm thirty-five years old," Moon said, and Remo seemed to know what he meant. He heaved his back against the fence, so that the nearest posts creaked off plumb.

"Well," he said, "maybe they got to blow apart pretty soon, like from too much yeast or something. Hey, look yonder at your goddamn brother-in-law."

June Munger was at the back door, peering in, calling to *her* thunderously. They could see how his blank scalp had sunburned; it was crimson and would blister.

"Let's go to the car," Moon said.

"All right. But you help me remember, I got to sack up some of them extra Grape-Nuts pretty soon."

"What's that?"

"Spain's wife, she says her kids like 'em, and they ain't no need to waste. She aims to carry some home with her."

"My God."

They walked past the south side of the house, cutting wide around the mud from Brother's hose. Moon was surprised at how fresh the ground smelled. The earth had needed a washing, and it had taken a plodding old has-been to order it, and a

121

mental cripple to carry it out, and yet it had worked. There seemed something significant about it, but for the present, Moon didn't care what it was.

"Your notion about the store," Remo said. "They kilt it, didn't they?"

"Very dead."

"Hell, what do they want?"

"Remo, I'm sick of talking about it."

As Moon unlatched the Chevvy's trunk, Remo said, "Well, with all that dough Spain could buy hisself a hospital, I guess, but that wouldn't make him no doctor."

John Remo bent behind the car to drink first. Moon gazed up at the house, The Old Place. It was late enough to tell the sun would set red. Because it wasn't quite spring, darkness would pull down rapidly, like a blind. Moon wished to get away.

But the Mungers were still in there. Talking and talking, or kissing each other, or maybe still clapping all the slim hands. How gently they tore the flesh off him.

He shuddered. The terror was that a moment ago he'd told Remo the truth; he could no longer care.

VII

Moon lagged back, behind the dust of the others. He switched on the low beams, and he drove the road home very slowly. The light sprayed now and then over big jack rabbits crossing ahead of the car, their concave flanks showing plainly the cruelty of drouth. Stars were out, and for a quarter-mile, he watched one. A low, red one. He couldn't recall the old words, those that began, twinkle twinkle.

When did this happen to a man? This ability to look at Venus and think, it's only reflected sun? Always he had meant to care about essences. He could remember caring, down to the founts of his blood, about poverty and pride, sickness and hurt; about bad smells and Okies and, oh yes, about the talked-of, talked-of Millennium that had hung always in front of the Mooney family; the magic carrot suspended before the treadmilling mule.

The night had quieted the Chevvy, and, it seemed, his family. Texas had accepted a lift with China. Carol and Hannah were weary and silent in the back, and beside him, Bethel was a pale statue that occasionally blinked stone eyes.

Perhaps, Moon thought, the several drinks lay too alive in

his stomach; maybe they made him wonder who he was. Or it could be the sociologists—damn them, those professional cleavers of humanity—did know a few things. In the sudden evening chill, he thought he could remember the cold, raspy, ungloved hands of the midwife.

It happened in northeast Amarillo, in his father's square four-room house, this but a speck in the vast clutter around cheap warehouses and the enormous tin barns of the city's "light industry." Among others no larger, it had stood on a narrow weedy lot and on borrowed time, rotting away at the corners while waiting for one of the expanding machine shops to swallow it.

Most evenings, his parents had sat in a kind of juicy-lipped speculation about what outlandish price the house must one day bring. It was only until this event, this Millennium, that they must "live tight," and not one second longer. The suspense dominated, it raced his parents to the door whenever a stranger knocked. When they were gone, outlasted by the house, Moon had had to sell the place immediately to complete their lives and make right their graves.

But for himself, then, only Davis & Scarborough was actual and important. Davis & Scarborough Hide & Wool, its plant a tall whitewashed ogre doing grisly business just two blocks down the street.

At all hours, the rancid steel-bedded trucks crept in and out, like mechanical red buzzards, delivering the carcasses to be skinned and rendered for tallow. "Gut wagons," the kids called them. They carted in hogs and sheep and cattle, once in a while a horse, and whatever the cargo, they hauled also the stink and the flies. Big, green, fat flies, Moon remembered; so lazily content they could be thumped off by the least stealthy finger. And the stink—

Cass Street, some said, caused a permanent curl of lip on those reared there. The air seemed visible, its power stretched the nostrils. As a boy, Moon breathed it shallowly; he had ghastly green visions of what might be happening to the flesh that wasn't renderable. But he never quite yielded to Cass Street's air.

He had learned to stare up at the sun, until the glare made him sneeze. The sneezes exploded away the stink, and for an instant afterward Father seemed to have sold the house and they had moved away. It was a fanciful discovery. He coached the other kids. Once, four of them sat out a sunny afternoon on the curb, taunting the sun and sneezing until they bled. Then later, there was a ninth-grade English teacher who taught him to fight the stink differently. She guided him toward a certain cynicism, wherein Davis & Scarborough became the smell of life, something that had to be breathed, but which could be leered at and mocked.

Bethel said, "If you wouldn't mind going a little faster, Richard. The children are tired."

Dimly in the rear-view mirror, he could see his daughters. Carol sat very still; if she'd spoken since saying good-by to Brother and Remo, he'd not heard it. He wondered what sensation, of scent or touch or sound, filled her childhood. Good or bad, and would it linger in her recollection of her parents?

The hide-house odor could color, for him, even the memory of his mother. Short, husky Velma Mooney. Slopping about the house in the frayed black tennis shoes that were a therapy for her sore, always puffed ankles. Canning black-eyed peas in the greasy little kitchen. Baiting mousetraps, draping summer-soured bedding over the back fence for venting in the hide-and-wool air.

His father never thought of abandoning the neighborhood. He could curse Davis & Scarborough, in the language of a twenty-five-year brakeman for the Santa Fe. But until the Millennium, the house was handy to the switch yards, and to the temporary hall of the Trainmen's Brotherhood. Anyway, Gerald Mooney seemed to lose touch with the stink after he had his stroke.

That tragic Mr. Mooney, the neighbors were fond of saying. Moon didn't agree.

With his mother, he'd had to wait on his father, hand and foot. Gerald couldn't fasten a button or tie a shoelace; he couldn't raise a spoonful of stew safely to his mouth unless aided. He had to be bedded and bathed. He mixed words. He lost his ability to read. Velma mourned him as if he were dead, yet complained at the burden of him and about his new way of thought. Moon, while saddened by the calamity of the stroke, liked his father better.

When in good health, Moon's father had been unable to sit down to an ample meal without lecturing on the crime of gluttony, just as though he weren't about to commit it. Nor could he let an evening pass without loud prophecy of the fall of the "moguls" and the ultimate ascension of "the little man."

But after the stroke, his were such wonderful ideas. Sitting out his days in the wheelchair the Brotherhood pitched in to buy for him, Father pretended to study, always with a copy of *Liberty* or *The Pathfinder* or the Bible spread on his lap. Often he called Moon to sit by while he described what he had not read and then expounded on it, shaping it into a new learning. Moon loved him; it was wonderful.

"Son, what folks are bothered about, at the root, is the Creation. All their troubles go back to there, you see. Well, let me tell you how it looks. When the Lord made this earth, it wasn't no bigger than the state of Rhode Island, if it was even the size of that. He fixed it up a manageable size, you understand; just roomy enough for them two He put on it.

"After a spell, He seen the world was going to be sinful, and Son, you're old enough to know the facts, and the fact just boils down to Adam getting into Eve's britches. Well, the Lord figured out death, then, and He added it to a man's back. And He decided a man's body might as leave turn to dust.

"You begin to see the scheme, Son? There was more and more people. But the earth got bigger every time somebody died, so as in a little while, everything was balanced out. Well, here's what we came to. Big lot of people, all sinful and bound to die, and a great big ball of dust for 'em to live on."

Velma condemned it, as the sort of tall story told to tempt the Eternal Fires; she never guessed that Gerald meant it.

Summer afternoons, when Moon rolled his father down the block to the Conoco station, there where Cass Street vanished into U.S. 66, he might hear the concept again. And if a wheel of the chair left the sidewalk to touch bare ground, Father would yell, "Lookout, don't be running over all those dead folks!"

Moon would park his father beside the cold-drink box. With the nickel his mother had given them, he bought a sweaty-cold Dr. Pepper. Then, while his father sat sunning, eyes closed, mouth sucking at the bottle, Moon would sink down against a gasoline pump to wait. If Moon thought how good the drink must be, he had to think, also, how his mother promised, "Your time is coming." And to watch 66 move by—this was free.

He liked the Okies best. They chugged along west, old cars strapped with bedding and rub boards and paper suitcases, and some had signs, "California or Bust." Moon wished to go with them. Sure, they were poorer than he, his mother said. And she had compelled him to see that the Okie kids were tired and dirty, and their grown-ups harried and afraid. But he was glad when they stopped for water, or to steal old tires from behind the station, and he bet they hardly noticed Davis & Scarborough, so quickly were they gone. Whatever Mother said, one thing was plain. If the Okies had gotten into a stink of their own, they knew enough to run from it.

Usually, while wheeling his father home, Moon could listen to the newest of his ideas. How the mongrel that trailed them was nearer to God than anybody, since he was made of love and affection, and nothing else; how Moon, because he was growing up, ought to be told that nothing is so sweet about a woman as her feet; how the Depression could be braced up to and killed if everyone in the country would just spend four dollars cash, at the same instant on the same day; how the dust storms could be ended, if only each man, woman, and child in the Bowl got the energy to tote out a few pails of water and pour them on the ground. And how, likewise, even Mr. Roosevelt could be put a stop to, if only one patriotic young man would step up and put a bullet in his heart.

Moon recalled his mother as busy, dutiful, yet a somehow disenchanted woman. She saw to it he stayed in school, that he was mended and scrubbed and paddled, and she aimed him with a shove toward a particular mark which had been established long ago by an East Texas family named the Clacks.

Moon lived by the shadow of the Clacks without ever getting himself informed on them.

"Mother, who are the Clacks?"

"The *Clacks,* that's who. Finest people that ever breathed."

Moon deduced that the Clack children had been brilliant at school, obedient and mannerly at home, constantly mindful of their elders, and, in net result, had made amazingly successful adults. A word about the Clacks was expected to cut him down a peg or two; to make him humble and malleable.

He had been in his second year at Hardin-Simmons, on his father's insurance money and his own athletic promise, when his mother died. He could remember how, during the long bus ride home, he had thought compassionately, for the first time, about her worship of the Clacks. There might have been a Clack she longed to marry. Later, at the funeral, believing this let Moon think his mother's life tragic; it freed him to grieve deeply.

She lay "all gussied up," as she herself would have said, in a lavender shroud, her face powdered and strangely sweetened, just as if the house Millennium had come at last. Moon found he missed her, and missed the most those things that had always irritated him—the stained muslin aprons, the Clacks, the maddening squish-squash of Cass Street air as it pumped in and out the tin eyelets of her tennis shoes.

Moon shook himself; perhaps Remo was right, maybe he was giving himself pity. Why else did he look back in time to dwell upon the old specters? How much better, he thought, if instead of measuring time by accounting what is past, we could use a calendar that gauges only what remains of it, so we might think only of what's ahead to be done, like so-many shopping days until Christmas, buddy, and you'd better get to humping. It seemed he must convince himself that today's time, tomorrow's time is all that counts. Even if it's to be limbo; a void marking off the hours, slowly, toward the end of an Estate-in-trust.

Bethel turned on the seat. "Carol, is something wrong?"

"No'um."

"You're very quiet."

"Yes'um."

"Isn't Hannah asleep?"

"Yes'um."

"All right. We'll be home soon."

Seldom, Bethel realized, had she seen her husband chewing gum. Except, he was chewing gum the first time she ever saw him; she'd almost forgotten that.

She watched his face, just half lit by the faint orange light reaching up at them from the instrument panel. His jaw ground slowly, as God's jaws do, or isn't that the mills? But they ground hard, the muscles rolling like parallel cables. He would look furious, she thought, except for his lip. He had it out in a miff, like a pouting puppy. He looked beautiful.

If hurt about The Camera House, if angered at her unlucky timing about the car, he should at least have approved the cuff links. They were expensive and unusual. She had relished knowing about them in advance, the secret hers with Spain, China and the others excluded. It had pleased and touched her when, after Richard made his way outside, the others insisted on sharing in the gift. Now, she regretted allowing it. In her excitement, she'd not suspected their kindness would make it seem she had been looted of something.

She struggled against resenting them, for the deed, or for what was said. Of course, Texas had meant nothing; indeed, hadn't she tried to call the words back? She'd spoken just as Richard cleared the kitchen, while Bethel herself yet applauded her husband; she'd asked lightly enough, "Now what sort of a 'vert' is he?"

"I—don't understand."

"Oh, you know, Beth. Introvert, extrovert, per—oh, I'm sorry, that's not clever, is it? Forgive me."

It stung like fire. Bethel had but slimly curbed the words that leaped to her lips, *And what sort of "verts" are we?* She, all the others, had been "verts" of a kind, once, and they'd revealed it to each other. Texas should remember that best; for years, her presence made them all remember.

The big funeral coach had appeared on the road, this road, shortly after lunch. The five of them had stood in the yard, watching it come. They were dressed in their best, and the effect was to make each of them more awkward as they moved about, just keeping clear, while the two young men from Gray Bros. put Papa in a corner of the living room. On directions whispered to each other, the young men banked a few floral pieces about Papa; they raised the bronze lid slowly, as if fearing it might squeak, and they propped it and draped it over with a veil of wispy gray. Then the young men bowed stiffly and went away.

Through the afternoon, a few people drove out, cutting speed as they caught sight of the house, lest they raise a disrespectful dust. They parked silently, they approached the house, hats in hand. Bethel thought them the wrong people. No neighbors bearing covered dishes. No one from school. Just people who were obliged.

She couldn't even call the names. Men from the big majors that then paid only a dollar twenty-six for Papa's good crude; men from the pipeline company that moved it. One, the elderly geologist who, back in the early 'twenties, first mapped the Munger producing sands, and following him, his awed and embarrassed and totally misplaced young wife. A discreet sampling, too, of Papa's employees, indentifiable by department, together expressing sympathy like elected spokesmen. And Mr. Williams-the-lawyer, whom Papa had trusted.

As though organized and coached, they entered the house

in sets. They looked down into the coffin, at Papa in his new suit, at the two ugly green marbles on Papa's watch chain. These were Papa's gallstones, worn for years where other men displayed Elks' teeth or Phi Beta keys or miniature caterpillar tractors. Gray Bros. had left them, because they judged them to be unpolished gems. The family left them, out of a lack of courage to take them away.

The visitors did not linger, Bethel remembered. They only glanced, as if to demonstrate that they held no cheap curiosity about a rich man dead from a dog's disease. As each returned to the front yard, he sought out Spain, and held out a hand and said, "If there's anything I can do?"; one buyer of crude remarked, additionally, that although it was a terrible time to face business, he felt he must point out that there were pressing crude contracts that now would have to be reexecuted, and with a war on, there could not be a moment's lag in oil, for sake of the boys over there.

May's late dark had come before the family was alone. Quietly they ate the supper of cold cuts China had thought to provide, and they spoke tentatively of the future for Brother. They settled who would sit up the night and who might sleep. Then they found themselves standing about in the living room, empty of words, looking at each other, and at Papa. Bethel knew that any of them might have done it. As it happened, the voice was Texas's.

She, the eldest, advanced on the casket and put her closed hand on the metal counter of it. They saw her bend down toward the swollen, bleached face.

Texas said, "So there you are, Papa."

The words hung hypnotically among them. Behind her, Bethel heard China sob; China would not yield to what the rest of them had no will to fight.

In that moment, what sort of "verts" were we?

They stood in the room like a community of remorseless murderers. Behaving as if each had helped put Papa in his corner, as if each were an avenger. It was smug and cold. For an instant, Bethel thought Papa hadn't died of the dog bite.

131

He seemed dead because his children had united their hate and brought it to bear on him in a single force. She had fled the house in a horror that was for all of them.

She knew all their memories. Spain, wincing at Papa's voice: "You goddamn kids, you done your chores yet? You, Snake, I want them hogs fed; you got to be hollered at all the time? And don't you put in, Meliter. He does look like a goddamn snake, don't he? Look at him! Six feet long, big around as my thumb. . . ."

Or Texas. That day in the kitchen, not long after the oil. In the summer; that was 1926, named ever after, The Oil Year. Papa came in the back way, smelly and staggering. Texas hadn't even turned from the dishes at the sink. Maybe she had looked like Mama. She was as tall, almost as heavy, and she was in a feed-sack dress by Purina, just as Mama wore. Maybe they did look the same.

Papa was fresh from Amarillo, where all the oil people drank and swapped and jockeyed, and he shouted something 'gleefully, about another drilling and the celebration of it, and he sent a rough hand scooping up under Texas's skirt. She turned with a meat fork in her hand; Bethel thought she almost stabbed him.

"Jesus, I thought you was Meliter!"

And if it had been Mama?

Bethel felt chilled.

You should not speak of "verts," Texas.

The car straddled a rabbit. Bethel looked aside at Richard; he hadn't noticed.

Her mood was deteriorating; she recognized the cheerless aftermath that followed all Sundays spent at The Old Place. While there, it was good. Brothers and sisters she loved, each loving her. But as now, driving away? The associations of the old house could come surging after her; they overtook and smothered her under ugly memory. Of homemade print bloomers, peanut-butter buckets for lunch pails. Braided hair too ratty to be combed. Of fright at coming home, dread at leaving for school along the furrow Papa ordered Spain to plow across the field so they'd not lose their way. When she remembered, The Old Place seemed to echo still with Papa's drunken, timbery shout, "When I speak to you, then jump, yu' little snotboxes! Else I'll slap the dogwater out of you!"

From the dining room, Bethel might look into the kitchen, and she would remember Mama standing there over the stove, a box of Arm & Hammer raised over the iron cooking pot: Papa called it "degassing the beans," and the ugly phrase made the event itself indelible.

If she turned the other way, she must see Papa's beaten leather couch, where he slept in his clothes after liquor, and nearby, the high-backed chair where he sat, a bottle on the floor beside him, to read boomingly out of the Atlas if Mama was trying to read aloud, instead, from St. Mark. Bethel thought the soiled, blue-backed look of the Atlas returned to her more clearly than Papa's face.

There was the Sunday when Papa summoned a bootlegger named Hank; "Sit a spell, Hank, sit a spell and we'll talk."

Bethel could recite every word.

"Now Hank, take my first woman. Nary a kid from her, and she was pore at cooking. But look around you now. Got me a pretty good bunch of little snotters, ain't I? Me and Meliter got six of 'em before we found out what was causing it."

Hank squirmed decently; he began trying to get away. Perhaps he could look beyond Papa and see Mama in the kitchen, where she bent over supper that waited on the stove and dropped quiet tears that spat as they struck the stovelids.

"See 'at big 'un there? That's Texas, she come first after them two stillborns. Sired the day I was fifty-three, an' named her right after this big country. And that next 'un, see her? That's Laska, she come next. Picked her straight out of the Atlas; 'though I nearly went homesteading in 'Laska one time. She's mostly boy, one of them kind that split when they oughta sprouted.

"June, he showed up next. I didn't have no hand in naming him; Meliter done that, on account of he was born in June, and I wasn't here to watch out. And that one there, that's

Bethel. The skinny one. Fixed her up straight out of the book, too.

"Bet you never thought of it. There's Bethels in Maine, Kansas, Kentucky, Missouri, Tennessee—and a bunch more places. I figured to put one in Texas, and like I tell the kid, if you seen all the Bethels, you've seen half the world.

"Them two little 'uns, yonder. Spain and China. I figured them was places I was never going to see no other way. China, she's the prettiest one, see her? Got the prettiest name, if you think about it, by God!"

Bethel looked aside at Richard. He drove faster now. She thought of scooting along the seat, putting her arm about his shoulders. The notion quickened her breath. . . .

"Big ganglin' gals," Papa said. "They'd of been good wives in my day. But they ain't no demand for the knuckledy ones any more."

This last was what she had remembered the day she met Richard. All of them except Papa and June and Spain had found places in town by then, and anyway, Papa was downstate at a meeting of Independent Producers. So with China, Bethel had dared "go patrolling" for the USO. Since it was almost Christmas, the regulars were reluctant to work, although the crowds of servicemen on leave had turned Polk Street khaki. At the service club, Mr. Holland told them, not a sandwich had been eaten or a ping-pong ball broken. He asked China to get out and "bring them in by the droves," and the way he directed himself to China, Bethel felt she was along as a chaperone.

They drove Mr. Holland's car up and down Polk. They collected a load of Air Force men and delivered them. At the first signal light on the second trip, they saw First Lieutenant Mooney.

Huge and trim, he looked, if much too young to be an officer. He stood at a curb, splitting a stream of shoppers that flowed around him.

"There's a target," China said. "You ask him, Beth. It's your turn. Quick, before the light changes."

"I don't enjoy this part of the job."

"Don't be so shy, honey. I'll bet he's dying for some Coke and ham salad."

"Well—"

"Oh, look, Bethel!"

Bethel craned. Richard stood straight and handsome, as if posed for a Marine Corps poster. Except he had puckered, and was blowing a great pink balloon of bubble gum.

"Marvelous," China laughed, and she put her face to the window. "Hello, Lieutenant. My sister and I are shanghaiing people for the USO. Have you some time?"

There was war and Christmas all around, and sunshine. Bethel felt the mixture quickening her blood, and she watched the young Marine with excitement. He spat away his gum and stepped toward the car.

"Want to come?" China said.

He glanced at the signal, which was changing. "Right now, you mean?"

"Yes. Come get in; we have to hurry."

They held back exasperated traffic while he climbed into the back. Bethel was pleased at how he squashed down the cushion. And just like the soap operas, he did smell mannishly of bay rum.

"Does this really have something to do with the USO?" he said.

Too quickly, Bethel put her arm along the seatback, so he might see her armband, and she wished she had not flushed. China laughed easily.

"Oh, it really does, Lieutenant. I'm China Wallace. This is my sister, Bethel Munger. We're recruiters."

"I see. And I apologize."

Bethel sat stiffly, feeling immense, coveting China's smallness and sweet, glib tongue. Because of China, they quickly knew his name, that he had Christmas leave, that there was an R on the end of his USMC and he was glad of it; that this was his home town.

"Maybe you'd prefer just a lift home," China said. "Your people will—"

"No," he smiled. "No family."

"Oh, I hope you've found a place to stay."

"I have, a hotel. Mangiest one in town, I imagine."

It was the first time Bethel experienced her sudden and shattering concern for him. Her thoughts placed him in one of those shoddy places Papa spoke of as "whore-tels," and it made her miserable. "The town is very crowded," she said.

They sat at one of the rock-topped, wire-legged fountain tables Mr. Holland had borrowed for the duration and six. China opened and brought the Coca-Colas. Richard smoked, watching them as they told of Mr. Holland's frustrations which centered, just now, on the Air Force boys, who already were leaving.

Bethel thought him beautiful. She said, "Did you have plans for your leave? I mean, the USO has a service—but of course, you know the town."

"Yes." He took his gaze off China. "I noticed your names are different. In war, I think, we're all allowed bad manners. So, which of you is married?"

"My sister is." Bethel blurted it, and felt a fool.

China smiled. "I'm Mrs. Frank Wallace."

He finished his drink and got up.

"If you go," said China, "Mr. Holland may shoot himself."

"I hope not. There's a movie I meant to see. Maybe I can get a seat now."

Bethel rose, then sat down again. "We're—supposed to urge you to come back."

"Thank you."

China said, "There's a dance here tonight. Girls coming up from the college. You should come."

"Will you be here?"

"We are substitutes on the committee—"

"Munger," he said abruptly. "Are you the oil people?" His eyes were asking Bethel, and she nodded.

"I don't see the connection, Lieutenant."

"There isn't any. Well—good-by."

He was gone. China laughed softly, and Bethel could have wept with shame.

"I'm sorry, China. Truly. I acted like—like a bitch."

China patted her hand. "No. Like someone about to get a crush."

"Oh, I've barely seen him!"

China's pretty face still smiled, but she was serious. "Why not, sweetie? You've wanted to meet somebody. And you liked him. You ought to set sail, have a good reckless affair. It would be wonderful for you."

"I'm not on a manhunt!"

"Of course not. But you can relax. Just relax."

"He won't be back, China. I'm sure of it."

That evening, Bethel was pouring pitchers of hot water through the coffee urn when he came in. Their eyes met, but he did not speak or wave. Shortly, she saw he had found China and was being introduced to Frank, who reacted sourly; Frank hadn't wished to be dragged along. Then Bethel lost all of them for a time. She felt abandoned, until she saw the big green uniform come threading through the couples, mostly bored girls dancing with each other. Several, Bethel noticed in outrage, smiled and spoke cleverly as he passed.

"Coffee ready?" he said.

"Yes, just finished." Bethel decided he was neither sleepy nor dissipated. The puffs around his eyes were there, that was all, and she liked them. He looked, she thought, rugged and bleak and very solemn.

"Thank you," he said, touching her as he took the cup. "At a dance, I think we ought to."

"I've—I've never danced in my life, Lieutenant."

"You're kidding."

"I am not."

"It doesn't matter. I can teach you to do it poorly."

"You mean here? In public?"

"No one will notice. If I recall, you asked me."

She took off her apron and went with him to the middle of the floor. She could look down on the heads of the college girls; above them, she flashed an appeal to China. China only smiled. She stiffened at his touch, and he laughed. He held her strongly; he said, "Just retreat every time I charge," and she said, "I can't seem to tell about the music," and he grinned, "To hell with the music," and they were dancing.

After a while, he held her farther away, yet their heads remained close as she watched her feet. His hand on her back was hard and powerful. It guided her in a way that made her seem light. For a while she worried that she must look entirely hicky, that probably she moved in a sort of comic spraddle because her feet seemed never to come together. Then she no longer cared, and he took her closer. Dancing, then, was the smell and touch of Richard Mooney, the shock when his thigh touched hers, a frightening sweet sin.

"You aren't so much of a character," he said.

"I beg your pardon?"

"I've heard of your family for years. I thought you were all supposed to be characters."

"I wish you'd—that's not very kind."

"No," he said. "But I meant it right."

She said, huskily, "Would you say China is a character?"

"No."

"What would you say? Of her, I mean?"

"That she's beautiful."

"Oh."

"Don't you agree?" he said.

"Yes. My sister is lovely. Everyone thinks so. And she's married." She bit her tongue for its obviousness.

He laughed, and stepped on her, and apologized. His cheek touched hers, and there was the shock, but she did not draw away. He began to talk, and she listened, dancing now, she thought, as easily as a teen-ager.

She didn't miss a word. He had made a mistake, coming back to Amarillo on his leave; yes, he was at Dago, no, he'd not been overseas, which proved the error in that saying about there being just two kinds of Marines, those coming and those going. A platoon commander, yes; and no, there was no one he wrote letters to.

She kept thinking of China's words. Have a love affair. The sky was falling; she hoped he knew it.

He had coffee with her and left with the evening but half done. After that, she sat with China. She talked; she felt hot and giddy.

"Did I look—silly, out there?"

"Oh, no. You did fine. I watched you every minute."

"He doesn't like Amarillo too much."

China laughed. "You're pretty as a doll; you should see yourself."

"I think he's very stable-looking, don't you?"

"Handsome, I'd say."

"I bet he never comes back."

"Did you tell him where you live?"

"Yes, but he didn't say anything about—well, he didn't even say he heard me."

China was delighted. "You'll see him," she said. "He's a little lonely."

"He didn't seem lonely to me."

"Well, he isn't sticky lonely," China said. "But he did try to—I mean, all men in the service are lonely."

China never faltered—in speech, or at anything else. Bethel's lips trembled. "He tried what?"

"Nothing important, sweetie. It was before you danced, anyway."

"Tell me."

China studied her for a moment. "It's so little, Beth, that I don't mind explaining. I just said he was lonely, or hungry, or something, because while I was showing him the place, he tried to kiss me."

"Oh."

"Wait, honey. That's wrong, he didn't try. He just asked if he might; husband or no, he said. He didn't touch me, and we laughed about it. He's been having a dull leave, that's all."

For a night and a day, the shine was off. She hadn't cried;

she discovered she didn't care very much, and it was a relief. Then he called.

He had missed his movie after all. They saw it together, from balcony places so fogged with cigarette smoke she almost fainted. Afterward, something made her tell China, "He tried to kiss me too." It wasn't quite a lie. He had kissed the palm of her hand good night. The hero in the film had done so with his clandestine love, and Richard was making fun. But she had begun to know him.

He angered, on a dinner date, because the heels she wore made her as tall as he, which pained her. He told her of boondocks and an alcoholic CO and an obstacle course that killed one of his platoon, and she was fascinated. She learned he was twenty-two, and her heart broke at being irreparably twenty-five. He had a habit of probing bluntly for truths; often he asked her to explain herself on things she'd never even thought of, and he waited patiently as she tried. However inadequate she felt, she suddenly liked herself better. It seemed he was bringing her alive.

On a cold evening, after a late walk through Elwood Park, he did kiss her. If just once, very hard. Briefly she thought of his uniform and almost panicked; she felt him on the verge of asking her to his "mangy" hotel, and it struck her she had at hand no immediate reply. Which seemed to mean she would consider it, and she felt guilty and abandoned and a part of wartime. What would China, or the others, think of that?

On a Saturday, the first after Christmas, he took her to dance. He seemed restrained, thoughtful. But she talked and laughed. When he took her home, she had time to think about it. She had been almost daring; she had said things she had never thought of before, and so many had been amusing they were both surprised. That week removed her from The Old Place. She understood she was purging herself of the old, packing in the new. She would die if he died, live if he lived, and there it was, put clear and straight.

On a mild still evening, one of the summery ones that make

Panhandle people disbelieve winter, they met at Frank's drug-store. They drank bad coffee.

"What tonight, Bethel?"

"Anything. I'd like anything."

"I wish I had a car."

"We can get China's; she'd be glad."

"You have plenty of gas stamps?"

"Well, Frank does. He's a hoarder, I think."

"This weather," he said. "We ought to go for a drive."

They drove the blue coupe that had been Papa's wedding gift to China, keeping the windows down although they were chilled. They followed an almost vacant 66, on eastward. Past the shell-loading plant, and the air base, both built since he'd been gone. On through the identical little highway towns; each with a service station marked also "post office" and "bus stop"; each with a grocery, a few shabby little houses. Every town, however small, showed a cluster of wrecked and junked automobiles, which Richard thought inexplicable, and each had a grain elevator beside stock pens, clogged, this season, with tumbleweeds.

He pointed at a towering, round-binned bank of elevators. Their concrete sides gleamed white under the moon. "There's the best architecture in America," he said. "Clean, honest, and functional."

"I didn't know you knew about such things."

"I don't," he said. "It's just something I heard, and remembered."

She liked him to talk this way. They passed through one crossroads town after another, each clinging close to the highway as if for its life, yet entirely dark as though life were already gone. Bethel didn't believe it when ahead she saw Shamrock, which was ninety miles from home.

"Do you mind?" he said.

"Oh, no."

He smiled. "Let's get coffee," he said, and turned in toward a café.

"You Marines, you must live on coffee."

"What do you live on, Beth?"

"I didn't, until now."

"What—?"

"Nothing."

The place was stuccoed yellow, to match its appended motel. Inside, it seemed jammed with bronze horses and miniature Stetsons and all the queer tricks the tourists are expected to buy. To get a booth, they eased around a wire rack of giant-size postcards. He offered her a cigarette.

"I still don't smoke," she smiled.

"I forget. You don't drink, either. You didn't dance. Is that Baptist, Bethel?"

"No. We—Papa doesn't believe in religions."

It seemed important to him. "How about you," he said. "What do you believe in?"

"Is something wrong, Richard?"

"No. I was thinking, that's all. My leave is over pretty soon —not that this is tragic. In war, nothing is tragic, really, because everything is. But—"

"I think it's tragic."

"It ought to be," he said. "But I was thinking, we ought to get acquainted the rest of the way. If we're going to."

"All right. What do you believe in, then?"

He wasn't smiling. "I don't know, exactly. I know better what I do not believe in."

"Tell me that," she said.

"Hurt. I do not believe in hurt."

"Just that?"

He nodded.

"Me, too, then," she smiled.

"And that's all, for you?"

He was searching, wanting. Suddenly, she yearned only to supply. "I think I believe in happiness. Yes, that's it."

"Just lately?"

She nodded.

"The love kind, you mean," he said, and she nodded again.

He lit a fresh cigarette. She reached, to crush out the earlier one he'd forgotten. "Bethel, a few miles more, and we'd be in Oklahoma."

She held her breath.

"Would you like to go, Beth?"

"There'd—not be so much to see."

"Almost nothing," he said. "But they don't have that three-day cooling-off period. You can just jump when you want your feet wet."

She took her hands down to her lap, so he might not see them tremble. "Richard, you're talking of getting married."

"Do you want to?"

"You mean—now, tonight?"

"Yes."

She was warned; he did not believe in hurt, and he knew she loved him. Both soft and hard, she did, with everything her years had saved up. She did not answer. But she must have made a sign.

Sayre, Oklahoma. The county clerk, not even irritated at being roused from bed. The silent, unreal lapse before the faceless JP opened the door. The drab, rapid reading of the service. The sight, beyond the little man, of the bride and groom figurines on the mantle. Not until they were back at the car could she think.

How sickeningly horribly awful, to have a war going on! He would do this, and go away. War, so that her wedding had caught her in cotton underpanties and laceless slip. She cursed the Japs and Mr. Bowles because she was wearing no hose. But she was married; she, the skinny one.

He started the car and pointed it back toward Amarillo. She looked down, and there were the license and certificate, sticking up from her hand. Like flags, like tickets for something for which she'd stood in queue all her life. The moon was gone, and in the dark of the car, she began crying.

"Why did we, Richard?"

"We wanted to."

"Are you—in love with me?"

"Yes. That's why, Beth."

"Then it's all right, isn't it?"

"It's just right," he said. "I promise you."

There were the unpleasant mechanics, then. Getting to Amarillo, checking Richard out of his hotel. Hunting out a motel, feeling the manager's eyes on her ringless hands and on Richard's uniform. She ached with shame, until they were alone.

They stayed the four days remaining of his leave. Hiding out, Papa ranted of it later. Perhaps so. She called no one, except China; she asked her not to tell, not yet, which was a sort of hiding. But it wasn't acting the bitch, as Papa said. Papa did not know. They were together in pink space, in a thinkless, seasonless, almost foodless removal. And she wasn't unloved.

Old-shoe Bethel. Her hair straggling wild, her nails unfixed and breaking, her skin uncreamed. Yet her heart singing at how pretty she had become. With Richard, there was appetite for moments and seconds; she regretted each hour gone while anticipating rapturously the one to come. Time counted; it amazed her that, before, she had wished it away.

"You've barely said you loved me, Richard."

"It's a hard word to say."

"I don't think so."

"Hard for a man, I mean. For me, anyway. I guess there have been too many tuneless and toneless and tiresome songs, all just beating the word to death."

"Please, Richard—"

"All right. I love you. But since the war, it means mostly sex, doesn't it?"

"Oh, no. I'd dislike it meaning that," she said. "Except, if it means our sex."

"You are a little bit crazy," he said.

She lay back in his arm, watching him smoke.

"Richard, what are you thinking?"

"Huh? Nothing."

"Do you wish—is it China you wanted to marry?"

He twisted toward her, looking at her hard, and she hated even having a tongue.

"I shouldn't even answer," he said. "But the answer is no."

She could not help it. "I mean, don't you wish, even a little, that it was China. Here, this way—?"

He kissed her. Gently, but so—so fundamentally, she thought. She helped him make it that way. He had an unexpected winter tan, gotten, he said, at a place called Muscle Beach. It glossed his big shoulders, the thick arms that lifted her from bed, or into it, so easily she was no longer ungainly. Her mind romped with what happened, shocking her. She liked him whispering at her, "wench!"; she thought if Papa should somehow appear, she'd say to him, "Ask Richard if he is really married; ask him if I'm good in bed! And Papa, do see how handsome he is!"

On their last evening, they dressed and went out. They ate ravenously; they drove a while in China's car, they went quietly back to their tousled rooms.

"Bethel, maybe I should meet your family," he said. "Or you'll have to explain me when I'm gone."

"Let's be by ourselves."

She started to cry, for crying, too, was new to her, and time could be mourned when it was short.

They listened to the scratchy little radio. At first, just brassy swing records that a disc jockey dedicated right and left. Then at midnight, a softer music, untinkered with by the announcer and enriched by sentimental violins. There was nothing to do, or to say. At the same instant they began preparing for bed, and she was glad they didn't pretend not to look at each other.

He came to her suddenly, before she found her gown. His arms closed around her, on the tune, "Street of Dreams." She stepped away with the music, and they danced. She laid her cheek on his shoulder. She felt the sad-sweetness all about them as they turned in one spot between bed and wall. The crowded little room seemed the whole world, and an ending one. They clung as if to their honeymoon, and it seemed final and right to be aware, but unaware, of their nakedness.

Tomorrow he'll be gone, she thought. A long time gone, before he loves me enough. But he will love me enough, because he must. Now, just dance, Bethel. No missteps, no imperfection between us. This time will never come again.

The farewell ached in her throat, still she was filled with peace. It was a loneliness and yearning, sinking deep, but not yet hurting. There was the touch of breasts and souls. She let her few tears smear away on his shoulder. The music went on. Her feet grew cold, and she tired. They kept dancing, around, around, around. When she was exhausted, she tightened her arms and rested on him. Then she slept. She could feel his breath, she heard the music. She was every woman, loved by every lover, and dancing him good-by was all she wanted in a dream.

The sun awakened her. She looked about, startled, at a room that daylight made cheap and strange. She felt of his pillow, and it wasn't warm. She wondered when he had gone.

Moon drove carelessly through the city's sparse Sunday evening traffic, and he thought, I've researched myself right up to Bethel and the war, and what about that? He remembered first, always, the triteness of the war. This he had known at the time, quite as well as he saw it now.

There'd been a world only livable because of its well-meant, stupid, and overworked attitudes. There'd been a worn-out language for it all, and this had filled every train and bus station; it loaded the pages of every letter written in a barracks and X'ed at the bottom for mailing home. Consciously, Moon had worked at refusing it all. He had not played war, especially not in his courtship of Bethel.

No whine to her about grabbing life by the pants before the pants were shot off. No proposition asking her to put herself in storage, to wait in the dreary romantic void where millions already waited, or pretended to wait. He hated all the wedges.

146

He had never threatened her with failing to return, and never, thank God, had he exploited her with that sure-fire, corny "This is it!"

None of the war platitudes, then. Yet without them, hadn't he still made the trite bargain?

No, it wasn't war-trite, anyway. He had wanted to marry Bethel Munger. He'd not been blind that she was too tall; he'd known she might have taken any man who asked her. Why, then? The oil money? Of course, the Munger wealth had been in his thoughts, because he was twenty-two. But he'd kept it out of his decision, hadn't he? The truth was, and had to be, that he'd wanted her, and she had wanted him. That was all of it. He burned to make the marriage do.

He rubbed his eyes; they stung from thought or the night road. His head was aching as he stopped in front of the house. Bethel held the doors for him, and he carried his sleeping daughters inside. He put them on their beds, each a slack and rumpled bundle. He took off Hannah's shoes and socks and spread a blanket over her. Her stern face frowned at him through a half-sleep, and she mumbled, "Don't treat me like a baby, Daddy."

"Be a baby while you can," he said. "You'll be a long time grown."

As he removed Carol's shoes, she too aroused to look at him. She did not speak, and he thought she must have been dreaming a sad dream, for she seemed ready to cry. He kissed her forehead and went to the kitchen.

Bethel said, "Are you hungry, dear?"

"No, thanks."

"I can make coffee, anyway, and a sandwich."

"Not for me."

She stood at the cabinet, watching him. Her brow was milk-white; she looked very tired.

"Richard, I don't know what to say. I'm—sorry about The Camera House. I hope you can see that Spain was right, that—"

"I see."

She said, "I want you to understand. Everyone was so proud of you, and I thought the cuff links—"

"They're fine," he said.

"Then it's the car. You do need one, and everyone was ready to see that you got it. But the Cadillac—you know it's not the money Spain thinks about; there's so much more involved, and—oh, I wish you'd stop chewing that gum and tell me what's wrong."

"Please, Beth, we're both bushed."

"Why can't we talk?" Her voice had risen sharply; her tall body had cocked like a whip. "I might tell you something of great interest to you; you might like to know China is having a baby!"

He stared at her. It took a moment to believe it, then another to understand that he was peculiarly outraged. He said, "Good for Frank," and it amazed him how he hated his partner so suddenly and irrationally.

"Forgive me, Richard, for—for throwing it at you that way. I only want to talk about everything, to—"

"Everything is fine."

"Oh, like sin it is!" Her eyes closed, her teeth ground. "And for God's sake, won't you stop that eternal scratching!"

He got off his stool, feeling sorry and shy, now; afraid to touch her. If Mean Week had come, heaven help them both. He wasn't ready.

VIII

The first week of March—not so blustery, not so dusty, not so anything other than dry—arrived with foreboding. When Moon awakened on Thursday, it was in an instant awareness of his wife. He turned toward her already knowing. No mistake, the chemistry was showing.

Even on her sleeping face, it was apparent. Definite small trenches drew outward from her mouth like spokes. She held to sleep with desperation, or pain; the stress of it gathering her brow, making her look spent, and too old.

He crept from bed and tiptoed through the house to his coffee. They had retired together. But as though by voodoo, he saw, the bottle of pink pills had appeared on the shelf.

Mean Week. God give us calm. Give us endurance, and the use of our brains.

On impulse he got down the serving tray and made her breakfast. Slice of ham, an egg that luckily scrambled nicely, toast cut in neat triangles, coffee, strawberry jam. He wished for a rose as decoration, then felt silly over it. After starting to the bedroom, he reversed himself and added a tumbler of water. It occurred to him he might put one of the pills beside the plate; then he found the sense not to.

Bethel was awake, her head raised and propped against the headboard. She frowned at the tray.

"Hi," he smiled.

"If that's for me, I didn't intend to eat."

"Here, let me pad you up. For once, I think, I've cooked successfully."

"Take it back. I don't want it."

"You should eat."

She said through closed teeth, "Richard, don't wheedle me as though I were a child!"

"Oh, come on," he persuaded. "Let me set this in your lap. I'll bring my coffee—"

"Put it on your own lap. You made it; you eat it."

Oh, hell, he thought, and he took the tray back to the kitchen. Which was how this week's despair began.

He sat down over cigarettes and coffee. He had committed his first crime; so they were off and running. The usual prospect was before him. The days of vicious exchange, of carefully disguised attempts to escape each other. Then, beyond these, the hours of tedious repair, when each quarrel would be walled off into the past, just one cautious brick at a time. And eventually they'd reach the state of self-blame and self-effacement called "making-up." This climaxed, always, in a night undertaken with emotions yet raw and exposed like severed veins. They cauterized with tears and with the raging frantic physical apology that was their anger, their need, their hurt and regrets. Until this night, Mean Week couldn't really end.

Moon wished they were through it all, wished today was the last of the cycle. At the end they always met each other as subdued, forgiving, much-appalled people.

He gathered his clothes and dressed in the bathroom. When he looked in on her again, she seemed not to have moved.

"I hope you'll feel better," he said.

"I feel great."

"Beth—I can stay a while, get the kids off to school."

150

"I take care of the kids."

"Well, is there anything I should bring from town?"

"Bring anything you like."

"Please, Beth. Let's be sensible."

"I'm never sensible; haven't you found that out?"

When every clock ticks only toward the death of a trust in May, and it is March, time is cruel. The way to do is think little of it, and go to the movies.

These days, Moon broke away from home early, unlocking the store almost at sunrise. He read something, if merely the brochures from Eastman Company, until Frank arrived. Then they made coffee and drank it and bickered. Moon waited for the earliest plausible minute and excused himself for lunch. When he got to the street, he felt at large, if not free, and the lift was as though he had a job to do. He made a considerable enterprise of it.

The first mission was to find a café where he had never eaten before. A hamburger diner, or backstreet chili house; often one of those places where men eat with their hats on and women fill their jaws too full. Moon would have a poor meal, then sit smoking over the dirty dishes, watching customers come and go and checking and rechecking the time. Then, just before one-fifteen, he tipped fabulously and began his stroll along Polk Street. From there, he worked at a pure problem in tactics.

He walked the whole street, glancing casually at the billing beneath each theater marquee. When he had elected upon the target, he walked past it a time or two, arming himself for the approach.

To see a matinee movie seemed a cheap, guilty thing. An afternoon was made of important hours; in them, essential people bore down at their work. Thus Moon could not barge up to a box office; he had to ease up, then dart quickly and unnoticed inside. The program should have begun, so the house would be dark; the back row must be chosen, so no one could sit observingly behind.

151

There must be, further, no disclosure of intent until the last possible moment. You held the correct change for the ticket in your hand; if someone stood ahead of you with the cashier, you strolled on past and made another run. You neither spoke nor looked at the girl or the ticket taker; you just transacted the poor business and scatted for the dark.

Once inside, you made a careful ritual of tearing up your ticket stub; this way, you carried no betrayal in some forgotten pocket. You sat quietly because motion draws attention, and if someone happened to come and sit near, you could put your pocket notepad on your knee and hold your pen above it and you looked exactly like the newspaper reviewer, hard at work.

You stayed through the film, however bad, and then a bit longer, so others wouldn't be leaving as you did. Usually, you took the fire exit that put you on a sidestreet or into an alley. And before stepping out, you lighted a cigarette, so that the first person you met saw a man smoking, as theater patrons aren't allowed to do.

It was much, Moon thought, like slinking toward the maw of an enemy dugout, looking, then sneaking away unseen. This was his thought while going. When emerging, he hated himself as much as he had while inside. He could only think, this is what it means to use up a day instead of using it. This is derelict; why isn't it possible for one to be only a little bit adrift? During each show he vowed not to see the next, and this was foolish! "Never swear against anything," his mother said, "or you'll surely do it," and this was true.

Frank Wallace wasn't deceived, but he made only a scant point of it when Moon got back to The Camera House. "Long lunch, boy? Or did you go to the talkies?"

Thursday night, Moon had supper in town and went on to Marine Reserve meeting. He stayed until the last dog died, so that when he reached home, Bethel and the kids had gone to bed. On Friday, Spain telephoned asking Moon to go with him to buy a power mower.

A reserved stubby salesman, doubtless a paragon among

Sears' finest, stood by with arms crossed while Spain stooped and squinted and rapped here and there with long pale fingers.

"Uh, I wanted you to reinforce me, Moon; I can't say I'm the great shakes when it comes to machines. I'd appreciate your opinion. You just toot your honker on me if I'm wrong, but I would say this one is your better quality equipment."

"It looks all right to me," Moon said.

Spain seized the mower grips and dragged the machine from among others, out into the aisle. He cocked it over on one side.

"Your salesman, here, can fill you in—but here's your side-cutter, for trimming against your walls, and that's your solid-cast aluminum chassis, which I'm told is sort of a bonus on your mower of this price. This giz is your governor, and you have three horsepower here in your four-cycle Briggs & Stratton." He straightened, his skin colored slightly from having bent so low, and he looked at Moon speculatively. "Uh, I'm inclined, off the cuff, to dive in on this model, unless you see I'm off base...."

They completed the purchase, to the surprise of the salesman, and Spain rolled the mower out to the front curb where Harry waited beside the old truck. Grinning broadly, Harry hefted the mower aboard and drove away.

They walked to a moderate, respectable cafeteria for lunch. Moon ate lightly while Spain consumed the food from a crowded tray as if performing a bothersome chore. The pale eyes bore down thoughtfully. Observing him, Moon was struck that the chairman was somewhat ambidextrous. Spain's right hand motored his fork, but the left one sent pieces of roll furrowing through the gravy.

"Uh, Moon, did you see the little piece in the paper?"

"No. About what?"

"Well, we went before the county commissioners about our road deal, and there was a paragraph about it on page two. Uh, if that's your customary thing, it's hunky with me. But there were three or four other supplicants, and I didn't see them mentioned in the paper. Just by way of keeping the board's ear to the sounding board, I wondered if it seemed to you the editor might have his stinger out, so to speak?"

"I doubt it," Moon said. "What about the road?"

"Well, that's what I wanted to get our heads together on, though I do appreciate your help about the mower. The commission took it under advisement, which I understand is the usual start. Mr. Williams-the-lawyer was there to sort of bird-dog things, and in his view, we need a good follow-through. From here on in, your thing to do is push her on home. Now, uh, I'm snowed up to the eyes, got this tax quarter pounding down on me. . . ."

He paused, waiting. Moon said nothing; be-damned if he'd make it easy.

"Uh, well, the crux is, I'd appreciate it if you'd just take hold of this thing and nail it down solid for us."

Moon said, "What do you want me to do?"

"Uh, your commission meets again this coming Monday, and Mr. Williams will be there to sort of catch hold of your tone. After that, we can get our marbles together. And I do want to say I appreciate this. Your board will be tickled if you can shake these peaches off the tree. . . ."

Moon left him at the table. He walked directly down Polk and executed one abortive pass at the Paramount before, on a second, less hurried run, he slipped inside. He sat in the dark two hours before returning to The Camera House.

Frank Wallace was pacing, in a sweat, demanding where he'd been. An unscheduled directors' meeting was on, he could gather no hint of its business. "Hell, Moon, there's just eight weeks left; what if they're talking about how to divide?"

It seemed ridiculous that after thirteen years of waiting, Frank had suddenly gotten impatient.

"I don't think so," Moon said, "not in an emergency session."

"They might." The old druggist sat down, got up quickly, and walked his office again. Moon followed the damp, reddened face; he wished Frank would wipe away the smudges that reflected dully on the rimless glasses. China's husband—

"The baby," Moon said. "Doesn't that change things?"

Wallace stopped, his jaw tightened. "Not one goddamned bit!" He strode off in seething laps around his desk. "What do they expect us to do while they sit up there deciding on *our* money . . . ?"

Moon grasped, then, that Frank must have been drinking all afternoon. He grinned at his partner-in-law, picked up a new Rolleicord from the desk, and he said, "We might take pictures of each other."

If the hastily called meeting of the clan excluded Moon, it concerned him too. This time The Old Place was not the site. It was a downtown meeting. And the meeting before the meeting took place at Laska's. They were all upset, but Laska the most.

Sometimes Laska said to her sisters that she had known only one entirely unique day in her whole life, and that was when she was nine. To Bethel, who had shared it, the events were terrifying, but the more memorable for it.

They had played together in the back yard the whole forenoon. The electricians were there, finishing up, and they had proved to be patient men who answered little-girl questions.

Laska and Bethel dashed about in races for the scraps of new wire. They snatched them up almost as the workmen snipped them away. It was a soft wire they could bend into dolls and pistols and bracelets that coiled several times around their wrists. Too, they got hold of tools, until the men demanded they be put down. It all was a part of the anticipation. A dozen times they dashed into the house to speak to Mama's back while she canned a new bushel of tomatoes.

"Mama, does it really work?"

"It will, when the men are done."

"They're done; they're fixing to go away."

"Then it'll work."

"Well, can we burn 'em now?"

"Later; your father said we mustn't waste."

"For just a minute, Mama?"

"Wait until tonight, when it's dark."

"Well, how long is that?"

"A long time," Mama said. "Run on out and play; you're in my way."

They stared up at the ceiling, at the yellow cord and glass bulb dangling from it. It could not be possible. Oh, people in town had electric lights. But here, out home—Laska had to keep looking at the wires to be reassured.

Papa had gotten together a little money, and as always, it was to be spent on more land. But before he could decide between two adjoining pieces, Mama's white lamp, the one with the big rose painted on the side, happened to split and catch fire in Papa's hand. The kerosene sprayed over his arm, burning stubbornly there until he finally beat himself out. He cursed, and took several drinks, and he had the electric wires building out from the highway almost before Mama could tear up clean feed sacks and get his arm wrapped.

Everything about it was miracle.

On into the afternoon, Laska rummaged about beneath the black wires; with Bethel, she walked the shadow lines on the ground between the house and the huge, new black pole. They gathered bent nails and chunks of broken porcelain, valuables the workmen had left behind, and they kept asking each other if, when Papa got home, he'd change his mind and have it all taken away.

When a breeze came up, the wires started to sing. The girls looked up and listened; it sounded like the music of sunlight. Then Brother came home from wherever he had been, and he helped them carry Papa's old ladder up from the barn. They propped it against the house, and sure enough, it reached the two white knobs and the place where the wires were stripped and shiny. Laska went up first, for she had thought of the ladder. She touched a wire testingly, and Bethel cheered, for it caused the lines to wave all the way back to the pole, and to sing more brightly.

Laska shook them harder, then, and she died.

Electrocuted, Mama and the others always said when they told about it; Laska heard them tell it a thousand times.

Everything so still, the sunshine still singing. Being on the ground, and safe there, but without having fallen. Having no breath, but not needing it. Laska knew when Mama came to lift her, but she could not feel her hands. She lay on the back porch, in cool shade; she could tell Mama was slapping her face, but it was all right, because it did not hurt. Everything was smooth and unbothered and sort of hunky-dory.

Mama bathed her feet, which seemed mixed-up, for Laska felt clean already. Then she floated into the house and onto Mama's bed, and suddenly everyone stood around her. Spain, Texas. Bethel and China, who were crying. Mama said, "Laska is gone. Spain, you must go to town and find your father. No— Texas, you go; Spain has a hole in his shoe."

Laska marveled at how they all watched her; at how nothing hurt. There was just a ring and buzz in her ears, sounding kind of nice. Then Brother began scolding her saying she shouldn't make Mama cry. Suddenly he charged the bed and he hit her in the stomach with his fist. At once, the buzz went away. Her stomach convulsed, and she had to holler.

It was God's wonder, Mama said. They hugged her, after touching her at first only gingerly. They wanted to know how it felt, being dead. They recounted for each other what had happened, each talking as if the others had not been there. It was wonderful.

Laska realized how remarkable she was, ultimately, when Papa told it to the bootlegger: "Goddamn, Hank, she was dead, dead as a doornail, no lie! Reckon she'll live forever, now, if once't is all anybody has to die."

It made Laska think she was immortal, her death already behind her.

She walked the top rail of the lot fence, as Spain and June never dared. She climbed the windmill tower, to wave down with both hands at Bethel and China while they screamed with fright. She waded the patch of quicksand underneath the river bridge, exactly where Papa said he once lost a horse. Laska, the others bragged, wasn't scared of anything.

It was good. She hunted danger as if it came in flavors; she told Bethel what strange dresses she would wear after everyone else was dead. She planned with them the care of their graves. No one opposed her. For a time, not even Papa struck her. The only trouble was, play wasn't much fun, any more; she needed bigger things. If you cannot die, you can do anything, and the only reward must happen in the faces that watch you.

Laska had to think hard, the way people got used to her stunts as soon as they were done. One afternoon, she got Papa's big shotgun out, behind Mama's back, and took it to the feed shed. "Shoot me," she commanded Bethel and June. When they would not, she begged them; at last, she cursed them, with all Papa's words, for spoiling the day. June she almost hated. He had struck her and made her more than human; people praised him for it: "Poor boy, he did save his sister's life." Laska thought he should take the gun; instead, he ran from helping her.

Soon, they stopped saying Laska was brave. If she could not die, then for her courage was not possible. Gradually Laska saw how this was true, and the daring wasn't good any more. The zest went out of it; her infinity became a discrimination inflicted upon her. She cried about it at night. She even said a prayer that she might die a second time, if not too soon. Still the misery dragged on through the summer. She resigned herself to it completely. Then, in late August, Papa changed everything.

Every year, Papa marked a date on the calendar as the deadline for getting the children ready for school. When the day came, he felled himself with a mule's dose of calomel. Next, Mama got hers. Then he primed the rest of them. For days they lay in bed or staggered about, green-faced and gagging. This year, Laska retched to listlessness, grew feverish, and almost died. She came to death's brink, recognizing the moment when she could drop away or remain. She found in it nothing so peaceful or charming as during her electrocution; she felt only mortal, and terribly afraid.

So ended her magic. She felt tricked. Her electrocution was undone, and she was left with just the daredevil's big scars and big muscles and not unbreakable bones.

"Laska," Bethel said again, "don't blame yourself."

"My God, who else?"

They were in the largest of the Munger houses, in a vast paneled rectangular living room beneath a ceiling ribbed with foot-square varnished beams. Laska sat on her curving gold divan, blowing clouds of smoke on which Bethel coughed. Across a triangular table from them, in an underslung chair meant to complete one of the decorator's "harmony groups," Sid Glass covered his eyes with his hands.

Laska spoke hoarsely. "It's always been me—let me say it. My electrocution, everything—it's like Papa always said. The way we had to have Junior, the—"

"Laska," Sid shut her off. He heaved his shoulders and rubbed his hands as if to clean them, and he said to Bethel, "If I understand, Carol didn't tell you this until today."

Bethel nodded. "I—I don't think she meant to tell it at all. I knew something was wrong when we drove home Sunday night. I—"

Sid said, "But nothing happened. Nothing really, did it? I mean, kids are always curious. From what you say—"

Bethel looked at him impatiently. "I told Laska all I know about it, before you got here. It's not—I do hate to describe it. Sid Junior said something, and took hold of her, and she ran away."

"Where did it happen?"

"In the barn. I think Selma had gone to the bathroom, and I suppose no one else was watching the children."

"Is Carol in school today?"

"Yes," Bethel said. "She seemed better, as soon as she told

159

me. I couldn't be sure, but, well, she did sound more like herself. I mean, saying 'Skit, skat, how about that,' and all those other silly things they pick up at school. Believe me, I didn't come over to accuse Junior of—of ruining her. It's just a nasty little thing I thought you had to know about. And I'm not blaming anybody. Laska, you do understand that?"

"I know he should be punished, Beth. But I couldn't lay a hand on him."

"I don't want that," Bethel kissed her sister. "I'm thinking of—well, some sort of control."

Sid took up one of Laska's slim brown cigarettes. "What did Moon say about it?"

"I haven't told him."

"Why don't we call him out here?"

"Sid, I don't mean for him to know. Not for a while."

"He's as concerned as I, or as any of us."

"Richard would have a fit," Bethel said, "I know he would. He's got a temper, especially where Carol is involved, and he might do something—I mean, well—we oughtn't to let this get any bigger than it is. Later on, it'll be all right."

Laska said, "What do you want us to do?"

"Oh, dearest, I'm not asking anything. I was furious at first, and we're all upset. I think we ought to go downtown; Spain says we should come. Maybe he, or China, will know what's best."

Sid shook his head. "Didn't you just say it's not as important as all that?"

Laska got up, broad-hipped and thin-limbed and very tall in her worn bluejeans. "I'll have to dress. Sidney, you'll come with me, won't you?"

"Not if it's to be handled this way."

"I'll—need you."

Sid studied his wife a moment. "All right," he said. "But I'll be the one—and the only one—to talk to the boy."

Bethel's brow was furrowed, her hair needed brushing, her face hadn't been made-up. Stiffly she said, "Laska, this isn't a good time for me. May I have an aspirin?"

160

The meeting was grave, then tearful, then calm. Because Spain appeared more deeply troubled than any of them, it continued an hour. Uh, to make no bones about it, your occurrence here was unnerving to everyone. But, your emotional side to such things was only your radius matter that ought to be sloughed off. The key was that there be no recrimination; blame was never the ticket. Instead, when something unpleasant hit the fan, you had to get busy and tack on your patches. Now —although the one-two-three of what took place needn't be reviewed, it was essential to steer a new course so as not to stub your toe on the same problem again. To get back on track —any of your books will tell you your, uh, physical curiosity in the adolescing boy is the norm, not your exception to the rule. Which was dealing strictly with your facts. So, a discreet silence about the whole thing, beginning with the completion of this meeting and continuing henceforth, was your first sound bet. After that—and this had to do with the sunny side—your board should plan together toward the positive remedy. Now —with the whole thing thrown out on the table in the light of day, there'd be no reason to go off half-cocked, no danger of handling the question off the tops of your heads. So, everyone should feel free, feel free. To begin with, by way of a concrete suggestion before coming to a vote. . . .

It was agreed the small military school at San Antonio was an excellent one; that Sid Junior should go there as quickly as he could be enrolled.

IX

Moon suspected that he was beginning to absorb more and more of Frank Wallace's attitudes. At least, through a weekend made difficult by Bethel's tension and Carol's abrupt and unexplained withdrawal from him, he kept coming back to a speculation on the emergency meeting of the Estate's star chamber.

Unlike Frank, he didn't mull and grouse and voice ominous estimates of what had taken place. Still, Bethel had told him nothing, so that as often as he looked at her, his dogged curiosity increased. The conference was a sly and clouded thing that had occurred behind his back. Such thought seemed parallel to Frank's; it alarmed Moon as a symptom of deterioration. He had only to recall the sort of man Frank once had been, and see what Frank had become, and he would pimple with fear of the road which seemed to be opening now in front of him. Moon realized he could become the kind of creature he saw in the coffeepot; perhaps, even, one who toyed at blasphemy and pornography while waiting out an estate.

He resisted, but by Monday, his irritations at all phases of his life were congregated in a sum. He drew no guise over his mood; he felt prepared to meet Mean Week head-on. Across from him, Bethel saw to their breakfast. She hadn't spoken, nor had he, since their rising.

The children were eating with eyes on the clock, although already dressed for school. Hannah watched them all with a rare light in her pale Munger eyes; it was as if she found Mean Week and her sister's recent reserve a needed stimulation. Carol sat quietly, her China-perfect face drawn as though she were tired or ill, neither of which struck Moon as possible.

He compelled Bethel to look at him. Point-blank he said, "What was going on, Friday?"

"Sidney Junior is going off to school."

"It took the whole family to arrange that?"

Carol excused herself and left quickly. Moon watched her; he missed suddenly her jazz language, her bold little quips, her gay teasing.

"Bethel, what's wrong with her?"

They looked at each other until Hannah, too, left the kitchen. Then, as he knew they must, they quarreled. With Bethel, he knew, it was only Mean Week. With himself, it seemed a hunger for combat, of any sort, in any direction, and he could not satisfy it. It astounded him that he argued coldly, even intelligently, using witty and merciless sarcasm, yet at the same time hoping to leave no lingering meanings for later and bitter resurrection.

He quit his breakfast unfinished; he left three of his usual four cups of coffee undrunk, and he prepared hurriedly to leave. He returned to her when he was dressed. She sat at the bar, her head propped.

"I'm sorry, Beth," he said.

"You're always sorry."

"I'm getting off, now. Because the new help is coming today, and there'll be some breaking in."

Bethel's reply eased him; its tone was her apology. "I hope you won't be late, Richard. There's Symphony tonight. And you are to go to the dentist at ten this morning for your checkup. Don't miss, or you'll have to wait weeks more."

Moon frowned. "About the concert—"

"You'll want to go," Bethel said. "We're sitting with China, and I know you wouldn't want to miss that."

"Oh, God," he said, and he turned and went out.

On the drive to town, he felt mean and cheap; selfish, petty, and vain, in need of punishment. He wondered what Bethel was thinking, and the question reminded him of a college roommate he'd once had. The fellow was a handsome, competent ass who committed himself to one overly dramatic flirtation after another, each one filled with the breakings-up and gushing forgivenesses of an overwrought play. "So after you fuss with a woman, you worry about how she feels. Well, take it from me, she feels exactly like you do; she even thinks the same things. In a fight, where's the difference between male and female?"

By this formula, Bethel felt guilty and sorry, just as he did. The idea was comforting; at least, some things they shared.

"I'm in love with you, Beth," he said experimentally. It did not make him feel better.

Moon saw the Birdsong woman as she walked past the plate glass, almost missing The Camera House before catching the sign on the door. He disliked the look of her; it chaffed him how she compelled him to ogle her fantastic figure; he resented that she, a stranger, should represent his lie and his rebellion. Something about her put his defiance of the Mungers in a class with Frank's pictures, so that he felt depraved at sight of her.

He understood he would have to admit his deception. To blazes with Spain, but he must tell Bethel.

Mrs. Birdsong wore the same clinging black outfit as on the day he had hired her, even to the fox fur which Moon guessed was expensive because the thing refused to look dead. Her thickly made face carried the same tough recklessness he'd puzzled at before, underlaid with the elusive hint of grief. He wondered if he weren't afraid of her.

She smiled, in a pleased cynicism that revealed her aware-

164

ness that his glance had been drawn to her incredible bosom, and she said, "Good morning. Do I begin by sweeping out?"

Moon said, "Have you settled things with Horvath?"

"I've quit. If that settles anything." She set her large handbag on the counter, burst it open, and took out an oval mirror the size of her palm. She frowned at herself, shoved at the bush of too-black hair, then exchanged the mirror for a Kleenex which she sniffed into.

She said, "I shouldn't have called you that Sunday. Do you remember what I said?"

"Yes, of course. But I'm not cutting the salary, as I told you."

"Good." She laughed, in a flat, hard way that made a by-word of it. "I'd had a bad night. Teddy gets too damned generous after bad nights. Well, shouldn't we get busy? If I'm to clerk, I ought to learn the prices. And the books—what about the books?"

"I've gotten them out," he said. "In Frank's office. They're a mess."

"Who has kept them?"

"Well, Frank and I. Spasmodically, I'm afraid. You'll find them next to useless."

She looked around the shop in one sweep. At certain angles, he thought, her face was almost crude. It was the cheekbones, he supposed; she could have been the Indian side of a nickel. "In there with the books is fresh coffee," he said.

"I'd say I ought to start a new set, if they're as screwed-up as you tell me. That would mean an inventory and accounting —a whole fresh start."

"Can you handle such things?"

"I can handle anything," she smiled.

They sat down with the big square mugs Moon had bought at a dime store, the desk and coffee steam and mutual curiosity between them. His eyes kept falling to her figure, maybe because it was so exaggerated in company with the strange, unrelieved face. He said, "I've only got one more point to make about your salary, Mrs. Birdsong. I—"

165

"You may as well call me Teddy," she said. "It sounds baby-ish and delicate, but people call me that."

"All right. You'll have a check for seventy dollars, less withholding, each week, and the rest must be in cash. You may have understood that earlier."

The thin lips grinned. "I guessed it," she said. She was looking about the office. "I miss something."

"That—picture, I suppose. Frank put it away."

Frank had called to say he'd be very late. China was suffering morning sickness, and he would stay home awhile. "So you get first pinch, Moon. Let me know if they're falsies."

The woman said, "He is the one that married China Munger, isn't he? Used to be a druggist?"

"Yes."

"She's beautiful."

"Oh," he said with some of the challenge he'd applied to Bethel, "you know China?"

"Just on sight," Teddy Birdsong said. "Everyone knows her on sight. Everyone loves her, I understand. Christ, she is a pretty thing."

She held out her cup, and he refilled it.

"Coffee," she said, "and a hundred a week."

"That's vital to you, isn't it? The money."

"You have a winter coat, don't you?"

It took him aback. "Why, yes."

"I don't. And didn't I tell you I'm a cold materialist? If not, I meant to."

Materialism wasn't much part of the things he puzzled over in her face; he very nearly said so.

She leaned forward, bobbingly, and took a ledger in her lap. "If you're ready to explain—?"

"I've got to go out in a few minutes. Dentist. So if we can put this off—or, Frank can go over them with you when he gets in."

She consented with a shrug. "In that case, you better show me the stock, and the price code and so on. Or I might sell you out at a loss while you're gone."

They went up front and got at it. Twice, customers for roll

film came in; otherwise, the work went uninterrupted. Behind the L-shape of the counters, she walked in the mince and unbalance of the sleeve skirt and tall heels, and to ignore the motion of her hips seemed impossible; you could avoid it as you avoided the sun. She took cameras off the shelves, read the tags, thumbed through the little booklets attached, and her lips moved silently as if she were committing nomenclatures to memory.

When she turned from the shelves to lean elbows on the counter while holding some bit of paraphernalia in her hand, her great breasts rested atop the glass. The gesture revealed her constant awareness of him; it suggested she had long since made a single appraisal of all men and now placed absolute confidence in it. To use her assets as a taunt, Moon decided, was habit become her nature. Still, the inconsistency in her face, the sadness-with-anger, as he approximated it, belied her claim on wisdom and answers.

He doubted she really ran her life, any more than he did his own.

"The inventory ought to be soon," she said. "It shouldn't take long, some evening after closing. Tonight; is that all right?"

He shook his head. "Frank and I have a date for the symphony."

"Well," she smiled. "Music lover."

"No."

He thought of Bethel's face, as seen across breakfast, and he wished he need not take her tonight. She was right when, in Mean Week, she accused him of reluctance to go out with her. But the cause was at a tangent from what Bethel thought. He felt, simply, at such times, that their hurts and shames showed on their faces, and he did not like them seen and recognized.

"Frank really likes to go," he said. "I'm indifferent. I'll see if I can get free, if Frank is willing."

"The two of us can do it," she said. "To you, that may sound like a proposition."

Frank came in, then, walking rapidly through the back and

167

up to the partition. He said, "Eeyo; how's the coffee?" and he did not so much as glance at Teddy Birdsong.

Moon took him back to the office.

Frank sat down with a sigh, old-mannishly letting himself drop the last foot of the way, and he said, "How you doing with the squaw, boy?"

"Come on, Frank. Her name is Teddy Birdsong."

"Well, Teddy, is it?" Frank grinned. He picked up and looked at her application form. "Billie Ted, it says. Makes me think of Belle Starr, or Tugboat Annie: can't imagine why."

"Now listen to me, Frank." Moon spoke low in deference to the flimsy walls. "I don't know what you have in mind. But leave her alone. None of your bright jokes, or those stinking films."

Frank kept grinning. "Don't you worry. I wouldn't touch her with somebody else's ten-foot pole. What's she doing, up there?"

"Learning prices. She wants us to take inventory, for a new set of books."

"Hell," Frank snorted, and he did not attempt to keep his voice down, "that's a dilly of an idea. We still got everything we ever stocked, ain't we?"

At her desk, The Old Girl sat in a rare instance of idleness, her eyes taking the long view through the office suite. She watched Mr. Jacobson, working over there in shirtsleeves, as he shouldn't, but her thoughts had nothing to do with him. She was apprehensive, for Mr. Williams-the-lawyer was closeted with Mr. Munger on matters solemn-faced for them both, and she thought their conference should have ended a good while ago.

Her nose tweaked, up and down in a spasm of tiny muscles, like a rabbit's. The gesture aided breathing on the drouth-dusty days that just murdered one's sinuses. Further, with Miss Northington, this winking of nostrils was something of a tick to express the loyal anxieties she had assumed on behalf of her employer. Today it reflected Mr. Munger's difficulty with the county commission.

The Old Girl had never attended a commission meeting, nor had she ever met any member of that powerful and stubborn body. But she had seen their pictures in the paper, and it seemed to her memory that each one of them resembled Mr. Jacobson very strongly. So she glared severely at the auditor, out of her low regard for the county authority.

She held a sort of a bead, drawn fine, on the county commissioners. She hoped she wasn't despising the commission members, but rather, the thing they had done.

"To live fully," her father once said, "you have to do some hating. It's an emotion too powerful to miss. But there's a trick about it you have to learn. You have to hate things, not people. Mostly, we hate people because we fear them or blame them or are envious of them, and that's the error. To enjoy hate, and make it work for you, you have to hate the fear, hate the blame, or hate the envy: just hate the things, apart from the people. Then you can hate at ease, hate with cleanliness and morality, which makes hate and loving, both, all the richer."

Very well; The Old Girl made sure of her target. She pointed her ferocity toward the commission as a political inanimate.

She bit her teeth into a Munger pencil. Mr. Munger had paced the reception room for an hour, waiting until Mr. Williams-the-lawyer got in from the courthouse. They had exchanged quick low speeches, and Mr. Munger had gotten the look of hurt and disappointment almost at once.

Now, Mr. Munger's door hid them. But behind it, The Old Girl felt sure, Mr. Munger was behaving calmly, bravely, as he heard whatever unwelcome news his attorney was reciting to him.

Spain Munger kept his chin on the flexible, but unflexing, truss of his hands. "Uh, Mr. Williams, I'd like you to wipe my cobwebs for me, so to speak, on the words your Commissioner Dawson, uh, resorted to."

Mr. Williams-the-lawyer owned a talent for looking stuffed and huffy, which he wasn't, and for appearing misfit to any and all chairs, which he was. For years—actually, as far back as the Munger family could remember—Cicero Williams had endured his hairless red scalp, had dwelt in his rolly short body, with great humility. Recently, however, Mr. Williams-the-lawyer had borne himself less apologetically. The change occurred when Cicero Williams II, nowadays spoken of affectionately as The Moose, suddenly bloomed to magnificent proportions and began winning football's golden A's in a stadium that rang with adoring moose calls. In the wallet of Mr. Williams-the-lawyer, there were photographs and documents proving that Mr. Williams-the-fullback was his offspring. These were produced at every opportunity.

Presently, Mr. Williams-the-lawyer sat miserably before Spain Munger. His was the shattered composure of the messenger who, while believing he has brought good news, discovers with a jolt that he has delivered bad.

He sorted the tip of his tongue over his dentures. "Well sir, it occurred only casually, I think. Mr. Dawson directed it as a question; as I recall, he said, 'The Munger family does keep somebody sick out that road, do they not?'"

"He chased that goose no farther than that, did you say?"

"Yes sir. I remarked then that if it were to be the petitioner's burden, instead of the county's, to supply the justification for paving the road, we would like to know what would be required. Another commissioner remarked that the county would need no help; that the highway patrol would be asked to put one of its traffic-counting machines up out there. If I may offer an opinion, Mr. Munger, we could scarcely ask for anything better."

"Uh, thank you. Now, would you say, in view of the water you've seen under the bridge in your time, that this is normal procedure?"

"Yes, I would. Of course, the commission doesn't always bother with a statistical study, when certain friends are involved. Naturally, some paving is done on the bias."

Spain had grown more pale, as often he did just when this appeared impossible. His gaze bored past the lawyer, at the closed door.

"Mr. Williams—and I'd appreciate your frank answer, and I

170

know you will produce—do you think the situation here has put your directors on the spot in, uh, some sort of a comparison of status with your other rural landowners?"

"No sir, nothing so serious as that."

"Uh, yes. Then to finish this ball of string—there was no other reference to my brother? Which as you can see in your own mind is an example of your slur based on your back-fence brand of talk, and I think we'll agree a hundred per cent on that."

"There wasn't any other mention; no sir."

Spain stood up. "Well, I wouldn't want you to, uh, fly the belfry without my saying how the board appreciates your, uh, filtering out for us here, and if there's any new thoughts that occur to your head, you feel free, feel free." He followed Mr. Williams to the door. He returned to his desk, slowly, and interlaced his fingers to control their trembling.

It was obvious now the paving must be won, in light of your big picture. But at the moment, this consideration was driven aside. In twelve years, Spain was sure, no one had let fly such public mention of Brother. You could not see the point of it, this Commissioner Dawson poking a finger into the chink in your armor plate.

He telephoned Mr. Remo. "Uh, Mr. Remo, your paint will be sent out today; Harry will deliver the goods, and, uh, I hope you'll put Mr. Munger right on to it, and you'll remember, your best nut to crack, uh, might be to paint your barn."

Spain lit a cigarette.

The old words were suddenly in his mind: A mattock is like a hoe.

The double-bitted, iron-headed old mattock stood against the back of the barn for years, rusting and unused. Each season, its hickory handle rotted a little more; each summer, the runners of the stickered, yellow-flowering goatheads ran across its blades. To Cecil Munger's little snotters, the tool was forbidden, and when tiny, toddling China once asked what it was for, the old man said, "A mattock is like a hoe, except it's a

171

heap harder to man. It's what you'd whelp out if yu' bred a pick to a garden hoe, and don't let me see you younguns messin' with it, or I'll whale your mother's blood clean out of you."

Papa himself had never taken up the tool; the mystery was how it got on the place, and why it was allowed to stay. Papa hated all instruments that were intended to break the land's natural sod, just as thoroughly as he despised the men who put plows to a country meant only for grass.

Thus, every one of them watched expectantly the day Papa laid hold of the mattock as if it were vile and brought it up to the back yard. Mama had, the previous day, made one of her rare stands against her husband. She wanted a garden, wanted fresh vegetables for her children to balance off the starch of the constant potatoes and beans. When Papa swore and refused to disturb even a small piece of his ground, she had moved out of his room, and even his hand across her mouth hadn't brought her back.

Papa hadn't touched liquor the day he got the mattock, for he had spent it scraping out firebreaks just inside his fences. He was dirty and irritable from the work and from his reflection on the night spent in a solitary bed.

He drove the mules, Jack and Judy, into the lot, unhitched them, stripped them, and kicked Judy in her sagging wet belly for standing in the way while he tried to hang the harness on its pegs. He raised loud hell with the children upon discovering that they'd swung on the gate until a hinge tore loose. Then he came up the path, wiping his forehead but forgetting beads of sweat and dirt strung about his neck, and he stopped at the cistern. He drew and drank a half-bucket of the shingle-flavored water.

He groaned, and he suddenly shouted at the house out of knowledge that Melita would be in the kitchen, since she always was. "Hellfire, Meliter, why stir up God's natural sod fer a few goddamn onions? Won't grow nothing, no way. A man can't take his rest, if he's got a woman around. These damn kids, they look fat enough to me."

172

She did not respond.

Papa discussed the matter a bit longer, shouting each word of it, and finally the voice from the kitchen said, "Just as you please, Mr. Munger," and even Bethel and China knew Mama meant to spend another night in their room.

"Where do yu' want it?" Papa yelled, and he went and got the mattock.

The children gathered, at a distance, spellbound. Papa was going to use the mattock; he would dig up a garden. He chose a spot north of the barn, where he could be sure the first freeze would kill whatever Melita might have planted, and began.

Before each swing, Papa glowered at the children. Then, on a particularly vicious swing, the mattock head struck a buried rock. It glanced, ringing loudly; the shivers of shock ran up the hickory and stung Papa's hands. He swore and slung the tool away.

Then the children stood in a curious semicircle, gazing down at June. The mattock handle lay across June's chest. A queer dent had appeared in his forehead. Later, someone pointed out that it happened at six in the evening, when June was six years old, and it was the sixth month, so there was never much worry about remembering the date.

Papa carried Brother inside and put him in his bed. Mama sat on the edge of it, holding a rough red hand to Brother's plump cheek. She stared, but did not cry. Above the heads of the children, she said quietly, "I hope you're pacified, Mr. Munger," and it seemed she never mentioned it again.

For weeks, Mama never left the room in which Brother seemed quite dead. The house cluttered itself, each Munger rustled his own meals whenever he wanted, and Spain remembered to feed the animals. Papa lay on his leather couch, day and night, drinking steadily through. He seemed a stranger, because never before had his drunkenness been silent.

Brother was different, from the moment he awakened that hot afternoon. He looked funny, the way his feet turned out; he sounded silly, because he had forgotten most of what he knew, including the names of his brother and sisters. He forgot to go to the bathroom. But he had learned something, too; he could make them love him as, until then, only China had been loved.

His sisters made him their puppy, their baby calf, their kitten. Papa himself removed June beyond the others. No scoldings, no razor strap, no chores, and no school at all. Even on the drunkest days, Papa had a gruff sort of kindness for Brother. He let June trot at his heels when he worked; he played the harmonica for him in the evenings. And, if June cried, Papa found somebody else to knock the dogwater out of.

Spain loved June as well; he understood, as Mama said, how "you don't love them any less." But toward Papa, Spain's heart was set finally, the day a neighbor man said to his wife, "That old sot sure did for his kid, didn't he? Yes, a mattock— that's sort of like a hoe. . . ."

Spain crushed out his cigarette and pushed his buzzer.

The Old Girl arrived quickly, her dumpy body uncannily quick, her eyes bright with readiness.

"Uh, if you care to have a chair, Miss Northington—"

"Thank you."

"Before it flubs out of my mind, would you get in touch with Mr. Mooney before noon, and, uh, I'll talk on the call?"

"Yes sir."

"Now, uh, we won't need your notepad, and if—I hope I'm not horning into your work, whatever you are doing?"

"Oh, no sir."

"That's fine. Uh, as I've said before, Miss Northington, when it comes to your family corporation, your giz is, you ought to lick a finger and stick it up in the wind, so you have your ear to the pulse of things, in a manner of speech. It came to my thinking we might, uh, just visit a little while—"

He squinted; in his 4F vision, it did seem Miss Northington had cringed a bit, and that was the last how-do-you-do he cared for, your employee who cringed from you.

"You are," he said, "in touch with a representative chunk of the people, don't you agree to that, and if your silly question deserves your silly comeback, I hope you'll feel free to shoot straight from the top of the deck with me, and be frank as the facts come, just however they may hit the fan. . . ."

The Downtown Club, erected, perhaps significantly, in the space between Amarillo's largest bank and the even taller building where could be found Merrill Lynch, Pierce, Fenner & Beane, had been awarded a red stone face that was most tastefully plain. This home-away-from-home for the city's fifty-five millionaires, plus a few hundred others not so gilded but as hopeful, fronted on an approved sidestreet and permitted, democratically, an alley to pass along one of its sides. Unmarked by any sign and entirely glassless, the club gave an outward impression of determined modesty. Inside, its governors allowed wealth to run the more normal course.

For a thousand a year, if your manners and resources and circle of fellowships met the criteria, you could walk right through the corroded bronze door. Inside, you found air conditioning, heat conditioning, humidity control, the scent of imported perfumes, and the comradeship of the Panhandle's lions and their lionesses. These dollars bought you the privileges of an unmatched cuisine, of drinks at an illicit bar which would never be raided, of basement privacy for poker and dice among the jolly men who elected the sheriff and sometimes had him in as guest, and for you and yours, there were luxurious lounges, party rooms, and conference suites.

The Downtown Club placed a member next to all manner of things to come. He knew when and where to invest in a property speculation. He could outline the route of the next expressway, predict the future of city paving, or point to imminent city annexations, and zoning changes. Ordinarily, the club member could identify the next local office holders and could spell out their real interests, apart from the mish-mash they broadcast for public consumption. And the club itself could direct the voting of the legislators and the Mr. Congressman, without going to the bother of writing a letter.

The city paid no salaries to its mayor and commissioners, an economy precluding government responsibility for all save the rich. These found the Downtown Club a pleasant and carefree ground on which to transact public business. Once a thing was decided upon, it was no trouble to reenact it formally at City Hall, where there wasn't any air conditioning or humidity control; where in fact, there was just plumbing, and this pretty old-fashioned.

The school-board members, too, found the Downtown Club ideal. Especially was its relaxed, secluded atmosphere desirable when the matter at hand was the circumvention of the desegregation order, or a decision on which section of town should have the next new junior high.

Club membership entailed other advantages. You could park a Cadillac in fire lanes, or, you could just blatantly double-park anywhere in the immediate vicinity and go ticket-free. You could be sure your hat would not be stolen. You could dress most casually, if you chose; the fact that you'd gotten inside was testimony enough of your propriety and substance.

Moon stayed away as much as he could. Spain Munger used the club often.

They were the Munger members. In Spain's eye, about a 33⅓ per cent representation of the family seemed appropriate, which meant two full memberships. One he sensibly took to himself. Moon got the other as the surprise recognition of a civic errand well accomplished, very much as more recently he received the diamond cuff links. All the Mungers partook of the privileges, through guest rights and the club's generous view that membership was a family affair.

In response to Spain's call, Moon walked over just at noon. Spain waited for him in the first foyer. The chairman looked bony and long where he sat in a low Danish chair, and Moon frowned. Something about him seemed different.

"Uh, glad you could bust out and come," Spain said. "I hope this doesn't throw a wrench into your applecart?"

"No," Moon said, and they shook hands. He located the difference, then.

Spain, who never wore a hat, held one in front of him. Moon had to smile. It was a broad-brimmed, big-crowned Stetson;

176

one of those costly tan umbrellas known as a Texas hat and worn in Amarillo by men of distinction.

"You've gotten a hat," Moon said.

Spain squinted his embarrassment, and it struck Moon the hat had been a cautious, difficult decision. Beyond Spain was a wall rack covered with forty such hats, and again Moon had to grin at him.

"The old hair," Spain said, "it's thinning out, and it came to my head that if I'm to hang on to enough to shake a stick at—"

Moon said, "I bet it looks fine on you," and he thought, I can't wait to see how fatuous you'll look.

"Uh, I've put the clamps on a table for us."

They entered the vast, white-clothed dining room. Spain led through it, to a corner table. Moon ordered Greek sausage and salad; Spain, the filet mignon he always had at the club, since this was the noon specialty that the board of governors liked to feel was world renowned.

Moon looked directly through Spain's thick glasses, exploring the pale eyes; he felt annoyance at the placement of the lean hands beneath the chin, he wished the blond hair, which indeed was very thin, would stop wafting up and waving in the drafts of forced-air heating.

Spain said, "Uh, I thought we might put on the feedbag, and get our thoughts together on your project about your road. To get clear, Moon, I ought to say your deal isn't just, uh, jim-dandy right now. But I wouldn't want to give the impression we've already run into a flopper."

Moon had forgotten the road. "The county commissioners met this morning, I suppose."

"Uh, yes. Mr. Williams, that's Mr. Williams-your-lawyer, was there, and I have his report. I think it's the time, now, to get the project on the pot or get it off, which I'm sure will be your thinking—"

"You want me to argue with the commissioners?" Moon said it too loudly.

Spain reddened, and sent his pale gaze about the room.

"Uh, Moon, if we can keep our voices down—that's your Commissioner Dawson, the man eating over there."

"I know him. I didn't know he came here."

"Uh, well, he's up for membership, and on our sponsorship—"

Moon stared. "Yours and mine, you mean?"

"I did nominate him, if you don't mind."

"All right. Why?"

"Uh, one of the tricks you'll learn in touchy affairs, you don't nail your opposition to the cross; not if you can lead them up to the trough and make them drink. I ought to say, here, that your Mr. Dawson doesn't know who is sponsoring him. And I hope that greases your scruples right down to the nut. By-the-bye, Moon, I admire your attitude—"

"I'm satisfied," Moon said wearily. "Where's the point?"

They sat back as the Negro waiter in stiff white jacket laid monogrammed linen and served their food. When he bowed himself away, Spain said, "To take hold of cases, Moon, the county is having the highway patrol set up one of your traffic-counting machines on the road, and the decision will be on your traffic count out there. Uh, to barrel right at it—Mr. Williams says that seventy-five per cent of the time your bold stroke is your winner in politics, and I'll bet you agree to the hilt on that."

Moon sat dumbly. He did follow; he'd been a Munger-in-law long enough so that he could. The suggestion was disgustingly clear. The errand boy was getting his instructions; he would execute them, too, however unprincipled. He almost swore. But there was Bethel. The guilt of their breakfast quarrel still hung on him like a yoke.

Tightly he said, "So you want that traffic count—adjusted."

"Well, as I hope to pinpoint for your mind, your political tactic is an, uh, imaginative cup of tea; never doubt it. Of course I'd not ask you, Moon, thinking of you as I do, to swallow any bitter pills—"

"When do they put the counter out there?"

"Tomorrow."

Moon gathered the napkin off his lap and stood up.

"Uh, your food there, that looks good—"

"I don't want it."

"Uh, if you said what—?"

"I'll do it. Good-by."

"Wait, if you'll hold on, Moon, I thought we might kick the ball around about your car situation, while we have the chance. Uh, I have always leaned your way pretty heavy. . . ."

Moon left him. He walked out rapidly; he swore like John Remo as he reached the street. Then he tried to locate some shred of humor in it. But he could think of nothing, except how inane Spain would look in the new hat.

X

The City Symphony presented a University of Oklahoma soprano; she was large and brunette, her voice was undisciplined and good. Moon listened poorly. He was separated from Bethel by the still, attentive figure of Hannah, who seemed to be serving as their Mean Week buffer, and he missed Carol. Unlike herself, Carol had begged to be left at home. Moon was sorry he'd not stayed with her.

He thought of her as he gazed along the row at China. China was as his daughter would be one day. The prospect excited him. Then he looked at China without thought of Carol. He watched until it seemed wrong, and after that, he whiled away the concert with his attention on Frank. His partner-in-law grinned and frowned with the music, which Moon couldn't reconcile with all their ugly hours at the store.

At intermission, while Bethel lectured China about choosing a doctor and having an examination and about walks and calcium tablets, Moon had tried to talk with Frank. Not even speculation on the trust got a response. However incredible it was, Frank appeared ecstatically deafened.

As they hunted out their automobiles on a dark parking lot, Bethel talked cheerily with her sister. Moon thought he would tell her about Spain's paving plans. But she lapsed immediately into a scowling silence as Frank and China drove away, and he said nothing. He hoped they might get to bed without a quarrel.

The telephone was ringing as they entered the house. It was eleven-thirty. Moon answered gruffly.

"Uh, Moon, I've been trying to get you; there's an emergency to be jiggered with, I'm afraid, we'll have to hop on it tonight, according to my thinking, anyway...."

Let the errands pile up. Moon listened feelinglessly. Harry was in jail; he had given Spain's name, and the night captain had called. If gotten out right away, Harry would show less prominently on the chief's morning report, which was what your newspaper-beat reporters used as a springboard into their dirty little stories. But if Spain himself went down and paid the fine, that would defeat your purpose, wouldn't it?

Bethel and the children were already in bed when Moon ended the call. He went in and kissed Carol, who hugged him suddenly with graceful warm arms; very warm and sincere arms, he thought, and they helped his mood. When he bent to Hannah, she shrank from him as though she wished not to but was constrained, and very quickly she said, "Good night, Daddy," and turned her back.

Hannah, he supposed, was beginning to reflect Bethel in this time of chemistry.

He looked in on Bethel, who had left the bed lamp burning for him. Her eyes were closed.

"I've got to go get Harry out of jail," he said. Bethel did not reply, as if this were as routine as putting Foxy out for the night.

"Good night," he said.

He waited at the streamlined new sergeant's-desk in the streamlined, monotonously moduled new police station, until Harry was brought out. Harry appeared entirely sober; he was dressed handsomely in dark trousers and plaid sports jacket. They were outside before either of them spoke.

"You have transportation?" Moon said.

"Yes sir, I got the truck, out yonder at the club. But Mr. Moon, I'd shorely appreciate it if you'd carry me home. I reckon I got some foolin' to do, toward my wife."

"What happened?"

"Well sir, I don't rightly know. First thing I knowed, the hall was full of law, an' they taken a whole batch of us. They even taken Li'l Richard, hisself."

"Who's he?"

"He's the band leader, sir. It was him, playin' the rock."

"You mean you were just having a dance, and the police came in and arrested everybody?"

"Well sir, it was just about like that. Disturbing the peace and quiet, that was what they said, though I didn't notice much disturbing, myself. Li'l Richard, he's still in the jail, like he'd done somethin', and all he done was play an' sing."

"You say there wasn't any trouble?"

"Well sir, they was one nigger got cut a little, but the feller that done it, the law didn't take him. Mostly, the law didn't approve of the music. I reckon Li'l Richard is some different."

Moon grinned. "Being different will get you in a jam every time."

They got into the Chevvy. "Now, home, did you say?"

"Well, yes sir, if you don't care. I can get the truck in the mornin'. It's behind the Pink Tiger, an' nobody is gonna bother it."

"What's this about Carrie? Where's she?"

Harry rubbed his purple hands together as if washing them. "She stayed home."

Moon started the car and drove toward Fourth Street, which would lead to Harry's small, neat house at the edge of The Flats. "The sergeant mentioned a woman you were with. Are you trifling on Carrie?"

"Well, yes sir, I guess I was. But Carrie, she knowed about it."

"You mean she doesn't mind?"

"Oh, yes sir, she minds, all right. It's good for Carrie, though."

Moon glanced aside. Harry was gazing straight ahead, and he had folded his hands so they were hidden in his armpits.

"How do you figure?"

"Well, Carrie, she's the prettiest gal in The Flats; always was. An' sometimes, that makes her think she's the onliest one. A man can't let his woman figure like that, if he wants to live with her. Now, Laura Mae, she's the blackest ugliest gal they is—so I taken her to see Li'l Richard."

Moon sought the logic of Harry's matter-of-fact revelation. "Where is she now?"

"In the jail, I guess."

Moon said, "You've done this before, it sounds like. What does Carrie do about it?"

"Well sir, nothin'. We get along fine, Carrie and me. This here, it's just when she commences getting bossy over being good-lookin' like she is. Now when I get home, me an' Carrie will have some words, all right, and then we'll have a real good time."

Moon let the cook out before the little house where all the lights were burning. "I'm mighty sorry I put you out, Mr. Moon. I reckon Mr. Spain is gonna be put out with me some, to boot. But me an' Laura Mae wasn't doin' nothing but dancin', and I'd be much obliged if Mr. Spain knowed that. I don't know nothin' about that cuttin'!"

Plainly, Harry was confident of tonight's marriage therapy, but afraid for his job.

Moon smiled. "I'll tell him, Harry. Don't worry about it."

"Thank you, sir. I sure thank you."

How, Moon wondered, would this wise man handle matters if his wife were plain, or thought she was, and if Laura Mae were beautiful? Probably, Harry would deal with it just the same.

Teddy Birdsong was sitting on a high stool in back of the counter the next day when Moon returned from lunch. Her silken legs were crossed, one slim foot bobbing up and down, and her false lips were forming figures soundlessly as she burrowed through The Camera House books.

"Where's Frank?" Moon said.

"He went home. He said his wife wasn't feeling well."

Moon did not remove hat and coat. He thought of the job ahead, and wished there were some excuse to postpone it.

"Mr. Mooney, we could start the inventory this afternoon," Teddy Birdsong said. "There's almost no business; maybe it won't have to be done at night."

"I'll be out all afternoon," he said sourly.

She shrugged, and her breasts demanded his glance. He was tempted to say something about her clothes. Today she wore a red suit, fitted quite as closely as her original costume, and her white frilly blouse was carelessly sheer. He had no doubt, now, that her entire wardrobe was intended to reveal her, and he blamed it for the constant reaction she caused in him.

He went back to his office, got a fresh pack of cigarettes and his car keys, and returned to the front.

"I expect you better plan on closing this evening," he said. "I probably won't be back."

"Oh? Do I need a key?"

"No. Just shut off the heat—at the thermostat, over there—and set the night lock."

"What about the cash?"

"Just leave it in the drawer." He started out the front, then remembered the Chevvy was in back.

"If anyone calls," she said, "can I tell them where you are? That is, if you intend to tell me?"

He stopped and looked at her. The devilishness was in her eyes; the cold laughter beamed at him, as if she knew his mission, or had guessed it, neither of which seemed possible. She shook the bushy hair; she got off the stool and stretched, with a cigarette in her hand. Ashes dropped from it.

"Ashes in your hair," he said.

"Oh."

"Look," he said, on impulse of the sort that had given her the

184

collusive salary, "I am going to the country. Would you like to come along? We could close this place."

"Close the store?"

"That's what I said."

"You *are* in a temper." She picked up her purse, walked through the partition to get the fox fur. Moon felt a moment of indecision—a warning. But, rationalize, as this woman recommended. All right, he wanted someone to talk to because he did not wish to think. Shortly, he would believe that on this errand, companionship was a necessity.

Moon drove broodingly out of town. The day was bright, sunny, but with a tinge of winter making the car squeak. With the heater turned on, they were too warm; with it off, they became chilly. As he reached the highway, she said, "It appears we're heading for the Munger farm."

"Just part way," he said.

She looked at him amusedly. "You didn't mean to bring me along without telling me what we're doing, did you?" she said.

"It's a stupid thing."

"I didn't ask to come. Tell me what it is or just take me back to the store."

"You'll see." He derived a small pleasure from opposing her.

She sat deep in the seat, well away from him, as they turned onto the caliche road. She looked smaller than ever, yet still quite top-heavy. She unbuttoned her snug red suit coat, and she looked brazen.

She saw he had been watching.

"All right," she said. "Size thirty-nine."

He reddened.

"It's all right, really," she said. "Women's dimensions are public property. You need only read your newspaper."

He said quickly, "I see you wear a wedding ring."

"At times," she cocked her head suspiciously. "When I need it, I do; when I don't need it, I leave it off. But I'm not maudlin; it's no memorial to my husband, if that's what you think."

"It was just a remark," he said.

"Tell me, what are you and I doing out here? I probably don't object; but I'd like to know."

He had to look at her, and because he did, he struck a blunt outcrop of gyprock in the road. The car bottomed and jounced, and he braked it down.

"I am supposed to drive up and down the road here, all afternoon."

"Whatever for?"

"There's a traffic counter out here—let's watch for it. You see, the directors would like this road paved."

She laughed. "So that's how you pave a road."

"It's how this one will be paved, if it ever is."

She lit a cigarette and considered the matter with eyes fastened on him.

"This wasn't your idea, I'd bet."

"No."

"Spain Munger's?"

He said nothing.

"Of course," she laughed, "you had lunch with him yesterday. And you don't like this a bit."

"Would you?"

"Why, I do like it," she said. "Hell, at this salary, I'd like most anything."

He noticed he was getting used to her oaths, even those that were most uncalled for. He accepted hardness by disbelieving it; being tough is always counterfeit.

They drove a mile in silence. On either side the yellow grassland Old Cecil Munger had spent his life protecting appeared to need him. The mesquite was leafless and gaunt, the creosote bush feigned death. Only the cactus and sage had color, and this seemed to be under a coating of dust. Before them, along the road, white dust devils stirred and went skipping. Teddy Birdsong waved a hand at her window.

"All this belong to the Mungers?"

He nodded. "The old man got it together."

"Is it true he was an old sot?—oh, there's your gadget." She pointed at a steel box half-hidden in the ditch ahead. A

186

rubber hose extended from it and across the road to an anchor in the opposite ditch. She said, "What do we do, drive back and forth? Or do we just get out and jump up and down on it with our feet?"

Moon drove over the hose and on toward The Old Place. When he could no longer see the instrument in his rear-view mirror, he stopped, backed the car around, and drove back again through his own dust.

Teddy Birdsong sighed as they crossed the hose a second time. She stretched, scooted lower in the seat and extended her legs. "This is going to be exciting."

The afternoon, it struck Moon, wasn't unlike those frittered away at movies. This was equally surreptitious, however sanctified by Spain Munger. Moon had the same sense of offending time, the same unease of spirit as at all the gloomy matinees.

"I guess you think this is funny," he said to Teddy Birdsong.

"I think you take it damned seriously," she said. "Sure, it's absurd, taken by itself. But it's smart, if it gets you what you want."

"Cold materialist, didn't you say?"

"That's what I said."

He lighted their cigarettes. "Where do you come from?" It had occurred to him suddenly that he didn't know.

"It's stated on the application," she said. "Jessup, just a hundred miles down the road."

"I know the place. Why did you leave?"

"Everyone leaves Jessup."

"You make it sound like a disease."

They thumped across the hose again. He coasted a hundred yards, then began his U-turn.

She yawned. "That made three, if you're counting."

"Do you have folks in Jessup?"

"Just my mother, since my father died. She teaches school. And my husband's family is still there. At least, my father-in-law was, the last I heard." She laughed. "I only go back when I need a treatment."

"I don't get that," he said.

"You would, if you'd ever lived there. At home, people practice misery as a religion. They keep telling each other how everything has gotten so bad it can't get worse. Then, they get busy and make it worse. When I go down at all, it's just to see how much things have worsened. It makes me feel better about myself."

"You make it sound great."

"Oh, it is. Every time I'm there, I find the drouth is worse, the government is giving less and less to fewer and fewer, and everyone is planning to starve to death."

"You're exaggerating."

"No, I'm not. They tell me all about the funerals I shouldn't have missed, and exactly how long the final agonies lasted. I get a description of every new cancer and heart attack, and every business that's gone broke. All such good news as that. My mother is as bad as any of them. She tells me about having a nastier brat in her home-room than ever before, and how her back pains torture her at night, and how the doctor bills on those change-of-life shots are ruining her. She shows me how the roof is leaking in the same old place, and points out all the bagworms about to kill her evergreens, and I'm informed how she has to chop her own weeds, and how the same tire on her car goes flat every day. She says the world has gone to pot, because all the high-school kids are marrying as soon as they turn sixteen: just awful, she says, to see pregnant girls standing at the blackboard doing algebra.

"I never get the chance to put in any complaints of my own. Hell, by the time Mother stops for breath, I don't feel I have any troubles."

They approached the counting machine once more.

Thump.

"Four," Teddy Birdsong said.

"If this is some of your rationalizing," Moon said, "what does it offset?"

"Nothing. I just hate the little burg, that's all. I lived twenty years there. In all that time, no one ever prospered—at least, they never admitted it. It was always 'if we make a good crop.'

And if the cotton did make, then it was 'if we could get a decent price.' Nothing in Jessup has ever changed. I remember my father and mother best of all for all their bleating about low teaching pay, and neither of them ever tried to do one thing about it. They just bitched in tune with all the other bitchers, and we kept going it poor. I don't care for poverty."

She smiled, a sudden humorless smile. "Do I sound real bare-fisted?"

"You do."

"Good. I like to let 'em have it the few times I get the chance. You know one thing I can't get over? My music lessons. We couldn't afford a piano. So I took a lesson a week. The teacher gave me a paper keyboard. I was supposed to practice on that, and to imagine the sounds for myself. My mother made me sit at the dining-room table for two hours a day, whacking my fingers on that sheet of paper, and she wanted me to sing 'dum-de-dum's' so she could be sure I was concentrating. My God, think of that! And she and Father thought I disgraced them because at recital time, I couldn't play anything.

"And 'expression'—all little girls in Jessup take 'expression.' Poems and gestures. I had to practice all this before the mirror. That's how jackassy the whole business was."

Moon drove more slowly, so he might watch her. She had "expression," now, if she but knew it. Something terrifying showed through the thick make-up and leaped from the cold, unpretty eyes. He thought he saw in her an absolute ruthlessness, yet still with her was that odd air of sorrow.

The car rolled across the hose.

"Five," she said.

"It's pretty stylish to blame parents for everything, isn't it?"

"Oh," she said tartly. "Your parents were perfect?"

"I think so," he said, for there was yet a long while to drive.

Her voice was lower. "Actually, I loved my father. I used to dream of marrying him. He seemed so wise, keeping his books upside down on the shelves, so people couldn't read the titles and want to borrow them. And I liked the way he smelled, when I was small. The truth is, I didn't resent my mother, either. She was better-looking than I, but kind of prim. I had her for third-grade penmanship; you know, where you do the ovals and push-pulls in 'muscular motion.' All the kids thought of her as a sourpuss. The truth was, Mother was an idealist. Some people can't stand being idealists; it makes them mean. Of course, I must say I've liked Mother better since she got mean; makes her different from the inky-panks, who are all such hale fellows—"

"I beg your pardon?"

"Oh, the inky-panks?" Some of Teddy Birdsong's severity broke with her grin. "They're certain people you have in hick towns like Jessup. Hell, the inky-panks are a whole society, with everything geared to that hacking and sawing and picking and singing that sounds like 'inky-pank, inky-pank, inky-pank' —if you can stand listening to it at all. The boys grow long sideburns and wear cowboy hats and boots and belts with their names engraved on the back. On dates they take you out and show you their cotton, and they giggle most of the time and try to put their hands on you. There used to be a dance hall upstairs over a chili joint where the inky-panks gathered. You got your wrist marked with a rubber stamp when you went in. They'd have an inky-pank band and sand sprinkled on the floor. You could grind and scoot around all night, with time out once in a while so the drunks could get room to fight."

Moon said harshly, "I don't believe that's all there is to your town."

"Well, in the fall you could hear the gins humming all night, and smell the cottonseed cake and the burrs being burned. And on Saturday night, the band would march downtown and play in front of the drugstore. Everybody came to town. The people who had cars sat in them, and the rest of us walked around and around the courthouse square—my God, I've walked it a million times, meeting the same people every time around, passing the same cowboy movies and onion smells, putting just the right twitch in my rear so the people in the cars would talk about me. I used to go home so tired I was about to drop and wonder what the devil I'd been doing."

"What were you doing?"

She smiled. "I think, now, I was building muscles. Just getting strong enough to get the hell out of Jessup. I—well, here's the dumaflochie again, Mr. Mooney. Is this six, or seven?"

Moon had thought he only tolerated her long recital. But he was aware now of every word, and affected by it. There was a kind of bright perception in her bitterness.

He stopped the car on the hose. He backed, then went ahead, then backed again. The metal box in the ditch clicked, clicked, and clicked.

"Oh," she said, "an inspiration!"

"I'm simulating a whole line of traffic." He said it with a sudden ferocity. Then he slid into an aching, pointless wrath. He rocked the car cruelly, crashing the gears. The Chevvy jerked to and fro, snapping their necks; it struck a roaring rhythm. The rear wheels spun up gravel, the hose bumped beneath the car, the counting machine echoed each beat with a click. He pounded the road, the car, and the tube as if to kill them.

He realized he was driving savagely, that he was shaking. The compartment stunk of exhaust. Then Teddy Birdsong yelled, and he saw he had thrown her hard against the dash.

He stopped. He dropped a hand from the wheel, and the other from the gear lever. He was perspiring, and panting, as if the car had burned his energy in place of its own Munger petroleum. He turned to the woman.

She panted also, through the painted-on lips that were agape at him. Her big cheekbones had flushed, the bushy hair had tangled. He seized her by the shoulders and kissed her. Long and bruisingly. He felt her immense bosoms heave against him; yes, Frank, she is real! In revulsion he shoved her from him. He looked away from her, quickly, and heard himself say, "Are you hurt?"

Teddy Birdsong laughed at him.

He got out of the car, and walked around it. The rear wheels had stopped on the hose. He leaned against the trunk, breath-

191

ing deeply. After a moment, Teddy Birdsong alighted and came around to him. She handed him a cigarette already lit and marked with her lipstick.

"I'm sorry," he said.

She shrugged. "Don't be a fud. You do what is necessary."

They drove the afternoon away. He took it so slowly they raised almost no dust. Twice he drove on, miles beyond the counter, to within sight of The Old Place. He caught a reflection from the near wall of the barn, as if Brother had indeed begun to paint and was using the aluminized variety. He did not look directly at Teddy Birdsong again.

Once he stopped in a low saddle of the road, and they got out to stretch and smoke. The woman looked about, chose a clump of mesquite, and climbed through the fence and was gone for a time. Moon watched dumbly; he tried to imagine Bethel, or China, doing this. The thought aroused a guilt that felt like lead. He wished he had called Bethel, had asked her to come out and ride with him. Perhaps, he thought, at another time, Bethel might have come. She might have wanted an afternoon of aloneness with him. But not this week. If he'd called her, he was sure, they would have argued.

The run became a monotony. A constant groan of the Chevvy's old bearings, the road rumble rising up through the floorboards, the whine of the transmission as he shifted. And Teddy Birdsong in silence, her unsweet perfume becoming oppressive, her sheathy clothing and dense make-up now only facts that were tiresome and uninteresting. Even Moon's thoughts settled into a groove, something like the ruts in the road: this is a new low, this the lowest low yet, boy. You can call me Frank Wallace.

It surprised him to see, during a fiftieth or hundredth U-turn, that the sun had gone red and was poised for the abrupt flaming plunge that, in this season, brought darkness so rapidly. He glanced at the fuel gauge; the gasoline, too, was nearly gone.

His voice sounded foreign to him. "I guess we may as well call it a ride."

192

Teddy Birdsong stirred as if from a nap. "I've lost track," she said. "How many times did we cross it?"

"I don't know. Enough, I guess."

He drove back to town. She spoke once more of the inventory that shouldn't be put off; she wasn't doing anything this evening, and after her afternoon off for an outing in the country, she ought, probably, to work tonight, and she would, if he'd just give her the store key.

He delivered her to a cold-faced buff brick apartment house not far from downtown. It had a pinched and pained look, from the way its greater and finer neighbors to either side crowded bullyishly against it.

He stopped the car and she smiled at him with a too-amused turn of the boyish lips. "Well, thank you, I think," she said.

As she scooted out, he looked frankly at her knees because, he was sure, she intended him to. She shut the door and bent her face to the window. "May I have the store key?"

Moon took it off the ring in the ignition and handed it to her. "Do I have to help?" he said.

"You're the boss," she said. "Suit yourself."

It was dark when John Remo tied a cup towel around his vast middle, so the grease wouldn't spatter his serge, and got out the skillet. He attacked the supper problem grudgingly; cooking, sometimes, got to be the sorriest piece of his job. He took a long sack of sausage from the refrigerator, along with a dozen canned biscuits and six of the fresh eggs that would stand up high when fried.

The sausage had just begun to sizzle when Brother came inside. His overalls were smeared silver; there were finger streaks of metallic silver across his cheeks.

"Honest, Mister Remo, ain't they comin', China an' all them?"

"I said no, dammit."

"But I seen ole Moon's car, out yonder on the road I seen it, Mister Remo; I seen 'em coming out!"

"You're full of prunes. Now, go get washed up."

193

"Ain't they never gonna come out for no Sunday dinner, Mister Remo, an' no star chamber—"

"You can shut that up, that star chamber stuff. I told you about that."

" 'Scuse me, Mister Remo; I sure don't want your tit stuck in no wringer, only, how come they ain't coming out, China an' all them, if I seen Moon's ole Chevvy on the road—"

"Goddammit, go get washed!"

For Remo, it had been a slow and tiring day, and he had a wind-burned skin.

"I don't care none, about no washing up, Mister Remo." He extended the fat hands, almost solidly aluminized. "But I don't know if I can get off this here paint, Mister Remo."

"Get that can of coal oil on the back porch. That'll take it off."

"Boy, I will, Mister Remo. You're a good sonofabitch, all right!"

They had gone shopping for shoes during the forenoon, taking the Cadillac the sixty roundabout miles to Pampa, as Spain insisted when there were clothes or groceries to buy, and the happiest Munger had set off a furor.

The slob, damn him; he'd opened his penknife as soon as they sat down at Thom McAn's, and as quickly as the shocked young clerk handed him a shoe, he stabbed his bunion slits into it before trying it on. The clerk, with a Navy anchor tattooed prominently on the back of one hand, had been about to yell for the police. But Remo got out the Munger roll, and he paid for each pair Brother tried. At last they got out with three pairs, two of them two-tone golf shoes, and Remo had paid for eleven. They treated themselves to steaks, and Remo picked up a bottle of Old Forester before they returned home.

He had allowed Brother his afternoon run of TV sob stories, then had browbeat him into beginning with Spain's paint. The big bald ninny had sung "Jesus Loves Me" so steadily, Remo thought, that even Christ must have wearied of it, and he had painted for hours on one small patch of barn wall. The job would have to be finished, now it was begun, and it might take a month.

Remo turned the rapidly shrinking sausage patties and mashed them out. Hot grease snapped onto his hands, and he felt it but it did not hurt. He wondered if, for some reason or another, Moon had been, actually, out there on the road today.

"Boy, we fixin' to have some Jello, Mister Remo?"

"You see what we're having."

Brother reeked of kerosene. "China, she says I get a big kick out of Jello, Mister Remo."

"Go wash."

"Can I get me that bird dog, that 'un we seen over at Pampa today, huh, Mister Remo? China, she don't care—"

"I told yu', no."

"Well, Mister Remo, Kittypoo, she ain't much account, sometimes, an' if—"

"Spain don't like dogs. You forget it."

Remo took up the sausage on a platter and began breaking the eggs into the grease. Two for himself, four for Brother June. Then he swore, for he'd forgotten to put the biscuits in the oven.

Brother said, "Ain't they comin' out no more, Mister Remo?"

"Hasn't been long since they came. You just hold your horses."

"Oh, I aim to keep my britches on, all right, Mister Remo; only Spain said we could go see *Break the Bank* an' *Li'l Abner*, and we ain't went yet, Mister Remo, and paintin' on a barn, that's not what I crave to do much, Mister Remo."

"You got to paint the barn before we go. Spain said that. Besides, we got to wait till we get some tickets. I told you that fourteen times."

"You sure did, 'scuse me, Mister Remo. When you reckon China an' all them is comin' for Sunday dinner, Mister Remo?"

"Easter, maybe."

"Boy, that's when I get all my eggs lost, ain't it, Mister Remo? Ain't that next Sunday, Mister Remo?"

"No. April First, this year. April Fool's, come to think of it. That'll make it your day."

"How long is that, Mister Remo?"

"Not long. Dammit, I said go wash!"

He put the plates on the table, looked in at the biscuits that would be late, and sat down to wait. He picked up the new letter from Pennsylvania, and before opening it, had to grin at the address. His mother kept making her point, even from this distance. His name was written out in full, and the *lewski* of it was twice underlined.

Damn, he bet she was lonesome.

"You're very late," Bethel said.

Moon's dinner was on the table which was otherwise clear. Bethel had eaten with the children; their schedule of baths, homework, and television toward a nine-thirty bedtime was rigid and their mother never allowed it tampered with. But she had kept an attractive meatloaf meal warm for Moon. One thing, even in Mean Week, Bethel cooked extremely well.

"I'm sorry."

She wore her robe and underneath, he supposed, her pajamas. Likely, she'd not dressed all day. It kept him cautious, although he thought he saw a lessened tension in her face, foretelling the inevitable trend back to normalcy.

He dealt with his food lightly, unable to relax under the closeness of her attention. After a while she said, "I suppose this is one of those times you can't stand meatloaf."

"No, Beth. And please. I've had a rough day. And I ought to go back tonight."

"Oh, is there a business boom?"

"I think I told you. We should have an inventory, that's all. An evening or two should do it."

"Do something about your hand, Richard."

"What?"

"It's bleeding."

It puzzled him. He had scratched his palm mightily, and quite recently, but the curious and inexplicable events of the day had stifled any consciousness of it.

"Since you expect me to nag you," Bethel said, "I suggest once more than you see the allergy doctor."

Moon got up. Withdraw from the kitchen, withdraw from

his wife, retreat from the prospect of another wrangle or, at least, from this promise of a more bitter one. He wished this one evening, Mean Week or Hell Week or National Pickle Week or whatever, to pass in agreeable company or in none at all.

He turned out of the kitchen, realizing he had decided to help Teddy Birdsong with her inventory, and he said, for what good there was in it for Bethel, "I'll get a little iodine."

He walked through the living room, barely seeing Hannah where she sat with notebook in her lap. He opened the bathroom door without having noted it was closed, and Carol emitted an electrifying little shriek.

He looked at her, shocked to the floor, and unable to move.

Carol was naked, standing with one foot yet in the tub. She seemed to have been stretching for a towel. She stood stunned and still, one slim arm reached out, her fine China eyes broad in surprise, her face florid.

There was an instant, and he knew it, in which the mischance might have been undone. But the sight of his child—except she wasn't a child at all!—held him there. He saw her get a towel, drop it in her haste, then sink with a splash back into the tub. She was bending her face to her knees, trying to wrap herself in her arms, and she cried, "Oh, Daddy, get out!" as he backed into the hall.

He shut the door. He seemed to have undergone, in mere seconds, the whole advent of middle-age. His daughter remained before his eyes, an undreamed-of, unprepared-for young woman.

He had seen how her skin glowed pink; how the faint breezes of white steam rose off her. Her new, small, plainly defined breasts; her limbs no longer gaunt but subtly curved, and about all of her, the incredible new shadows.

He leaned against the wall. Carol, just eleven years old. Through the door, he heard her sob.

He thought of her as he'd seen her every day, in her little-girl dresses—how could Bethel have done that, or not thought to tell him? Carol was changed, somehow gone from him. He felt dowdy and hoary and crotchety and old, and he groaned, for now it seemed she had stared back at him with a horror that had almost become hysteria. It struck him she could not know he'd been only amazed.

He leaned on his fists against the door. "Baby, I want to talk to you—"

"Oh, please go away!"

He winced at the sound of her. "Listen to me, Carol; I just wanted some iodine. I didn't know—I mean, you surprised me, that's all. You're a pretty girl, Baby."

She screamed, "Go away!"

He almost broke in on her, to slap her, to make her listen. "Carol, it's nothing!"

Bethel turned him from the door. She split it a crack, looked in. "Richard, what have you done?" she said, and she went in quickly and shut the door and clicked the lock.

Moon sat in the car, almost retching on the foul taste of his cigarette.

All the baby pictures were in his billfold; there was the face of a sweet small child, caught as it had been when she used to cock her head toward the sound of thunder and whisper in awe, "Listen, Daddy; the Lord is moving his chiffonier!"

Beth, Beth, set this right! You should have told me; I should have known, for Carol is mine!

Suddenly he was drained out, empty. He felt nothing at all. The complete husk, then; the ogre in the coffee urn, the colossal flopper of floppers. The discard.

He started the engine.

Your giz is, you have no giz at all.

And—skit, skat, how about that?

part two /*XI*

XI

Back there on May 9, 1943, a conspicuously hot day if you considered the month to be the end of spring rather than the beginning of summer, they held the funeral for Old Cecil Munger. By every intent, the service was indistinct from all others in its objective detail. But those present could say they sensed a certain uniqueness, perhaps due to the economy of tears, or to the undisguised curiosity that hung like a scent in the air. Everyone speculated on this. And many minds marked the occasion simply because for once, all the rich Mungers, except one, sat in public display.

It was confirmed that the seldom-heard-of son named June had been forced to remain out at The Old Place, much against his will. A career lounger from the waiting rooms of the Texas Employment Commission had been obtained to sit out the day with this absentee. This talkative fellow related, later, how the big fellow wept—no, cried—just exactly like a baby; how, after the other Mungers departed for the church in the Gray Bros.' black limousines, and before you could say "Jack Robinson," this June took a running jump into the cistern.

The man stood down there in breast-deep water for hours,

sulking, sobbing, refusing the ladder and every persuasion sent down to him. Not until his pale kinspeople returned did he allow himself to be hoisted up again into the light of day. And this came only upon his sister China's gentle and earnest and unimaginably tender supplications.

The incident brought back to mind the tale which said Old Cecil Munger once jumped or fell into the same tank, shortly after the accident that maimed his elder son. Which, if true, likely caused the broken ankle that caused the crooked foot that caused the ever-after limp that caused you to notice the unkempt old rum-pot more frequently than you would have otherwise.

The sitter-of-that-day couldn't help telling the two stories in couplet. Dirty linen was due its airing, he avowed. And in the same admirable candor, he admitted this was a fine point on which he and the Munger family didn't see eye to eye. Which, as he explained to the man who gave him his weekly unemployment check, was the reason, no doubt, that the Mungers had never invited his services again.

The Reverend Justin B. McLean's throat constricted. Noticeably, he feared. He depressed his chin down over the disturbance; perhaps if he manifested serenity long enough, it would come.

The occasion sat so heavily upon him that his face had heated dry; particularly did it smart in the area of the birthmark. His body, too, was like something borrowed, and atop it all, his good Baptist militancy—which he thought of, ordinarily, as being the most part of his soul—seemed shrunken to a germ. He felt that the many eyes now turned on him must see that, for the moment, he was a charlatan.

Reverend McLean's two boon years of dispensing hellfire and damnation from this pulpit hadn't prepared him to speak the final charities over Cecil Munger, or over such a fortune.

"Oh, relax, good parson," Mrs. McLean had smiled while kissing him out the parsonage's side door. "You're okay. You're just a little smidgen unnerved."

Unnerved, certainly. He'd been nowise as upset when, with

his rather unprogressive new theology on him like a pious pallor, he preached his try-out sermon before this same critical congregation.

Only, today it wasn't the same congregation.

He crossed his legs, and let his gaze move about selectively until it sorted out his wife. Mrs. McLean sat in the far back row, frowning at him for playing the real dickens with the bladish creases she had pressed into the black funeral trousers. His wife classified all things; these were, inflexibly, his funeral trousers. He had, also, Sunday morning trousers, and Sunday evening trousers, and visiting trousers, and going-to-deacons'-meeting trousers; even some loafing-around-the-house trousers. He owned one pair she'd not labeled and which he pleased to regard as just plain trousers trousers. But soon, he felt sure, Mrs. McLean would designate these as his off-to-war trousers.

His thumbs somersaulted each other in his lap. It did seem his wife should have had in ready reserve a pair of dependable, rites-for-a-rich-sinner trousers.

Where was the US Navy, he wondered. He wanted the Navy; he lusted for it. He wished *Mighty Mo* would come sailing down the middle aisle, its great guns saluting him, its crew to snatch him aboard in a cargo net or something, its screws to drive him away from here fast, to Caledonia or such other far place whence he could write forlorn and lonesome and very warlike letters to Mrs. McLean.

He wished . . . but here, here, Brother McLean! Be no coward, you are God's man.

He wet his lips.

The huge bronze casket rested on a chrome carriage just beyond the altar rail. Its dull gloss lifted through a shaggy blanket of plumosis and Boston fern and giant mums, the fragrance of which waned short of him. Beyond The Remains, he could see the Munger family. The bereaved ones.

As was his funeral duty, Reverend McLean extended them a sympathy via the gravity of his eyes. The offering seemed to reflect right back at him. They refused comfort. Or maybe, for some indefinable cause, they were refusing him.

He changed his legs once more.

Comfort. He had the notion these Munger people needed comfort about as much as they needed holes in their motionless blond heads. His shoulders shuddered at such mental sin, and, in attrition, he beamed his comfort at them again.

The Mungers sat tightly against each other. Did they have to pack all their long bodies into that one very short front pew? They were still, fair-skinned, flat-waisted, prominently boned. And tearless. The men kept their arms uniformly crossed, for lack of elbow room; among them one superb-looking young Marine whom, Reverend McLean thought, he must remember to jest at if the opportunity came, since such is the Navy tradition toward the "bellhops." Beside the Marine was the tall girl called Bethel, breathing through parted lips in a way that caressed her man without touching him, and the minister felt there was pure beauty in the plainest woman if her beloved is just home from the war.

The other Munger women formed a uniform row of veiled black hats and each held, in appropriate black glove, a war-scarce Kleenex at the ready, as if challenging him to make them weep.

He supposed he was being unfair. The family had been kind to him. They would pay him fifty dollars. They expected that value in suitable remarks, to be spoken with dignity over their father's paralyzed and, literally, dog-bitten old remains.

Reverend McLean wondered if they'd heard he was going off to war. Perhaps he ought to have told them; to have explained, there *is* a war on, and I am going to the Navy next week, but of course I'll do the best I can with the funeral—and in the war, too, needless to say. But I have had a great deal on my mind, getting ready. It's difficult for one to know what one should say. . . .

A hundred million; imagine it!

He had all but begged Brother Bellew, the bald and pensioned old pastor emeritus, to replace him in the service. "I'm so new here, Brother Bellew. I've never met this family. And I'm getting my chaplain's commission next week, so I've much to do. I'm buying uniforms, I must shop for an identification bracelet—"

Brother Bellew had laid a heavy flab of arm around him. Brother Bellew declined, but with hasty amplifications: now, far be it from the old workhorse to evade whatever assignment, however humble, his fine young successor might find for him; that, you can count on, preacher, but you will understand that in the Indian summer of a man's life, meaning advanced age, of course, which is naturally not to be confused with senility, you may lose, well, sir, lose some of the normal controls, and you must wear, ah, well, a rather bulky fixture that makes standing in a pulpit prohibitive, just utterly prohibitive, chuckle chuckle, but son, why worry, you will do splendidly I am sure, you need but bear in mind that Mr. Munger was among the true pioneers of this great Panhandle country and the founder of the largest fortune I know about, and it occurs to me, young man, that you may ferret out here a God-given opportunity, for in the cause of His Name we know no limits, and in this case, if we hark to the angels, doesn't it seem that "some of the family wealth, or at least the pretty tithe of it, may yet find its way to the church and the glory of the Lord? Now, Justin, the bereaved will be seated there before you, sensitive for the moment that they sit also under the brows of Eternity, and at a time of mourning, we need nothing so much as a redirection. . . ."

All this may have sired Reverend McLean's sense of being in a fix. Or, it could have been aroused a few hours earlier, from his own discovery that Mr. Cecil Munger had never sought out the Gospel, but preferred to cauterize his immortal spirit each day by drinking down two quarts of whisky, which he took undiluted and unsecretively. The hundreds gathered here had this knowledge, Reverend McLean could not doubt. Did they wait, then, to see how he might preach such a soul up to the Gates and beyond?

He drew his breast-pocket handkerchief and wiped his face, despite the cautioning frown of his wife. He had to fight down the urge to reply to a yawn he noticed on the face right beside her. Unfortunately, he had been up very late last night, asking frank questions and receiving frank responses from the Munger daughter peculiarly named China.

At his own troubled request, Sister Wallace had called to recount something of her father's history. Over strong coffee in the parsonage's new breakfast nook, they talked a long while, quietly. Sister China had seemed to like him. She looked and smelled and sounded lovely; he had to think, whatever her home training, that her memories of her father were exceptionally Christian.

With Mrs. McLean sitting aside, taking down his notes, he had been temporarily at ease.

"Little things, perhaps?" he said. "Such as might suggest your father's gentleness toward his family."

"Oh, let me think. There was one time I remember, when he had shot a wolf. He carried it on his shoulder three miles, to get it home so we kids might see it."

In his heart, Reverend McLean loved her for it: this woman who read generosity into a hunter's boast.

"Sister Wallace, I had in mind something more—more sentimental. I know it's difficult to think, at a time like this."

"Well, there was Papa's music. He loved to play the harmonica. We used to sit on the floor around his chair while he played. It was wonderful."

"Can you recall anything in particular he liked to play?"

"Oh, yes. 'Little Annie Rooney' was one. And 'Old Gray Bonnet.' And 'Run, Nigger, Run.' Oh yes, almost every time he played 'Whispering Hope,' too."

Reverend McLean seized on it. "That was his favorite hymn? Something he was fond of?"

"Why, yes, it was. He 'frilled it up,' as he used to say. Gee, when we knew Papa was feeling good, we used to dance around the chair, the way he played it. He—"

"You danced to that glorious old hymn?" Reverend McLean stiffened. "I feel that isn't quite the thing we are searching for. If you'd tell me just the things you'll cherish in memory, I'd be grateful."

She thought a moment, her fine features becoming even more fascinating because of it. Suddenly she said, "God is love, I think."

"Indeed, Sister Wallace. There's no better definition."

"Well, Papa said things about God and religion that I know he didn't mean. I mention it because I'm aware—we are all aware—that you can't help but have heard of this. But he was full of love. I doubt that anyone, except my mother, could see this. Oh, my Brother June felt it, and I did. Papa loved the land. He would have died for his land, he loved it so much. And his children. He cared so much, I think, that he never dared show it. There are people like that, aren't there?"

"I'm sure there are."

"Papa liked to read to us from the Atlas. He gave us 'characteristics, elevations, and populations.' Especially the ones that went with our names, don't you see? He'd tell about the Great Wall of China, for me. The bullfights, for my brother Spain. And he surely loved my mother. There's something I remember. We—none of us expected it. Beside her grave, when he made them let him look at her one more time. He wasn't like—like any of the things you hear, not then. He told the funeral people 'To hell with the custom,' because he did talk that way, and he bent down and looked at my mother's face. He kissed her, and he said, 'Good-by, Meliter.'" Mrs. Wallace had begun crying, so softly it did not disturb her voice. "That was Papa, under the skin. Do you understand that?"

Reverend McLean had been considerably confused by the anecdote. It matched no concept of Cecil Munger, drunkard–sinner–lost soul, that his discreet but diligent inquiries had produced. This young woman's saintly sweet face compelled him to accord doubt's benefits where he might, for the moment. But his strict ecclesiastic conscience forbade any acceptance of mere words of farewell to a dead wife as proof of a belief in the Hereafter. From such as Cecil Munger, a kind word might indicate nothing more than a fill of pagan liquor.

"I can remember, when I was a little girl and no one else was around," China Wallace was saying, "how Papa liked to muss my hair. Sometimes he took me with him in the truck, and if we saw a road-runner, he'd drive like sixty to see if we could run it down. Don't you think—well, you understand, don't you?"

"I understand," Reverend McLean said.

He hadn't, not at all.

Today he couldn't even recall the wonderful shine on Sister Wallace. Out there in front, she looked like the other Mungers. She appeared inseparate from them. Together, he thought, the Mungers alloyed themselves into one many-limbed many-eyed person, indivisible from the big land and big oil that the service, in effect, would dedicate to their unity.

A hundred million, for better or worse.

Reverend McLean got out his notes.

The choir, edited down to its ten better voices, was arriving at the closing stanza of "In the Garden." Reverend McLean had suggested this to Mrs. Wallace without explaining his reasoning. His seminary considered the hymn the safe old reliable whenever the deceased hadn't been on terms with the Lord, for its poem did rhyme out a hope left unqualified by the woeful judgments.

Damp-handedly, Reverend McLean riffled through the note cards. Each was precisely typewritten by Mrs. McLean. With exasperating prankishness, she sometimes smuggled some overbold thought of her own into his notes. He had learned to beware. Now he glanced up at her again, and she gave him the slight shake of head that signaled, Don't Be So Fidgety. He semaphored back his Roger by scanning slowly the sanctuary which this crowd made so small.

Every pew was snugly occupied as were the special collapsible chairs added to the rear. Through the open windows he could see tobacco smoke and hear restrained voices, meaning that many latecomers intended to pay their respects from the shade outside.

Reverend McLean failed to get good grasp of it. Even the better of his two revivals, the one last August when forty-seven souls ventured forward for rebirth, hadn't attracted this attention.

"The Mungers weren't people who mixed much," the

emeritus Brother Bellew said. "The old man left folks alone, and he saw to it that they let him be. I can recall, back before the oil, seeing his old pickup rattling around town on a Saturday with dirty kids piled in the back like cotton pickers. I wanted to help; my heart went out. The church ladies rummaged up clothes to take out to the children, and all that. But we never really touched them. They just never mingled, that's all."

Well, then why was everyone here? How did a pastor speak over a lecherous old land miser, before listeners arrived only to learn what sort of sermon befitted a hundred million dollars? Quickly, Reverend McLean purged his thoughts as, once more, unpreacherly.

The Navy. Maybe after the war and the Navy, he'd be better in situations like this.

The choir finished. Reverend McLean sighed secretly and went to the pulpit. He placed down his notes, straightened a copy of the expensively engraved obituary in front of him, clamped his palms over the oaken sideboards, gazed up at the dirty ceiling plaster while the crowd completed its coughing and rumbly adjustments of feet, and at last he began to read.

The obituary, which Gray Bros. Mortuary seemed to have circulated through town like a Dollar Day handbill, struck him as very clumsily composed. He hoped the shadings of his voice improved it.

"Cecil Rogers Munger, born April 2d, 1858, in Tipton County, Tennessee, the eighth of the eleven children of Samuel and Maggie Rogers Munger, none of whom survive, and died May 7th, 1943, at Amarillo, Texas, at the age of eighty-five years, one month, and five days.

"Mr. Munger departed his native Tennessee in 1888 to pioneer in the Texas Panhandle, where he established himself in various land and ranching enterprises. . . ."

A hundred sections, a hundred million.

"In 1890, Mr. Munger joined in marriage Miss Eula Perkins, of Tipton County, Tennessee. This good woman preceded her husband in death on October 19, 1908, leaving no offspring."

Surely the Gray Bros. could afford a more gifted writer, wouldn't you think? Reverend McLean read on.

"Later, Mr. Munger entered into matrimony (oh, good gracious!) with Miss Melita Jane Graham of Amarillo (thank heaven they had omitted the date, for as Brother Bellew happened to know, the old snorter had been romping away in the bed of his second marriage before the first Mrs. Munger grew cold), and to this union were born eight children, six of whom survive.

"They are Miss Texas Munger of Amarillo, Mr. June Munger of Route Six, and Mrs. Laska Munger Glass, Mrs. Bethel Munger Mooney, Mr. Spain Munger, and Mrs. China Munger Wallace, all of Amarillo."

Except for a sterile statement of place and time for the funeral, which Reverend McLean did not read, only one other line remained: "Mrs. Melita Munger preceded her husband in death on August 4, 1936."

There, save for matters distasteful, you had the whole eighty-five years of Cecil Munger. A man boiled down to a few squares on the calendar and to the enumeration of his issue. Reverend McLean wondered if the Gray Bros. could sum him up by the same formula if the war should claim him.

He turned back to the hard, peaked dais chair flanked by its two smaller replicas. He sat down, crossed his sea legs, folded his hands on the deck his lap made, and waited for them to strike up the special music.

Intriguing, about the Navy. Was it true: did they really weight the feet with enormous shells, and spill them overboard like in the movies, with guns blowing off in salute, with tears glistening in the eyes of a crusty old skipper, with ship's company arranged in solemn statues of immaculate white attention?

Whiteness. Before him, Spain Munger was a variety of it. Hair thin and downy and almost white. White skin, etched white frown. The man's shanky overlength looked misfitted to the pew, and his youth—he was only twenty-three, hadn't

Mrs. Wallace said?—was unapparent, as though its bloom and ripeness had been set aside, deliberately: there you were, youth conquered like an ailment.

Well, however he preferred to watch Sister Wallace, this Spain Munger was the one to please; the man seemed ready to tally up the platitudes until satisfied of having received the money's worth. . . .

Mrs. Tracy Kellow, of the crop-and-casualty-insurance Kellows, stood and began her solo: "Ivory Palaces," in place of a "Whispering Hope" these strange people might dance to. Mrs. Kellow was a tiny gray woman whose round full mouth was a faucet of sad music; it could, on call, outpour a sincere and fetching kind of melancholy. She wept while singing at funerals. Without turning to look, Reverend McLean knew she was weeping now.

He could see the Bereaved Ones were not.

XII

In the years since their marriage, Bethel and Richard Mooney had maintained membership in three of the national book clubs. This rapidly populated an entire wall of their living room, and soon there was a sizable spill-over of flashily jacketed novels on the innermost shelves of the garage. To begin with, Moon had read every book.

The experience was bewitching and new. Reading on Cass Street had been scant, the air being inconducive as it was, and Moon found he consumed books as if frantically catching up. He went doggedly through the fact books, taking pains as one does while going about what is good for him. But the novels —these struck him alive.

They seemed mighty bonanzas of truth. He decided fiction was the parable of merciless self-examination. And if it came draped on an often-too-neat structure for most advantageous display, well, truth remained good, however you coated it.

During those first years after the war, while Moon yet regarded his in-laws somewhat humorously and before he grasped how no detail of the Munger big picture was less than grave, he made himself patient by reading, and the novels assured him all human problems are soluble. Happily, because he brought his mind to a book, it seemed all the formulas were there, demonstrated in a trillion lines of magic print. It should have led him to a comfortable, nice sort of creed. It almost did.

But he read on up the scale, as set by the reviewers, into Algren and Capote. As his innocence fell, he had to read on and on, through to the unmasking of authors as mere men who, it dawned cruelly, set down only their own truths because no mind is capable of more, and who then alerted you that one man's truth is apt to be another man's dirty lie, which warned you as subtly as the blow of an ax: Watch out, Wayfarer; for you, two heads may be better than one, but for me, too many cooks spoil the broth, and for the fellow over there neither cooks nor heads are worth a fingers-snap, and as you see, what is meant is that each crisis is utterly new, each decision without forerunner, each conscience equipped with justice enough, all of which tells you how each heart is isolated irreparably to fail alone, and listen, Mr. Disenchanted, if you didn't know this until now then your hopelessness is complete already, and you may now feel free to project it so as to discover that love is myth, sin nonexistent, God a tormenter, goodness no more than a puff of thin smoke, and loneliness the only reality, and since your wisdom has arrived at this near ultimate, please follow along one step more, and take an old second-hand brassiere (for sex) and hang yourself (for tragedy) from the elaborate chandelier (for irony) of a two-dollar hotel room (here's money) and make this a room for which you've not paid (pathos) and let them cut you down (in pity) and may they take due note of victory's sour smile (bitterness) on your lips and let them understand it's there because you traveled life down to just a few miles of bumpy road (philosophy) and let's hope they grasp, as well, that you (spark of honor) could never have both captured the truth and kept living. Or at least, you could not have lived and shown them such an unforgettable smile.

And here, Moon despised realizing, was literature's most

sophisticated ride. So in 1949, he threw a book against a wall and jumped off the tram. Now, when he read, he did not examine. The book was only fun. Or occasionally—when some odd scrap of time lay before him, begging to be used as if knowing how heartily he longed to accommodate it—the book became a utility.

Now, still in bed, he had such an interlude. He rested the utility on his naked chest. When he turned a page, he turned it carefully. He hoped not to disturb his wife.

At some indeterminate moment of the night, Mean Week had packed up and gone. He couldn't mistake the smoothness of Bethel's pale skin, so suddenly refreshed, as though from a regained infancy. There was an audible peace to her breath; a visible and contented falling-apartness of her slim length, now curled on one side and tucked down deep in bed and in untroubled sleep.

Sunday, the eleventh. Moon marked the date this March's sciences ended, so he might anticipate April's. He was relieved for Bethel. But this month, he couldn't feel particularly glad for himself. The last few days of her gloom and wrath may have let him feel less depraved than he would, shortly, when she awakened as though newly in love.

He glanced up at the silent, leather-padded clock. They ought to be up, plunging into their prechurch turmoil. But Beth would need, as on every recovery day, an hour or two of extra sleep. Besides, he admitted, his mind seemed disinclined to accept her gentleness as abruptly as it would come.

He lowered the book quietly, and from the bed table got his second cigarette. Perhaps it was the click of his lighter that opened her eyes. "Good book, dear?"

"I don't know," he said. "I've barely begun."

She smiled, and drew herself up to sit as he sat. "Oh, I slept well!" she said. "Good morning, Richard."

"You look—rested."

There were signals of Bethel's return from Mean Week that Moon expected, and liked. So many small things. Just now, the sign was the sheer nightgown she wore, and he was positive she'd been in broadcloth pajamas when they retired. One

214

wispy shoulder strap had slipped, revealingly. It was a disarray she had to be aware of, but she left it uncorrected and it became a part of her apology.

"I am rested," she stretched her voice with her arms. "Oh goodness, dear! We'll be late for church!"

He nodded. "I'd just as soon we didn't go. I can call Sim to fill in for me."

"Spain would disapprove, wouldn't he?" She wrinkled her nose.

"That's right."

She relaxed against a doubled pillow. "Hark," she said.

He had to grin. "Hark what?"

"Just hark, I feel good!"

He started getting up.

"Dear, where are the kids?"

"Still sawing logs," he said. "I'll bring some coffee."

As he put pot and cups on a tray, he confirmed that the brown bottle had vanished from its shelf, and as he returned to her, he noticed she'd not fixed the shoulder strap. She smiled "Thank you" at the cup he gave her, and she settled back holding it between both thin hands. Moon sat down on his bed. Then the embarrassed silence posted itself between them. He felt he should move first toward destroying it, but he hesitated to begin.

"Hot," she said, and she reached and put her cup on the table. "Richard, I'm—ashamed. And so sorry. All the fusses, and I can't even remember the things I said."

"It's all right," he spoke the old lines, "it was mostly my fault. We needn't bother to talk about it."

The Munger-light hair lay remarkably untousled and gleaming, each short wave having shed, miraculously, its dead look. Her hair struck him as being as fair and almost as pretty, just now, as China's.

"I'm a shrew and hussy," she said. "Richard, I know you couldn't tell it, but this time I did try very hard not to be mean. I—"

"You're here," he said, "and I'm here. Look, what about your coffee?"

"Oh, yes. Yes, dearest!" She patted a place on her bed. "Come sit here."

He moved across to sit beside her, and at once she took his hand. Another of the small obviousnesses reached him; she was unusually perfumed. She drew his hand to her, and she said, "Do you know what?"

"What?"

"I dreamed we went somewhere and danced."

"We ought to do that, sometime," he said.

She began suddenly to cry. He took and held her, kissing her as she offered it. She did not release him, and he turned his face aside. "Beth, my cigarette is about to burn the table."

"Let it."

"Beth, it's daylight, and the kids—"

"They're asleep. Oh, Richard, don't you know—?"

He did know. He kissed her, lightly, guiltily, and he put her back to her pillow. "Now," he said, "the coffee."

She winced, then smiled and let him return the cup to her hands.

They sat, each aware of how busily the other concentrated on sweeping back the regrets. They drank the coffee, and he refilled the cups. After a while she said, "I should be up, seeing about breakfast."

"Let's talk, Beth. Right now, while we can."

"About Carol, isn't it?"

"Well—yes. I've made a mess of it."

"It isn't as bad as you think," Bethel said. "It's—my fault we haven't talked about it before. But I did think it was straightening out."

Moon shook his head. "Did she tell you I tried to talk with her about it?"

"No."

"I did try. The day after, I think. It wasn't a very good job. I tried to explain—I haven't explained to you, yet, have I?— I tried to say I hadn't imagined she was growing up, and discovering it that way surprised me. I tried to tell her I wasn't ogling or anything like that."

216

"What did she say?"

"Almost nothing. Just that it was all right."

"Then it is, Richard."

"But it isn't. The way she said it—like we were strangers. She wouldn't look at me, not directly. Beth, it's driving me nuts."

"You are making too much of it. She needs time, that's all. It's very hard to be eleven years old; I can remember how hard it was."

He did not wish to be soothed. "I am saying, Bethel, that I can't even approach her."

"Oh, I know. But you are trying too hard. Don't make such a point of it, for one thing. You must treat her a little differently than before, that's all."

"I will. I'll have no choice."

She patted his shoulder. "Oh, here now. Just treat her like a young lady. Don't you see, she's frightened by what is happening to her. And ashamed. But however terrified we are of growing up, we all want to. We just have to make her see that rewards come with it. I'm putting her in teen clothes; I can allow her a little lipstick, things like that. But it's you who'll have to make her think she's gaining more than she's losing. She must feel she is prettier—and she is, don't you think? She must feel she is more interesting, that she's becoming better company. You can do that for her, Richard."

So solid-sounding, so intelligent. Straight from the parents' magazines.

"I've tried," he said. "The other day, I called her at school, asked her to meet me for lunch."

"That's good."

"No, it was rotten. She wouldn't come. They were having cartoons next period, *Father*, she preferred not to miss them, *Father*. Just dodges, and no take-it-easy-greasys, or later-alligators, or anything as usual."

Bethel laughed. "Poor Daddy Mooney. Can't you see, she's doing fine?"

"No, damned if I can see."

Bethel lay back, her gaze settling on the seam where wall met ceiling, and she frowned. She said, oddly, "I feel so sorry for Laska. It broke her heart to see Sid Junior leave for school."

Moon looked at her sharply. "You're not thinking of something of that sort for Carol?"

"No. But—Sid's going does have something to do with Carol, and it's partly what has upset her. I mean, you shouldn't think the accident you had is responsible for—well, what you worry about is less your doing than you realize. What I'm trying to say, Richard—"

"What are you trying to say? What's Sid got to do with Carol?"

Bethel sat up, she placed her hands on his arms. "Don't get excited, please. I've been waiting to tell you; there was an—an incident."

Moon caught the careful, break-it-gently concern in her eyes, and suddenly he seemed to be fathoming what she would say.

"I didn't tell you before because I was afraid you'd—well, it wouldn't have helped. Spain thought you needn't be bothered with the thing at all, but I never intended to keep it from you very long."

Moon's scalp crept, as it must with every new exclusion. Another prerogative of his had been lifted from him, to reappear as always—only belatedly and tightly wrapped in the finality of a conference-room decision.

"All right, tell me!"

"If you're going to rant and rave, dear—"

Moon struggled against shaking her. "That boy did something to Carol."

"Oh, almost nothing. Honestly, Richard. It was that Sunday at The Old Place—and Selma was sick about it when she heard; she thought she was keeping an eye on the children. Carol was in the barn, and Sid Junior came in. He—don't look so black, Richard—he had an impulse, I suppose, because he's not a bad boy. All he did was try to experiment, and Carol ran. It was over before anything—dear, if you're going to take it this way. . . ."

He was on his feet, grinding his teeth, glaring down at her.

"It was adolescent curiosity," Bethel said, "and Sid is gone now and Carol has almost forgotten it."

He had never been so near to striking her. His daughter assaulted or something, his father's privilege of outrage, or just of worry, preempted by these cold dumb pompous one-brained Mungers—

"You had a meeting on this, didn't you?"

"Richard, we got together on how to help Sid Junior!"

"You—you mustered your damned board down there in your goddamned star chamber and made policy on what to do when someone tries to rape *my* daughter?"

She was very pale; she looked at him with pleading. "I was afraid you'd be hurt and angry, and it couldn't have helped to have had a turmoil—"

No, of course not. Anger is too normal; it's a natural emotion.

Bethel bent her head; her thin shoulders shook. "Richard, I've never heard you swear that way. . . ."

Poor, hurt, frightened Carol. . . .

Moon could think of nothing to say, or do. Then he felt released. Free of the obligation he'd intermittently sweated under and hidden from, uncompelled to any accounting. His thighs had hardened until they throbbed. He rubbed them and sat down on the bed. He said, "We should have gone to church."

Bethel looked up quickly. She reached to put her arms around him. He got up and went out.

On Monday evening the Golden Spread had an hour of excitement; there was, for that time, a black and muggy and boiling sky to be watched. The clouds came trundling in from the southwest, and that was a sign; the temperature began jockeying up and down, which was another sign. The people of the city, now well convinced that the Panhandle was a drouth disaster area, just as the Congress kept saying, emerged from their new brick homes and stood in their handsomely 'scaped yards and leaned on their new automobiles and observed the show. With their neighbors, they speculated that this might be the drouth-breaker, and hooray, hooray, for the farmers and ranchers. Underneath, they hoped the clouds would blow away.

The thunderheads stood three miles high, their edges tinged that foreboding green. The flat bottom of the formation seemed so low a tall man might touch it. Out of this sultry edge hung the small fickle tassels of dirty air. Women located their children. They did so somewhat on the sly, never mentioning how near it was to tornado season.

Almost nothing happened. A gusty wind stirred, and a quick hard rainshower broke. Hailstones the size of peas appeared for a few minutes to be shooting out of the ground. Then the clouds grumbled away toward the northeast, and people welcomed back the drouth and returned to their television and told each other the Okies were apt to get quite a storm.

At The Camera House the next day, Frank Wallace searched the morning paper carefully, and he seemed outraged when he found no account of how some Oklahoma hamlet had been blown to smithereens.

"That cloud looked like a bitch," he complained.

"So it did," Moon said. "But it wasn't."

In Frank's office, neither the Christ's head nor the shotgun was in view. All the Mungers were in town. Spain had them in all-day directors' meetings which would continue most of the week. The tax forms for the quarter had been completed, much to Mr. Jacobson's relief and the family's chagrin. This was the "large business"; and every item was to be reviewed and threshed through.

"Moon, maybe they'll talk turkey this week. Did Bethel mention anything?"

"What do you mean?" Moon asked absently. Whenever the Mungers-in-conference occurred to him now, he seethed with speculation on what the talk must have been the day they settled on Sid Junior and Carol. All the nodding blond heads, the tedious words. . . .

"I mean the trust, and you know it." But Frank pushed the matter no further. "I hate tax week. China gets in late, and tired, and we wind up eating out. That is, I don't eat at all. No decent restaurant sells the junk my belly has to have."

Moon might have said he found the quarterly ordeal quite as dreadful. Bethel would come home vexed, perhaps unknowingly conscience-stricken over some of the board's decisions, and she would quote Spain on how the tax system forced one to unsavory methods as the only way to avoid knuckling under to anarchy. From her remarks, Moon judged Spain Munger believed any tax policies successful if they made the taxpayer only a moral criminal instead of a legal one; Spain thought lawmakers expected as much. Once, Bethel had quoted the chairman as saying he had begun to understand how even a capitalist could swallow a few Red ideas. Tax week was always frantic.

On Wednesday, it brought China by on one of her uncommon visits to the store. She was shining with talk. She wore a black sheath that disclosed her pregnancy clearly but somehow tastefully. The look and sound of her was so joyous Moon found himself relaxing without wanting to. She chattered about nothing; Spain was becoming interested in her idea for a party, and wasn't spring ripening beautifully, and didn't they think Spain was being such a good sport about the hat.

"How is that?" Moon asked.

"Oh," China laughed, "haven't you seen him in that hat?"

The Stetson, Moon thought, made the chairman look like a mushroom.

"We gals ganged up on him," China said, "and I think he got some fun out of it. Anyway, he gave the hat to Mr. Williams —that's Mr. Williams-the-lawyer. It was too large for him, but he took it home, and I think Moose is going to try it."

When she was gone, Moon said to Frank, "Has she been to a doctor yet?"

"No. She doesn't want to go."

"What's wrong? Is she afraid?"

"Hell, she's got nothing to be afraid of."

"You better do something about that, Frank."

"Any suggestions?"

Moon took up the morning paper, on the margins of which his partner-in-law had doodled many sets of bosoms, and he read the headlines. It was still disastrously dry, the Shriners were in convention, it was time for school-board candidates to file and a half-dozen already had. He scanned the school-board story, then read it. When he looked up, Frank was scratching his ear with a piece of his jigsaw puzzle.

Moon said, "I might run for the school board."

"You serious?"

"I don't know. I'd like to do something with my time."

Frank grinned. "Spain would pinch off that little brainchild in a hurry."

"I wouldn't ask him. I'd just go down there and file my name."

Frank studied him through the pink-tinted glasses; Moon saw him putting on, gradually, his fatherly face. "Don't be a chump, Moon. Listen to the old pro; this is no time for any horsing around. Hell, I wouldn't vote for you anyway."

"That," Moon said, "would beat me."

Frank pointed across his desk. "Hand me that purple piece there; I think it's the one I'm hunting. . . ."

Moon went to a movie that afternoon. As usual, he stalked it, but through the Technicolor Western called adult because one of the players was permitted to say "damn," he felt less cheap and wasteful than usually. The school-board notion, really but picked out of the air, stuck with him. He closed his mind to the pounding hooves and gunfire, and combed the thing over carefully.

Clearly, the campaign's only genuine issue this year was desegregation. The candidates would make no mention of it; they'd speak of bond issues and new buildings and increasing teacher pay and let it go at that. He knew he could make it different, if he wanted to try.

His pulse doubled its beat. *He* would collide with the integration question head-on. It struck his imagination as a glorious, satisfying way to lose. He could declaim quite simply that the color line must go, that the Negro children must be gotten out of their shabby war-surplus barracks buildings and into desegregated schools; he might protest that the Constitution, at one hundred eighty years of age, was now mature enough to be honored. He could talk with Harry, who was wise about such things, and evolve an outline for the mechanics of integration and present it boldly. Then, he could sit back and take a terrific flogging at the polls.

It appealed to him mightily. To commit himself publicly in a way obviously not decided by the Mungers.

Even his estimate of the aftermath brought heat to his blood. The Chest wouldn't have him for next year's drive; he would make himself utterly useless for a hundred other Munger errands. Spain, very probably, would turn gray overnight. But then, there was Bethel. With her, the issue would have nothing to do with segregation; she would care only that he had shut her out.

Until this, Moon had thought he was concerned with social rights; he had forced himself to think so. Now he yielded; he admitted his need was for retaliation. But his leash caught him up short. Anger wasn't enough. He owed Bethel no pain.

When he left the theater, the lightning was spent, the challenge worn thin, the intention almost gone. But the next afternoon he said to Frank, "Did you ever think of kicking your way out?"

"Huh? Oh, that school board again?" Frank was in shirt sleeves, and the buttons gapped over his stomach, which had been growling and was presently being tamed with warm beer. "You can't have an idea I haven't had a hundred times. But out means all the way out, boy. You ain't going any place until you're ready to go every place. Hell, you're not ready to leave your wife, or your kids."

"I wasn't thinking of leaving my family."

"Then you better sit tight, until they scatter of their own free will."

They sat looking at each other, and a trace of humor began

to show in Frank's eyes. Moon got up and took his hat off the desk.

"Where you going?"

"Into politics," he told China's husband, and he walked the seven blocks to City Hall.

The clerk was a small, middle-aged woman with deep voice and permanent smile. She put the form before him, and took up a desk pen, but when he reached for it, she held on.

"You are Mr. Mooney, aren't you?"

"Yes."

"Well, I have an urgent call for you. That is, you were expected, and you are to call this number immediately." She drew a telephone to her. "May I dial for you?"

Spain Munger, when he came on the line, sounded as if he'd run all the way. "Uh, Moon, there you are!"

Moon cursed Frank Wallace, reprobate, and now informer. Frank who liked to say at the in-law luncheons, "We guys got to stick together."

"What is it?" Moon said. His hand itched, and he scrubbed the palm of it up and down on his thigh.

"Uh, the directors are here, which is no news to your ears, of course—and, uh, to toe right up to the line, we've just been thinking about you."

Moon said, "Well, what do you think?"

"Not to mince punches, Moon, we did want to talk with you before your filing down there, on the off-chance your mind wasn't all up to snuff on developments. And let me say—and I don't think I'm letting any cats out of the beanbag—we, uh, appreciate you, Moon, and your job with the Chest, that's your real monument to my mind, and your decision you have here on your, uh, desire to serve your community, well, we're all impressed with that, too, a hundred per cent. We are unanimous over here, too, on your good qualifications for public office, I'm proud to say, and I don't think your voters could pick your peer—"

"Spain, I think they want to close this office shortly."

"Uh, yes. Well, I'd rather see you in person, Moon, when we've a bone to pick. But—well, you have to face your facts right in the eye, and fit them to your picture, and I have to say it doesn't seem in the cards we could win your election, not right now."

"I know that."

"Uh, good, good. I told your partner I thought you had a joke going. Well—"

"It's no joke," Moon said. "I'm going to file."

"But you said—uh, Moon, did you see Bethel at noon?"

"No."

"I see. Then, you and I have been talking at loggerheads, I'm afraid, and that's my fault, because I didn't get clear. Uh, you don't know about your road deal, then?"

"The commission promised to settle on it some time this week."

"Uh, yes. They did this morning, Moon, and your news is not what we had our hearts set on, I'm sorry to say. Now, to lay your chips where they may—the count on your counting jigger out on the road came in a hundred and twenty-three cars. Uh, this isn't to place any blame, and I hope you understand that right off. But your count there—the commission got in mind your jigger had been, uh, tampered with, and they denied the paving on the spot. The board appreciates your energy, Moon, and it doesn't make a blot on your record, so to speak. But your giz is, it, uh, puts your board up on the tight wire for a while."

"That's too bad," Moon said, and heard the ineptness of it.

"Well, as I want to make straight right off the reel; your losing your paving is rosy with us and it doesn't cut any ice on how your directors feel. But you can see how as, uh, a corporation and a family, we're skating on thin ground for the time being. And I don't think I have to put your ABC's to that."

"They want me off this phone, Spain. What are you telling me?"

"Uh, well, ninety-nine per cent of the time, your details over-

225

lap into your picture. One of your newspaper boys was, uh, in the front row at your commission meeting—and you know about those fellows. We did sort of keep our feet around here, and Mr. Williams-the-lawyer got right over to your news people. He got his finger in the dike, it's good to say, and the goof won't hit your paper. But of course, if we let it become political, the editor won't sit steady on his rocker. So your school-board race is sort of out the window. Uh, I hope you feel free to disagree, if you aren't sailing in my wind—but if you throw your hat in the bullring right now—"

Moon closed his eyes. A trump perfectly played, and he was done. To lose an election in martyrdom to civil rights—this he might wear like a medal. But to be buried under the scandal of an attempted petty fraud, and to drag Bethel and China and Carol and all the rest with him. . . .

Why couldn't men, as do women, just let go and scream?

"Very well," Moon said. "I'm back in the stable."

He walked out, growing more furious because the words he'd planned to use in a sort of announcement speech at Reserve tonight kept repeating themselves in his mind. Then, despite the hour, he got the old Chevvy from behind The Camera House and drove to The Old Place for supper with John Remo.

XIII

Moon telephoned twice before he got Bethel. "Oh, Richard, I'm glad you thought to go out there. Is Brother well?"

"He's fine. Does have a sore throat, from painting out in the wind. Remo is taking care of it."

"Give him my love. Will you be home soon?"

"It's Reserve night. I'll have to go directly there, I guess."

"Then I'll wait up."

"No, don't. It may be late."

"Richard—is it all right, about the school-board thing? I know how you must feel; I planned to talk to you as soon as I got home—"

"It's all right. Beth, do you suppose you might put Carol on the line? Just to chat a little?"

"If you want. But it would be very obvious."

"I suppose it would. Well, good night."

"Good night, dear. I am tired. . . ."

John Remo sat at the kitchen table, his rough hands winding a ball of gauze on the end of a stick. "Goddammit, June, come back here," he said.

"Ain't no need to bother none, Mister Remo, on account of my throat is feeling good, thank you anyways—"

"You heard me. Sit down."

Moon grinned at them. The hulking old cop tied the gauze fast, grunted his approval of it, then saturated it from a bottle of merthiolate.

"Me, Mister Remo, ain't I had a-plenty of them goddam swabbin's, wouldn't you say?" Brother said. He sat in the armless kitchen chair, his great flesh sagging over the edges of it, and Moon thought he was shivering.

"Open up," Remo said.

Brother hesitated, and Remo put a powerful hand on the happiest Munger's jaw and squeezed his mouth open. He rammed the swab in and rotated it rapidly. Brother coughed and gagged and wagged his head evasively. "Dammit," Remo growled, "get your tongue down; when I want my fist slurped on, I'll call that mangy cat."

Brother gagged heavily, and Remo drew out the swab. "That'll hold yu'."

Moon said, "Remo, you should have been a vet. Sid could use you."

"Boy!" Brother caught his breath. "We ain't doin' that no more, are we going to, Mister Remo?"

"Not unless you need it."

"You're a good sonofabitch, Mister—"

"You go on now, watch your TV. Another drink, Moon?"

"A little one." It would be his third. "Then I've got to shove off."

Remo poured the two glasses. There was a streak of aluminum paint on his cheek, almost paralleling the knife scar, and tiny flecks of it spotted the big nose. He sighed. "I'm sick as hell of this paintin'," he said. "But he has come further than I ever thought he would. Everything but the roof is done—"

Brother said, "Me, Mister Remo, I'd just as leave have me a speck of that whisky, if it's all the same—"

"You get in yonder!"

Moon drank, too rapidly for one who so seldom practiced, and for a moment his throat was incapable of speech. "Thanks for the supper, Remo. I've got to go. When you coming to town?"

"When they haul me in in a box, I guess. I wish you'd stay; I ain't heard nothing from town since you was here last time."

"It's the same—oh, I meant to tell you. Some of your old buddies picked up Harry a few nights back. I bailed him out. I gather they raided a dance and brought in everybody who couldn't run fast enough."

"Yeah," Remo said. "It's a new policy. The chief says if they boost up the fines by a couple hundred thousand this year, the whole force will get a raise."

"I heard about that."

Remo walked out to the car with him; he bent to the window as Moon started the engine. "Is *she* gettin' on pretty good?"

Moon grinned. "Why, yes."

"Well, no thanks to that goddamn Wallace, huh?"

Moon had to laugh. "That's right. Now, what little pink message do you want me to give her?"

Remo flinched. "Just mention to her how I told you to go to hell," he growled, and he waved and made an ugly grin as Moon pulled away.

Moon piloted the Chevvy along slowly, over road he now knew in detail, and in tracks he imagined he and Teddy Birdsong had worn deeper, and he reminded himself, most of the way, that he was headed for a dull and pretenseful Reserve meeting, where everyone appeared mainly just to sign for their pay and where drill was in snooker rather than in Arms or Rocks 'n' Shoals. On the highway, he studied the swing he ought to take, onto the loop that led directly to the armory, but somehow he continued straight ahead. Then he had to play that he'd made an oversight, and after that, gradually, he admitted to the other destination. At once he felt rotten, but he didn't care enough to change course. His good body was, indeed, quite hollow, which excused everything. Shortly he was

229

braking the car in the parking lot behind Teddy Birdsong's apartment.

He cut off the lights and had a cigarette.

It had begun on inventory night. The panacea for Mean Week; the hot, pleasant vengeance on all Mungerism. The first of many wakes for a lost sweet Carol now become, so suddenly, all the more a repeated China through this coincidental new dimension of being forever removed from him. Or maybe, Moon had to consider, it was nothing so justifiable. Perhaps his farewell to decency had begun as the simple inevitability he himself had ordered when, with a nose-tweak at judgment and intuition, he forced the woman's improbable name onto the Munger payroll.

At any rate, Teddy Birdsong.

He had sat at his desk the whole evening, burning stupid candles to his misery, while the woman worked away at counting the stock. She did not call on him for help; when, through the partition he occasionally heard her voice, she was speaking just a number aloud, probably while writing it down. At eleven-thirty she prepared to leave.

"Surprises me," she said. "I'm not even half finished. I'll try again tomorrow night." She rubbed her eyes. "Damn, I'm afraid I need glasses."

Moon said nothing, nor did he rise.

She said, "Your hair shirt is showing."

He glared at her angrily. "How does it look?"

"Sloppy," she said, and she stretched the painted-on lips in a yawn. "Good night."

"Wait. I can drop you off."

"I've already called a cab," she said, "but I wish you would. Going home alone, in the middle of the night, could wreck my reputation."

He frowned at the piquant, so-assured, too-close eyes, at the ridiculous arch of the faked pen-line brows. He thought, she thinks she reads me. She boasts; she asks, dare you, little man? She stands there less high than me, and top-heavy while my

230

eyes sting full of my own frightened and bare baby girl, and she poses for me in her tight clothes and her cold tough-as-tripe sorrow, whatever its name is, and she brags of all her talents for making big bitterness taste sweet to a man. Her mind is quite sure what will happen. Well—Moon vowed to take her home and do her the insult of not touching her.

"You want something on your hand?" she said.

"What?"

"It looks to be bleeding."

"Don't worry about it."

He cut the heater, switched off fluorescent lights that died grudgingly, and set the brass lock on the door. She went ahead and put herself in the car. They drove a dozen blocks through forsaken streets, saying nothing. Even at this hour, the city's was an imperfect silence. They could hear the strain and roar of the trucks taking the beltlines around town, and from behind them came the occasional squeal and blast as the boys in the hotrods went dragging down Polk. In one block, they passed a boy and girl walking, and the girl was laughing: as Teddy Birdsong suddenly put it, "She's laughing like hell, isn't she?"

They came to a row of apartment houses.

"Show me the place," he said, "I forget."

"Of course you forget," she said, "just since this afternoon. It's that one there."

She indicated no eagerness to get out. He watched her take a long cigarette out of a reptile purse, but he didn't extend his lighter until she asked for it. She inhaled deeply, and she scooted down in the seat as if settling to rest and purr a while.

"Thank you," he said, "for the extra work. I had meant to help. I could have gotten Frank to pitch in, too."

"If he had come," she said, "I'd have gone."

It appeared she gazed up at just the darkness beneath the car's ceiling. She had extended her legs, and she stretched them, and he noticed she had kicked off her shoes. The gesture enraged him. There was little light, but too much. He could see that her hose had ornamental seams, that she had crooked, beat-up, knobby little toes that seemed to have been stubbed against ten thousand table legs ten thousand times. There were high graceful arches in her feet. Nothing so appealing about a woman, his father had said. . . .

Then he wanted her. Like poles and magnets and affinities.

He got a cigarette from his pocket, and knew the act to be a part of reconsideration. Bound to happen, wasn't it, because he had sworn it wouldn't? He used the dash lighter, not daring to strike the Zippo that would illuminate his face. All at once, he had a sense of repeating. It seemed an old sequence. The place, the time, this odd unpretty woman, were as though they had occurred in this exact combination before. Even his appetite gnawed at him familiarly; even the taste and pace and necessity of breath were old, old things.

It struck him he was learning. Resisting, yet learning well. Don't the great emotions come in matched sets? Aren't they so closely akin that one, in the present, represents itself as another in the past? And aren't they, these hungers, engaged at a common genesis which is power? And aren't the powers, however rooted, of such a single blood that one terrible need can become another terrible need, all in an instant, without the least interruption of their force? Love and hate, the two sides of one coin. Said so often it was a cliché. Then why not fear and lust, sorrow and desire, frustration and aberrancy? Why not these? Just now, wasn't he proving these mechanics? Oh forgive me Beth, return to me Carol, oh bless us God; but wasn't his maddening regret, without his consent, relocating its might, downward from throat and breast to thigh and loin? Wasn't—but how could it matter?

"Oh hell," said Teddy Birdsong, "let's go inside."

Feebly he said, "I'd better get on home."

She laughed as she unlatched the door and slid out. "Suit yourself," she said. He followed her.

In the restrained night lamp's dingy light he saw only the fantastic curve of her, and he walked behind her, on through the entrance hall and up carpeted stairs.

The apartment was two floors up. It was kitchen cornered off from a meager dinette, a pink tiled bath with door open

232

and nylons drying on its towel racks, and a main room furnished for both lounging and sleeping. The pieces looked new, the carpet unworn.

"Sit here," she nodded at a low iron-legged divan.

"I shouldn't be here," he said.

"Rationalize, Mr. Mooney."

She crossed before him to a dressing table, stooped to a mirror and retouched her lips, then felt of her back with both hands. "All that reaching for the shelves—do you want a drink?"

"I guess."

She laughed at him, for his tone, perhaps, and from the kitchen she said, "Relax; it's been a long day."

She brought a tall glass half filled, handed it to him and sat down opposite him in an underslung armless chair. She put her shoeless feet on the coffee table.

"Where is yours?" he said.

"I'm not quite ready for one. Whisky sometimes makes an inky-pank of me."

"What do you mean?"

"Just that. My head doctor explained it to me. It's a hundred-dollar explanation—"

Moon sat forward, stiffened and abruptly high-schoolish. "A psychiatrist, you mean?"

"Oh my God, don't run! I went once, for fun. It wasn't, and I didn't go back. I wasn't supposed to, anyway."

Moon covered his nerves by trying the drink. "Strong," he said, and he could think of nothing more.

He watched her through half a cigarette. The queer mean-sad look came through the dense make-up; at moments it made the brown eyes appear utterly evil, so that he had to shudder. He thought he began to know her, then. One of these who wished to practice evil honestly and good only deviously, to make evil proud and make good ashamed. It was an ugly thought. He wondered why his mind, lately—

"Finished your drink?" she said, and she got up and took off her blouse.

"I—"

She laughed. "Just thought of something," she said. "I thought you Mungers were bone dry."

"They don't use liquor," he said foolishly.

She looked at him over a bare shoulder. "Well," she said, "you pumped me all afternoon. Now you can tell me about you, and those millionaires."

"I didn't mean anything," he said. "Just making conversation."

"Okay, so am I. Now, what happened to you today? Fight with your wife?"

"Well," he started to get up, "thanks for the drink."

"Oh, sit down," she said, "it's getting late." She sat down on the table, back to him.

"Here now!" he seemed to have said.

"Unhook me."

He should have hesitated, he did not; he should have thought, but he could not.

He said, "You feel very wise, don't you?"

Sitting in the car, gazing up at this light and that in the apartment building, Moon wondered if he mightn't yet go to Reserve meeting. He had decided on his evening back at the road intersection, but as so often it went, his choice was now being remade, as though he'd not dealt with it before.

One thing, he hated the look she would give him when she opened the door. The shrewd, unsurprised, of-course-ly look that placed him in Everyman's pattern. He had told her, on inventory night, that he'd not be back.

"Sure you will," she said. "At least twice more."

"You know a lot, don't you?"

"You'll come here three times, even if you don't like it."

She had begun drinking as he prepared to leave, and he had lingered because she suddenly looked quite different, and from his own drinks he'd aroused a reckless curiosity. "Why three?" he had said.

"Everything is in threes. Good or bad. Didn't you know that? Lord, Moon, you wear ugly socks. Where was I? Oh, the trinities. Religion, that's God and Son and Holy Ghost, and you

yourself, aren't you physical and mental and spiritual, and
don't we have just birth and death and the time in between?
My father told me all this; it's why one car wreck calls for two
more. Three necessities, food, clothing, and shelter, and three
sexes, and three parts of every day, and an earth just land,
sea, and air. Now don't ask me why we don't have three eyes
apiece, and three ears, and three arms—all right, Moon, laugh
at me! But you will be back!"

Now, here he sat.

This would be only the second time.

His mind's clammy underside kept nudging him; why not,
why not? Physically, Teddy Birdsong had been as magnificent
as she advertised—which was a thought Frank himself might
have had, and Moon almost gagged on it. Still, his flesh remembered wildly while his mind loathed her. The bushy hair,
big cheekbones, hideous make-up, as if she'd laid a comic mask
over a tragic one—these had faded. Her body was the memory.
She had been derelict and frantic and more needful than he.
He had huffed and sweated, freely, because they pretended
no romance, and he was sure he'd been debating, even at the
moment, on whether she was obscene, and he had concluded
afterward that she was not, for obscenity meant Frank's
films, or the tangle of hairy male flesh at the wrestling matches;
it meant these and just a few other sights he could remember,
among which, it shocked him to realize, had been the look of
his mother's unlaced, squashy old tennis shoes.

Moon got out of the Chevvy. That first time, he supposed in
a bit of self-ridicule, had been justified by his heartbreak over
Carol. This time he must call it something else. He squeezed
through a narrow passageway between the apartment house
and its greater neighbor, and he rang Teddy Birdsong's number.

At the store the other day, he'd said to her while Frank was
out for beer, "What am I to call you, anyway?"

"Teddy is the usual."

"It doesn't fit. Didn't you—that night, didn't you speak of
yourself as Billie?"

"Maybe."

"Then I'll—"

"Billie is what *I* use. It's something I'm saving. . . ."

She was holding the door for him when he topped the stairs. "Two," she said, "if you're counting."

He ignored it and went on in. The apartment was less tidy than before; she herself, it struck him, looked much better. He hadn't seen her, until now, with the make-up peeled away. It surprised him that she looked less hard, more youthful. He preferred not to tell her.

"What is it tonight?" she said. "Let me guess—we are punishing Mrs. Mooney!"

"Don't, Teddy. Maybe I just wanted to come."

She brought glasses; this time including herself. She wore a faded black wrapper that trailed the floor, and it explained the lack of paint; clearly, she had just finished bathing.

"I only wanted to know how uneasy I should be," she said. "What did you tell your wife?"

"It's Marine Reserve night."

"Cute."

"No," he said flatly, "it really is. I always go to Reserve."

"Why?"

"I belong, that's why!"

"I salute you."

"Look," he said, "I didn't come to fight."

"How true," she smiled infuriatingly. "But you do hang onto those Marines, don't you?"

"I've kept my commission."

They stared at each other, keeping touchily apart, while they drank. Gradually, satisfyingly, he came to feel that she was pleased he had come. He gathered it from the small adjustments she made to her chair, from the unanticipated freshness of her face. He stopped resenting her.

"Moon, what did you do in the war?"

Save for Bethel, rarely, and Brother often, no one ever asked. He watched the squaw face warily, but he found himself telling her about his platoon of gay and fierce young men, now all the gayer and more fierce from the passage of years,

236

and easily he called the names he'd been sure he'd forgotten. Because she listened, really listened, he told of the assault at Bougainville, and of the withdrawal that began as a rumor and developed into a panic, and he told her how his wild young men supported him, not in heroics but in practicality, when he decided—yes, in that jungle and swamp, *he* had decided— to carry out the orders. Moon could not reexperience the exhaustion and the steam and itch of the air, but he could remember how they'd won. He could have quoted the paragraphs of the citation, *en toto,* verbatim.

She got up as he finished. "Another drink, hero?"

"Dammit, Teddy, if we are only going to fight—"

"Let's do fight," she said. "Didn't you say that making love to me is more like fighting?"

"The hump we got was called Hill 712." Moon spoke as might a braggart boy. "The letter came from old ComSoPac himself."

Until very late they lay together, talking their throats dry. They traded bits and pieces; at their ease, Moon noted, because each was sure the other only partly listened; each knew he talked only for himself. It was, like the act preceding, only a furtherance of personal comfort, a deliverance of burdens. Their talk was not to be remembered; it occurred as privately as thought, and he never wanted it to end. It amazed him how, beside this strange troubled woman, and in this place where he did not belong, he could say Beth's name; how in this atmosphere of false peace, it could seem so clear that he deeply loved her.

He described a Munger-in-law luncheon; she told an inky-pank story. He recounted a Camera House stalemate; she related how her Ben died so unglamorously by upsetting a jeep. Neither, for a while, commented upon the property of the other. Teddy Birdsong got up now and then for drinks.

He lay watching her calmly in the bright light she switched on, observing, as if the owner of, the beautiful breasts and the whiteness. Perhaps he memorized; perhaps he wanted to remember so well that this need not happen again.

237

"God, I was barely seventeen," she said, "but I'd been work-ing in the dry-goods store for a year. I sold piece goods, and Ben sold shoes. He was a big man, not attractive at all. But he was clean, I remember that. Fresh shirts, neckties without spots on them."

She brought the glasses and she propped herself up beside Moon. Idly, as she talked, she tortured herself by touching the frosty glass to her naked stomach. She would scarcely lift it until she touched it down again.

"Ben and I necked a lot at the store, in the dressing rooms. But we wouldn't have married, except for Pearl Harbor. He enlisted, and Christ, I got patriotic. I told Mother to go to hell, and I married him. Everyone was doing that. Then after he was gone a few months, I wanted other men. You wouldn't understand that, would you? I didn't either, back then. But one Sunday at church, the sermon was about how mistaken it is to love the instrument of good instead of the good it-self.

"I had to think about that. I didn't love Ben. But I did love what happened to me when we were together. So I listened to the preacher, and I went out for the good thing itself. Not the person of good, don't you see, but the good itself. And I found it, too. Then Ben was killed, and I began to get his insurance —hell, I hope I'm not getting drunk."

"All the war marriages aren't bad," he said. "Bethel and I—"

"Oh, sure, you're wild about her. That's why you're here with me."

It startled him; he did not want the suspended judgments to come down. "If only she weren't all cycles."

"Why shouldn't she have cycles?"

"Well, I mean, hers so often match mine—"

"Crap," Teddy Birdsong said, "you mean you match yours to hers, with tricks like this. You lean on her, and spend her money, and blame it on her that you aren't quite a man— that's the truth, isn't it? And I'd do the same if I could; God, how I could lean on two hundred million!"

"You have drunk too much."

"So you are trying so gallantly to be in love with your wife! That makes me sick!"

"All right. Let's don't talk about Beth."

"You brought it up, mister. I think it's noble of you. Trying to love her, because you can't afford to leave her—"

"That's not it!"

"A lot of men I've known—" she began.

"You have known plenty of them, haven't you?"

"Hell yes, I have. Does that bother you?"

"No."

"Then please shut up. I was about to say a lot of men I've known really wanted their wives, but they didn't know it, or they didn't want to know it. Horvath, he's one, he goes pinching around because he's fifty-one—"

"We're brawling," he said.

"Who cares?"

They lay silent a moment. The mood of the bits-and-pieces had lingered on, for him, and he wasn't really angry, for his shell was around him. He said, "You started to tell about your marriage."

She drained her glass. "Sure, Mr. Mooney, that's what you expect of me, on an occasion like this, isn't it? What would you prefer, a comparison of abilities?"

"Oh, let's drop it."

"Sure, let's do, you parasite! And that is what you are, isn't it? That's your disease, isn't it? Well, if you want to play house with me—"

"Teddy, get off of it. You oughtn't to drink."

"I'll tell you one thing more, boss; you're lousy with diseases! Decency, that's one of them! A little sex, and you have to go to talking about marriage because the way your brains work, they're inseparable, and so you go to putting me to a lot of stinking damned questions. . . ."

Moon yawned and removed himself from range simply by stepping off, deliberately, into sleep. He awoke with a jolt,

239

in a sudden time-consciousness. He batted his eyes against the light until he could read his watch. It was almost four. He shook himself, and he looked across the room at the stunning sight of a different Teddy Birdsong.

Four A.M., but she had dressed, in a shapeless and plain print frock. Her back was to him. She knelt at the divan, her arms folded across her waist, her cheek pressed against one of the cushions. She spoke softly, sorrowfully, with thick tongue, and it sounded as if she said, "Be ye kind, one to another—"

"Teddy!"

She gave no sign of hearing.

He went to his clothes and dressed hurriedly. Her attitude was like prayer. A whole roof of begrimed conscience smothered down on him.

One-notedly, Teddy Birdsong was singing.

"You better get to bed," he said.

"Go 'way," she sang. "Jesus Savior, oh pilot me. Over life's—"

"Teddy, get up from there. You're sick."

"I am sick. Oh Jesus, pilot me. . . ."

He drew on his coat with shaking hands; he almost turned up the collar over the chill that spread across the back of his neck. He wished to run, yet it seemed he must not leave her like this.

"You've drunk too much," he said. "It's no time for—to do what you are doing. Please, get up."

She chanted her phrase once more. He grasped her shoulders, and she resisted him as if frozen. "Come on," he said. "And there's not any 'oh' in that line."

She looked at him. She was puffed and red and bruised. At the hatred in her eyes, he released her. "I am doing this!" she said thickly. "You go away."

She turned her face into the cushion, as though to suffocate herself. "I'm leaving," he said. "Come on, I want to help you to bed."

She clasped her hands together behind her neck, holding her face to its hiding, and she made whimpering, pleading, anguished sounds the cushion couldn't entirely swallow. Moon could not listen.

He turned to the door, weaving in his haste; he shut it hard behind him, he went down the stairs clinging to the rail against a dizziness that should have been slept away. An ache in his chest threatened to spill him ahead, and he walked more rapidly. Then he raced to the car. Beside it he vomited, and he wished neither of them had ever lived.

XIV

Spain Munger's pale gaze cautiously approved of the day. He had at hand, just now, something most unusual: a half-hour of free time. He was tired, but warmed with the not-common sensation of an approximate well-being. It had been months, it struck him, since the business of family and the corporations rested in such solid placidity.

You did yourself your real favor, he thought, if occasionally you eased off your spinning of wheels and inspected your blessings as carefully as, at your other times, you took your hard looks at your bitter pills.

The Good Friday weather beamed into his office, just as mild and bright as the TV forecasters had promised. Matter of fact, he'd had a call from home, for Mom wished him to pry loose for the afternoon to go with her, out into the good air on a picnic for the children. Except that you dared never sleep at your switch, he might have canceled appointments and gone. But staying in pocket, and keeping on your tiptoes, there was your key to your enjoyment of the occasional untroubled day.

Early this morning, China and Bethel had dropped in, just

242

to visit before continuing spring shopping, and he'd been pleased that it was only because they wished to see him. In fact, they had suggested he have a vacation, a certainly deserved rest, as they put it, and he had felt pleasantly touched and he had been cordial and kind in refusing them. He had been delighted, also, that he had some good news for them. A great deal of it.

Word had just come; your Railroad Commission was raising your oil allowable for April, guaranteeing a not-to-be-sneezed-at hike in the revenues of Panhandle Green. Then, he had just discovered what a remarkably shrewd deal the board had made on the new pipeline. For, almost as he arrived at the office, Mr. Cole himself of Parsons & Cole had shown up in much distress to beg a renegotiation of the contract. The ditch was crossing some unanticipated rock; the crews were threatening to strike for a fifteen-cent hourly raise, and to top it all, an engineering error had been discovered and some of the excavations would have to go as much as twenty inches deeper than the original work scheme contemplated. Grayly, miserably, Mr. Cole explained that even with a ten per cent increase in the contract price, a profit for Parsons & Cole appeared improbable, but they would ask no more.

Spain had expressed regret; he had explained himself to be entirely answerable to his board, and he had made clear how the board, in view of its big picture and its already executed fiscal plans, couldn't excuse Parsons & Cole from an explicit performance on the first-agreed terms.

He marveled that the cup was even further filled. On his desk was Laska's newest letter from Sid Junior. She had sent it along to him in joy. At last the boy seemed to be hitching up and liking; Laska need no longer forestall a visit down there for fear he'd make a scene to come home. Even Texas, so often in the gloom of that trial diagnosed as the middle-years transformation, had been cheery when she called last night.

Although Spain could not approve, he felt grateful to the therapeutic qualities of her new hobby. Texas had discovered that American industry is most sensitive; she had begun writing them letters. She reported candidly whatever imperfections she could discover in what she bought, and already a half-dozen packages had arrived. Just yesterday, as she related, there had come a whole case of assorted grinds of peanut butters, this the result of sending in a tiny stick found by Hannah in a jar bought by the Mooneys.

Uh, actually, your only bad omen on your horizon, it seemed, was your aftermath of your flopper Moon made on his road paving, plus your near-miss, on some inconceivable impulse, when he almost got into politics. The thought of it solemnized Spain. But the optimistic fact was, many days had passed, and no repercussions had come home to roost, and you could almost rest your mind on the conclusion your newspaper people and your city clerk intended to keep faith on their pledges of silence. Still, Spain saw no harm in keeping his ear to the pulse.

Through many of Spain's days, he endured the dread of some crouching, waiting catastrophe as terrible as only the unknown can be. The vague, powerful suggestion of such an enemy drove him through these times; he wrapped himself about every Munger and around the Munger name itself, and he saved the carefully made big picture by hiding it within his own being, beyond the view of calamity's brittle yellow eyes. It seemed in such times that his will and energy alone kept those he loved from plummeting back to their beginnings, kept the idle lies from becoming active truths. Anticipation of some dire event caused him to chill and sweat, but he feared as much his own lapse during some weary moment; one instant of oversight that might permit disaster and destroy him with the blame. It was on such a day that Spain had ordered Mr. Williams-the-lawyer to prepare all the papers for a simple May reorganization.

But today, the apprehension was small. It pleased him to consider the end of his task; to think that, come May, each arm of the family might be ready to hold its own reins. This way, he foresaw rest, and time, and peace, and the bells that rang in your bonnet when you knew your hard job was well done. Thus Mr. Williams was preparing, also, a mountain of documents toward the dissolution of Old Cecil Munger's trust.

Spain squinted at his watch. He had thirty-two minutes before seeing the insurance man about the group policies for the employees. When there was time, you were on safe footing if you used it at looking down your rat holes and drowning out whatever weaknesses you might see. He rang for The Old Girl.

"Uh, Miss Northington, if it'll not mess up what you are doing, and if so, just feel free to speak right up, well, there is just time to have lunch in today, and I thought you might want to go downstairs for sandwiches, and we can have them in here."

"Oh, yes sir," she said. "Is there anything in particular, Mr. Munger. I mean, any certain files you want?"

"Uh, no; nothing like that. I just noticed it is about time for the old feedbag, and I thought, if you cared to, we might, uh, just visit a little while. . . ."

"Aw dammit, Snake," Papa said the day Spain had the fight at school, "what's it gittin' you, settin' so thin-skinned all the time? Where yu' think I'd be, I ask you, was I always keeping my feelin's on my sleeve? Look at me, back there in '17. Three-quarters German an' a quarter English, at a time like that! What you think people said to me? Did I ever have me a fight? Hell, no! Before they could start on me, I said, 'The Kaiser is a sonofabitch,' and then I'd say, 'Them German kin of mine, they rig up the goddamn wars, an' then my limey cousins, they come along behind scavenging up,' and then I tole them, 'Me, I'm a Panhandle Texan, an' I'm raising the beef to feed our Texas boys who'll whip hell out of one side or the both of 'em, whichever needs it!'" After which, as Spain recalled, Papa got up off the couch and took him to the kitchen, to play poker a little while for the ten days' wages owing because Spain had been grubbing mesquite.

The High Plains claimed almost three hundred days of excellent flying weather each year, and this pre-Easter Friday was one of them. Eunice Casey, as the only passenger on Golden Spread Lines' Flight Number 2, commanded an especially good view of this huge expanse of sunny calm. Although she'd lived her whole life in West Texas, she could scarcely believe such days, simply out of her recollection of so many blizzards, so many blowing dusts. The little feeder line's glittering Twin Cessna rode along on silken air, and despite her worries, she found she was enjoying the trip.

The hometown Jaycees, bless them, had taken her off the tiresome buses and put her aloft for her biweekly trips to Amarillo. The time saving was enormous, and to her surprise, she found she didn't really mind having the fare paid for her by those very friendly young men. These were special times, filled with special means against special emergencies.

Gazing out her port and down the trailing edge of the wing, she thought the look of the land most incongruous with the public outcry. True, the pastures did appear skimpy and lifeless. But everywhere she saw great squares of rich green, where the winter wheat seemed to be doing quite well. On a few of the wheat fields, despite the lateness of the season, lazy red Herefords grazed, and she thought them hardly drouth depressed. Their downy white undersides seemed to swing almost to the ground.

Outward appearances, she knew, often indicate well-being where in fact a gargantuan difficulty exists. Her own case stood much in point.

She was Mrs. Eunice Casey, actually. But in Plainston everyone called her Miss Eunice, or they meant to when they made the title sound like "Miz," for it is necessary to think of small-town librarians as old maids. Only the community's oldest old-timers recalled either of her two husbands, and even they spoke of her as Miss Eunice, or Miz Eunice, the latter being a sort of neutral definition of her maidenly-unmaidenly state and applicable without offense against library dignity.

Last week she had completed twenty-four years of superintendenceship over the small blockhouse of books first given by Mr. Carnegie. And just yesterday, they'd had a small ceremony and given her a plaque.

The city fathers came in body; they seemed pleased that she accepted the token with a full flow of tears. She hung the plaque over her desk while they watched, and she could not stop thinking how gravely they presented it.

For some time, out of her direct access to rumors, she had known that her town intended an elaborate fandango for her next year. A twenty-five-year plaque, plus an all-day library party to be climaxed by a testimonial dinner. The premature presentation meant this glory day was canceled; it revealed the general conclusion that she'd be unavailable.

She wasn't ready to agree.

Her radical mastectomy was now almost two years old, and she felt quite well, despite the surgeon's three-year prognosis. Since the operation, she had come to Amarillo twice each week for her session with the radiologist. Most of Plainston's electorate knew her chest had been so radiated and baked and scorched that its flesh was mottled permanently black; this had been mentioned at the Jaycee luncheon when they adopted her as a project.

She wondered if the Jaycees had known she was about to ask for a raise.

The radiologist had a way of requiring his fee after each treatment, the travel became a costly item, and she had had to pay a substitute for the days she could not keep the library. After two such years, her savings had gone. It seemed, come to think of it, that the mayor and his friends were much aware of this when they brought the plaque. The citation in place of more salary; perhaps, even, their way of saying they considered her service to be near its termination.

If they thought Miss Eunice high-minded beyond any desire for money, they were practically correct. The trouble was she had come to that critical point where her financial peril matched her physical peril, in something like equal balance.

She sighed, and she forced her mind back to the enjoyment

247

of the trip. The airline was locally owned, and of the "feeder" status, which meant, she supposed, that its airplane couldn't help having to take off and land at Plainston on the rough surface that until recently had been a sugar-beet field. She did concede the comforts of the nice new plane and the many small considerations given her upon every flight. Just now, Amarillo came into clearer view, and she leaned nearer her window.

The city, however often seen, had a breath-taking quality for her. Each time, it looked larger, and newer, and busier, and from the air, less real. You could see nothing half so remarkable on the whole Golden Spread. The tall buildings, very red and very white on sunny days, sprouted up altogether startlingly from the flat open country, and toward them, in sudden convergence, ran the dark rails and broad glittering highways, and all about were the plaid pattern of streets and the crawl of thirty thousand automobiles.

Some of the Panhandle's small-town people, she knew, regarded Amarillo as a greedy, fat monster sucking the blood out of an emaciated country. Indeed, the city had never worn the face of disaster, however rainless the years. Still it delighted Miss Eunice to see all the handsome people in all the handsome clothes, all the big-city courtesies and habits in a land otherwise drab–folksy–rural. She did not think prosperity lewd, even in such sharp comparison with surrounding hardship. Rather, she imagined a little wistfully that someday the city's riches would overflow and go spilling across the whole Panhandle, so that in some future year, the difference between Amarillo and Plainston would be very small.

Since her very first call on the radiologist, she'd felt the city's magic might even hold an answer for her. As her plane circled widely toward the airport traffic pattern, she tried to pick out the city library. They had a new one, enormously staffed. The salaries, surely, would be quite high. She shook her head over the idea. It was already too late. Plainston owned her. The Plainston Bank held a mortgage on the home Mr. Casey had left her, and she owed delinquent accounts at several of the stores, although she'd not had a new dress all year.

The plane crossed an edge of the city, quite slowly it seemed, and they flew at an angle away from the airport. Always there was much time between arrival at Amarillo and the landing. Once the pilot, a Plainston boy she'd known since his babyhood, explained how the small new airline rated no preferences at the big city terminals. If schedules conflicted, the Golden Spread Lines flew the widest approaches. The pilot was as irritated as she, but as he explained, part of his salary came as stock in the company, which guaranteed him a "future," and for this he could put up with any disagreeable detail.

They came about far north of the terminal, low enough now so that she got clear view of vast grasslands and the helter-skelter of pumping wells. From the air, the pumping beams struck her as iron beasts that nibbled up and down, rhythmically, at the short yellow grass. The plane continued letting down—ah, she was learning so many of the airplane terms—until she began to see bare patches and great cracks in the earth. Perhaps, as so many in Plainston said, Mr. Eisenhower was a bit slow about substituting money for rain. But she still admired him, and had voted for him, and she had certainly enjoyed his book.

Ahead and to the right, she saw one of the checkpoints she had come to know as familiarly as did the pilots. It was a big, boxy, two-story house, flanked by a large cement garage and facing away from a shabby barn. Today, the place looked different.

She checked the small watch that dangled from a brooch on her blouse, then looked again at the place. The barn, that was it. Still quite clearly off plumb, and swaying a little in the roof, it was newly painted. She was amused; what farmer, she wondered, wanted a wood barn the color of aluminum? The sun burst off its walls, but the old roof remained unpaintedly raw. It should have had paint also, she thought. She could, however, excuse the poor devils. In drouth, a farmer was lucky if he could fix up any at all.

Then, as the plane turned gently into the final leg, she

caught sight of the barn roof's far slope. It appeared partly painted. Indeed, it was half covered with crude, brilliant lettering.

Miss Eunice gasped. She strained against the safety belt she liked to keep fastened all the way, and she read the two words again. She flushed stingingly. She drew back in her seat and turned her face away from the window. At that moment, the second pilot, who sometimes made this unremunerative schedule because regulations required it, appeared from the cockpit. His fresh young face looked queer, and he said, "We'll land in two minutes, ma'am."

"Thank you."

He looked at her questioningly, then started back up front. "Wait, young man," Miss Eunice said. She used the voice that sent children scurrying away from the De Maupassant shelf. "Did you see that—that sign?"

"Yes, ma'am. I'm sorry about that."

"Well, whose farm is that?"

"Ma'am, the First Pilot said he was sure you'd understand the company isn't responsible for—for any sights a passenger sees on the ground. He said you'd know we are flying the same course as always, and that we have no control—"

"You tell James to mind his diapers; I'm not so idiotic that I need such things explained to me. Now, young man, who lives there? Do you know?"

"Well, yes ma'am. I mean, no."

"Which is it?"

"The First Pilot—"

"Shouldn't you speak of James as the Captain?"

"Well, I guess, except in our classification—"

"Never mind. Who lives down there?"

"The First Pilot says the name is Munger. The Captain says, I mean."

"And who are they?"

"The oil Mungers, ma'am. Panhandle Green Petroleum, and outfits like that."

"Very well."

"I'm sorry it happened, ma'am. When we land, I'll sure make a report."

"All right. Hadn't you better get back up there and do whatever it is you do, before we crash and everyone is killed?"

"Yes, ma'am. Well, no ma'am; there's not any danger of a crash."

Miss Eunice accepted no help in alighting from the plane. She walked straight through the terminal building, to tell her cab driver that she was safely arrived and he should wait. Then she reentered for a word with the terminal's efficient-looking manager.

"You are sure of this, Mrs. Casey?"

"I'm certainly not imagining anything."

"Of course not. But if you could tell me, frankly, what the words are?"

"They aren't in my vocabulary. One does not repeat them. I suggest you take one of your airplanes and drive out to see for yourself."

"We haven't any aircraft for such uses," he said. "But naturally I'll have to inspect, one way or the other. Unless you can save me the trouble by being a bit more explicit."

"Well, there are just the two vile words."

"You know, I do agree with you, Mrs. Casey, that a lot of our aerial signs are annoying. My own last trip, I saw an amazing number of barn-roof ads. Purina Chow, and Garrett's Snuff, to name two."

"Believe me, this is nothing of the sort." In exasperation, Miss Eunice decided upon boldness. "I am a librarian. It is my duty to read every variety of books. I don't say I read trash, mind you. But the last time I encountered such language in print was in a work called *From Here to Eternity*."

The manager reddened; she knew she had scored.

"Thank you," he said hastily, and he reached for his telephone. "Get me the city manager, at once." He meant for her to hear his half of the call, but she would soon be tardy for her appointment, and she got up.

"If you'll wait, Mrs. Casey—"

"I'll be back in two hours."

The cab driver found her difficult to converse with, this trip. For months now, he had driven this little woman on a regular basis; in his billfold he carried the typewritten table of dates and times she had provided to guide him in her service. At first, she had been dry and prim during the runs to and from the professional building. After a few trips, she relented to chat away the miles with him. He enjoyed it. His wife had had a cancer, once, which gave them much experience in common. Today, Miss Eunice declined any response at all.

The driver tried along several tacks before giving up. In his mirror he noted how stiffly she rode, how sternly she committed even her colorless lips to her thoughts. The sight saddened him. Perhaps she had learned her treatment was failing. By the time they reached downtown, he was convinced of this. He felt very sorry. Maybe he was too soft, but he couldn't help thinking. Lonely, unlucky old lady. Her slip always showing. A shame, a pity, if she has to die.

Richard Mooney had passed a weary morning. At noontime, the calls began, in cascade. The first brought him The Old Girl's strained, shaken voice asking him to hold the line for Mr. Munger, please.

Spain spoke rapidly, metallically. "This is important, Moon, and when your tail is stuck in a crack you don't namby-pamby around, and what counts is—how soon can you bring Bethel out to The Old Place?"

"You mean now, today?"

"Uh, within an hour, I mean, and if you have to shut down the store, I know your board will go along on that, and you can take my word of mouth for it."

Moon struggled at filtering out the thoughts and absorbing them. He said, "I don't know where my wife is. She went shopping with China."

"Uh, that's one cat skinned already; your Mr. Jacobson scoured them up and she's on the way home now. I'll appreciate it if you'll pick her up. When your situation turns coat on you out of the blue, you have to get a hustle on. If I sound like I'm, uh, popping the old buggy whip, why—"

Moon set his jaw. "What situation?"

Spain hesitated; he coughed thinly. The big picture was in jeopardy. "Uh, to hit it on the head briefly, your city manager telephoned and one of your lawyers, a, uh, Mr. Blassingame, called right in his tracks, and I understand he's one of your unscrupulous shake-down artists and there's your rotten kettle of fish. Uh, if you'll get Bethel out on the double, and tell Frank—no, China will buzz him up, since I've just talked with her. Uh, one more thing, if you'll bring a camera and some of those flash shooter gadgets with you? Now, I've got to speak with your city manager; Mr. Williams-the-lawyer thinks if I call him, man to man—"

"Wait." Moon tightened his fist on the phone. "Tell me what happened."

"Uh, what's that?"

"Is it Brother?"

"Well, June is involved, but not to lay your blame on the wrong shoulders, it seems to my mind your Mr. Remo put him up on this horse, so to speak. Uh, I know you have your warm spot for Remo, Moon, and I can say that ninety per cent of the time, your directors have been satisfied with him, which ought to be made clear, but your brass tacks are, he shouldn't have allowed Brother on top of the barn at all."

"Brother fell off?"

"Uh, no; I'm telling you he painted a sign on the roof, and you know how your aluminum paint shows up at a distance, and all your airplanes going over—well, to be frank, Moon, the sign is one of those, uh, obscenities he copies out of your comfort stations."

Moon's shoulders went down; he'd not realized how the suspense had lifted them. He laughed. "Let him paint over it, Spain. If you think it'll be seen."

"It's been seen, that's your facts of life!"

Moon's pleasure was instant. A wave of it. But as he grasped the implications, he felt sorry for Spain Munger, then sorrier for Bethel.

"The city manager saw it?"

"Uh, an airline passenger, a short while ago; a woman named Mrs. Casey, I understand, and she must have hotfooted it straight to your Mr. Blassingame's office. Mr. Williams thinks—well, he's afraid they'll be sending out an airplane for photographs. Uh, Mr. Remo is throwing one of your tarps over the roof for the time being; that's Mr. Williams's advice, and he thinks we ought to get pictures of our own, in event your lettering is so jagged it couldn't be read except by your dirty mind, if you see the giz there—"

"What are the words?"

"Time, that's your main cog right now; can you make it out by one o'clock?"

"If Bethel's ready."

"Fine. Uh, wait a shade; it strikes my mind we needn't have the children out, I know you'll stamp your okay on that."

As Moon cradled the phone, it rang again. Bethel sounded broken; he imagined her there in the kitchen, trembling, propped against the cabinet, her pale face ashen. "Richard, I'll be ready when you come for me—you have heard, haven't you? Oh, poor Brother. And the kids. Who'll I get to stay with the kids?"

"No one, Beth. They're too old for sitters. Just make one of them responsible."

She sobbed; he couldn't have mistaken it.

"Now, Beth, please don't fall apart. It's nothing a little paint won't fix. I'll be right home."

He only got to his coat before the telephone went again, and he grabbed it almost gleefully. Business boomed, deals were afoot, emergency clouded all horizons. It amazed him that Brother's newest defection came as something he needed.

"Hello," he yelped.

"Moon, my God, it's me!" John Remo said.

Moon laughed. "You got troubles, Remo?"

"Hellfire, that goddamn chucklehead—"

"I've heard."

"I only tried to take me a bath. Wasn't in the house but a half hour, and not one damn minute more! I ain't had no chance to explain that, either. He's fixin' to fire me, Moon."

"Did he say that?"

"He might near did. This fat slob; I'm a mind to stomp the grease out of 'im!"

"Don't yell," Moon said, "you're exploding my ear. Just relax, and I'll bring you a drink."

Remo's big voice growled. "I'd be obliged. If I'm gonna get canned again, I might as leave get soused over it. I got a mother to take care of."

Moon said, "I don't think you'll lose your job. That is, unless old Brother is burning down the house while you gab on the telephone."

"Tame as a lamb, damn him," Remo said. "Settin' in there looking at TV, like he ain't done nothin' and the world is his'n. If he didn't bruise so easy—"

Moon laughed. "I'll see you shortly."

"Hell yes. And I ain't looking forward to it!"

Frank Wallace paused at the door, coat in hand, on his way out, and he was grinning broadly. Moon could smell his beer. "Eeyo," Frank said, "this is the year!"

"How much do you know?" Moon said.

"Same as you, I guess; China called me at the Monarch. She didn't know what he wrote on the barn. Or she wouldn't say. What was it?"

"I don't know. The unveiling isn't until one o'clock."

"Ready to go?"

"You go ahead. I've got to load a camera."

Frank turned toward the back, then paused. His vein-meshed face sobered, and he said, "Remo's out. He's had it coming, the crooked bastard."

"Right on the beam, aren't you?"

"Sure. He was a crooked cop, wasn't he? And I'll bet you a hundred he's been swiping from the kitty."

"Lay off him, Frank."

"I'm not getting into it. I was just saying that next to your squaw, he's Number One on my list."

Moon said hotly, "That about makes me Number Three."

Frank grinned and shook his head. "Nope. I love you, partner. See you at the diggings."

Moon glanced at his watch and returned to his office. He dialed Estate offices twice before he could get a line. For twenty minutes he had been so busy he perspired. It felt heady and good.

"This is Mooney," he told The Old Girl. "Put me on with Spain, please."

"Oh, he's in conference right now." She sounded next to tearful; Moon judged things were jumping high up there.

"With whom?"

"Well sir, Mr. Williams-the-lawyer is in there. Mr. Munger said I should take numbers for call-backs—"

"Okay. But put me through."

"I don't know. If you'd explain to Mr. Munger—?"

"I'll tell him I threatened you."

Moon pictured the chairman and president. In such a crisis, pale hair wildly tousled and pink scalp showing through; pale face drawn lean and gray, bony hands bridged restlessly beneath the fleshless chin, the weak eyes pinched narrow behind the thick glasses and faded to the color that was scarcely more blue than skimmed milk. And across the desk from him, the harried and wary advisers, speaking cautiously and with every phrase gingerly qualified.

Spain's voice came on. "What is it, Moon? We must hurry."

"It's important. About John Remo. Have you fired him?"

"Uh, that's not my cupcake, Moon. That's for your board to gnaw on when we come to it."

"Of course. I don't want to step out of line, Spain. But there's something in this connection we shouldn't overlook."

"Uh, if we can hurry on, Moon. Texas and Laska are already on the way out, I think—"

"All right. First, I think Remo has done pretty well, if I've a right to an opinion. But beyond that—fired people often go out pretty bitter. If you think, you'll realize how much Remo knows about—about family affairs; things he won't talk about as long as he has a job."

"Uh, well; now that is an aspect, I agree with you there a hundred per cent. Uh, you do kind of keep your finger tabbed on him, don't you? Would you say, off the cuff, that if he left us there'd be—"

"No," Moon said. "I'm talking possibilities, that's all. And I've not gotten to the main thing. Suppose there is a lawsuit. Remo is a primary witness, and he can be a friendly one, or otherwise."

"Uh, yes; yes! I understand that," Spain said, and his tone meant he'd not thought of it at all. "Uh, that does touch on your bedrock, doesn't it? Moon, I appreciate your coming right down the aisle when you've got something on the ball, and your directors are right with me there, you can bet your bottom boots."

The action, the quick election of a target and the immediate concentration of fire upon it, undoubtedly with success, filled Moon with elation. However small, here was decision and execution; he joyously loved himself for having thought and acted. It gorged him with such benevolence that he said, "I'm sure you had thought of it, but I felt I'd call to make certain."

As he got his coat on, Bethel called again.

"Richard, aren't you ever coming?"

"Right now, darling. This minute."

Darling, he had said.

He took a Rolleicord off a shelf, detouring around Teddy Birdsong to get to it. Using the counter, he loaded a roll of film, put two more in his pocket. Quickly he rigged a flash gun, found a carton of bulbs, and hung a light meter around his neck. When he looked up, Teddy Birdsong stood in the center of the shop, watching as if about to break into laughter. She had a hand braced on cocked hip, in a way that pointed his gaze downward to one small ankle-strapped shoe.

"Big doings, huh?" she smiled.

"I imagine you've heard as much about it as I," he said.

She nodded. "I'm that way."

"Are you getting a kick out of it?"

She acknowledged his coldness reversely, responding to it as if flattered. "Hell, Mr. Mooney, I love to see important fat in the fire."

Her squawish, clown-painted face looked up at him with a subtle mocking; she tapped a whorish shoe, so that her breasts undulated slightly, and she kept the knowing, infuriating challenge before him in the upturn of her false lips. He glared at her. In these seconds of fast blood and sharpened mind, she only barely tempted him. Just barely. Except, if she should stretch her arms above her head, he knew, he'd have to remember vividly their terrible last night, and whenever he reflected on this, it seemed he himself had somehow caused her to be as she was, had led her to distill sex and prayer into that weird complex. He shuddered; he could think of the event as a kind of black mass not greatly different from Frank's evil painting. And now, for the first time, it struck him that Teddy Birdsong threatened to become his counterpart to the old druggist's Christ head; she could be his own dark blend of deity and sensualism.

He swore he wouldn't allow it. He shut his eyes on Teddy Birdsong, and he bent his thoughts to Bethel. His wife was in her period of peace, but hurt and needing him.

"What's your beef?" Teddy said. Her sad-hard brown gaze stared him back, the thin-plucked brows arched up too confidently.

"Damn you," he said softly.

Her expression did not change.

"I didn't mean that," he said. "Nothing is your fault. I'm sorry, but it'll be best if after today, you don't work here. I'll trust you to lock up for me—just go home whenever you please."

Her eyes only widened a little.

Moon hurried on out back to his car.

XV

The Mungers—full ten per cent of Amarillo's millionaires—took sorrowfully to the rough road that by Moon's error might never be more smooth.

He drove Bethel's quiet year-old sedan over knots and pits in a haste she didn't object to. Beside him his wife sat silently, facing ahead. Perhaps because the Mungers were not yet together, had not yet merged their identities, he gave her an unqualified, honest sympathy. He even yearned toward her; he pitied June Munger with her, he longed for kinder words to say.

She wore the handsome suit of her shopping tour, and the shoes that made her too tall. The scant make-up had been spoiled by tear ribbons down each uncurving cheek, and she looked drained and tired and not young at all.

"Bethel, it's not so critical as you think."

"Poor Brother," she said. "I love him. But when he—when something like this happens, I could almost slap the dogwater out of him, and that makes me feel just rotten and dirty."

It startled him; he'd not heard such a phrase from her before.

"Oh, I'm sorry," she said. "I needn't have said that."

"It's quite a term."

"It's horrible."

They passed the accusing spot where the traffic counter had lain, and Moon supposed they'd be the first to reach The Old Place. They had seen Frank and China, with Texas in back, stopped at a highway gas station, and everyone had waved.

"It's Good Friday," she said.

"Yes."

They topped the slight hill that brought The Old Place into sight. They saw the barn, glittering silver in the sun, so that it looked larger than the house. Neither spoke. Then shortly they identified the queer look of the roof's near slope. It was under a dark green tarpaulin which, despite the almost complete windlessness, appeared to billow up and collapse as if, underneath, the barn were breathing.

"The board will simply need to hire some painters," he said, and at once wished to recall it. It was he, this time, who sliced them apart. His stroke that ended the closeness.

"I—I don't know what Spain has in mind," she said, and the division was complete; his wife had joined the Mungers, and he felt like a boy among the Clacks.

He slowed the car. They overtook a curtain of white dust left by someone who'd beaten them, after all. Through it Moon saw clearly, now, the swish-swash of brush strokes that proved the barn to be Brother's job. Leaving their car on the parking area were Sid and Laska, he in a trim business suit and she in blousy slacks that accented the inches by which she towered over him. At the front corner of the house, Brother's sun-blistered head bobbed near Remo's cropped gray one; the happiest Munger appeared to fight the old cop's grip on the blue paint-smirched overalls.

"Oh, my Lord," Bethel gasped.

She left the car quickly, to hug Laska, to stare at the struggle between June and John Remo. Moon watched a moment before getting out. Brother's fat face was in terror, his round body quivered as he tugged toward freedom. Clearly, old Remo had intercepted him at the manhole end of the porch.

"Hello, Moon," Sid said. "Too bad."

Moon went on alone toward the house. He grinned at Brother, and the pink face appeared to lose some of its panic. Abruptly the struggle ended, and Remo shifted a big hand from the overalls to one of the shapeless fat shoulders.

"He aims to git under there, Moon," Remo panted.

June wheezed heavily; sweat ran off his freshly shaven chin. His shirt was clean but its tail was out and white fleshy rolls of him showed through the unfastened plackets.

"China is on the way," Moon said. "She'll be here real soon."

"She's really comin' out, ain't she, Moon?"

"She's on the road now."

"Well, I don't care none myself, I'll say that, but me and Mister Remo, we done et our Sunday dinner last Sunday—"

Moon smiled at him. "We didn't come to eat, June." He thought suddenly of China's easy, mandarinish little figure, kneeling beside the porch, and the gentle coax of the voice she directed underneath, into the darkness. "We came to see you, actually. And you look fine."

"Well, I guess I do look fine. Mister Remo, he said I had by-God better look fine, didn't you say I by-God ought to, Mister Remo?"

Moon said, "You don't have to hold him, John. He doesn't want to get under the house. Do you, June?"

The blue darkened and richened in Brother's eyes; it glistened there as if from inner tears, and Moon could see him arriving slowly at resolution. "Boy, I didn't say I was gittin' under no house, Mister Remo, but I don't know if Kittypoo is under yonder or not, if I don't look under yonder, and boy, Mister Remo—"

"Here they are," Remo said, sadly, and he turned Brother free.

The Wallace car was parking. Brother's mouth opened. He raised his arms, laced his hands behind his head, and went to meet her.

"He doesn't seem as usual," Moon said.

"Hell, I had to get a little rough with him. Fact is, I was

trying to get him to the bathroom; he's been out here just dancing, about to wet himself."

"I didn't know he did that."

"Today he would, I think. That's the first time he ever wrestled me. And the last time, I guess."

"You sound like you have your bags all packed."

Remo grimaced. "Would have, if I'd had the time."

The big hands went into the blue serge, the homely heavy-lidded eyes looked beyond Moon, watching closely as China Wallace kissed her brother and exclaimed at how nice he looked and how terribly she had missed him. Her fresh sweetness seemed to wash upslope to them.

Moon turned to look. She wore a black silk maternity dress that made her hair all the fairer, almost blinding in the sun. Laughing delightedly, she was stooping to pick up a tiny white hat Brother must have swept from her.

"Goddamn," Remo muttered.

Moon nodded at the road. "Here comes Spain."

"And here goes ole Remo."

"I think you're wrong," Moon said. "If you aren't, I did remember the bottle."

Remo glanced at Moon speculatively, then together they watched Spain's contortions as he ducked his head and fetched his long frame out of the car. "Looks like 'Mom' stayed at home," Moon said.

Remo whispered, "If yu' know something, tell me now."

"Firing you wouldn't help anything. And I think Spain knows it."

"Ain't many that'll hire an old man," Remo said. "An' it's just me to look out for my mother."

Spain went jerkily into the group beside the cars, and Sid and Frank excused themselves and moved idly away. Spain carried his great rancher hat, returned to him because Moose Williams wouldn't be caught dead in it, and he clutched it conspicuously in front of him. One pale hand held a roll in the untrained brim but could not keep the crown out of the way.

Spain bent to kiss each of his sisters. Not one of them smiled.

"Lookit my boy," Remo growled.

Moon grinned. Brother, like a miscreant child, circled about each time Spain turned, keeping himself behind him and from under the pale eyes of discipline.

For a moment, Spain squinted up at the house. Then he said something and came leading the group toward Moon and Remo. The solid front was established, Spain and his sisters were one. Except for China, the Munger women matched the tall man's strides. Moon resented them for it; particularly, he hated how Bethel looked suddenly without grace. She walked as if stretching each step to reach the crest of the next furrow. At Moon's side, Remo sighed at this perspective of the many advancing upon the few, the big ones marching to their feast upon the small ones; and Moon understood exactly how he felt.

"Uh, well," Spain said, and he shook hands with Moon, then with Remo. He looked ghostly and weary behind the thick glasses. "I appreciate your coming out, Moon, and let me say if there wasn't enough notice to shake your stick at, well, this brand of foul-up is bound to put that kind of pressure on your valves."

"It's all right."

Remo's nose shone mountainously in the sun; he was watching China, frowning at the change in her figure. She smiled at him, and he said, "They's coffee in the house, ma'am. Wasn't nothing more to fix, but I guess you all have already ate."

"Coffee is just what I wanted," China said. She turned to her sisters, and in her flawless, intuitive tact, suggested: "Let's get out of this sun before it ruins us."

She held Brother's hand; she pulled him along with the others, on inside. John Remo got out his broken pipe, polished it by rubbing it alongside his nose, then uncertainly put it away.

"Uh, Moon, you brought the camera?"

"It's in the car."

"Well, to get down pell-mell to your chores, wouldn't you say we ought to get your pictures while your sun is on the roof?"

Moon went to the car. As he returned with the equipment, Laska and Texas appeared on the porch. Laska had a mug of coffee in one hand, a flattened brown cigarette in the other, and in her striped slacks she recalled and made almost credible the rumor that one of the Munger girls shaved.

Spain told her, "I'm going out to the barn now."

"Wait." Laska spoke huskily. "We've been talking about that. We are all a family. I think we should all see what Bro— what has happened."

Spain reddened slightly. He said nothing. He turned, and he led them in file around the house, past the patch of mud that endured despite these years without rain. They marched wordlessly by the dead, trash-filled old cistern, then along the dry path toward the lot where white chickens pecked about. At the gate, Spain paused.

"Uh, Mr. Remo, if we can see your gidget from here—?"

"No sir." The old Pole's face flamed now, down to his tight fresh collar. "You'd have to go on into the lot. That's how come I never found it myself; I didn't have no call to go into the lot."

Spain squinted and frowned. He fumbled at the gate latch and went on through. The women held back. Moon glanced at Bethel. She was as pale as Spain; her thoughts might be his. Moon stared, commanding her gaze to him. She met his eyes, but her expression did not change. He could not alter a line of it. He shook his head and released her, and he looked up at the sun, letting it make him sneeze. Then, he watched the high trail being cut aloft by an invisible jet; a long spill of white foam, the wake of a free man. Only Moon noticed, and he resented the others because of it.

Remo propped a ladder against the barn and turned. "Mr. Munger, I think—well, it ain't what you show to ladies."

Spain considered. The long arms folded themselves across

264

his back. A narrow palm supported each elbow, and with the toe of a glistening brown shoe, he scattered a small mound of Grape-Nuts.

"Uh, my sisters wish—the board will need to shake this down to your bare facts. But your thought there is good. Maybe, if we viewed separately—yes, that would be the best beam to sail on. . . ."

The women agreed silently, then turned back toward the house. China wasn't among them. As Moon wondered about this, he heard her. Her voice echoed in the old kitchen, in banter with Brother; feeding him, taking her Beloved onto her wings and flying him about up there where she lived. It struck Moon as right that China didn't care to come out, or to see.

When the back door closed after his sisters, Spain said, "Uh, well," and he paced straight ahead to a position near the center of the lot.

"I'll need help, rollin' that tarp," Remo said.

Moon stowed his camera atop a fence post and followed the hulk of blue serge up the ladder. "Watch 'at third step, Moon."

The ladder popped and creaked. But Moon thought, how quiet it is. Sunny and bright and still; even the dove and sparrow hawks waiting, spellbound, to appraise June's masterpiece. He saw Sid and Frank enter the lot, and felt they must have been sent out at the last moment. Almost creepingly they put themselves at either side of Spain and a few feet behind him. From the top of the ladder, the three men looked to be in echelon and at parade rest. Moon watched them lift their faces and crane about, searching the sky for aircraft. Then Spain coughed and signaled the barn.

Moon and Remo squatted cautiously on the steep roof. Each unlashed a corner of the tarp. They climbed up slowly, dragging the heavy oiled canvas into a fold. As they strained upward toward the ridgepole, the crude ten-foot letters broke out into the sunshine. The words glittered the ancient admonishment perpetuated by generations of small boys who write with chalk on sidewalks. Quickly Spain signaled again, his hand making a chopping motion, and Moon and Remo brought the tarp down.

Spain turned in a full circle and strode from the lot. Sid followed, and only Frank lingered to shake his hands like a boxer and grin.

Moon and Remo sat on their heels at the lowest corners of the roof, gazing across at each other as the old shingles crackled beneath them.

"God, Moon, I hate for *her* to see this." He added, hurriedly, "And Mrs. Mooney, too, of course."

"I don't think *she* will."

"It's their choice, I reckon. But damn, I don't see why none of 'em can't take my word—"

"Shut up, Remo."

Spain had reappeared, leading the women. Just Texas, Laska, and Bethel. Moon watched them come. Why couldn't Bethel have let it go?

Halfway, which he must have marked as the point of no-return, Spain quit his sisters and returned to the house alone. The women came on. Moon looked down at his wife. The fun, the action, the noontime sense of strength, were dead, and his wife was a stranger.

The sisters formed at the center of the lot. Laska stood, feet wide apart, at the forward point of their triangle. Moon and Remo avoided sight of each other as again they made the hard climb up the roof slope.

They heard Laska say, "I hate this barn; sometimes I wish it would burn."

Moon turned at the ridgepole, sat down on it. Bethel was already going out the gate. Texas put a handkerchief to her face and fled. Laska stood unmoving, alone.

"Moon," she called. "If Mr. Remo can hold that cover by himself, won't you come down a moment?"

Moon got down quickly. Laska's strong hand drew him close beside her. "You must see it from here," she said. He looked up. The letters, almost unintelligible close upon them, read easily from here.

"Pictures wouldn't help us at all, would they?"

Moon shook his head.

"That's what Spain thought. I think we all agree, and he said tell you we should forget about them."

"All right." On impulse, he said, "What was that you said about burning the barn?"

She still held his hand, and now she squeezed it. "It's—the thing Bethel told you, about our kids. Richard, I never did say how sorry I am, did I?"

Moon's face stung. He shouted up, "Turn it loose, Remo."

"Richard, Carol has about forgotten it, hasn't she?"

"I don't know. I got in on it too late."

"Bless you, I know. But I think they're both all right now. We had planned, except for this mess—Sid and I meant to go to San Antonio tonight. To spend Easter with him."

"Have a nice trip."

She released his hand. He watched her great broad back and her Munger ranginess as she went slowly out the gate, and he felt he wronged Sid by how long he stared after her.

Moon climbed the ladder once more. He helped John Remo fight down the tarp against a breeze that had excited itself into a vulgarly gleeful wind. They lashed the corner ropes tightly.

Remo grunted. "Is it about to turn cold?"

"The Easter spell, I guess. Remo, I don't see how you got this thing up here, by yourself."

"Didn't. Brother was with me. Hell, for once't I had 'im humping."

They got to the ground. Moon lit a cigarette. Remo stared toward the house.

"He ain't said nothing yet. About firin' me."

Moon said, "Nothing turned out as funny as I thought. Let's go to the car."

Remo wagged the bullish old head. "I reckon they'll send for me, pretty quick now."

"Come on. They'll have to talk a while first."

As he raised the sedan's trunk lid, Moon caught the new-car

smell still trapped there. He uncapped the whisky without removing it from the paper sack. They sat down together, their knees hanging uncomfortably over the bumper.

Remo took the bottle and crushed the sack to fit it. "One good thing," he said, "*she* stayed in the kitchen. Making June some Jello, I guess." He leaned out, clear of the lid, and turned up the bottle. He held it long, then brought it down with a groan. He wiped on his sleeve, and gazed at the smoke lifting off Amarillo. "Jello," he muttered. "An' kissin' all over the slob, I bet."

"Probably."

"I ought to of killed 'im."

"Remo, your heavy textures are showing."

"Aw hell; where'd you ever hear that expression?"

The Old Place, without its run-through by Harry and Carrie, smelled of dust and an almost vile animalism that seemed to radiate from the downstairs bedrooms. Spain was glad no one mentioned it. The need was to get the group to sitting formally without lost motion. If you dallied and dillied, if you took notice of your surroundings, if you recalled the past days in this house when the scents were of liquor and crock jars filled with half-cured cheese, then you invited pessimistic thought and you blew your hope of successful decisions right out the window and good-by. In his experience, Spain had learned that with a family board, the members' common background tended to misguide; there was always the hazard of unanimous error.

He felt the risk to be greater today. The board, except for China, hadn't shaken off its shock. Spain wondered if he'd at last gotten an ulcer.

The president-chairman sat at his end place, the new Stetson atop the table to his left, and he bridged his hands for his chin and waited behind his most thoughtful face until his sisters turned toward him.

"Uh, if the board pleases and we can snap to order—"

"I suppose I have the minutes," Laska said.

"—and if you all agree, we might proceed the first shot out of the box as, uh, just family, in view of your snarl of affairs, which I might say aren't a hundred per cent bad, however messed up they may seem."

"I'd just as soon not bother with minutes at all," Laska sighed. "But if it's to cost anything—is it?"

"Uh, well, if the board sees tooth and nail with what has sprung to my mind, it will involve some money, but let's just saw off that bridge when we get there."

China said, "Don't let me forget, darlings, I have some eggs on to boil."

"Eggs? Lord, I've missed lunch, but I'm not that hungry."

"They're for Brother; he's so afraid he'll have to miss the egg hunt this year."

"Please, uh, if we can keep order, and address your remarks to the chairman, we can get our knots threshed out in jig-time. Now, to bring your summary up to date, you've all seen your joker on the roof, and from the first jump, when the city manager called me—"

"Why the city manager?" Bethel said.

"Uh, to fill in your mind there, the city owns the airport, and this woman's complaint went straight up to his bailiwick. Now, Mr. Williams, that's Mr. Williams-the-lawyer—"

"How come he sent your hat back?" Texas said.

Spain frowned and licked his lips. "Uh, it didn't fit his Moose, I'm told. Now, to set aside your alarming psychotic facts of this incident and tackle the urgent storm over our heads—let me lay it on the dotted line. And Mr. Williams agrees with what I'm about to propose as our best stand to take. I've assumed the liberty of bringing along a set of checks, so your job here can get rolling."

"Just a minute, please. A check on what account? We ought to establish what board—"

"Uh, as a matter of fact, these are drawn on the Big Plains primary account, but if we can comb things out first as just family folks—"

"You *are* speaking of pay for some painters, aren't you?"

"Well, no."

Bethel said, "Let's open another window. Does anyone mind?"

Spain controlled himself; he realized today's tensions demanded patience.

"Uh, Mr. Williams believes, on your grounds of about fifty per cent information we could raise, that your Eunice Casey pirate here, this library woman, is your typical breed of adventuress. And to set your facts out frankly, she probably wasn't so, uh, offended by the barn as she is impressed by the resources of this board. I'm sorry if seizing the horns this way grinds too hard on your ears. But, to continue—I understand your Casey woman is a sort of deadbeat, and she has some medical bills saddled around her neck. Mr. Williams is sure she'd sign a waiver, if we can agree to pounce on her quickly with cash on the barrel."

"Give her money," Texas said, "just for riding an airplane over our barn?"

"Well, you have to fit your shoe to whatever foot gets stuck in your face, and as Mr. Williams points out—and let me state that he's dead center on the ball, here—we can be spry about it and at least circumvent your shyster lawyer she's gotten hold of."

"I suppose," Texas yielded. "But I dislike any little thief, just looking for the opportunity to—"

"Oh, no, Texas." China's protest was gentle. "We don't really know that, do we? Perhaps she's just someone in trouble."

"Uh, be that as it lies, I'm now asking this board to approve—"

"Lord," sighed Laska. "Which board?"

"Let's say, to make our hay faster, Big Plains. On your tentative basis, anyway. Uh, I'm asking this board to approve these checks, which you can see are drawn in your stairstep amounts from five hundred up to your ten thousand dollars, which should cover the range where your negotiation is apt to fall, I believe. Then, on your authority, I suggest that Mr. Williams and I hop over to Plainston this evening and talk to

270

your Mrs. Casey man to man. Mr. Williams thinks your whole lawsuit could be nipped in the nub tonight."

"I don't know," Bethel said, and they sat a moment in silence.

Spain cleared his throat. "Uh, let me say it's not any pumpkin pie to swallow. But unless we are quick on our toes, your original petition could be filed tomorrow, and your subpoenas would come flowing out, and most likely, you'd face your demands for depositions, not to make mention of your actual trial."

"They'd—they'd have to call Brother, wouldn't they?" China asked hushedly.

Spain nodded. "All of us."

"I move," Bethel said, "that we authorize Spain and Mr. Williams to go—I move, I mean, we approve the checks—actually, I move we do what Spain says."

"Second."

"Uh, thank you. If everyone would say 'aye'—?"

"Aye."

Already, Texas's pen scratched at countersigning the checks.

"Thank you; I'm glad we're a hundred per cent on that. Uh, now, to wind up—"

"Oh, goodness," China shot up from her chair. "The eggs must have boiled dry!"

She brought in a saucepan filled with eggs and placed it on the table. "There!"

Spain squinted hard at his watch. "Uh, to push ahead on all four cylinders, we've got to take your long view about—"

"Hey," said Laska, "will someone explain to me about the eggs?"

"Sure, honey. We—"

"Listen"—Texas straightened from the checks—"won't there be some expense in the trip to Plainston?"

"Well, your Mr. Williams will bear his own expenses, which you'll recall is the clause in his contract that applies to such as you have on your hands here, and as for myself, I'll meet that hurdle out of my own pocket—uh, I anticipate what you intend to say on that score, and I appreciate your thought be-

hind it. But let's say we'll talk about your reimbursement problem at a later meeting, when your time element isn't such a
ball and chain dragging your feet. Now, Laska, your eggs
there—"

China had placed several eggs on the table before her and
was passing the others around. "Everybody take one. Careful,
they're hot. Decorate them pretty as you can."

"What?"

"Oh, Tex dear, there isn't a speck of dye on the place. So I
thought we might use pen or pencils. Just draw something
on them. Poor Beloved, he isn't fussy."

"But we always have the hunt on Easter afternoon."

"Uh, to get you ironed out on that, Brother can't be gotten
off without your egg hunt, and as Mr. Williams says, your time
is pungent to get him on out of state, just as a backstop in case
your bargaining with this library woman fails to come to a
horse trade. I hope the board won't mind, but as your chairman I did reserve plane space for this evening, and that should
get June well over the hedge before your shyster can drive
out here."

"Where's he going?"

"Uh, New York."

"He's dying to go," China said. "For that show, *Li'l Abner*."

"Uh, time is pretty short—"

Texas said, "Who is going to take him?"

"Well, under your circumstances, Mr. Remo is your man,
don't you agree?"

"I don't. I think we must discharge Mr. Remo."

Bethel said, "Richard likes Mr. Remo a great deal."

"Well, this is something we can't pass by. China, I know
what you are thinking. But if you had gone out to the lot with
us—"

"I know, it is horrible."

"Uh, if the board pleases, this touches on the question I
hoped we'd not have to deal with today, in view of your time
marching on. But there are your ramifications I doubt you've
had the chance to drink in. Uh, just grabbing this by the nap,

272

I believe we'll have to keep Mr. Remo, at least for the time being."

"We should be fair," China said. "Brother did it, not Mr. Remo."

"But where," Texas said, "was he at the time? Sneaking around to drink booze, the odds are. I know I've smelled liquor on him more than once."

"He was bathing, darling," China said. "He does have to choose his times for such things—"

"I don't like to put anything in the minutes about a man's bath."

China held up an egg, laughing at it softly. "Can anyone tell I've drawn a duckling?"

"Uh, please—"

"If a man is undependable," Texas said, "he should be dismissed. I don't want to sound stubborn, of course."

Spain spoke thinly, wearily. "The first reaction on my part was the same, but after your wheels got to clicking, the point came home that ninety per cent of the time, Mr. Remo does passably well. And, if he should become a witness in your, uh, litigation—well, there's your friendly witness or your hostile witness to take into account. As a further side of the coin, to act against Mr. Remo at this moment might, uh, appear to concede this woman her point, or so Mr. Williams puts it."

"I hadn't thought that far. But I do think we could have that man in. It seems he deserves some what-for, at least."

Laska asked, "Are we voting?"

"Well—and if you don't see eye to eye, then fire right out and say so, of course—my thought is that your prudent path here is no action at all. And that's not to say your bone is buried so deep you can't air it out a later time."

"All right. Let's do something with the eggs."

Bethel said, "Shouldn't we arrange to get some painters to work on the barn?"

"Uh, it's my experience that your professional painter is your gossipy type, by and large, and besides, you'd not want to increase your list of witnesses, in case the worst hits the fan. Now,

I'd not like throwing up a fence around your discussions, but in view of the time squeeze we're under—if the board will trust me, I'll take charge of the painting and clean up your dirty linen there."

Laska said, "Fine, but we ought to note which board appointed you."

"Uh, I want to say before we adjourn, this hitch we have to face is the fault of your chairman, since I went to sleep at the switch, but I have tried to keep all your safeguards up, and what I'm trying to punch home is, I hope we can keep our confidence even with our backs to the brimstone, so to speak—"

"We simply must settle something about the minutes."

Then Spain threw up his hands and shouted. "If you'll all just button up your claptrap interruptions and stop putting the bee on your chairman's back, I'll get your chestnuts out of the ditch before the day is out! And if you want to be on your own come May—!"

"Spain!"

It hadn't happened before, ever. The women stared at him. He had risen to his feet, his fleshless knuckles had cracked down on the table, and already, one was turning blue. He stood there, pale as death, himself aghast.

"Oh, my darling," China said. "You're so tired. . . ."

Spain shook himself. His voice was a whisper. "There's no excuse for your outburst of that brand. I'm sorry."

In the interval of silence, the Munger women looked at each other; each knowing the other to be stunned and frightened. Then China said, "We've all been so upset. We love each other too much to—well, good gracious, let's do hurry, so Spain can get off, and Beloved, too."

Laska had been bowing her pencil between her hands. Now it snapped in two. She said, "Forgive me, Spain. I've nothing more to say, except I had hoped we might talk a minute about our lawn party, since the weather is getting so pretty. But, skip it."

"Uh, no, no." Spain was contrite, yet surprised and shaken by what he had done. "I'm glad you brought that up, and it

274

pops to my head—and I do try to keep my ear to the wind—
it comes to my mind your successful social affair might be just
the giz at your delicate time like this. Uh, may I be the one to
move that the lady members of this board act as a committee
of four to kick your tentative party plans around? And of
course, we can review a little later when we've seen what rises
to the top."

They smiled at him. He went around the table, clumsily,
and kissed each one on the top of her head. China hugged him,
and smiled. "May I be chairman?"

"Uh, of course, unless your condition—"

"Which reminds me," Bethel said, "at three months, dear,
you should be having a doctor."

"I—oh, there's Brother. Let me call him in; the rest of you
can hide the eggs."

Texas Munger got up last, and as they started outside,
grouped closely together, she told them she understood June
to say that Mr. Remo had stuck some kind of a rag down his
throat several times, and she announced that a punishment of
this severity was a matter she intended to learn a good deal
more about.

Moon and Remo stood against the fence, watching the
scurrying and confusion in the yard. The tall fair Mungers
hustled about, scattering eggs rather than hiding them, and
they went at it without banter; indeed, they were stoic. Moon
offered no help. Easter couldn't happen except on Easter, nor
Christmas except on Christmas, not if you wished the special
atmosphere to be there.

At the back of the house, Sid Glass concentrated at putting
a golf ball. He used one of Brother's clubs, and he seemed to
putt well. Frank, with an admission that his stomach was
"boiling," had gone to the car to try for a nap.

"They could have got me in there," Remo muttered. "Let
me tell 'em my side of it."

"Stop worrying. Spain hasn't said anything to you, has he?"

"No. But they always send for me."

"Look; they're ready."

The Mungers gathered about the cistern; they watched with pale eyes and folded arms as China dashed about with Brother, collecting the eggs for his pockets, and unlike The Old Place Easters Moon could remember, Brother was almost grim about it. Although he talked ceaselessly to China, and laughed a little when she laughed, June appeared to miss the noisy enthusiasm of all the absent Munger children. Or perhaps he felt the weight of Spain's gaze as it tracked him. Very quickly, it was through. Or almost.

"Ain't but 'leven of 'em, China. I counted two times, and you tole me it was twelve, didn't you say that, China?"

"Yes, Beloved. We'll find the other one."

They trotted about, Brother heavily, China in dainty, lovely contrast, and they peered into the clumps of dry grass and under the edge of the house, and they checked behind each fence post. Ten minutes passed. The Mungers waited, not assisting, as if unaware that for June the lost egg had become the most precious.

"Sweetie, we'll have to let that one go," China said. "We don't mind, do we?"

"Didn't you say it was twelve of them eggs, huh, China? I ain't got but 'leven in my pocket, an' you tole me—"

"All right; don't you worry. We'll find it." She took Brother's hand, leading him about, and Moon thought her eyes looked a little frightened.

"Hell," Remo said softly.

Moon threw down his cigarette and moved out from the fence. He began to search. He found the egg almost at once, deep in a roll of rusty wire beside the barn. He picked it up, and as China led Brother to him, saw its shell was covered with neatly inked dollar signs.

"Oh, thank you," China said. "Thank you, Richard." Then she looked at the happiest Munger, and suddenly her lips trembled, and her eyes filled with tears.

When Moon looked up, the Mungers were dispersing toward their cars. Spain kissed each of them, then came hurriedly toward the lot. Remo got up off his heels to stand stiffly. While an airliner went across, Spain's pale gaze passed over their heads. Then he said, "Uh, Mr. Remo, how quickly can you be ready to leave?"

The old cop flushed; he stabbed his pipe into his teeth. Moon winced, with shock; with the expectation that Remo would swear.

Remo said, "Right now, I guess."

The tarpaulin cracked suddenly in a gust of chilly wind; it sounded to Moon like the explosion of his helpless anger.

"Uh, fine; just fine," Spain said. "You'll want to pour on your coal, since your plane leaves at five-fifty, and you get to New York, as I remember, somewhere after ten."

Remo took his pipe down; Moon sought to meet the pale eyes, but there was only the sunglare off the thick glasses. "Uh, your plane tickets you can pick up at your TWA office, and they're paid for. I know this isn't much notice to prime your pump with, but your ball can bounce that way, as I know you understand. Now, I understand your tickets to that, uh, that musical show—they've not arrived?"

"No sir, they ain't."

"Well, there's your bind," Spain said. "But once you get there, you can find a solution; I think I can count on that, and if you have to stay over several days, just feel free, feel free. Now, on your cash situation—"

"There's plenty of money," Remo said. "Mr. Munger, the reason that sign got painted—"

"Uh, the clock has me by the short hairs, if you don't mind. At least, there is the lesson to draw from the ill wind. We can come out like a rose, with everything reasonably hunky, if this caper sharpens you to the hazards you have to watch out for. I hope you'll keep your eye glued throughout this trip."

Remo said, "I'll look out for him."

Moon leaned back against the fence, indefinite on why he felt disappointed. Perhaps he disliked this gratitude in John Remo, this quality of voice which, in a man so harsh, seemed like crawling.

"Uh, you will have to hurry," Spain looked at his watch, and the old cop jerked into action. Like an overloaded truck he chugged for the house.

"Good man," Moon said.

"Uh, yes."

"Are we ready to go to town?"

"Well—if I can hold you a minute more, Moon—we've put the gray matter to your situation, here. And believe me, I hate to ask, considering how imposition on good nature is a thing I try to avoid, generally speaking—but if you've nothing planned for the remainder of the day—?"

Moon stared at him; at the genuine discomfort around the thin mouth, at the complete weariness that seemed to affect even the thin blond hair. He seemed to sense what was coming. You suffer when you give it to me, don't you, Spain? You suffer, but you give it to me, anyway.

"Uh, it's the feeling of the board that your, uh, repair of the damage is the earliest fish to fry, which I know you can see. And anyone outside the family, well—you are getting to be the right arm of your Estate, Moon, and don't think I don't appreciate it, and as for your school-board business, that's a minor bobble down the drain. I want you to know, uh, know how good it is to count on you in the hard pulls—"

"You want me to paint over the barn."

"Uh, I'm tickled you're willing to help. I'm sure a couple of hours will do it, and I'll be glad to drive Bethel home, so you'll have a car when you've finished up. Now, your feasible plan might be to leave your tarp up until after dark, in case of airplanes, and I'm sure you're clear that just some smearing over will fill your bill. The board will want to get a painting contractor later on down the line, or that's my present thinking. . . ."

Moon could see the women waiting at the cars. They watched, perhaps, for the effect of this schooling on a man whose marriage might have been but the mere search for oil. Or perhaps they were curious as to how eagerly he would earn his keep, how humbly he could reach into the toilet for his

278

pennies. Except, Moon was sure, they never thought of such things at all.

"Uh, I appreciate this, Moon," Spain was saying, "and your Cadillac deal has been on my mind, and if you still feel interested there, I hope you'll just drop a bug in my ear—"

"You better go," Moon said.

"Uh, yes." Spain turned away shankily. Beyond him, Bethel waved, then beckoned Moon to her, and he pretended not to see. He tried to imagine her fighting the others on this. But, no; to her, there was no grinding heel, no comedy. It struck him she might even be proud that *her* husband, not one of the others, had been elected to this—what could he call it?— this vital assignment.

Moon went to the house. The Old Place was a thunder of activity. Brother scrambled about, Remo swore roundly through the hole in the wall. Moon went no deeper than the kitchen. He poured the dregs of a stale pot of coffee and sat down with it. He dug at the itch of his hand, as if to assuage his itch of mind.

In one of the rooms, a crash. Remo swore.

"Marryin' Sam, Mister Remo, he's the one I aim to look at; won't he be up there, in New York, Mister Remo?"

"Git that goddamn golf stick out of your suitcase."

"I wasn't aiming to take my goddam golf stick, Mister Remo, except if you don't care none, I just as leave have one, to knock the eggs me an' China found. China, she's a good sonofabitch, huh, Mister Remo?"

"Put in your gray suit. And fold it good."

"Boy, we're really goin', ain't we, Mister Remo? China, she said lookit that Umpire State building on the roof, Mister Remo."

"You're wadding up those shirts, dammit."

"Reckon them coyotes is goin' to eat my chickens agin, Mister Remo?"

Moon took his coffee to the hall. Remo was bent over his bed, assembling, organizing, and packing with surprising neatness.

"What are you doin' here?"

"I," Moon said, "am a barn painter."

Remo straightened, slowly. "The hell you say."

"Yes. The unanimous choice."

"I'm sorry, Moon, sure enough. You oughta boot my rear."

"Boy, Mister Remo, I knowed you was jokin', about booting my ass for me; China, she said it was just joking an' you wasn't ever aiming to boot my ass, Mister Remo."

Remo winced, his great fists clenched, and he was livid. "You said that to *her!*"

Moon laughed.

Remo swore and picked up some change, a watch, his revolver, pocketed them, and drew on his coat. "I guess I have to hustle, Moon. I wish I could help you. You saw the paint, out back, didn't you?"

Moon nodded.

"They's some salami in the icebox. Here, catch." He tossed a ring of keys. "Two's for the house, the others fit the cars. In case you want to take a Cadillac across the pasture."

"I might, at that."

Through the hole, Remo yelled, "Don't put in them overalls, dammit!" He closed his own suitcase, and was ready. "Moon, I guess this is about the first trip I've wanted. My mother, she's in Pennsylvania, which ain't far. If I wasn't on touchy ground, I'd try to finagle something."

"Go ahead, see her. No one will object."

"If I knew what to do with him, I might try it. She don't write very often, and she kind of likes to chew on me once't in a while." He picked up his bag. "Hell, it's past five. Moon, gimme back that shiniest key. Come on, June, let's hit it."

They took the newest Cadillac, and Remo said, "Sorry," and they were gone.

Moon sat down again in the kitchen. After a moment, he caught himself licking a scratch on his palm, and he was revolted by it. But he'd been in thought. No, that wasn't so. He'd tried to think, but his head had filled with odd bits. And these, it seemed, were stagnant. China's tears of compassion for her Beloved. Bethel's earlier tears. Remo, for the first time not a rock but afraid, and crawling. Teddy, entirely uncaring that he had fired her. And buckets and buckets of paint. He sat a half hour, and listened to the quiet until the phone rang.

There were tigers, who devoured the earth now, and lambs to inherit it later: wasn't that how it went?

"Hello."

"Oh, Richard dear, are you about finished? When will you be home?"

"Good Lord, Beth, I haven't even started."

"It'll be late, won't it?"

"It doesn't matter."

"I'm sorry I didn't even think about your dinner. And you missed lunch. The kids and I could bring something out."

"Don't bother. Listen, Beth. Whose idea was this?" He wanted mightily to hear her say she had opposed them.

"There wasn't any other way, Richard. I thought Spain explained. And Frank isn't strong. Sid would have volunteered, I think, but he isn't young, either—"

"Let it go. I asked a stupid question."

"I hope you won't be too late."

"It's a big barn." He asked numbly, "How did the kids make out?"

"Fine. They feel real adult about it. I'll wait and let them tell you."

"They won't."

"Richard," her voice lowered, and softened; it was muffled, even, as if she had cupped her hand around the mouthpiece, and she said, "I wanted you here tonight. I think you know I did."

"I'd rather be there."

"Then I'll wait up for you," she said.

"Don't. I may paint all night."

The wind grew stronger and colder. Moon got the bottle; he drank deeply and unskillfully against the dusk. The Old

Place smelled bad; worse than Cass Street. The fog of Laska's smoke hung about. And in there on the table, Spain had forgotten his big Texas hat.

Moon put a smear of iodine on his jungle rot. Then he got into Bethel's car and drove to town. The lights were on in Teddy Birdsong's apartment.

XVI

When she opened the door, he saw the peculiar baked-on sadness. It lay hardened about her eyes, at the ends of her mouth, and he thought it a part of her top-heaviness. It seemed she should teeter from the cold weight of it. She did no more than lift one surrealist brow. "Well, little friend," she said, "third time is charm."

He shrugged; why should he fume, any more? There were too many mysteries. He said, "I want you to come with me."

He drove her through Amarillo's boisterous Friday nightness. She gazed out at the jalopies, the ducktails and ponytails of the teen-agers who, once weekly, preyed upon every theater and street and drive-in in town, and upon everyone's nerves. Moon smuggled her along no back routes. He drove straight down Polk. As they cleared town, they fell into casual talk. By the time they reached The Old Place, he felt only lightly troubled. He hoped that, like Teddy, he was learning not to regret. At least, not fatally.

They found rye bread. They built three-decker sandwiches of Brother's tough mousetrap cheese and Remo's salami. They sat down in the kitchen to eat out of hand. Crumbs stuck to her garish lips, and he laughed. Their ease, here in the Munger homeplace, interested him. You'd suppose the new atheist, having spat upon the altar, must immediately wrestle with hysteria. But he felt no foreboding. As Teddy said, you rationalize, and work at it, and you get you a thermostat.

She swallowed an enormous bite and said, "I judge I'm being unfired."

"You've got mustard on your chin."

"You looked sort of silly, Moon. Jumping around with all that camera stuff and telling me I was fired."

"Maybe. But I meant it. At the time, I mean."

Her nose shone, the big cheekbones appeared oily already, although she had attended to her mask as they left the apartment. "I would have come to work as usual," she said. "And you'd have kept paying me."

"No, you wouldn't have."

"Don't be so dense. You should know I'm unfirable."

"If I understand what you mean—" He frowned, "I don't like to be clubbed."

"What does it matter? I need this job, at least for a while. After which, Dicky boy, all you millionaires can go to hell."

"Don't call me that."

She laughed. "Christ, I've forgotten my matches."

He lit her cigarette, then his own.

"Did you have Horvath gouged this way?"

"No. He wasn't like you, Mr. Mooney. His was true love. Wait, I'm not ready to fight." She stretched, in the unnecessary way she had, compelling him to look at the crew-necked black jersey. "I've been out to dinner, now I'm ready to work. How the devil do we paint in the dark?"

"Badly, I predict."

"About like we paved the road. Are we ready?"

"No hurry."

She smiled. "Did you bring me out here to paint, or just to help you get the silver spoon out of your throat?"

He said, "I can take you back to town."

"You aren't any fun, are you? Let's paint."

They got up and went through the dining room, where the Munger chairs remained in disarray, and on to the bedrooms. "We can find some work clothes in here."

"You find them. I want to see this place. Everyone hears about it, you know."

From Brother's tumbled closet he took two fresh pairs of the huge bib overalls and a pair of faded blue workshirts. As he laid them out, he heard the sharp hard heels clicking overhead, then down the stairs, and his guess that she would be disappointed pleased him.

He drew on the overalls over his clothing. They hung out slackly around his middle, and reached no lower than his shins. The shirt went on as blousily. When she came in, she winced at sight of him.

"Crumby damned place, isn't it?"

"Here, put these on; they'll save your dress."

She held up the big denims. "Tell me about this June— these are his, aren't they? People say he's half goose and half fox."

"There's the shirt." She stripped off her dress and got into the work clothes. She looked more bundled than dressed. He rolled up the pants legs and the sleeves for her.

"It's drafty," she said. "I'll probably freeze to death."

He found her a heavy khaki jacket with sheepskin collar before they went out.

"I wish we had a light," he said. "That roof is pretty steep. Maybe you better stay on the ground and hand me things."

"No dice. I haven't seen the handiwork."

They stood over a clutter of paint buckets left beside the back stoop. He gathered brushes from a can of kerosene, and studied the buckets in the light from the kitchen.

"Looks like silver or red," he said.

"Red," she said. "It'll wake up the place."

They carried the paint to the barn. Moon climbed the ladder and unfastened the tarp. It skidded of its own accord, snagged once, then dropped off to the ground. "Too dark," she said. "I can't read it."

"It wouldn't shock you much."

"I'm coming up."

"All right. Watch that old ladder. And bring the paint."

The breeze was diminished, as Panhandle winds always wane after dark, but it needled them icily. Moon's hands numbed before he dipped the first brush. He heard her rustling about, somewhere near the center of the roof, and he thought, what if she should fall off?

"God, it's big," she said. "We'll be all night."

"What are you doing over there?"

"Reading," she laughed. "A letter at a time. It's beautiful, the sentiment—"

"Shut up."

"I saw your camera, down there on a fence post. Will it take pictures at night?"

"No," he lied.

She came toward him, moving on all fours, more cautiously than was necessary. "I'm freezing."

"Take a brush. Any brush."

"Moon, I'm really cold." Her voice quavered. "We ought to have a fire. If you made a fire, we could see to paint. If we're really going to."

"We're going to."

He climbed down. Stumbling in the dark, he moved a pile of scrap lumber from behind the barn to the center of the lot. He stacked it high, on the spot where Spain had stood for his quick pale look at calamity. With kerosene, Moon set the pile off. At once Brother's chickens aroused. Orange light came up so quickly he feared he'd overdone it.

"How's that?" he called.

"Not warm. But light enough to see."

Before returning to the roof, Moon got the whisky from the kitchen. She met him at the top of the ladder. "I'm a poor drinker," she said, but she took the bottle at once.

He found a broken shingle, stuck the bottle through it, and they began to paint from opposite ends. The fire seemed to hiss at their backs, yet he could hear the chatter of her teeth.

"Teddy, go back to the house. I can do it."

"No. I want this."

"What does that mean?"

"Dammit, let's paint."

He got a glimpse of her face. Grim, sharp, Indianish in the firelight. Candles always flattered Bethel. But Teddy Birdsong —he did not look at her again.

They smeared and sloshed away, working steadily nearer each other. He slowed with cold, his eyes stung with the wood smoke. He heard the woman's periodic little gasps, the occasional sniffle. Twice he went down to stack more wood on the fire. He kept thinking, Remo must be a liar. Brother could not have done this in a half-hour.

"Where does your wife think you are?"

"She knows where I am."

"And when we've finished, you'll run home and jump right back into her bed and board?"

"Why don't you leave that alone?"

"Give me a cigarette—if I'm not too frozen to smoke it."

He turned, and found them only a yard apart. He supposed an hour or more had passed, and his mind had scarcely turned, as if in a deep freeze of its own.

"You go on down," he said. "I'll paint in the gap."

He began joining their work rapidly, with wide sweeping arcs of the brush. He hurried while she stood beside the fire and almost sadistically shouted up a description of its warmth. He made the last stroke, then one more, and dropped his brush. He put the liquor in his pocket and went down on feet clumsy with cold.

In the kitchen, while coffee perked, they got out of the ruined clothes. She stood against the stove, warmer than he, but not warm. Half nude and spotted with paint, she looked less than tough, he thought. Certainly, less sure. Suddenly, he laughed at her.

She frowned. "You're giving them hell tonight, aren't you?"

"There's paint in your hair."

"Oh, I thought so. Get it out."

Using Remo's fine old straight razor, Moon chopped out a handful of the black bush. For a moment, he held the trimmings in his hand. However coarse it appeared, Teddy's hair felt electrically soft, very worth the touching. . . .

"Well, do you plan putting it into a locket?"

He threw it away and brought back a rag dampened with kerosene. They scrubbed off their spots before he poured the coffee. She sat down to drink; she let him add a bit of whisky. Moon stood at the stove looking down on her. The channel between her breasts narrowed and deepened each time she lifted her cup.

Moon thought, a little inanely, I owe Frank Wallace a million apologies.

Mr. Williams-the-lawyer must have dozed the moment they drove out of Plainston. He rocked loosely in the seat; certainly this good man slept soundly now. Mr. Williams had gone through a long day, and Spain didn't mind that he rested.

The chairman kept his gaze on the highway. His vision was even poorer at night, and he hewed alertly to the centerline; that was your main do-hicky about automobile safety, anyway. It was almost eleven o'clock, with forty minutes more of road. Nevertheless, he thought he might call the board with the news as soon as he got home. Perhaps word of the settlement would add some peace to their rest.

He shifted his legs; they ached. But weariness, he knew, was the fiddler's price. You worked, you tried to cut the mustard. You kept a modest face on your triumphs, because people expected that, and you grinned through ordeals, since people liked that too, and whatever roof fell in on you, then you did still have the reins in your hands. Which, he decided, was something he'd think about again, sometime when he was fresh and could define it more clearly.

He blinked his headlamps and raced around a creeping produce truck. He shivered, not at having discovered the truck so tardily, but in realization that the board might have slipped into any one of several biffles today. Texas, if encouraged, would have gone to court. She and Laska might have voted to fire Mr. Remo. Bethel, to judge from her surprising reaction when she learned of his talk with Moon, would have brought in some blabbermouth painters, no matter what. Even he himself had gone through a short loss of perspective. Only China had been herself—radiantly, gently, turning the rest of them back toward solid middle ground.

Spain believed his sisters would be satisfied. On the negative side, the thousand dollars did amount to almost an hour's production of Munger crude. Besides, at the last moment, your Mrs. Casey had revealed her malignant condition, and there was the plain indication she'd be unable to force her case onto a civil-court docket during her lifetime. Nevertheless, Spain had given her the check. He mistrusted birds in the bush; when amid pitfalls, he preferred to butter his bread on the safe side.

He sighed, and decided to think of the transaction no more. You had to push on, now, toward mopping up your aftermath. He enumerated: your airport people, your shyster lawyer, your friends of the library woman—in jig time, so many could fan the blaze in all directions. The tentacles sprouted, they grew and came at you, and you chopped off where you could, and you hoped you'd missed only a few.

The car topped the last grade to the caprock. Almost home. Spain glanced aside, at the attorney who had been Papa's, and he was suddenly impatient with him. Mr. Williams threatened to snore.

"Uh, Mr. Williams."

"Oh—yes, sir! I might have dropped off—"

"Uh, I wanted to say before we get to town how the directors appreciate your putting your shoulder right to the grindstone today, so to speak."

"I'm just glad if I helped, Mr. Munger. And I'm glad we were successful. That is, if it seems to you we were."

"Uh, yes. But, uh, just to flick about and see what we catch— what would you say about your public-relations position? Just as a projection, more or less?"

"Well—I can't see we're badly hurt."

"I'd be the last to get on the brink just over your malicious rumor, Mr. Williams, and I'm sure you'd be the first to stamp your amen on that. Uh, what I really meant, I meant if we've got some sweeping under the rug to put our heads to, then I'd appreciate whatever thoughts you have in hand about that. You know you can feel free, feel free. . . ."

"Why do you say, 'a cowboy is a cowboy'?"

Moon laughed; the liquor had thawed him, then heated him; he felt he'd never been so nearly drunk. "Because you and I painted the barn."

She lay on Cecil Munger's couch, languidly, almost sullen. More sad, now, than hard.

"Daddy was educated," she said, "down to a fine edge of ignorance."

He kept laughing; it seemed riotous, the joke on Remo, for they'd found his reserve supply. Two bottles, hidden high atop a rafter in the barn.

"Teddy, how come every time you say something worth thinking about, you tell me it's something your old man said? That's a lie, isn't it?"

"Go to hell."

"I want to go to bed."

"Go on. But take me to town first."

"What do you mean?"

"You know what."

"You want what I want. Or you wouldn't have come out with me. You didn't have to come out."

He bent toward her, and she pushed him away. "I've drunk too much. Leave me alone. It feels rotten."

"There's more coffee."

"Oh God, not that kind of rotten. Take me home."

If mistily, he did see something new, spreading beneath the cold-hard-sorrow of her, and he shook his head. Shook his mane, that should be, and he snorted himself a snort, and crouched for his charge. He heard his whisky laughing, be-

290

cause he was wild and free; now and in this place. Still, that look of her. . . .

Well, put your gray matter to your giz, boy, and in a minute she'll be hunky. Now, what would your veteran lecher do? That's Frank, come to think of it. All right. What would old Frank do, if he stood here, in your shoes—new shoes, it happened, spoiled with red paint. Frank the pharmacist, the old faker who, despite all his filthy pictures and warm beer and cruddy stories, may never have claimed any woman at all, aside from China. And oh, goddamn that Frank; China was pregnant and so lovely, even Remo loved China, that dumb Polack did. But well, if old Frank had a woman, and she said, "Take me home," wouldn't Frank just offer her another drink?

"Boy," he said, and he found her glass and handed it to her. "Here, fix your thermostat; that's your bone to chew on!"

"Leave me alone."

The odd look, as if she'd lost all the make-up. "Teddy—"

"Get your hand off of me!" She screamed it.

"You don't even know I can get mad," he said—

She struck him across the mouth. He stood over the couch, peering down at her. She twisted away. She snatched the afghan over her nakedness, and hid herself against the leather.

He blinked. So much to drink, when he never drank—how could he know what he'd seen? Still, it had seemed a transformation. Hadn't her cheekbones been smaller and less rouged, weren't the brown eyes moist and unglinting? He hated that they'd drunk at all. He wished he might think. If he might have a good look—

He caught a bare shoulder and wrenched her over. She struck at him, and he intercepted her arm. He looked at her face. Not squawish, nor bitter; not anything. She was someone gone down all the long dusty roads, and no one he knew. He retreated, growing desperately sober. He saw her slide slowly to the floor. She drew her knees beneath her; her cheek lay against the carpet, and she cried through closed eyes.

"Teddy, get up. I'll take you home."

"Oh, Holy Jesus. . . ."

He wanted to run from her. He understood now why she never wanted to drink, why there was always both evil and sorrow about her. Had she been born with her conscience in reverse; were her inhibitions on backward? Did these forbid her all talent for love and faith? If it were so, if then she drank the dark inhibition away, couldn't normal conscience suddenly arrive to lash her with its thousand accumulated whips; mighn't it be torturing her now with a total, undeserved agony?

The hypothesis of a soul created left-handedly chilled him. Then he refused it; he would not believe in monsters. Instead, he tried to recall her inky-panks, her betrayed husband dead beneath a jeep, the ovals and push-pulls—all the symptoms that might be clinically explainable. To blame these was suddenly vital. Nothing was so necessary as to affirm for himself that she, and all others, originally had a choice.

He rubbed his eyes to clear the mists. Still Teddy Birdsong looked the same, and he wanted to cry out because the judgment upon her was so awful-cruel-foul-stinking-rotten. She lay moaning, her being an animate tragedy.

"Oh Jesus, come to me," she whispered. "Come to me."

Moon went to her. "Billie, I'll help you. Let me take you home."

At this name she reserved for herself—maybe, he thought, for the self she was now—she raised blindly toward him. He lifted her, he began dressing her. A piece of his mind sought to intercede for her. He urged it on; pray long and well.

He carried her outside to the car. She was limp and heavy against him. As he put her into the seat, it struck him he'd not felt her breathing. He seized her face in his hands. Then he said, "Thank God," for she was warm and asleep.

XVII

On into late April, the Golden Spread put up with being dry. A real pistol of a season, Old Cecil Munger would have called it, had he been alive. Already the newspapers recounted that seventy per cent of the wheat lay in abandonment; that the salvation, if there was to be one, depended upon rains for the row crops of sorghum being dusted in atop the dead wheat. Even Amarillo, its prosperity still unaffected, talked less tongue-in-cheekly of the disaster.

On the ranches, the stubborn grasses thinned rapidly while showing a brief effrontery of green before parching away to dusty gold. Whole herds were unloaded on a frightened market, and beef became cheap, then cheaper, although you'd not have known it when you toured a supermarket. A few of the cattlemen who mined neither gas nor oil became less frequent around the Downtown Club. Perhaps it disturbed them that, in such a time, the body of governors had thoughtlessly raised the menu price of sirloins by two dollars. They intended no offense; it was just that all the governors, except one, were in oil.

For the Mungers, there passed a time of peace. The star

chambers dealt with little that seemed crucial. China suffered one severe and violent siege of nausea, but it passed just as a neighbor started to summon help, and she got right out of bed laughing and clapping her hands because for the first time, she had felt her child move. The family heard of this in detail; they teased China over her surprisingly old-fashioned ideas on child-bearing, and they accused her jokingly, yet with traces of concern, of avoiding a doctor out of a modesty that might lead her, instead, to a midwife. The Glasses spent a full week at San Antonio, and although Laska did not propose it, she obviously believed the Peacock school had reconstituted Sid Junior into such stability, already, that he might as well come home. Texas won a-whole-year's-supply for placing seven-teenth in nationwide competition to christen a new detergent, and a pretty good paragraph about it appeared in the morning paper. She was quoted as saying, "Of course I'm very thrilled."

More relevant to the big picture was the accolade for Spain. His twelve years of Chamber of Commerce membership, most of it spent at the small drudgery of the minor committees, suddenly dividended. He became a director. In elation, and after a quick telephone canvass of your board, he volunteered The Old Girl as a gratis part-time clerk for the Chamber and he gave her a twenty-dollar raise. Bethel endured a particularly critical Mean Week, then began again to exhaust her husband with love.

Frank Wallace yawned. "Sleepy day," he said.

They sat in Frank's office, which Moon supposed was, in its way, a world, and they drank coffee by way of pursuing their joint career. Moon listened for whatever sound Teddy Bird-song might make up front.

Last night, Reserve night, he had taken her to the smallest, dreariest highway café he knew. It was late; at the door a boy was barking the next day's paper. The bare head, the small dirty face, had caused Moon to pause. Perhaps it was because he'd driven out by way of Cass Street. But he worried that the boy had no coat, that his lips had blued with cold.

Moon paid a dollar for a paper while Teddy pulled at his elbow. He resisted her, to watch the boy walk away toward a brightly lighted truck stop a vacant block distant. Teddy Birdsong said, "Stop staring at the boy."

"I can't. It's a damn shame."

"Why do you say that?"

He peered down at her, at the false face and false iron veneer, hoping to see what he at last knew to be underneath. "Doesn't he strike you as—as a shame?"

"Oh Christ, Moon. You mean desolate little street waif and all that? Sure, but why pity him?"

He shrugged. "Skip it."

She spoke with sudden heat. "Who do you think you are, pitying people? You're the one who keeps preaching to me about the beauty of our system and all that. If you believe what you say—that boy is, right now, what all our wonderful self-made men claim they used to be. My God, you ought to be envying him. He's self-making himself, isn't he? He's on his way to greatness!"

He thought, I hate her; she wants to be hated.

She laughed. "If he doesn't grow up to make his million, he can marry it. Come on in, I'm freezing."

"Teddy, I'm getting a little sick of—"

"Don't be so damned pure. And turn me loose; I'm going inside."

They ordered hamburgers from a pimply waitress who never stopped clucking her tongue in time to the whangy, jukebox music. He kept glaring across at Teddy, thinking how good, at this moment, it would be to hit her; how with his fist, he might put something new into their lives. She lit two cigarettes and handed him one of them. "Isn't this sweet of me?" she said.

"Teddy, do you have to keep ruining everything?"

"Oh, don't be a fud."

"Or an inky-pank?"

"Yes, by God. Lately you act like a missionary, or something. You're getting what you want from me. Let it go at that."

He looked away from her. At such times, he felt the cheapest.

He thought of Bethel, and unless he could grasp as well a quick vision of Spain Munger, the guilt would make him sick.

"Besides," Teddy was saying, "I don't know what we're arguing about." She laughed. "Why Moon—maybe you're in love with me! The standard male must always remake the female he wants, isn't that true? Have you begun jacking me up to your level?"

"I was only talking about that kid."

"All right. But be consistent."

"I am consistent."

She loved provoking him. "Really? Why, just the other night you gave me all that stuff about enjoying moments. Pursuit of happiness tips; getting the good feel and good smell and good taste out of each second."

"That has nothing to do with this."

"Yes, it does. That kid is a moment; enjoy him. That's exactly what I'm doing. 'Teddy,' I am saying, 'isn't it nice to be better off than that alley rat?' "

"That's the meanest thing you could have said."

"Oh, how much do you know? The boy may be getting his kicks out of underprivilege. There you are—maybe he's got your talent for this moment-by-moment pleasure."

Moon stood up. "Let's get out of here."

She shook the black bush of hair. "Not until I've had my hamburger."

Moon had sat watching her eat, unable to fear or detest her quite enough. If he could blot out that evening at The Old Place. . . . Since then, it seemed he must forgive everything, however she put or did it, else he would have become no one at all. . . .

Frank said, "You know anything about the board meeting? I mean, besides the party business?"

"That's all of it, I guess."

"Moon, there's less than a month left."

"You never forget it, do you?"

Frank scratched his stomach where perhaps it was burning, and he said, "Don't tell me you and Sid don't care."

"What will you do, Frank, if it happens?"

Behind the tinted glasses, Frank's eyes closed; it struck Moon he must look like a very old man when he slept.

"I'll kiss you good-by, buddy. This town won't ever see me again. I'll catch half the trout in New Mexico."

"I keep thinking we may never see the day, Frank. What can they gain, if they don't need independence from each other? As it is, they may be getting what they're after."

"Maybe—"

"Haven't you seen Spain lately? He's riding on air."

"Okay. But at least, without the old man's strings—well, what if you and Sid and I got together?"

Moon laughed.

But Frank persisted. "Oh, crap, Moon. We just have to agree, for once, and stick to it."

Moon studied the serious, unnoteworthy face of this senior Munger-in-law. He said, "What do you hear about the party?"

"You really mean it, Beth? Cornbread and beans?"

"Of course. There'll be so many to feed. And Spain says that since we've no precedents of our own, we should walk lightly. Besides, novel parties are stylish these days." She patted his hand. "Poor Richard; we've gone so few places you don't even know what people are doing. The Adamses gave a hot-dog dance—Texas says they had champagne, too, but then, they are drinkers, I'm afraid. And there's been this whole rash of chili suppers; you know, after symphony and Little Theater. So, if we have red beans, as a sort of a theme of this awful drouth—don't worry, not just beans by themselves. We'll have chow-chow and onion and things. Everyone will be delighted, won't they, dear?"

Moon was dumfounded. He couldn't envision the Downtown Club's whisky drinkers and lobster eaters gathering about a bean pot and a jar of buttermilk, not even if the beans were

Boston. Still, he recognized in the idea the loyalty to the picture, the plan. A social event in neat harmony with the pattern, austere rather than miserly, all whetted down to sufficiency and purpose. He refrained from expressing an opinion.

Bethel took up her pink kitchen notepad and began checking off her list of reminders. "China is seeing to this, and let's see, isn't Laska telephoning about that? Oh, Richard, before you get away—there are a few things I'd like you to do, if you will. . . ."

The board gathered daily, for a week, in the great red chamber. Uh, if you meant to poke your spearhead into your world of society, well, the prudent consideration was to guard against the big splash. If first you bore at the top of your mind that your flopper was the sleeping dog to watch, then you could begin thinking of success. Now, you couldn't invite everyone in town, yet you needed to keep a peeled eye toward those left out. Your social venture is only the stepchild of your business venture, and if you latch onto your party with your business mind, then the whole blow-out is a lead-pipe cinch to jell.

The women loved it. Alternately, Bethel became exuberant and distraught; it startled Moon what an added dimension this gave her. She looked to him for advice, she grew more interesting, and despite himself he found he was taking a positive attitude toward this first Munger party.

Automatically, the Glass house won designation as the site. It had size, it admitted to the Munger resources, it stood in the only impressive neighborhood. But the lawn was far from large enough. Swiftly, the board of Big Plains Investment Corporation moved to negotiate for and buy, at $6,500, the weedy, unlevel vacant lot next door. Then Big Plains took bids on fencing the new property, and awarded a contract on a rush basis. Harry and the new mower were sent to clear the tumbleweeds and create a garden, or the illusion of one, in just six days.

"Bethel, you'll have to offer liquor."

"You know we couldn't do that. If we laid aside a basic principle, just to cater to a handful of drunkards—"

"They aren't drunkards. It's just that at parties, a lot of these people expect a drink."

"Oh, don't worry, dear. We'll have everything they could decently want."

Harry managed only to skin the new lot bare; the new chain link fence gave the whole the appearance of a cage filled with dust. The board ordered two truckloads of sawdust to serve in lieu of grass, and a carpenter was hired to build a dance floor of pine planking. Laska went into bargaining with several hillbilly bands, among them Red Wines and His Castro County Cavaliers, Billy Samples and His Texas Plainsmen, and Ernie Favors and The Gila Canyon Boys. Then, almost as a deal was closed with Red Wines, she switched, with committee endorsement, to Jelly Watson and His Prairie Ramblers because Jelly, for twenty-five dollars extra, could supply an expert square-dance caller, one willing to cancel another engagement only because Mr. Watson had married his sister. Further, The Ramblers furnished their own PA system.

Together, usually in the Mooney kitchen, China and Bethel worked on the list for invitations. Spain furnished a cross-section list of the Downtown Club, in addition to the names of the Chamber directors, the Democratic and Republican precinct chairmen, and a representative listing of important Estate employees. From Texas came the names of the symphony board, the Federated Women, and a careful selection from Amarillo's banking and merchantry. China brought in certain church deacons and the good sideburned preacher, Reverend McLean. Laska prepared the out-of-town list, which included, principally, the management families on the Munger ranches. The aggregate reached more than three hundred. Once it was calculated, Spain dispatched Harry to buy a hundred-fifty pounds of beans.

"My God," Teddy Birdsong said, "inky-pank music, isn't it?"

Moon frowned at her. "Where do you hear such things?"

"From your partner. Once in a while, he speaks to me. When he's angry, or has heard a dirty story."

"Teddy, you are getting an invitation."

"Good! Have I arrived?"

"There's nothing special about it. Most of the employees are being asked."

"Along with the upper-crust? Jesus, what a mixture."

"Teddy—I'd rather you didn't come."

"I hear the Munger ladies are having refresher courses at Arthur Murray's."

"That's a lie."

"Don't blame me," Teddy Birdsong laughed. "I only heard it, that's all."

One evening, mild and warm, the board inspected the party grounds. The dance floor, created hastily by laying two-by-fours and sheeting them with boxing plank, sloped curiously; perhaps dangerously, Spain feared. But such was the configuration of the lot. A score of redwood picnic tables were arranged around it; electric wires had been strung on temporary poles and already, naked bulbs hung in place. The lights set off speculation on the bug problem; a careful measurement of table space resulted in the discovery that the beans must be eaten "in shifts."

"Now, uh, Harry—."

"Yes, sir!"

"Uh, I know you have your menu rigged to the gills, already, and that's fine, that's fine. But, uh, there's a little trick, for your beans, and I'd appreciate it if you'd remember it. Now, if when they're about cooked, you'll treat them with your baking soda, you'll make your dish more agreeable, and I'm sure you'd planned to do that, but I thought I'd call your attention, just in case."

"Yes, sir."

Harry had risen, for the occasion, to the glory of executive capacity. In addition to Carrie, he had a half-dozen of his preferred friends from The Flats to help cook and serve, and for all of them, the board had rented white jackets. Harry was happy, but he did try, through Moon, to suggest an enlargement of the food plan. "Fried chicken on the side, that'd be good. If I put it to Mr. Spain, since he loves the heads to crack, do you think—?"

"No."

Harry had a thirty-foot serving table of redwood—"Uh, redwood runs you four cents a foot cheaper than pine," Spain had discovered—from which to dispense the Munger hospitality. The table was piped with gas, so that cooking in the great aluminum pots found at the Army Surplus Store could be accomplished on the spot. Frank, on commission from China, had found even a large baking oven which, mounted on bricks, promised to make the cornbread preparation equally convenient.

Bethel said, "Richard, maybe we should have considered a catering service, just to make sure."

"Harry knows what to do. Here, let me help you lick those stamps."

On the Tuesday afternoon before the Saturday of the party, Spain called The Camera House, sounding tired but assured, as though matters were beautifully in hand.

"Uh, I hesitate to impose, Moon, except everyone does seem tied up, and I appreciate how we can depend on you when your old clutch goes to slipping. The fact is, June got word of the party and, uh, insisted on attending. The blunder was, your Mr. Remo allowed him to phone China, which I think happens after almost every trip—well, to shorten things, I wonder if you could drive out there?"

"He wouldn't listen to me."

"Uh, that part is all settled, I'm glad to say. We're letting him take another little trip, out to Los Angeles. I was thinking, uh, they'll need some money, and no one is free to shake loose and take it out. Now, of course if you've got any irons in the stove—?"

"I can go."

"Good, good. If you'll stop by, Miss Northington will have the envelope. And, uh, by the bye, Mr. Remo has his instructions, but I'd appreciate it if you'd emphasize that he may as well get off today. You're sure, now, that this won't throw a kink?"

Frank stood by, grinning, until Moon hung up. "Messenger service?" he said.

Moon nodded.

"You don't look sore."

"I'm not; I wanted to see Remo anyway. He wasn't asked to the party, and everyone else was."

"That old bastard. How much money are they sending him?"

"Spain didn't say. But you can afford it."

He started the old Chevvy, which thundered because its muffler had rusted out, stopped off for the envelope, and then drove out to The Old Place. Brother's balloon form was out front; he used a chrome-shafted club to drive rocks toward the road, one of which struck the roof of Moon's car.

Remo appeared from the house as Moon parked.

Brother said, "China an' all them, ain't they coming?"

"Not today." The sleek new Cadillac had been pulled around to the front porch, and its trunk lid was propped up. A set of effeminate blond leather bags sat ready on the porch.

"Hi, Moon," Remo said. "Lookit him, dammit."

"What's that on his clothes?" Brother wore shiny summer-weight slacks, these girt low below his paunch, and a brightly flowered sport shirt, both already spotted with grease.

"Cat food," Remo said. "He's strung it out all over the place, so's that cat won't git hungry. Hell, there goes a whole case of the stuff, and the coyotes will come get it, quick as we're gone."

"You sound vitriolic," Moon grinned. "Has it been rough?"

"You don't know the half." The old cop stared out at the sloven, sweaty figure of the happiest Munger who, now, was almost forlorn in a hushed "Jesus Loves Me." "You watch yourself," Remo yelled. "Moon, they oughtn't to have told him about that party. Come on, I got coffee."

As they entered the house, Moon noticed a scatter of new holes cut in the front wall. Remo snorted, "Pretty quick we'll be living in a basket. I told Spain that, too. He says let 'im bore."

They walked on through, back to the kitchen. Suddenly the coarse face broke into a grin. "You done a lousy job on the barn."

"Didn't I? It was a cold night."

Remo put cups on the table. "Thing that I wondered about was them two pairs of dirty overalls. And my whisky being missin'."

"You sound like a policeman."

"I ain't pryin'; I was just curious. The way one pair of them overalls was rolled up so short. Look," Remo closed his great hands together, and he gazed solemnly through the mismated eyes, "if you're in some kind of a switch, Moon—well, me, I can lean about any which way for a friend."

Nothing so close to a statement of affection had ever escaped this crude hulk of a man. Moon thought, I could get along well in a world of John Remo's, a world where guise and cunning and fluctuating lines didn't exist. He said, "You got a long drive, John. But I wish I were going with you."

"Why don't you? If I told Spain that ole Brother hankered for you to come along—"

Moon shook his head. "I'd rather have gone to New York with you. I've never seen a Broadway show."

"Hell, there's where you ain't missed a thing. Nothin' to them, outside of stuff you can't swaller. Like when a boy and girl starts making love, an' about the time it gets good, one of 'em busts out singing. They'll stand there face to face and sing real loud, right up each other's nose. You ever see courting like that? When I'm watchin', I have to scrounge down in the seat, like I wasn't there. You ever get that way? Where you get so embarrassed for the actors, on account of they ain't embarrassed at all?"

Moon laughed. "Don't be a realist, or you'll miss all the fun. In art, you have to make a few surrenders."

"Art," Remo grunted. "Let me tell you, when I first commenced on the force, I got a city park beat and in the summer I had to go around shaking the kids out of the bushes. Rattle a couple of 'em out of one hedge, and right off I'd ketch the

303

same two in another one. Anyway, I seen plenty of the kind of art we're talking about, and I never seen a one of 'em break out singing to the other."

Brother's spherical face appeared at the back screen. "Ain't we ready to leave, pretty soon, Mister Remo? China, she says hurry up, and take time to see them birds, Mister Remo!"

"You go put them satchels in the car."

Moon looked questioningly at John Remo, and the gray head nodded. "Yeah, *she* called up, to talk 'im into going. Told him we'd go to the San Diego zoo, where they got a big cage of birds."

"Mister Remo, you don't aim to stick me in the jailhouse this time, do you aim to, Mister Remo?"

Remo shouted, "Go on, put the bags in the car."

"What did that mean?" Moon said.

Remo reddened and swallowed some coffee. He lowered the cup and said, "I did put the ox in jail for a while. Up in New York."

"Good Lord, Remo. After all this mess about the barn—have you lost your mind?"

"My mother's town is just a little ways out of Philadelphia, and I got to thinking about it. I fixed it to keep him taken care of while I ran up there a little spell, that's all. It wasn't nothing; they didn't put his name in the book, or anything. I guess it was a dumb stunt, huh?"

"Did you see your mother?"

"She wasn't home. I figured I better not wait, on account of I did leave Brother in the pokey. I guess I ought to of waited; she's pretty lonesome up yonder, an' she don't have any more blood kin. But one thing, Moon. I bought my own train ticket up to Philadelphia. And the little dab I left in her mailbox, that was my own money, too."

Brother yelled, "Mister Remo—!"

Moon followed him around as he made The Old Place secure. Last, he unplugged the TV, against the spring's crashing electrical storms, and closed the front door.

"Sorry to rush you, Moon. But if I fool around, until he gets to thinking about that party—by the way, is it really going to be a bean deal?"

"It really is."

"I'll be damned. Well," Remo put out a big hand, "I'll see you."

"Have a good trip."

"Hell, I won't. For a little while, I'd just like to stay home and fight the cockroaches."

Not until the party Saturday did the great error become apparent. It struck the Mungers through the women; first Bethel, then China, as they began considering how to dress. Moon had only reached The Camera House when Bethel called, almost in tears, and begged him to come on home. "What will I do; it's my fault," she quavered.

"Call the others," he said, "and I suggest you agree on something. Don't worry."

When he entered the house, she had indeed called the others. It appeared a board meeting progressed, tensely, in his living room. Spain sat in Moon's lounge chair; his bony hands held one of the invitations, and the pale gaze held fixedly to it.

Moon said, "Pardon me," as if this weren't his home, and no one responded.

Moon looked about him. Texas and Laska sat on the divan, pale and looking thunderstruck. Bethel, in the chair opposite, held Amy Vanderbilt's *Complete Book of Etiquette: A Guide to Gracious Living* on her knees; her finger ran up and down the indexes. Only China looked at peace. Her lovely face smiled to all of them; Moon thought that she might actually be amused.

"Blame me," Bethel said, "I was chairman for invitations. I don't know what I was thinking of."

"Uh, your nut, here, is not to lay responsibility, although this is the sort of, uh, oversight that your planning should have scotched against, but rather, to speak bluntly, it's to decide just what britches to put on. . . ."

Moon left without excusing himself; he thought not even

305

Bethel saw him go. On the way back to town, he reveled a little in the mishap, if for no other reason than that the gathering of the clan made it theirs, not his.

The invitations, with message printed within the outline of a bean, had given no indication of dress. In Amarillo's immature society, hosts were expected to say "formal," or "informal," or they said "semi-formal," a vague misnomer that was taken to mean something in between. As it was, each guest faced independent choice on what seemed the proper dress for cornbread and beans, and each must risk conspicuousness. Shortly after lunch, Moon and Frank heard the decision.

Uh, you did have a lot of hosts, and you could strike a homogeneity. Couldn't it be handled so every guest, whatever he wore, would find himself in keeping with a host; wasn't that your ticket?

Frank and China drew casual wear. Sid and Laska would appear in the rustics of their square-dance club, since there might be, to some, a definite suggestion of Western dress in the wording of the invitations. Spain and Selma would appear as if ready for church. And the Mooneys would go formal; Richard did look very dashing in his tux.

Moon thought his assignment preposterous. Top hat and tails on a vacant lot. God save the Munger Estate, boy, and pity the lesser appendages!

He felt certain he would hear of his tuxedo forever, wherever good fellows gathered. Frank began it; Frank was so maliciously delighted.

A block from Laska's, Moon heard the whomp and scream of the music through the car window. "Lord, what's that noise?" he said.

"Richard, please don't be that way. That's Mr. Watson and the Prairie Ramblers. And they're very good, really. It'll be a nice party, and I hope you'll change your mood."

"Oh, man," Carol said from the back seat, "we'll wake up all the neighbors!"

"Laska's neighbors are among the guests," Bethel said shortly. "And if you want to stay, young lady, mind your manners."

Moon hadn't known, until the last moment, that the children were coming. Even Spain's trio of small ones. They were to be fed early, then stored inside the house where, through the windows they might watch the party and listen to the music.

As they parked, the Ramblers abruptly upped their volume; guitars and more guitars, bottomed by a heavy drum, came chording through a potent speaker system. Moon thought of Teddy Birdsong; surely this should turn her back at the gates.

"The caller came all the way from Portales," Bethel said. "They say he's awfully good. People just love to square-dance, I think."

Spain greeted them on the concrete driveway, kissing Bethel's forehead, then shaking Moon's hand as if he were the honored guest. They were the last of the family to arrive, he said; it appeared the guests would be stylishly late, the food smelled delicious to your nose, and all was well. Still, Spain's pale brow had set inflexibly, and he folded the long arms across his back as he led them onto the lot.

Unluckily, an almost chill breeze had risen, after an entire week of summery evenings, and it knocked up small puffs of sand and a great deal of sawdust. Nevertheless, the place looked, Moon thought, remarkably festive. At the last moment, someone—probably Laska—had covered the lights with paper bucket shades, and rows of chairs had been added around the fringe of the markedly sloping dance floor. On the bandstand, Jelly and the Ramblers glittered in sequined Western finery, and the fat fellow himself had begun, already, to grin professionally at everybody.

A handful of guests stood about, waiting, as Sim Vermillion put it, for "a chow line to form," and they watched, in amazement or awe, the further warm-up practices of the Prairie Ramblers. Sim shook hands with Moon. "Glad to see you," he said. "I was beginning to think I'd be the only dinner jacket."

Moon moved away, toward Harry's ready buffet. Three ten-gallon pots steamed over the gas jets; between them lay mountains of corn sticks and corn muffins. At either end were the platters of sliced raw onion and wooden bowls heaped with a green relish. China Wallace stood with Harry, laughing, tiptoeing up to smell at the lip of one of the great beanpots.

She was altogether beautiful. Moon paused to appreciate her. He had thought her beyond enhancement, yet pending motherhood had clearly added a breathtaking quality. The sweetness that lay in her face now throbbed there, poignant and dramatic. Her collarless blue cord dress swept outward from shoulders to a hooped skirt, and the effect was almost perfectly conical. Close around the slender pale throat lay a sparkling chain necklace and a jeweled comb was just back of her ear and twinkling against her hair. When Moon reached her, she stretched up to kiss his cheek, and the skirt hoop bumped against his shins.

"Where are all the customers?" he said.

"Late, I'm afraid."

"There aren't many—"

"Eighteen, so far."

Moon looked about at them. Mr. Jacobson-the-auditor, and his restless little wife; Mr. Williams-the-lawyer and Mr. Williams-the-engineer, each with spouse; beyond them, alone, The Old Girl, and standing aside from her with arms folded and lips pursed against the apparent prospect of dancing, the Reverend Mr. McLean, who in some detail Moon couldn't identify created the impression of a stern and graying Elvis Presley.

At least, the payroll had checked in on schedule; there was Martin, from the mammoth New Mexico spread four hundred miles away, and Moon thought he recognized, also, the Garrett brothers who ran the Double O in Colorado. The rest were in a close group with Sid Glass. These, the Amarilloans.

Moon said, "I don't know, China. It's past eight o'clock."

"Good evening," Jelly Watson bellowed, so that the PA shrieked with feedback, "grab your gals and let's go! Nothing stirs up an appetite like a good country hoedown."

Moon flinched, just avoiding a grimace as the Ramblers attacked their instruments. The output was deafening. Immediately the bandsmen became identical, even though two wore full beards. Each man leered with joy; each set off a boot into a lively stomp; each kerchiefed throat was aroused by the irresistible beat to issue its shrill rebel yell.

Jelly motioned to the listeners and shouted. No one advanced upon the canted floor.

Moon smoked and watched; he didn't notice just when China slipped away. People coughed on the sawdust. A few new guests arrived, paused at the gate, stared, came in and shook hands with Spain and Laska, then withdrew to remote corners until they might get away. Texas tried to stimulate a line before the food. People allowed themselves to be served, then walked away uncertainly, trying not to look down at the tin plates afloat with red beans.

Moon's throat began to hurt.

He sat down with Sim and Mary Vermillion and began to eat forcefully.

"My stars," Mary said, "somebody didn't salt the beans."

Moon groaned inwardly. He remembered how conscientiously the Mungers now monitored China's diet; they wanted no recurrence of her old salt attacks during this delicate time.

Oh, in God's name—

The supermarket Anholtzes appeared at the gate, wearing their banquet dress. Over Sim's shoulder, Moon saw Tootie Anholtz blanch and freeze before, in sudden rage, she turned and pulled her husband back into the dark.

For an hour, it continued. People came, others went. Jelly Watson developed great sweat rings under the sleeves of his fancy orange shirt; his fat chins dripped as he began to browbeat dancers to the floor. Someone said, "What's this; are they vegetarian, or something?," and the brash young son of the county judge inquired of his date, "Is that a bottle of catsup, there, or is it red corn liquor?"

Harry appeared at Moon's elbow. "Where is Mr. Spain at, can you say, sir? They ain't eating the beans!" Behind him came Bethel, a tower of pale anxiety, and she tried to smile. "Dear, everyone is having a nice time, don't you think?"

He squeezed her hand. And to reassure her, he ate, immediately, a great chunk of ham just discovered in the beans.

Moon did not see Teddy Birdsong until she sat down beside him. "Balls of fire," she said, "what a hassle!"

He gave her a cold look. "Have you eaten?"

"I've managed not to, so far." She turned her hard brown look to the clash and whang of the Ramblers, and she shouted at his ear, "Inky-panks, Mr. Mooney. You shouldn't have gone to all the bother!"

It's not quite a fiasco, Moon thought. Not a riot, and no one will call the police.

In less than ninety minutes, Amarillo society had presented its advance guard and this had had its look, had strained its manners, and was gone. Only the nervous, obliged people remained, and for these, the music ground on. Out on the floor Mr. Williams-the-lawyer attempted to polka with The Old Girl in his arms, and over her shoulder he glared at those of fainter heart.

Moon retreated with Sid to a darker table, and they sat with coffee and cigarettes. "What happened, Sid?"

"I don't know. Maybe liquor would have helped."

"Where are they, in the house?"

Sid nodded. "They're all in the kitchen. I feel sorry for them."

Moon gazed in envy at this inexpressive little man who, in such infrequent committals as this, only gained in dignity and the clean air of peace. "I don't know what I expected, Sid. But I'm sorry too."

A strand of gray hair had fallen down over Sid's forehead; he rested his weight on one forearm and with the other hand he kept lifting his cup, turning it, and setting it down again. He said, "It'll kill Laska. This is her house. And Spain, all of them—"

"Wait, Sid."

A young woman came toward them. She hesitated a few

310

feet away, then smiled and came on. She introduced herself as the society reporter by showing them her invitation. "I must get all the names right," she said. "If you'd not mind spelling out every one of the host group, I'd be grateful."

Quickly Sid said, "Glass, G-L-A-S-S. I'm the only one; Dr. Sidney Glass."

The girl looked at him warily, then smiled. "Thank you. I have to go now. I had a lovely time."

Moon frowned incredulously at this suddenly larger, suddenly handsomer man. Sid Glass, so trodden upon that even his marriage bed could be put on timetable and his son exiled by action of the board, could now elect himself as whipping boy and do it without pause for thought. Moon wondered if this unheard, unseen little man simply lacked all memory of wrong, and at once he knew better. You only covet the knack, the trick of it; you wonder how he brought it off, what detail of mind or heart opened the channel. Moon felt childish and inferior. Something good had happened, and he'd had no part in it.

He started to speak, and found he could say nothing.

Sid stood up. "I went in, a while ago. Spain asked that you and I kill it, whenever we can. Is now all right?"

"Yes."

"He sent out a check, for the musicians. I'll tend to them, if you'll see about Harry's crew, and the guests."

They parted, and Moon went across to the steaming kettles. Harry stood behind them, a ladle in his hand, his dark wine eyes dull with misery. Moon smiled at him. "That's all, Harry. Do you have an idea, about disposing of the food?"

"No sir." He looked about, as if to spy in the relish or onions the cause of failure. "Nothin', unless I throw me a late party somewhere in The Flats."

"Do that. Take the truck, and tell the boys they'll all be paid tomorrow. And thank you, Harry."

He crossed the lot, to the last cluster of guests. It might have been any meeting, in any place, for the elite of the Munger employees. The lesser ones, like Teddy Birdsong, were gone. He drew The Old Girl aside.

"We may as well call it a night. If they see you leave, Miss Northington, they'll know it's all right to go. Do you mind?"

She nodded. Her loyalty, always so earnestly ready on the sturdy plain face, burst up at him. "I'm pleased you asked me," she said. "If I may inquire, is—is Mr. Munger all right?"

"I haven't seen him. Thank you, and good night."

Sid and Moon stood together, hearing the automobiles start and move slowly, respectfully away; watching the Prairie Ramblers assemble paraphernalia which they packed into trunks, each to be inspected by Mr. Jelly Watson before its sealing.

"I haven't seen Frank."

"He got away, home, early. His stomach."

From the house, they heard the run and romp of the children. These, the future of the big picture, remained unaware of what, tonight, seemed to have happened to it.

The bass fiddle left last, and they stood alone on the party ground. Sid said, "Looks like a carnival that's just moved," and Moon shut off the lights.

They walked together around to the rear door and let themselves into the house. All the blond heads sat in half-circle around Laska's nook table. A few half-drunk Cokes were before them. Children's feet and voices made happy noise beyond, in the den. Moon's gaze sought out Bethel. She had been crying.

Moon said, "Everybody's gone."

It wasn't yet ten o'clock.

Something in the den tumbled over with a crash. Moon saw Spain's body twitch. His chair lurched, and his tight high voice exploded through his hands: "Goddamn, Mom, can't you tone them little snotboxes down!"

Distantly, through the ugly ice of shock, Moon heard Selma Munger's wounded whisper pleading with the children. In the kitchen, nothing moved. The president's words seemed visible on the table.

Moon looked at Bethel's bent head. Sid will know what to do, he kept thinking; Sid will know, and he'll do it.

Then China began laughing. The perfect creature, the keeper

of the magic, laughed softly. Then lightly and more lightly. Nearest her, Texas and Bethel seemed not to hear, and Laska barely turned her head. Moon felt his hair bristle. The sounds couldn't be China's. Except they were. The laughter gasped toward a dangerous rhythm; Moon saw welts of tension lift on the smooth fair arms and climb upward.

He crossed the room and raised her from her chair. She turned her face into his shoulder. He stood there, looking down on the children of Cecil Munger and holding China while she wept.

The party was over.

XVIII

Texans, particularly those of Houston and Dallas, keep alive the old saw about Amarillo being defended from the North Pole by just a barbed-wire fence. These, the noisiest of Texans, as Spain Munger pointed out, were to blame for your smoke-filled-room kind of talk which convinced everyone that Panhandle weather is the world's worst fright. The statement got him appointed to one of the Chamber committees charged with combating this myth.

The idea was thought to have cost the Golden Spread its full share of new or relocating industry and many tourist dollars, and nothing, it was agreed, could be more malicious. Steps were necessary. Foremost, the Chamber undertook the suppression of certain weather news, under a theory that the occasional nasty day is strictly a family affair. In addition, it launched a dogged, often fierce counter-propaganda effort, the backbone of which was the advertising placed with the Houston *Post*.

The Sunday following the Munger party bore the Chamber out. It was sunny, blue, windless, and of the tallest sky. The people of Amarillo felt smugly sure those poor, damp-rotted coastal swamp-dwellers to the south never even dreamed it so good. Spring colors brightened the church crowds, and during the afternoon, parks were overrun.

The Mungers went to church in brave execution of their post-party policy. Afterward, Richard Mooney considered tennis, then rejected it. He settled on his bed, away from the loud television which was, for the children, the zenith of any weekend, and read through Bethel's newest novel.

It wasn't the first tale he'd encountered wherein a character needed, at times, to be alone; wherein a man felt a compulsion to think, in the hope of knowing. But from this point on, it seemed to Moon, writers always got the matter all wrong. They gave the hero a sensitive wife who approved of solitude, or a shrewish one quick to shatter it. Sometimes Moon wondered if authors were celibates—if, instead of women, they married one another. So little did they know. For instance, Bethel never dreamt he might wish, for an hour, to hold his soul separate from her own.

She spent the day interrupting him, pacing the house, speaking sternly to the children. She came in to ask about the book, to wonder if he'd like to take a drive. And she made a few calls on the telephone. It might as well have been a day black with storms. Moon was glad when it was gone.

Early on Monday, they sat at the table with the morning paper before them.

"Richard—why wasn't there anything, in the Sunday paper? Wouldn't you think, if they meant to have their fun—?"

"For heaven's sake, Beth. Persecution isn't their business. There was nothing on Sunday simply because society sections are printed on Thursday. And—well, here it is."

"Oh, Richard!"

Gently, he shook his head at her. "You'll be disappointed; it's almost nothing. Here, in the 'Ladies and Gents' column. Just one line. It says, 'People are talking about: the gorgeous metallic gown Sarah Hart wore to Junior League ... the unusual yard party at the Sidney Glasses the other night. . . .' "

"That's—all of it?"

"That's all."

"But—there'll be another paper this afternoon."

"—which will say nothing at all." Moon yawned. "Why did we get up so early?"

"I'm sorry, dear. I was—restless. Anyway, there is a meeting of the board at eight-thirty, and I'll have to rush. I hope you will drive me to town."

"Sure."

"Dear, you've been so good in all this. I don't deserve you—"

"Please, Beth."

I love you, Richard.

I know that, Bethel. And maybe you don't believe it, but I've never stopped trying. . . .

She kissed him, and he said, "I guess we'd better break out the kids."

"All right. But what would you suppose that means, actually? That 'people are talking about. . . .'?"

Spain remembered that it had been about this time of year, well short of the dog days. Papa had been all cupped up, being fresh from town. Brother and Spain watched him come skidding the old truck into the yard; together they backtracked as he rammed the vehicle into the cistern corner of the house.

"Turkey cock, back down the road!" Papa yelled. "First goddamn wild turk in ten years! Don't stand there, Snake; where's my gun?"

"In the closet, sir, I think."

They stood aside, yet within the dread aura of rum and wildness, while Papa went tumbling through the house for gun and shells. He came slamming out back, cursing that the turkey had not promised to wait, and he fell to all fours to hail the old mongrel bitch from beneath the stoop.

"I see yu', every goddamn rib of you, I do; come out!" Papa probed with a hoe handle; then threw brickbats and a Mason jar or two. Brother got atop the stoop and pounded his big feet on the floor. The old dog came creeping out at last. With red eyes, she looked at each of them before lying down. Then, as Papa vowed to stomp some vim into the scarred, ring-wormed

316

old carcass, the animal growled and lazily set her worn teeth into his thigh.

For a moment, Papa danced and swore and rubbed against the pain. Brother whipped himself with laughter. Papa spat and lifted his gun one-handedly and let go the charge of shot that cut the dog in two.

Spain leaned against the back wall of the house, dizzy and nearly retching. He thought to look at Brother. June's small-boy grin had hardened in place. Suddenly, as if crumbling, it fell away, leaving just the terror. He stared down at half a dog lying near his feet. Then he went running, hard toward the empty yellow pastures.

Papa sat down on the stoop, rubbing his wound. Without a sound, he poured the bleeding gash full of St. Croix rum. "Yonder goes your brother, Snake," he said. "Whistle 'im back, goddammit, 'fore he gits hisself lost."

"I've never learned to whistle, Papa."

"Ketch 'im, I said! Dammit, Snake, yu' want us to hunt 'im all night?"

Bethel and Laska were there to run, too. Laska, who could outstride them all, cornered Brother underneath the creek bridge and held him, both arms hugged about his face, until they could start him back toward the house.

In two weeks, Papa began drinking and pacing away his nights. He would countenance no help until, in early May, he made saliva faster than he could swallow. Spain and China rode along in the ambulance. They'd scarcely gotten him into one of the curious, backwards hospital gowns when, in a convulsion like an eerie battle for his soul, Papa fractured both his legs. After that the paralysis advanced hourly, climbing coldly upward toward the moment in which it must strike and kill his brain.

Through the long night hours at Papa's bedside, Spain tried to assimilate the meanings of this final, revolting oddity being laid upon the Munger name. Only sixteen per cent of persons bitten by a rabid animal actually contract the disease, Laska's husband said, and the most part of these were children. But at eighty-five,

Cecil Munger was dying of rabies. Spain had to think of other old men, coming to their times. Accepting heart attack, or cancer, or a stroke. But nothing so common for Papa; nothing so unattractive to all the quick tongues and long-remembering minds.

Papa had been strung out in a chest-high bed, beside the sunny windows of the costliest, most secluded room. Everything was painted a drab green, as if this were the color of death. From the hard chair of waiting, Spain could see Papa's thin, hairless legs, their shattered bones left unset, and over them the web straps buckled tight against the impending valedictory convulsion.

By the second morning, Papa could move only his head. He began the day swearing about it. Slowly, in revulsion, Spain shaved him.

"Mind what I tell yu', Snake," Papa said. "I'm going, an' I know it. So pay mind to me. Don't you lay me out in no church, do yu' hear that? If anybody cares who Cecil Munger was, let 'im look at the land I got, and count up my younguns I bred, and figure up the whisky I drunk. Let 'em see, by God, that I've got me a full pantry. A man's work, and what he gits for it, that's what he was. Yu' listenin' to me, Snake? Don't give me no show in no church!" Then, "I forget, Son. Didn't I shoot that lazy old bitch?"

Breakfast trays clattered outside in the corridor; there was the smell of fresh coffee.

"Best you take aholt, Snake. You listenin'? I got things fixed up with Cicero, where's you can't git into no trouble. But you take aholt; them other kids, hell, if yu' pissed in their faces, they'd think it was rainin'."

"The doctor said keep you quiet, Papa."

"They ain't no bad in having plenty, Snake; if they's any bad to it, it's in flashin' it around."

"Are you going to eat this morning?"

"You listen. Don't sell no land, no time. For a spell, you can't, an' after that, I'll goddamn bet you won't crave to. Now Snake—"

"Papa—don't call me that name, any more."

"Well, if you ain't the tart sonofabitch!"

Spain left the hospital. He jaywalked across the street to a small café. He ate breakfast before he telephoned his sisters; yes, Papa seemed to have gotten a little rest, the latter part of the night. Afterward, Spain put in a call to the Red Cross people. Good, good, it did appear the emergency leave for Bethel's new husband would come through.

When he returned to the hospital, it was wearily, unhurriedly. He climbed a flight of stairs, and opened the door of Papa's room. He seemed to have startled a pair of student nurses. They turned quickly, in a swirl of their blue mother-hubbards. Behind them he saw fresh linen stacked on an empty bed. On the floor was a pile of dirty sheets.

"Oh," one of the girls said. Then, "Please!" and she pushed him back out into the hall.

Spain leaned there for a little while, searching himself for emotion. Any sort of one. There was only an objectivity, directed at an interesting bit of new knowledge. It had never occurred to him before that, when a man dies, he dirties his bed.

He left the building, crossing back to the café to make all the calls. His sisters, first, then the Gray Bros. It struck him that he could defeat the very last of the oddities. He thought of a funeral, one with mourners and flowers, in a church where, at least by atmosphere, he might with the others decently, normally, bow in grief.

As the preacher, why not a newcomer and stranger, a man with new mind and ears clean of your backyard fence brand of thing? He seemed to remember, from the paper, the name of the newest. A young Baptist who, it was said, preached quite innocuously. . . .

Presently, Spain lifted his glasses and rubbed his eyes. He bent at his desk over Monday's first mail. The letter spread before him was merely a gracious note. Handwritten: "We had such a lovely time at the party; thank you for having included us," and signed by the Reverend Justin B. and Mrs. McLean.

Uh, to be candid, Spain had no recollection of the man's

presence. But then, the light hadn't been good. Besides, after thirteen years, your Reverend McLean would have changed. In Spain's memory of the service for Papa, he could recall the man well enough. That sermon had seemed to outpour from a boob.

Still—Spain pressed the creases out of the note—in such a time of loss and stress and bereavement, your nerves did hang by their frayed ends, and your judgments made then weren't your best, not by a long haul. Here he detected sincerity, a respectful courtesy sent up from your rank and file. The note was valuable. It could restore the hot spark of your board's thinking; it verified your conclusions about bread upon the waters. Later, he meant to get more clear on that.

The Old Girl addressed him on the intercom, announcing the arrival of the directors and their decision to await him in the board room.

He got up, put Reverend McLean's acknowledgement in his pocket, and squared himself up against the weekend's lingering fatigue. All in all, the big picture still developed; it endured. He forced himself to smile. You never allowed tangents to grab you by your heels. Actually, when your sky looked its blackest, you needed but to open your downspouts and—to borrow a term from Moon's pretty youngest—whambo, man, you found that very soon you were busy catching the rain.

Corinne Northington, her thoroughly disciplined hair stabbed full of short pencils, throbbed with sympathy's tender pain, with loyalty's fierce, ready militancy. From her battlement in the reception room, she guarded this tense and critical forenoon with extra care; she sent it along a course that tolerated no hint of levity, not even from the most lowly of the file clerks.

Mr. Munger had appeared thinner and more pale when, a half-hour early, he arrived. She had smiled at him quickly, seeing to it her glance approved openly of the broad Western hat. And, on the underside of her "Good morning," she inscribed with her heart, Count me with you, Mr. Munger; now, and tomorrow, and until the hour you wish me to die.

He had strode on past, toward his office. She took up her pad and listened for the buzzer. Until the directors began arriving, she had sat stiffly waiting. Then, though relieved, she worried because he hadn't summoned her.

With a slight incline of head, The Old Girl could see the shiny paneled door that now shut them away. When she directed herself ahead, she could glare her seniority, along with a certain recrimination, at Mr. Jacobson. And to her left, no callers waited, so that without rising she could maintain watch on the blinds in behalf of the carpet. She realized that this last was about all she was accomplishing.

She patted her bosom, and turned to the typewriter. Mr. Munger expected detailed abstractions from the lengthy bill that the Mr. Congressman would shortly introduce in hope of curbing oil imports. The work went slowly. Her mind wandered, her head was heavy with the stories. There was one phrase in particular: "beans as good as fire and water could make 'em. . . ."

Mr. Jacobson, she felt sure, had snickered at that.

At eleven-twenty, the great door opened. Mr. Munger led them out. For a few minutes, as always, the family stood in the reception room, saying the nice things they so affectionately had for one another. The Old Girl was touched. As Mr. Munger kissed them, she looked away, in case there were tears.

They left altogether cheerily. Then Mr. Munger, with papers in his hand, turned away to his office. He rang immediately.

The Old Girl put the ugly gossip from her mind; she fixed her smile in place well before she entered. It surprised her that on Mr. Munger's face there was seriousness but no dreariness.

"Uh, sit down, Miss Northington, if you will. If it won't be honking in on whatever you are doing, I have a letter, on your rush basis, if you don't mind—"

She sat down in heaven, all dread at once gone, the carefully made lies falling away.

"Uh, this is to your Mr. Felix Croft, your Managing Director, your Baptist Children's Home, and I must say, I can't offhand just reel off your address there: 'Dear Sir.'"

Mr. Munger paused, gazing ahead in thought. A twinge of

resentment, although resisted, arose in Miss Northington. This was new business; something, until now, held quite secret from her. She felt undermined.

"Uh, let's see. Uh, strike that, of course. Now. 'Dear Sir, uh, the board of directors of the various Munger interests'—no, let's whack that out of there, if you don't mind. Uh, 'Dear Sir, My sisters and I have taken note of your wonderful activity, and I am happy to advise you we wish to offer, uh, a more concrete expression of our appreciation. Therefore, we, uh, we pray you will accept the enclosed draft toward the support of your solid work against poverty and want among helpless children. Uh, you may feel free, Mr. Croft, if in your opinion this gift should receive, uh, tasteful publicity as a means of encouraging others. My sisters and I send our best wishes for your continued success in your solid front against poverty and want among helpless children.'"

The Old Girl's breath sped.

"Uh, if you please, you may slick up my rhetoric there, Miss Northington, and sign it 'Sincerely yours.' I suggest we use the plain Estate letterhead, and I think you'll agree with my mind on that. Oh, yes. You might add, 'enclosure: draft for fifty thousand dollars.'"

Miss Northington began to cry.

"Uh, if there's something rocking your keel—well, you know I'll lend a hand, just at the drop of a hat—"

"Oh," she said, "I've never heard of anything so wonderful!"

He cleared his throat. "Uh, yes, thank you."

"It's just beautiful, Mr. Munger! So generous and Christian, turning the other cheek!"

He came around the desk and touched her arm. His hand guided her gently to her feet and toward the door. "Uh, I appreciate your voice out of the darkness, so to speak. We all do. Now, I want that letter gotten right off, by special delivery. Here's your enclosure to put in it."

"I'll have it off in three minutes!"

At the door he dropped his hand away. She turned, looking up from the dumpiness she was aware of, to his fair and majestic height. Her heart remained filled. "God bless you, Mr. Munger."

Suddenly he frowned. "Uh, just one jiffy. I'm not sure I understood, about the other cheek."

"I meant doing this for Amarillo, after the way it laughs behind your back and says you're stingy and makes up all those funny stories—except they aren't funny, and—" She stopped. Too late, she realized with terror.

Mr. Munger fell back. "I—uh, I beg your pardon?"

Her tongue changed from careless to thick; she longed to chop it out. Lamely she said, "I only wanted to say this is so— so fine a thing."

He looked stricken. His face became milkier, but his ears had gone scarlet. The pale eyes flicked to hers, held, flicked away. He spoke in a strange voice.

"Uh, if it won't poop up whatever you're doing, we might sit down for a little visit. . . ."

Almost violently she shook her head. She spun out into the corridor, her sensible flat heels thumping. She cut into the women's room, butting the door open, her hands still clutching the notepad to her breast.

Spain gazed after her a moment. Then he laced his arms across his back and walked to the windows. He stood in the sun, stooped and shivering. He trapped and bit the lining of his mouth; it bled faintly as he squinted down at the street.

A mattock is like a hoe.

Moon walked along Polk Street. It was Tuesday, and dull, and necessary that he get away from The Camera House. For a week prior to the party, he'd scarcely spoken to Teddy Birdsong. Then, on party night as he drew China back from the verge of hysteria, and later while he talked Bethel to sleep in his arms, he had considered himself finished with his affair. Suspended between Teddy and himself was their incompleted trinity of intimacy, and he was sure they both kept thinking of it. But aside from the constant suggestion of her figure, she hinted at nothing. He felt grateful. Except her patient disinterest was becoming almost irritating to him.

He credited the woman with no remorse, certainly not the sort that he felt. It seemed more likely that in her queer bitter-harshness, she regarded his withdrawal as simply a natural interlude within a natural interlude.

She worked efficiently, with all the becoming concentration of the competent white-collar girl. She finished The Camera House's first inventory. She began putting the new books in order. She rearranged the shop, she changed the window display every few days. She took over the buying and mailings and bills. With it all, she still had time to spare. Often she detained some well-dressed customer with a surprisingly bright run of chatter. Her talents retired Moon and Frank into an even deeper limbo.

They swigged more coffee, nettled each other in more protracted debates about how best to split a hundred sixty million dollars. They wandered out more frequently, Frank for beer, Moon just for the street that removed him from Mrs. Birdsong's great utility and his own great uselessness. Besides, Frank grumbled ceaselessly.

With the woman about, China's husband could no longer while off time with his films. He protested by leaving his Christ's head on the wall most of the time. When Frank spoke of Teddy at all, it was as "that squaw," and invariably he proposed that they fire her. Moon thought the callousness, the automatic mistrust that Frank and Teddy showed each other, was preferable to what might have been. It pleased him to think that lovely China was safe from the offense he had committed against Bethel.

He wondered, then, how it would be when he told Beth about Teddy Birdsong. He would, ultimately.

He walked more rapidly, he made four blocks in which he could read three theaters' billings for the day. Then he turned on to the Downtown Club's sidestreet.

A woman is a pendulum. You must discover the rhythm of her, and then you can dare break her heart at one high side, and hope to pick up her forgiveness at the opposite one, and ever after you can expect recrimination when she swings to

the point where you hurt her, and you can count on a reforgive-
ness as she returns to the extreme at which she originally
pardoned you, and if your touch has been delicate, the balance
is undisturbed and she treats you pretty much as before. So
Frank Wallace said. But Moon doubted Bethel was this woman.
It seemed more likely that to set himself straight with her, he
must lose her. Or worse, destroy her.

It brought him to consideration of the perpetuated lie. If
the truth would destroy, then wasn't the lie the only kindness?
He believed, now, that the weight of the eternal lie would
torture him more than any sudden, purging release of the
truth. The truth seemed selfish, as it would make Bethel the
casualty; to carry on the deception appeared his deserved punishment. He shook his head; he didn't know. Somewhere along,
he had lost the ability to deal in ideas and morals, matters so
paramount once and so vague now.

Lately, all of Moon's thoughts were confused with people.
Each idea arrived in some person's clothing; whenever he
probed deliberately toward principles and solutions, his mind
kept bending back to the Mungers, to Teddy, or himself. In
such unabstraction, there was only disclarity. He wondered if
this were true for others; if everyone's dreams and fears and
regrets stand inseparable in thought from the persons involved
in them.

Probably not. Some people seemed to understand their beliefs
and thus can steer by them. He had to face the possibility that
his mind wallowed in personalities because he wished it to. Perhaps it was his device for blaming himself on others. To have
come to such intellectual decay frightened him, and it was a
fear that made him feel reckless.

He had come to the Downtown Club and entered without
being aware of it. The place was filled with women, handsome
ones in quality hair-dos and successful girdles and tasteful
clothes most certainly labeled White & Kirk, Blackburn's, or
Neiman-Marcus.

From the foyer, Moon could see no vacant table. The women
had packages on the floor beside their chairs; the feathers on

their hats made a forest. The dress shops must have been mobbed.

Moon had never quite fathomed the silent signals that ran, as though by invisible antenna, among the ladies of wealth. On certain days they appeared simultaneously for their tours of Polk Street. On other days, not one would be out. Never had he seen them shop coincidentally with the rushing, sturdy, budget-tense women from the country and from the city's barren FHA compounds. You suspected that a mystic, intuitive bargain had been made. Some days the town belonged to the high and the higher; on other days, these lent it to the worried washers-of-soiled-diapers who must sigh over price tags and who wore no hats.

He grew morbid. Suddenly his life seemed crowded with women, known and unknown. He turned and went out. He was in front of the Paramount when Spain hailed him.

Moon paused, letting the chairman come to him. Spain wore a shiny, shoulderless blue suit that threatened to wash out the lean face entirely. He came in long hurried strides, and Moon felt the old premonition. He felt also a certain defiance about it. It struck him that for each little errand, he had a kind of answer. For one, there was Teddy Birdsong. If he'd sworn off her, he could always unswear.

"Uh, glad to see you," Spain said.

They stood together near the curb. Spain, Moon thought, had never learned how to stand on a street. He folded his arms behind him, then in front of him; he tried propping his hands on his hips, and in all aspects he looked misplaced and awkward. Near them a newsboy hawked the first edition of the afternoon paper. Personages from Washington were coming out to inspect the Panhandle drouth disaster, which meant they would spend an hour standing in some dry pasture and try to look thoughtful while spitting sympathetically down the cracks in the ground.

"Uh, I'm glad to catch you; the fact is, I've been ringing up your home base." He was very pale; he had misplaced or forgotten his Western hat. Abruptly he was talking about the weather; he covered it in passionate detail.

At last Moon yielded. "Has something happened?"

"Uh, not to my knowledge, though I haven't heard from June this trip, and—"

"I had a postcard from Remo," Moon said. "They got into that TV show all right, and June got a lot of fun out of it."

"Fine, fine. Uh, your mention of Mr. Remo brings up the employee question I wanted to quiz you about, and I'll appreciate your help, let me say. Uh, it pays you to put your yardstick on your personnel now and then, and I know you'll agree to the hilt on that. My thought was we might discuss your Indian girl—"

"She's not Indian."

"Uh, I do seem to remember you set me straight on the beam about that. Anyway, under your premium salary arrangement there, I had hoped she would pan out to be gold—"

"She does a good job," Moon said.

"Fine. Uh, would you say, Moon, she's your material for promotion?"

Moon looked up sharply. The pale eyes were gazing past him. "What do you mean?"

"Uh, it's been the policy of your board to pull your employees up by their bootstraps from within your own organization, and I know you see the gray matter of that. I anticipate—I know I can count on you keeping hold of your discretion— Well, uh, we can expect a change at the office. Not on the spur of the minute, of course. But I've always felt your loyalty right down to the rock ribs, that's the real test of your good employee, right? And when you have some of your key personnel collecting your sickening dirt behind your back—I hope it's all right, Moon, if I sound off frankly—then you need to review your ace in the hole."

Moon leaned back against a parking meter. Was it Cicero Williams? Or Jacobson? No, Teddy couldn't possibly replace such men. But God, not The Old Girl!

"Are you speaking of Miss Northington?"

"Uh, as I say, for the time being we're just jostling this thought around. Of course, your management chores aren't always peaches and cream to administer—"

"Don't do it, Spain. You'd never get another one like her."

"Uh, about your Indian girl—"

"No; she's not for that job."

Spain's blond brows lifted, looking thinner outside the magnification of his glasses. "Unless I got my wires mixed up, I understood you to say—"

"She's good where she is."

Spain squinted about the street, as if to decide whether it was the place for anger. Moon wished suddenly to attack. He said, "How does this tie in with that donation to the Children's Home?"

Spain stiffened. "Uh, I don't seem to read your connection."

"You got a good press on that, and there's been nothing more said about the party."

The pale eyes glittered. "I'd rather you didn't—that is to say, your conclusion you jump to there is taking the wrong dog by the tail, and to be blunt where honesty is due, it isn't fair to your board. Uh, if your automobile or something is nagging at you, I want to make clear I've loosened my mind on that, and we're certainly eager to—"

"Let it go," Moon said.

They stood a moment without speaking. Spain shifted from foot to foot, then coughed.

"Uh, I've always believed, Moon—and I don't hesitate to make this clear—I've always felt that you among the whole group had the big picture dead center in your sights, along with the consensus of us. . . ."

Moon thought of Sid Glass as he had looked across the bean table that night. "What about Sid?"

"Uh, yes, of course; I make no bones there, I've always loved Sidney like a brother, and I'd be your first to say Laska—to inject a little humor—really frosted the cake when she added him to our number. Though I don't grasp your meaning—"

328

"And Frank?" Moon pushed it.

"The same with Frank, naturally. Uh, with all of you, though it seems to me your, uh, delicate discussion of this brand ought not be fired off on the public street, and I'd appreciate it if you'd walk along back to the office with me."

"Sorry," Moon said, "I'm going to a movie."

"Uh, I beg your pardon?"

"Would you care to come along?"

Spain seemed stunned; he squinted incredulously at his watch, then at the Paramount's box office. "Uh, well, no thank you, I've got to get back before the fat hits the frying pan. But I have enjoyed the talk, Moon, and I want to say I appreciate your points you had that landed on the mark, and I'd like to pay for your ticket."

Moon left him. He remained in the theater only long enough to drink a furious Coke in the lobby. When he got back to The Camera House, Frank was sitting at his desk toying with a novelty he'd found; a tiny varnished outhouse with spring door and occupant inside. Teddy Birdsong sat on a stool up front and made entries in a ledger. She wore a tan sheath of polished cotton and smelled of unsweet perfume.

She said, "What do we do with film on which the dates have run out?"

"Throw it away."

"That's poor business."

"The worst," he said, and he moved close to her. "I wish we could get out of here. Aren't your books in bad shape, or something?"

"No. Unless you say they are."

"Let's go." He shouted to Frank that they were taking the books to an accountant and would be gone a while, and Frank responded through the partition with a groan.

As they got into the car, Teddy said, "You're learning to lie real good."

"I have a good teacher."

"Thank you."

He drove out Sixth Avenue, slowly and miserably in a roundabout route he knew would lead to her apartment. He said, "What are you after? In the way of a job, I mean?"

"Christ, you aren't firing me again?"

"No."

She said, "I'm after the time when I'll have no job at all."

"What if Spain wanted you up at Estate offices?"

"You could kiss me good-by."

"He thinks you're getting seventy a week. Up there, that would be it."

Her smile wrinkled the make-up around the cold eyes. "I hadn't thought of that. But, think of the opportunity."

"There'd be no advancement."

"For me," she said, "there always is."

He hated her. "Don't impress me; I know you're rugged."

She twisted and put her back against the door and looked straight at him. "And you're glad of it, you damned capon. Else you couldn't take a running jump into my bed every time you tangle with those bone pickers and get your sweet sensibilities offended."

"You'll never work for Estate!"

She reached across, rummaged his lighter out of his shirt pocket, and lit her cigarette. "Oh, shut up," she laughed. "We both know you'll help me get what I please."

XIX

"Me, I just as le. ve you wasn't chapped at me no more, Mister Remo."

The car hummed along with all the built-in excellence of luxury engineering; the speedometer was steady at 90 miles per hour. John Remo drove intently; he watched how the mouth of the automobile seemed to suck in and swallow the paving, gulp after gulp, and there was a drowsy fascination to it.

"Boy, Mister Remo, we're really going lickety-split, ain't we, Mister Remo. Me, I bet we can do a hunnert, don't you 'spect, Mister Remo?"

"Turn your collar up, like I said. And leave it up."

They drove east through bright, mid-day Arizona. Remo kept calculating the distance home, not in miles, but in time. He meant to travel straight through the night.

Beside him, Brother chewed a fifth of cigar, and spat occasionally into a thermos bottle. The ox had spoken little since they raced out of San Diego; this time he, too, was afraid. Remo took comfort in that.

"Boy, Mister Remo, we gave 'im a real whoppin', didn't we? You're a real good sonofabitch, Mister Remo!"

"Take a nap," Remo said gruffly. "We're going all the way in."

" 'Scuse me, Mister Remo, but my neck sort of smarts, like, and if I bent my collar down, so's it wouldn't rub none—"

"Do what I tell you!"

"Boy I will, Mister Remo!"

Remo wrinkled his brow, against the glimmer of sun and haze down the road, and he thought, It's *her* that'll care the most; she who didn't have it coming. He cursed himself.

In all his time with the Mungers, it seemed now, he'd slipped from one error into another; each time, he'd thought he had finally, permanently learned. But whatever the lapses and their consequences, he had never lost the big slob before.

He glanced aside at him. With the gauze compress on his neck, and in the black sportshirt bought in Hollywood, Brother looked like a bald fat panda.

The days in Los Angeles had gone well. One at Disneyland, another at CBS-TV, the third saved for the boat trip to Catalina. Then the drive down the coastal highway.

Remo discovered, as they set out, that he wished as much as June to see Balboa Park. Or, more accurately, the birds there that China liked. "You mustn't miss the birds, Mr. Remo. Brother will love them, and you'll enjoy it yourself, I know." He had promised her profusely, the words flowing because she wished him this pleasure along with her Beloved.

Brother grunted to get a foot up on the dash. "It's sure a long goddam ways back home, ain't it long, Mister Remo?"

"Stop cussing."

They'd spent the first forenoon in San Diego at wandering about the city, although Remo detested walking. Brother was entranced by the sailors, and the town was full of them. The first fresh kid in dress blues had grinned at June and said, "Hi, Fatty." So as Remo followed, Brother paused at every bar and pawn shop to peer in at his beautiful, friendly Navy. For a time they stood on a dock and stared out at a moored flotilla of destroyers, and Brother ranted that this sort of boat had never turned up in his Grape-Nuts boxes. They ate lunch among more sailors in a grimy little barbecue cell off Pacific Square before going uphill to the park.

332

The day was sultry hot. Remo carried his coat over his arm as they moved from one animal pit to the next. It was late afternoon when they reached China's birds. Remo was exhausted. He sat down on a patch of cool damp grass, back from the pathway around the jungle of trees where birds cawed and screamed and seemed free, although trapped beneath a vast wire canopy.

He watched June Munger every second. Except for the moment it took to fill and light a pipe.

The first two hours of the search involved just the park and its people. After that, Remo went it alone, over the route of the morning walk, and it took him almost until midnight. He felt numb and futile. He went back to the hotel, had a drink, and almost put a call in to Spain Munger. Then he thought it through once more and went to the police station.

He sat with a sergeant in a game of cribbage, this occasionally interrupted as the officer was called upon to pay off winners in the afternoon's baseball pool. It was almost three when they brought Brother in. A pair of grinning young patrolmen led him by the arms while a giant Marine MP shoved from behind.

"You aim to whip me, Mister Remo?"

"Where the hell you been?"

An officer said, "We found him in the Square. Trying to buy some knucks, in that all-night hock shop."

"You ain't gonna stick me in the jailhouse, are you, Mister Remo? China, she—"

"Shut up." To the officer Remo said, "He's all right, ain't he?"

"Sure. But take a good look."

On his throat, Brother had a fresh tattoo.

"Ain't we going to stop noplace, Mister Remo; I got a pretty good ache in my ass, Mister Remo."

"I'll give you an ache."

Remo pulled the Cadillac into a fringe of the light thrown out from a squat adobe service station. "Let me look at your neck."

He pulled the bandage out and down. Brother's wound was inflamed and moist. The red and blue ink seemed to have

darkened, and around the edges, Remo saw a few tiny bubbles
of pale blood.

"Am I gettin' well yet, Mister Remo?"

"It's all right."

"Well, me, Mister Remo, I'd just as leave we et a hamburger,
wouldn't you as leave, Mister Remo?"

"Go to sleep."

Remo set the car in motion. For an hour he drove fiercely.
The night road became hypnotic. He grew drowsy, and he fell
to considering why he'd decided to rip off the entire twelve
hundred miles in one monotonous, tiring run. For one thing,
maybe he needed to make sure now and then that he wasn't
in fact unfit and old. More basic, he thought, was the feeling
that this was the way to wave farewell to his job. He intended
no crawling before Spain Munger this time. He drove hard to
get there and be done with it. To quit caring was easy, once
a man admitted all the caring in the world wasn't going to alter
anything.

He put his burnt-out pipe in his teeth. Somewhere along, he
had begun assuming that now he would leave Amarillo for
good. He didn't want to. But then, since '54, his town had been
only a recollection and the tiny bit of smelter smokestack he
could see from The Old Place. He'd go to Pennsylvania, which
he hoped wouldn't prove too Eastern, and his mother would be
tickled to have him there.

At the thought of her, he smiled. That sour old Polack needed
him, relied upon him. She could use him to rag at, to lecture
and browbeat; she would seize him as a club for beating back
her loneliness. Up there, she'd make him John Remolewski,
and he'd stand for it out of the same set of guts by which he
would have to tolerate becoming a nightwatchman. This was
the part that ran hardest against the grain. Nightwatching,
the last stop; the nothingness they reserved for fired cops and
used-up cops and all the unsmart cops who had believed they
would never get old.

Remo drove less hectically now. He wouldn't have retired
himself, not finally, until he stood before an exploding Spain

Munger. He began a remeasure of his situation, and for the first time regretted the temper vented against San Diego.

It had taken but an hour to find the place. A hole in the wall just off the Square, marked by an easel sign standing out on the sidewalk. Remo had taken off his coat and tossed it back onto the luggage. Shoving June Munger ahead of him, he went through a door that was the entire front. The tattooist lay on a bare cot at the rear, dozing off his busy night. He sat up quickly, a thick, squat man in stained T-shirt and a hundred tattoos of his own.

"Sleeping," he said. "Something you want?"

"Boy, he's the one, Mister Remo. This is the sonofabitch, all right!"

The squat man stared up at them. "Whatsa matter? You a cop?" Then he grinned recognition at Brother. "Hello, Fatty; I bet you got a sore neck."

"Get up," Remo said.

"Huh? Now looka here, big boy—"

"Get up."

The man scooted down, over the foot of the cot, away from them. "If the fat boy is yours, fella, then you owe me ten bucks. Them swabbies never paid me."

"I'll pay," Remo said.

"No cause to get hard, fella. I didn't like it neither. He come in with them sailors, and I worked on all of 'em. They said, fix him something different—"

Remo hit him. He reached and lifted the man up, and hit him again.

"Boy, lemme whop 'im a lick, Mr. Remo!"

"That's all. Get the hell back to the car."

Remo looked down at the dazed, gaping face. He dropped a Munger fifty between the man's knees. The man remained on the floor; perhaps he was there long after the Cadillac cleared town.

He hoped, now, that the fifty had been enough; that the man hadn't thought of the police. . . .

The happiest Munger snored through the night.

Remo's eyes were stinging from the last miles against the morning sun; they felt like a pair of Brother's holes in the snow as he put the car across the cattle guard and up to The Old Place. Brother slept on.

Before arousing him, Remo got his whisky from the trunk and stored it, high overhead, in the barn. He carried in the bags, opened windows, and turned up the icebox. Then he went back for June Munger. Remo herded the round staggering figure ahead of him, and he put him to bed with just one quick tinny clatter of the bells. Brother said, "Mister Remo, ain't China an' all them comin' out for Sunday dinner?" and returned at once to sleep.

Without disturbing him, Remo peeled the now-soiled bandage off the throat. He stood a moment, looking down at the round face which admitted its age if you saw not the baby eyes but the stiff copper eyebrows. Then he studied the whole effect.

China would see it, he thought, as he saw it now. The tattoo had taken something valuable. The innocence, the unworldliness, the peace of June Munger were gone. You saw just the dotted line, extending in a crescent across his throat, and the festered lettering above that said, CUT HERE.

Remo sighed, and in broad daylight, went to bed.

Bethel stood beside the bed as Moon awakened from a dream about an ice mountain. She was smiling, and she'd already put a glass of cold orange juice in his hand. "Almost eight o'clock," she said.

"Breakfast in bed? How come?"

"Carol thought of it, as something special for you."

Moon awakened the rest of the way. "That's not funny, Bethel."

"It's true. It's an overture or something; she was too shy about it to bring it in herself. She and Hannah made the tray."

He looked at the food doubtfully.

"Carol's coming around, Richard. She's beginning to understand."

Bethel wore a flimsy light blue dress identical to one he'd seen and admired on China, and as he gazed at it in puzzlement, she turned around for him and said, "Dear, I bought this to sweep you off your feet."

"It looks nice," he said. "Drink your juice."

As he drained the glass, she sat down on the edge of the bed. "Will you—will you really stay home today?"

It was Thursday, May third; word of his street-corner tiff with Spain had sped through the board, and last night Bethel had asked him to "take off a day and rest." They assumed him to have been short-tempered from being tired, and he'd not bothered to argue. It had occurred to him he'd not missed a day at The Camera House since Teddy Birdsong, that it would have been better if he'd been crippled or ill and had had to miss them all.

"I'll enjoy it," he said.

She smiled brightly. These past few days, he thought, his wife had been in some sort of revitalization from having shared in the first Munger philanthropy. This appeared true of the other women, except Texas who, Frank claimed to know, had pointed out in star chamber that fifty thousand dollars equaled eighteen thousand barrels, not taking into account gross-production taxes and all the other levies.

"What do you want to do?" she said.

"Anything."

"We could put on old clothes and set out the iris bulbs. And I'll make you a liverwurst lunch."

"Fine."

He exchanged his glass for coffee. She poured a cup for herself, and as they drank, he watched her. Every blond hair was in place, her make-up was faint but carefully done. He thought, this is good. Certain panels of his mind seemed to open and close, so that Teddy Birdsong and the Mungers were shut away, and he was at ease with his wife. He sensed rather than reasoned, and something clean and comfortable seemed in the offing.

337

"Sleep well?" she said.

"I had a crazy dream. One of those where you fall and keep falling."

"I had those when I was a little girl. I'd dream of walking the fence like Laska, and every time I'd fall. But not any more."

"What do you dream?"

"Just wild things. Mostly. I forget as soon as I'm awake. Last night, it was an airplane dream. Here, eat the toast; it'll please the girls if I bring back an empty tray."

Moon did as he was told, the sense of well-being growing.

"I just heard the airplane sputtering and I saw it fall into a tree. I ran out, and as I got there a little man came out of the wreck. I—do you think dreams mean anything, Richard? Spain does."

"They mean you're asleep."

"Well, this little man—he was dark, like an Asian, or an Indian, and he had a giant lizard that was as long as an automobile. But the lizard was friendly; he kept trying to nuzzle up and rub against my leg. Newspaper reporters and other people came, and everyone wanted to know where the little brown man and his lizard came from. Everybody crowded into a little house near the wreckage, and talked and milled around. Then I got hold of the little dark man's clothes and dragged him around wherever I went, so he couldn't tell anyone but me."

Moon stopped eating. She told it seriously, with small furrows between her eyes.

"I had the feeling I knew something the rest of the people didn't know, but when I tried to think what it was, I couldn't. I tried to tell the authorities about it on the telephone. I kept holding to the little man, and his lizard stayed close, smiling at me. While I was on the phone, someone came hurrying into the house and said the airplane had a Chevrolet engine. Everybody thought this was a very valuable clue. The little dark man just shrugged and said, 'I'll confess.' "

Bethel paused, embarrassed. "Well, what do you think?"

"Let's hear the rest of it."

"Oh, that was all. It ended right there."

"Then you better make up an ending for me," he said, "or I'll worry all day."

She laughed. "I really think the little man had just flown over from the greenhouse to bring me some iris bulbs."

An hour after Carol and Hannah left for school, the sun was high and hot. Bethel changed into a pair of faded shorts, which was something that happened but a few times each summer, since Spain believed shorts made a woman, uh, unnecessarily vulnerable. Her slim long legs, if startlingly white, were attractive. Except—and here Moon exercised what he thought his husband's prerogative—he wished she'd learn to wear a garter belt. For unknown reasons, the Munger women still wore elastic garters. These had depressed deep grooves around Bethel's thighs, like permanent scars. It struck Moon how a man needs to be proud of his wife, even in such details, and in the same foolish way he prizes his deer rifle or the new wax job on his car.

They worked slowly along the front of the house. Moon turned up earth with a spading fork, and Bethel set the bulbs. The planting, which kept the Mooney house abreast of others in the development, had been Harry's task in past years. But already the schedules of the new solid front about lawns made him unavailable. Harry was mowing every day, he was flooding all the lawns to wet them deep before the city's summer water rationing must begin.

Bethel talked ceaselessly, as if she'd saved up for this time. At the next board, they'd decide finally about this polio vaccine business, safe or unsafe, and if the former, then how marvelous it was, especially for Spain's very young children; and what did you do with the perfectly good little-girl dresses Carol would use no more, those that seemed too special to send to the Salvation Army; and Richard, don't you think it strange how unexcited Frank seems about becoming a father? You'd think he'd at least give in and go along with China on her evening walks, but anyway, wasn't it a relief that, at last, China had agreed to go to a doctor?

"I hadn't heard."

Bethel straightened up to rub wet loam from her hands. "We made the appointment for her, and insisted. We've been worried; she's been 'eating for two' and she's gained twelve pounds when she should have been dieting and taking calcium and things. I think—I think she's a little like a child about this baby, and maybe afraid of having it."

Moon was astounded at this sudden inclusion of himself in a Munger secret; astounded, too, at the supposition about warm, tender China. It occurred to him that her mothering of June all these years revealed how wholly she yearned for a child—

Bethel colored slightly, she put her hand on his arm and started to say something.

"What is it, Beth?"

"Nothing, really. But while we were speaking of her, I did think—I mean, there's something I've not said to you. About you and China that night, after the party."

He whirled to glare at her. "What?"

"Well, I wanted to tell you I thought that what you did was all right, honestly. She did need somebody, and Frank wasn't there—"

"Oh good God!"

"I—I knew I shouldn't have mentioned it, not that way. The point I really wanted to make was that it vexes me sometimes, how Frank is always disappearing. . . ."

They'll never understand, Moon thought. Never in their lives will they see what it is that makes a man run.

He shook his head at her. Then they worked silently, turning the corner of the house, continuing the bulbs in a modular pattern that duplicated exactly the one adopted by the insurance salesman in his identical edging around his identical house next door. It was difficult for Moon to let the subject lie. His urge was to speak harshly. But he thought of Teddy Birdsong; he remembered his lost right to judgment on anyone. He said, "What are you going to do about the trust?"

It failed to startle her; she squatted down again to her work. "We have a few days left to decide." Her voice softened. "What do you want us to do, Richard?"

"I want out."

"I knew that, dear." She packed the earth around a bulb with exaggerated noisy blows of her open hand. "So that's how I'm going to vote."

It amazed him how calmly, simply it came. "How about the others?"

"I think I'll be the only one."

He reached down to touch her hair. She turned her head under his hand, keeping contact as she looked up at him. She blinked at tears.

"This sun is cooking me," he grinned. "Maybe I should get a big hat like Spain's." He drew her up, heard her knees pop and laughed about it as he kissed her.

They were idling about the yard together, hunting a reasonable location for the few left-over bulbs and discussing at length each possible site, when John Remo's call came.

Assembly at The Old Place occurred immediately. Under a hot sun, the gathering exchanged sad kisses before moving upslope from the hard-driven automobiles to the manhole end of the porch where China, in faltering voice, brought this new misery from beneath the house to face them.

The solid front raised its eyes, it gazed at the tattoo necklace of its Beloved as if beholding a corpse. The corpse abided the scrutiny bleakly while scratching its crotch and protesting in a whisper, "Me, I don't care none about a little old sore neck, China, and besides, how can I find Kittypoo anywheres?" The board, your stunned units of a stunned whole, appeared unable for a while to absorb this dose, this giz of a Munger throat asking to be cut. Then in the tight unity of disaster, the tall people turned away. Like a train drawn by the long legs of Spain Munger, they climbed the familiar steps into the familiar house.

True, a hundred per cent so, this was a slate that would be hard to clean, but when someone laid you below the belt, you had to sort out the pieces while taking steps against your employees who committed such floppers for you, and you had to get busy fixing your clock. Uh, well, didn't everyone agree your minutes for today could just go to grump, so you could get right at your chores? Now, of course, your Mr. Remo was the derelict in the woodpile and ought to have been fired straight out of the box, and we all agree there are no more pros or cons to that. But you do have your interim with Brother to think of, until you can lay hold of your more competent and more loyal replacement, so the course to take would be to act only half-immediately with your just retribution, giving Mr. Williams-the-lawyer time to seek out your new man to fill in Mr. Remo's shoes. Well, if we're all of one thought on that score, the important booboo to get at is your dotted line on Brother's throat, and though there's not been time to put many feelers out, you do have some experience to draw from right in your own backyard. Uh, Mr. Williams's Moose got a tattoo on his shoulder the night he graduated from Junior High by just the skin of his eyes, and they solved that by your surgeon up in Denver who specializes in nipping your tattoo messes in the bud, just by picking out small tidbits of skin at a time. So there's your answer staring you in the face. Uh, I beg your pardon? No, to freshen your memory there, your medical and dental on Brother has always been drawn from his entrusted share of the Estate, keeping you clear of the corporation funds. And now that we begin to see the light of day, I know we all feel better about this lowdown inexcusable state of affairs.

Brother was driving away golf balls. He hit them to the west, so he might watch how the south breeze curved them. The same wind whipped the new white silk scarf China had knotted about his throat. It was one of a half-dozen scarves, costly things from Blackburn's, that Spain had thought to bring out in his briefcase.

"It don't matter, Moon," Remo said. "No crap, it doesn't. I reckon my old lady needs me, anyway; she don't know a living soul back East."

"I hate it, John."

"It sure changes 'im, don't it? Funny, how I never much

noticed the look he had on his face, not until he didn't have it no more."

That's precisely how it is, Moon thought. You never know for sure what is good or bad until it's past. "You're getting sentimental, Remo."

"Go to hell." The old giant was kicking up dry earth with one of the big soft shoes; one of his hands jangled change in his pocket. "You want to walk around to the barn, Moon?"

"I don't want to drink."

"Me neither."

"It makes him look like a jack-o'-lantern, in a way. That's what I've been trying to think of."

Remo grunted. Suddenly he said, "I ought to tell somebody something before I leave; might as well be you. For a while, you better keep an eye on that ox. I guess it sounds like a helluva thing, but he just might turn up with a dose of clap."

"You don't mean that."

"Well, I don't know it. But he was loose in San Diego all night with them two sailors."

Moon shrugged. "He doesn't know up from down about such stuff."

Remo shook his head. "He knows the ropes. I swear I never taught him anything; I guess somebody ahead of me got 'im started. But on these trips I've had to let him go a few times. Not often, that's the truth, an' only when I had to, so's he wouldn't grab some woman on the street."

"If Spain knew that, he'd kill you."

"I reckon. Anyway, the next man that comes out here ought to know about it. Hell, I can't get Brother to say if he hunted up any goody out there—goody, that's what he calls it—but I figure you better look out for a couple of weeks."

Moon watched the listless swing of Brother's driver against a battered tuna fish can. Remo's revelation seemed to have changed June further, beyond the ugliness of the tattoo. Moon could imagine the happiest Munger shut up in some hotel with

343

God-knew-what-sort-of-a-woman. Perhaps with Remo standing watch outside.

"I don't like knowing about it," he said.

"Yeah. *She* wouldn't, either. Looks to me like Spain is the only one that really thinks of that; he acts to me like he's got an idea what kind of trouble the family could have."

Moon kept gazing at Brother, surprised at how shocked and hurt he was. He tried to shake off a feeling of distaste; he thought of Carol's bright little dismissal, "Skit, skat, how about that?" And of Bethel saying, "You don't love them any less."

Spain came out of the house, paused on the porch to shade his eyes, then strode toward them, his pale head bowed as though to force along tired or unwilling feet. They waited. Moon lit a cigarette.

"Uh, if you don't mind, Moon, I'd like to try one of those."

Moon gave him a cigarette and held the lighter for him. "Thanks." The chairman drew ineptly, exhaled loudly.

"Uh, Mr. Remo, let me say I appreciate—all of us appreciate—what a stemwinder of an experience you've been through, and we all have a real warm spot for you; let me make that clear. Now, I've presented your, uh, problem to the board so as to blow the chaff off, and I think you'll agree we've got to improve your condition here, and that's the only giz to shoot at. Anyway, to shell right down to the meat of it, your board's thinking is that you'll need some help out here, and the vote was to track down a good man to relieve some of your burden off your shoulders. And let me get straight, we all hope the result will take some of the worry off your back."

Remo took his pipe from his mouth; he poked at it with a forefinger too large to go down into the bowl.

"This is not to say your assistant is your permanent arrangement to rely on; we'll have to see how the cookie crumbles and keep matters in a state of flexibility, so to speak."

Remo said, "That's fine, Mr. Munger. I'll leave when the new man shows up."

"Well, I appreciate your decision there, and I want to say the board had sincerely hoped you'd be manning the switches out here for a good many days to come." He sighed. "Uh, Moon, I haven't seen Frank around."

"He's keeping the store."

"Uh, good, good. I am glad that you could drop everything right on the spur, though, and get right out here."

The women had emerged. Brother met them and was kissed, and Laska complained hoarsely that the white scarf was already soiled. Spain went to join them, his downy hair blowing, the slack arms folded across his back and one hand dangling the tan Stetson.

Remo watched the women, his coarse old face seeming almost dreamy. *She* was in the center of them, smiling, speaking, allowing the warm heart, the natural sweetness, to flow out from her core of grace. The wind pressed her maternity dress against her, yet she remained beautiful. She raised a gloved hand to wave at Remo and she called, "Good-by."

Moon wished more of her; wished she might have remembered to cross to them and offer the touch of hand and personal smile that Brother's keeper had come to wait for as if for the blessing of a saint.

"Well," Moon said.

"Hell, what happened?" Remo said. "Did I quit, or did I get the boot?"

"I couldn't tell."

Bethel came extending her hand to Moon, and he took it. As they walked away, he thought she might have spoken to Remo. He said, "I'll keep in touch, John."

"Yeah."

Moon put his wife in the car. She looked drawn and cried-out. He said, "I've been thinking; maybe your little Asian flyer was a wetback, and his lizard was really a dragon, and—"

"Oh, please, let's don't talk. Let's go home."

XX

"Stars and Stripes Forever," booming out of a new phonograph, blasted Remo up from his rest. He leaped to the watch hole over his bed, and through it glared at June Munger. Brother was naked and marching fleshily about his room under the propulsion of his new "sailor" music. Remo swore. Today, he vowed, this chowderhead would learn something of labor.

By ten they had cleaned out the chicken house, despite the many timid "Them chickens, Mister Remo, they don't care no heap about this"; they had gathered the litter of the yard for burning, contrary to Brother's "Me, it don't look so trashy to me, Mister Remo"; and they had washed all three of the Cadillacs—"If they're all dirty, Mister Remo, I guess we could buy us a new 'un, couldn't we buy us one, Mister Remo?"

"You can latch your fat trap and keep humpin'. Next, you grab the hoe and get at them weeds."

"I don't mind no weed choppin', Mister Remo, only it makes water bubbles on your hands, an' China, she don't like me to have no water bubbles, Mister Remo."

"Jump, or I'll put bubbles on your rind."

346

It felt ill-tempered and good, this hurried, hard completion of a job of work, this spurt toward the finish before the advent of one John Remolewski, nightwatchman, who would but sit or pace out his life in a stagnancy of wishing away time.

Shortly before noon, the odd automobile of the mail carrier —wheel and gearshift installed on the wrong side—appeared on the road. Remo walked downslope to meet it at the mailbox. The lean, ununiformed carrier had agreed to pause long enough, when The Old Place was abandoned, to feed and water Brother's Leghorns, and Remo paid him. He put the money away quickly and handed Remo the mail. There was the new Sears catalogue, out of which Brother would order some gift for China, and a letter from Pennsylvania.

Remo studied the envelope's unsteady scrawl, he grinned sourly at the "lewski" portion of his name, under which his mother had drawn her scolding double underline.

Usually her letters acknowledged money he had sent, or recited the agonies of age as manifest in the most recent night of cold feet and indigestion. Or, she took pains to remind him of his evil irreverence toward good Polish lineage. Nevertheless, he anticipated her letters pleasurably; no one else ever wrote at all.

His mother wrote almost as she spoke. Remo, when plodding along the shaky lines, could think he heard the irksome hisses upon each word; he could envision the set of bad dentures lain aside on the writing table, so that she might dictate the letter to herself.

Carefully, as he walked back to the house, he tore off an end of the envelope. He sat down on the front porch, to keep June Munger in safe view, and spread the pulpy, blue-ruled tablet pages open on his knee.

"Mr. John Remolewski, Dear Son John," it began. "It is unhappy I was gone out of my place when you brung East the idiot fellow and I do not see you. Since you have not say you will come, so it is you to blame for this, and I am not to blame about it, and I wish to hear not so many complainings. The money comes late this time, which was almost so I lose my lights by shutting off, except Mr. Eddings be good help about it.

"When you come to fiddle around in my mail box, I was went out in the fresh air in the country. Mr. Eddings take me automobile riding before in his big car which is good as new. So I tell you do not send the money any more because Mr. Eddings have a very best job in the electric plant every day but Saturday and Sunday and nothing is owed to anybody. He give me ten dollar bill like a present quick after the wedding which was very good ceremony like the Old Country. It was had at the Oujeski house where is a big size parlor and which was afterwards big party give to me by Mrs. Vladocek and her four nephews up on their farm. . . ."

Remo swallowed.

"You will be glad, as Mr. Eddings is very healthy man and sixty-four years of age and also may buy new house to live in quick as union make rich electric company sit up and say is uncle. . . ."

His mother was seventy-eight.

Remo folded the letter slowly, along the old creases. He let the sudden sweat trickle down into his eyes, and he thought, it isn't the truth. Oh, damn her, damn her. Hadn't he sent her up there to be miserable and lonely?

He didn't know the time; two hours, maybe, since he went out to the barn, though it made not a good goddamn, for his brave blood ran fast and hot, and old happy Brother was around some place, and if he got lost, any good cop could find him, and it was good to be the worst wet-nurse in the world, the whole stinking world run by dirty stinking little reporters and the richest asses that ever ate briar, and he knew for sure, if he kept trying, he could make this glass balance atop the others; Remo could do that, if Remolewski never could. Moon, that sharp-looking devil, if he was here, you'd light him off like a fuse; he loved *her* too, if he did follow his wife around like the echo of her heels, and damn, what Texas-born man wants to be a Pole or an anything else besides a Texas-born man, old

348

witch; you could explain that to *her*, hell, you could explain stealing a hundred dollars to *her*, if she wasn't all the time kissin' on that slob and making him Jello and Easter eggs: Hey, Beloved, where you at, where you at? Sure, they'll come out for Sunday dinner, the whole mess of 'em—come on, where you at?

Teddy Birdsong said, "Last night was Reserve night, wasn't it? What happened?"

"I went to Reserve."

"Hooray for virtue," she said. "But you might have called. I got soft; I had some sandwiches made for you."

They worked at the rear, unpacking a replacement stock of fresh film. Moon peeled the boxes while she stood by, confirming the invoices.

"This is the last one," he said.

"So you'd rather not talk about it. All right, I congratulate you. I—"

"Leave it alone."

She met his gaze with the expression of hard, painted mockery; with a shrug she knew put motion into her thinly covered breasts. "Okay, Mr. Mooney. We might talk about tattooing."

He straightened. "Who told you about that?"

She laughed. "Don't you know I'm like one of the family?"

He carried an armload of the film up front and put it on the shelves. The door stood open to capture a southwest breeze which whined mildly as it entered.

"What did the Mr. President say, about giving away the old film?" she asked.

"I haven't told him."

They had sent the out-dated stock to a camera club, upon Teddy's suggestion, as a gift that might earn repayment through new business. Already, several of The Camera House's competitors had heard of it, and indignantly they were undertaking to teach him the facts of business life, fair trades, and the Unwritten Code.

"He won't like it," she said.

She was right. Spain would think of means to undo the matter, as soon as he happened to sense the Polk Street disapproval. Moon wondered if Teddy had learned so much so rapidly, or if her estimate was merely by way of exploration. Behind him, he heard her greet someone, and he turned. China Wallace was hurrying in through the door.

"China! Come in—this is Mrs. Birdsong, Mrs. Wallace."

China paused, nodded to Teddy, and turned a pale and scarcely composed face to him.

"Is something wrong?"

"I—I wanted to see Frank," she said.

"He's out. Barber shop, I think." Which was what Frank had said when he left; it meant, ordinarily, the Monarch.

China looked about the store uncertainly. She wore another of her blousy dresses and a tiny hat; her hands held tightly to a white wicker bucket of a purse. "Richard, I must talk to you."

Moon glanced at Teddy. He said, "Let's go to the back." He led China through the partition and into his own office, a place almost strange to him, since the coffee stand was in Frank's. They sat down, she just on the edge of the chair, and he said again, "Is something the matter?"

"Oh, it's Mr. Remo. I'm afraid he's—ill."

"What? Here, let me call out there—"

"No, wait. It isn't that kind of ill, and I've no idea what Brother may be doing. You see, Mr. Remo telephoned me, and he sounded very—well, he sounded irrational."

"Have you told Spain?"

"No, there's been so much load on him lately. If we could locate Frank, he and I might run out."

"China, what's wrong with Remo? Do you mean he is drinking?"

She nodded. "Just a few minutes ago, he called. I tried to find out if Brother was all right, but he wasn't able to make much sense. I'm scared silly. But I don't want to alarm the others so soon after all this other. And Mr. Remo may really be just ill."

350

Moon got up; he'd never seen Remo drunk, nor did he now quite believe it. He said, "You'd better not wait for Frank. I'll go with you."

"Oh, please do. Frank isn't strong, anyway. I mean, if there's anything that has to be done—"

He felt a foolish flash of pleasure. He took her arm and they hurried out back to Moon's car. The alley sun fell on her, lighting the ash hair as he backed out and got the car in motion.

"Don't worry. Remo hasn't a mean bone in his body."

"Oh, I know that. But poor Beloved, he might wander off. You know, he did set a fire once."

He drove hard, with great thunder from the unrepaired muffler attracting eyes to them. "You haven't called Bethel, either?"

"No."

"Why, really, China? You like Remo, don't you?"

She nodded. "He's been so—so faithful, really. There's been so much trouble, but he isn't to blame. Brother gets—gets less controllable, doesn't he?"

He reached the highway, and shortly was cutting off it onto the old road. The Chevvy roared and banged, then grew light on its springs as if touching only the high spots. China said nothing.

Moon said, "Why do you think Remo is drinking?"

"He told me. It was one of the few things I understood. He said he was celebrating a wedding."

"Whose?"

"I don't know."

Moon felt a disappointed, unactionable sort of anger against Remo. "Do you know why he called you, China? I mean instead of Spain, or someone else?"

"No, but I'm glad he did."

"Because he has a crush on you, in a clumsy schoolboy way."

"Please, Richard—"

"It's true. He'd love the chance to put his coat in the mud for you."

They came in sight of the house. On the sunny south side, Brother stood showering himself with the water hose. He wore only tennis shoes and candy-striped shorts; they could see how his shoulders had sunburned crimson, how the bald head gleamed red inside the high-clipped halo of hair.

"Oh, thank God!" China said. "Poor Beloved."

Chiner, old Cecil Munger used to pronounce it when scolding her for climbing up to his lap, or when telling her, antagonistically, how special she was. "Chiner, lookee there," Papa pointed one Sunday in the last year of his life as, together in the old truck, they chased after a Cadillac which was crashing along astride a wire fence, "look at 'im rip up them posts!"

"Oh, Papa, what will we ever do with him?"

"Well, one thing, you don't get sore at June. Keep that in mind, girl; Brother only likes to play. He ain't never goin' to hurt nobody, on account of he don't hate nothing, an' I'll brain anybody that—Jesus, look at 'im go!"

"We'll never catch him."

"Sure we will. An' you younguns, you better learn how. When I'm gone, you got to look after 'im."

"Oh, I will, Papa."

"See to it. Brother, he's sort of beloved of God."

From Papa, that was surprising. She said, "What do you mean?"

"It's in the Atlas. Says over in India, a dimwit is like a holy man. Folks all say he's beloved of God, and they watch out for 'im. It's how Brother is, an' I know best how it ain't no fault of his own."

"I'm glad you told me that, Papa. I wish the others could have heard—"

"Oh hell, will yu' look at that sonofabitch eatin' up that fence! Hey, June! Damn you, when I ketch you, I'm going to peel your hide!"

Beloved. . . .

Moon slowed the car for silence; he crept it onto the cattle guard and across. Brother appeared not to have seen them. He was laughing and he stuck the hose into the waist-band of his underwear, and two streams of water gushed out the legs.

"China, you wait here. I'll get him into his clothes, then you can come on."

"No, Richard. You go to the house for Remo. I can manage best, we don't want him scooting underneath when he sees you."

Moon coasted the car up near the porch and stopped. They got out together, out of June's sight, now, but within yards of him. Moon hesitated. "He might be a little wild, China. If he's scared."

She tried to smile. "It's all right."

Moon went inside. From the living room he could see straight through to where John Remo lay shirtless and groaning on the kitchen floor. Moon went to him and turned him over. "Hey," the old Pole sighed, and he looked up dully through the heavy wrinkled eyelids. "Moon, old stud—"

"You jackass," Moon said. "Get up." He pulled on a thick arm that yielded slackly, then dropped it. There was broken glass about, and a gash bled on Remo's forearm.

"Come on, Remo. Before China sees you."

Moon got him half up, then dropped him as he heard China scream. He pounded out the back and around the house.

Brother's arms were locked about his sister in a great flabby hug. His body pushed hard against hers, the new tattoo leered over her shoulder like an extra grin. China's little hat was gone. Their feet slipped in an ugly dance. Moon saw them fall hard, Brother's nudity on top. The big man was laughing, his white flanks and thighs quivering. China fought wildly, screaming. Moon seized the round water-slick face and pulled Brother's head back. June grimaced, but didn't let go. Moon yelled at him, he kicked a heel into the soft ribs. Brother only grunted and rolled, pulling her with him.

"Richard, the baby!"

Moon swore, he wrenched futilely at the shapeless arms. He wedged a hand between them. Brother threshed, pulling Moon down and into a tangle that wrestled in the mud. It was then Moon smelled the whisky. In panic he yanked an arm free and jabbed fingers at the wide blue eyes. The bald head jerked back, and Moon smashed the face with his fist.

June Munger released her. He giggled weakly. He turned heavily over onto his back, and he lay there with his arms spread, naked belly heaving, the child eyes half closed.

Moon bent to China. As he put his arms beneath her, she pressed her face hard against his shoulder. Her body shook, but she made no sound. He took her up like a broken doll and carried her into the house. He put her on the couch. The look of terror and revulsion remained on her face.

"I'll call a doctor."

"No, don't. Please don't; I'm all right."

"But we have to. The—"

"The baby is all right. I'd know if it wasn't."

In half an hour he attended to Brother and his keeper. Then he and China faced each other like stunned survivors. China had washed her face and combed her hair. A bruise blackened one of the fair temples, streaks of drying mud clung to her dress.

He said, gently, "It was my fault. It never occurred to me he might have gotten some whisky."

She looked up, across the kitchen table at him, and he saw the small red bruises appearing around her lips. The marks of cruel kissing, edging a mouth that seemed, now, to retaste the terror. "I—I don't know what to do," she said.

"Are you sure you're all right?"

She nodded and got up, moving unsteadily toward the refrigerator. "I'll make us a cool drink."

As she filled glasses with ice cubes, Moon went again to the bedrooms. John Remo lay on his back, mouth yawned open to accommodate his great breathing. One foot hung over the side of the bed and was set firmly flat on the floor. He appeared not to have moved. In the next room, Brother lay curled on his side; he had turned, and the icepack had fallen off his nose. The nostrils had bled only briefly, and the swelling wasn't great.

Moon returned to the kitchen. China had cleared away the whisky bottles, and at each place was a tall glass of ice water. "Both asleep," he said, and sat down.

China shuddered. "I almost came out here alone."

"But you didn't."

"If it had been Frank. Frank couldn't have—have stopped it."

"But it wasn't Frank. It's over."

She touched her glass. "Thank you, Richard." Then she said, "I drink gallons of water when it's this hot."

"Damn that Remo."

"I read his letter," she said.

"Me, too. But I still don't understand."

She took a sip of water. He saw that her hands still trembled, he noticed bruises on the slim white forearms. She said, "Poor Spain. I'm afraid he'll not be able to stand this."

"You mean to tell them, China?"

"I don't know."

Moon rubbed a swollen knuckle; he thought of Bethel, the way she would put hands behind her to grip the cabinet whenever Remo called. "What you said, coming out," he said. "I think you are right."

"Oh, Richard, God bless you. You don't want Bethel hurt."

"I don't want her hurt." He meant it, more deeply as he said it than he had known. "Look, Remo will be on his feet in a few hours. June too. I can stay here until they are. You could take my car back to town. We'd not have to tell anyone, at least, not for a while. And I can call Bethel, tell her Remo is sick and that I'll stay out here overnight."

China looked at him queerly; for a moment he could not sense her certain uniqueness, so that she might have been any of the Mungers. "Why will you do this, Richard, when you hate us so?"

"I don't hate anyone."

She put a hand to her forehead. "Oh, forgive me, Richard. I'm not myself. I—"

"It's all right."

Everyone loves China, he thought. Except that now, his mind seemed to experiment with this definition of her; it said to him, abruptly, today has changed her, or changed me. There are new terms: China is desired by everyone but me, and how is that? It lay boldly in his thought, at once more clear than the sight of her face drawn by shock, or the hideousness of Brother's form over hers. She seemed disrobed of her magic, her saintliness. Henceforth, he realized, he'd be China's friend, not her worshipper. He had seen her when the sweetness was weak, when the perfection was imperfect.

"It's past four o'clock," he said. "If you feel like driving, maybe you should go now."

"Yes." She got up; she smiled at him.

He picked up her crushed hat and the muddied purse and put them in the car for her. He held the door as she got in daintily. She shook her head, and her shoulders shuddered once, then were stable.

"I can't tell you how I feel, Richard. But, from my heart, believe me, I'm so thankful for you."

"Do you feel—comfortable, now?"

"Don't worry about me. I've promised everyone I'll see the doctor tomorrow."

Without the old awe of her he said, "China, you hate the thought of that, don't you?"

She did not answer.

"I'm sorry. Drive carefully."

She beckoned him down to her. She kissed him lightly, small-girlishly, on the cheek. He watched her away, conscious that his pity for her—hadn't this been a horror, hadn't she lost her Beloved?—was late. Even now, as it arrived, it was shallow; it seemed that he wasn't deeply afraid for her. Perhaps it was because her special allure was so newly gone.

He walked back to the house. The hot sun fell on him; a hundred sparrows descended to nip at puddles in June's little swamp, or to inquire of the ground what had happened here before flying away to disperse the ugly news. Moon watched them a moment and grew aware of an unexpected

356

contentment in himself. His mind went darting at it, to understand but preserve it. He pondered whether, by the blow of his fist, he had become some sort of a functioneer. Actually, the events had determined the action. Like the nights with Teddy or the drinks with Remo, this had occurred outside the Munger surveillance. If the board had been in session, would he have thought or acted at all?

Here, he decided, was an unlucky habit. Whenever he dared think of having won, his mind examined the victory so coldly that it became a defeat. He felt deflated, exhausted, but the curious germ of satisfaction did not fade.

He telephoned Bethel. She reacted with fright because he was at The Old Place; then she accepted the lie that Remo had a touch of ptomaine. He bid her good evening and good night. As he looked in on the sleepers again, he wondered why her voice with its slight, lingering rural accents had sounded so good to him.

XXI

With plumbers, Amarillo rated as a good town. The city's special atmosphere was such that the do-it-yourself mania never did, or never could, bite into the skilled trades. Scores of plumbing firms prospered. When a faucet leaked or a drain stopped, the distressed householder might choose his relief from dozens of possibilities. Between the larger of these, competition was rough and spirited.

At the top of the heap stood the T. J. Cowles Company. The owner, spoken of by his friends as "Bowels Cowles," which summed up both his profession and physique, and known to his employees as "Big Jesus" because he preached perfection and thought he had attained it, was wholly responsible for this success. He was a wit and a fighter, one of those coarse, shrewd, sloven yet likeable men who build and who overawe others. He had an enormous capacity for work, a barefoot kind of language accepted as picturesque rather than vulgar, and a personal force that, unprecedentedly, had put the plumbing trade into a country club. Mr. Cowles owned the precious competitive knack; he was dual. He could shine as an executive in one moment and as a working plumber the next.

As usual on this Saturday morning, he was short-handed. He

358

kept a five-day week for half of his crew, to avoid time-and-a-half, and today the others happened to be tied up at making sewer taps in a new subdivision. When the lady on Fannin Street called that the bottom had dropped out of her water heater and her house was being flooded, Mr. Cowles assigned himself to the call.

He never asked anyone to wait; the company's advertising motto promised service "sooner than immediately." He handed the office to his bookkeeper and pulled on a pair of starched overalls over his seersucker suit and roared off in the oldest of his repair trucks. Before thinking, he started out on the most direct course to Fannin Street. Then he grinned at himself for slighting his own policy, and he circled the truck around to make his swing through downtown.

The practice was something he had picked up from the ambulance people. For years, these always managed to go screaming and careening down Polk, whatever the hazard or inconvenience, so that thousands might see which company had been preferred in this obviously severe emergency. Mr. Cowles had painted huge signs on his trucks, and he required that his drivers negotiate the street with every air of anxious urgency.

He swung the panel wagon onto Polk from Third and hurried south with much roar and rattle. More than a few shoppers turned to look. Soon, Mr. Cowles expected to add a new sign across the rear of every truck, saying something like "There Goes Another Cowles's Plumber to the Rescue."

He struck the lights at Fifth, Sixth, and Seventh Avenues just right, and he switched to an outside lane for a good run at the signal on Eighth. A policeman waved him on, and he accelerated. Then a small ashen-haired woman on the curb looked at the signal, and at the truck, and stepped out. He stomped the brake. Tires screeched, the truck slewed sideways. Joints of pipe and a hundred pounds of wrenches clattered off shelves in the back, so that he heard nothing else.

But he knew he had hit her.

He ran around the truck. She was small as a child, she had a lovely delicate face. She lay on her back, a maternity dress spread wide over the brick paving. "My God, I had the light," he told the gathering spectators.

The policeman was racing to his callbox. People streamed off the sidewalks. Cowles knelt to look at her. As he started to lift her, someone in the crowd shouted, "Don't touch her; that's what the Red Cross says!"

Two doctors in white jackets came out of the Professional Building, one running and one walking.

Cowles said, "She stepped right in front of me. Right in front of me! I wasn't going over twenty, and she stepped right square in front of me!"

The crowd opened to let the doctors through. The older man who had walked picked up her wrist. "She'd just left my office," he said. Then, "Won't you people move back, please?"

"I saw it happen," a woman's voice said loudly, "I was just coming out of Levine's when I looked up, and wham. . . ." A man at the inner edge of the crowd looked at his watch, frowned, and began plowing his way out, and he commented, "She doesn't look bad; just bumped a little, and she'll be all right."

In twenty minutes, China was dead.

The stupefying news ran along Polk almost as rapidly as it found and cut down the Mungers. It assembled businessmen on streetcorners; a second crowd formed at The Scene. An odd moratorium fell on all the wry old Munger tales. Everyone loved China. She the pretty one; in fact, the very loveliest among the fifty-five: shouldn't someone think to shut off the music at the Downtown Club? Maybe they ought to close the bar. T. J. Cowles himself had been driving the truck; he had a heart attack at the hospital, he was getting oxygen, it was said.

At The Camera House, Moon first disbelieved. Then he was mildly excited, and after that, steady and detached. He prepared to go out to the hospital methodically. The whole thing was a drama; whatever he did was formal and theatrical. He moved through the day deliberately making the gestures and reading the lines. His throat constricted and remained tight, but otherwise he felt rehearsed and mechanical. Not until very late did genuine grief break upon him. Then it staggered him, it beat him with racking power, and he was ashamed and dismayed that for hours he had been only hollow.

Along with Sid Glass, he got the women home. He saw Texas to bed with a sedative; he held Bethel through her screams and convulsive chills until a third hypo finally got her off to sleep; he spoke to his daughters of heaven and the natural patterns and bravery and saw in their terrified eyes that they heard none of it. Laska dissolved into a strange pale state that alternated at weeping and cursing; she seemed to blame Brother for the accident, just as though he'd been driving the truck. Of Spain, Moon knew only that he had fled from the hospital and was at home. This time, they did not wish to be together. Each hurried to privacy, and Moon found this surprising and past explanation.

Frank Wallace had spoken alone with the doctor, had emerged to shake his head at those waiting to learn if there'd be a baby, and he left the hospital quickly. He appeared at Gray Bros. to choose the dimensions of the service. Without contacting Spain, he also talked to a man from the newspapers. He contacted Reverend McLean and established the last details. He had accomplished it all before Sid and Moon finished with the family and the hovering Munger employees. It was dark when Moon drove his partner-in-law home.

"You all right, Frank?"

"Eeyo."

"I'll take you somewhere else, if you'd rather not be home tonight."

"No." Frank got out of the Chevvy. "Thanks, Moon."

"Look," Moon said uncomfortably, "I don't know how to say this. But I wanted to tell you you've changed my mind about you today."

"Sure. I'm an unfeeling skunk. Cold-blooded. Too indecent to bust all to pieces like I ought to."

"Not that. I meant it's good, how you took hold of everything."

Frank said "Good night" and went up the walk to his house.

Moon drove home. Carrie was there, setting out sandwiches for the children. Bethel remained asleep, lying extraordinarily on her back and breathing very deeply. He told Carrie he had to drive out to The Old Place, and he kissed first Carol, then Hannah. "No TV tonight, hear me? And when Carrie says go to bed, then go to bed."

"How does it feel to be dead?" Carol said.

"We'll talk about everything tomorrow."

"Hannah says Aunt China was to blame, she says Aunt China didn't even look where she was going. That's not true, is it? I mean—"

"Tomorrow," Moon said.

He drove through a calm clear night, out the road that seemed ancient and almost ghostly. He sat in the kitchen an hour with John Remo. The old cop listened; he wiped his face hard with a stained handkerchief, and he got out whisky and they had a silent drink. He said, "God, it's the good ones that always get it, ain't it?"

"The thing now is Brother."

"What does Spain want me to do?"

"I haven't talked to him," Moon said.

"Well, don't put that chore on me. I ain't the hoss to do that to 'im."

"Where has he gone?"

"Out to feed the chickens. He's been queer all day, Moon. No singing, no boring. He ain't touched his golf sticks that I know of. While you was talking, I was thinking about that. You can't tell about 'im; maybe he kind of knows about her already. I mean, maybe he gets hunches when things ain't right."

Moon rubbed his temples; his headache had begun to throb. "Sid and I talked about it. We thought he oughtn't to hear, not for a while yet. The family has had enough without June breaking out of here for town."

"Well, it'll be on the news, won't it? TV and stuff?"

"I hadn't thought of that."

Remo said, "I guess I could pull out a few tubes, put the set on the blink for a few days."

They poured more whisky and sat gazing at it. Abruptly Remo said, "Oh Christ, how could such a bitchy thing happen? Her, when the world's full of sorry bastards and sluts and—"

"Have your drink, John. You can't cuss her back to life."

"What's gonna be done about that plumber?"

"It wasn't his fault. You better think about Brother."

Remo groaned, he put the great hands over his face. After a moment he said, "Feels goofy, don't it, Moon? Sitting here this way, figuring ahead about that slob, like her dying starts something instead of finishes it. Me, I keep thinking, the last time she seen me, I was soused to the gills. What did I say to her?"

"Nothing. You were flat when we got here."

"Did she mention anything about me?"

"She read your letter, and she said she was sorry about your mother if you were, and glad about it if you were glad. And that was all. Anyway, that was one thing, and this is another, and they don't belong together."

"Hell," Remo said, "I'm not off my rocker, if that's what you're gettin' at. Someone like her dies, right after you pull a deal like I pulled, and you think about it, that's all."

"You won't get drunk as soon as I leave?"

"Damn you, Moon."

"I'm sorry." Moon got up. "I have to go. Fix it so he can't get the word, will you? In a couple of days they'll be in shape to decide how to handle him."

Remo nodded. He walked along out to the car. "Funeral's Monday, you said. I'd like to make it. Reckon Spain's new man will get here that quick?"

"I haven't heard anything about him." Moon let the old giant shut the car door for him. "If he should show up, you won't shove off without punching in, will you?"

"I don't know," Remo said. "Don't think I'd do that, but I might." He remained bent to the window, as if he considered whether to explain. Then he straightened and backed away.

Moon drove out slowly; his car seemed already to be falling into China's funeral procession.

On Sunday, the telegrams were pouring in. Some from the expected sympathizers, a few from persons no member of the family could remember or identify, plus a surprising number from high places. The wires were delivered to Spain's home. He read each one thoughtfully before sending it on the rounds among his sisters. At first, Spain took the messages in consternation. Soon they began to lift him. China left a vast chasm in the family, in the big picture. The condolences from mighty people did not fill, but they diminished the darkness.

Spain began to think the whole Golden Spread, and its limbs that extended to Austin and Denver and Santa Fe and Washington, shared the Munger loss. It was a good if not a joyous discovery, but had there ever been joy? He could remember only that in previous times, there had been lesser griefs. And always, at least, there had existed the closeness, the talent to agree, the solid front, the Munger chins setting in firm, identical fortitude.

Late in the afternoon, a lengthy and perfectly composed wire arrived from the governor. Spain was overwhelmed. He got to his feet. He read the message over and over to Mom, and on the telephone to his sisters. Suddenly China seemed to have been sacrificed for a cause, the same cause of these past thirteen years. She died so that those who remained would surely stay together. He shuddered at the suggestion that her passing had advanced them toward their end, but wasn't it a normal truth; didn't all clouds have your silver lining? China must always be mourned, and never forgotten. Still, with the messages in his hand, Spain began to see her death as a gesture on behalf of them all. Her tragedy had its triumph; she was invested in the Munger future, which made every goal twice as dear and abandonment twice as unthinkable.

Shortly, Spain got in touch with Gray Bros. He reviewed the funeral plan, directed several changes there, among them a finer and more costly casket than Frank had settled on. He talked with his sisters and afterward with Moon about his trip to the country and in appreciation of your sharp thinking about the problem of breaking your sad news to Brother. The shock of this greatest blow, this forever absence of the pretty one, the one most loved, was not put aside. But at last it was being dealt with. The Munger oneness rose, the bereaved would carry on.

Moon watched it happen, and wondered that Spain did not call the board together.

On Monday China was presented in the Gray Bros. state room. From Spain's house was issued a schedule for the viewings; each wife and husband were to go separately and remain briefly. Moon could make nothing of it. When Bethel's turn came, he took her arm and held it tightly so she'd not mind and asked her, "Why are we doing it this way?"

"Texas thought—we all thought, actually—well, we just felt it would be better if we didn't all gather there at one time." She alluded to something in the past, and Moon could not place it. He inquired no further.

China was beautiful. Pale and fair, dainty; sweet to see, as if the warmth so especially hers was immortal. Together they wept over her. Carol and Hannah cried for the first time, and Moon was thankful for their release. He had worried about them while understanding that for the very young, the painful fact is not accepted until seen. They stayed only a minute. Moon supported Bethel until they reached the car. Before he started the engine, he searched for and found what had troubled him. It was the dress China wore. It was ribboned, almost juvenile. For China, he thought, Frank should have chosen a soft, pastel shroud.

At two, the funeral began with music that filled Gray's new, high-raftered chapel. They heard it before they were shown into a screened-off booth flanking the platform. They sat removed from scrutiny of the audience, close together in the glass-faced chamber meant to swallow sorrow's sound. Moon held Bethel's hand, and he let his mind travel. To the service for his mother, now so vague in detail; to his father, now a part of the ground and perhaps believing yet that all the dead are walked upon and plowed up and irrigated and grazed over. He denied it for China. Never for China.

He did not listen until Reverend McLean's words began invading them through a wall speaker at their backs. The man's voice faltered as he read the history; again as he recited the Psalm. Moon recognized everything. There was a sudden reminiscence in the bronze casket, in the figure of the pastor, in the inadequacy of the words. Was there nothing, nothing, that hadn't occurred before?

Reverend McLean gripped the pulpit; he almost leaned upon it. He spoke too feelingly—he appeared personally distraught. It seemed to Moon, then, that the pastor had seen China too many times in his church; that he loved her as all men had, in an area not wholly included in Christian brotherhood. Moon remembered China's sympathy for the pastor's birthmark, how she had encouraged him to the sideburns. He doesn't preach, Moon thought. He mourns aloud. An anger stirred in Moon, and he debated the man. Death is new life, your words say, but your face disbelieves it. Beauty a permanency? Then why does your tone say beauty passed with her? Faith? How you speak of it: so feebly, in such small conviction—is it the same for you, poor Reverend, do you find also that faith comes slowly, piecemeal, while fear rips and gobbles and swallows great chunks?

In twenty minutes, Reverend McLean finished; he sat down with damp forehead rested in one hand. A man gray as Gabriel must be gray propped up the lid of the casket. The queue began.

They came forward by rows and sections, shuffling toward China, each bound to gaze down at the beautiful face, solemnly and not too long. Young men in charcoal suits whispered and nodded and signaled, and the file formed and moved. Moon hated that he could see it. Something of repugnance reached for him from this parade. Uneasy men, hands in coat pockets or crossed over prominent bellies. Women with best handkerchiefs flagging, careful to guard against awkwardness in this stop-and-start march. Each to pause only slightly, to look once at death's loveliest face.

It seemed to Moon he knew what each of them thought. Here

lies me, after one unescapable day or tragic night, yet I must prohibit the moment; I cannot allow it; how can I, me, endure such a sleep! Moon shuddered. Strangers glanced down at China, then shed their tears for themselves. Death is too long, and too lonely.

Beside him, Bethel lowered her head. Moon had to go on watching the line. It struck him how limited is the human spirit; how much greater if it might have been given one more capacity, how much finer if each being could weep even once for a loss that was truly separate from self. If there existed tears of such purity, how much, now, he'd want to release them. But there was nothing except to be calculatedly sorry, nothing but to think upon the brevity of the human moment and of the queue that must shuffle past us all; only the admission to make, that China wasn't China any longer, but was now all the dead who ever died, and not to be mourned back. He thought again of his father, keeping the wheels of his chair off bare ground. If they all came back, wouldn't it shrink the world?

Moon began to smell Frank Wallace's whisky.

The chapel emptied and was quiet. Only the pallbearers remained in their forward row; at one end, Mr. Williams-the-lawyer, at the other, Mr. Williams-the-engineer. The man who entered the family booth persuaded gently, "If you will, dear friends," and they arose and filed out. They stood then beside China. Moon did not look at her, he thought of her instead, in navy blue, squatting to coax Brother from beneath the house. Spain's voice said, "Good-by, Baby," and one by one, the Mungers put soundless kisses on the smooth cold forehead.

In disciplined sequence, then, the sunshine, the black limousines behind the black coach, the lagging drive to Rest Park and to the plot where Cecil and Melita Munger lay; the reading, the prayer; every protocol adhered to in the saddest diplomacy of them all.

Moon forgot his discoveries.

He held to Bethel. He wept shudderingly because China, who was beautiful, must be left alone in earth and silence and time.

XXII

The children had gone home with Texas, who did not wish to be alone. Moon drove Bethel back from the cemetery along a back route. When he spied a small green-fronted drive-in café, he turned into it. "I want some coffee, Beth."

"All right. Let them bring me a Coke."

She had taken off the black hat and veil; it lay in the seat between them. She looked tired and emptied and, in the dull black dress, very pale and blond. It occurred to him that now, his wife was the fairest and handsomest of the Mungers.

"I'll miss her, Richard. Every day."

"Yes."

"It feels so vacant. And I keep thinking, how strange. Like a cycle that was planned and started a million years ago. Something we couldn't touch, however we tried."

"I don't understand, Beth."

"This is the seventh. Thirteen years ago today, Papa died."

Moon hadn't even thought of it. Except for a plumbing truck, this would have been the decisive day. The in-laws' millennium, the end of months and years marked off on a prisoner's calendar. He wondered if Frank had forgotten also. No, Frank would not.

"I'm worried about Frank," Bethel said out of grief's closeness, or some extraordinary access to his thoughts.

"Where is he?"

"He left alone, though I did ask him to come with us. I imagine he went home, and maybe he shouldn't be there. Do you think he would come to supper?"

"Maybe. I can call him."

Moon left the car for the pay booth tacked at a corner of the café. He called China's number—no, Frank's—and allowed it to ring a full minute. Then he tried the Monarch. Mr. Wallace wasn't in; yes, he had been for a few minutes; no, positively, Mr. Wallace was long gone.

"No?" Bethel said as he returned to the car.

"He doesn't answer."

"He's been so—so poised, Richard. Hasn't shown how he feels. When he slows down, and begins to think—"

"Frank will be all right."

Moon summoned a girl for more coffee. He'd not drink it, as he'd not finished the first. But he needed just to sit, to let the talk go on. He started a cigarette, the one he had wanted so badly as they left Rest Park. He said, "You think so clearly at funerals. Things get pretty fundamental, for a while."

"Yes."

"I've been to only a half-dozen in my life. I remember now that each one was this way. For a while, most things seem small. You want to do something afterwards. Something direct, and right."

"Oh, Richard, I feel that way! I think it's why I'm worried about Frank."

He nodded. "With me, it's like wanting to get clean, all at once." He tensed as he spoke; his mind warned him. Stop, now. If you do not believe in hurt, stop.

They were silent for a time. Then they called each other's names at the same instant, stopped, and smiled at each other. "Go ahead," he said.

"Well, it's hard to say. But I feel so unright with China. As you say; like I wasn't clean toward her. She was so lovely, and

369

sweet. That was good, wasn't it? Good for me, because I could see it, and feel it. But since she—now, it's as though I had been jealous, or afraid of her. I—"

"Don't, Beth."

"I won't cry. But let me talk. It pleased me for everyone to love my sister. I wanted them to. Except you. I tried not to think—"

"Don't tell me, Bethel. I knew."

"Then you see, don't you? I mean, at the USO, you remember the time. And when Carol was born and she stayed with us. And when—oh, just all the times. I watched you, and I couldn't help it. While I loved her, I blamed her. Now she's gone. It's—it's like I caused it to happen."

"That's foolish."

"Not to me."

A flush had enlivened her face; she held her hands together in her lap. "You were wrong, Beth."

"Yes. I believe that, now."

"But you never did before?"

"Not until—until very lately."

There was scarcely a pause, scarcely a change in his voice. He simply heard himself beginning to destroy her. "I guess it's my turn. It's true, I've seen China just as some wonderful creature outside of the race, someone to look at and listen to. But what you think—what you thought of me, I've done."

She said, "Is that the—the prologue of the unfaithful husband?"

He turned to her; it was incredible. She knew. Her eyes met his, unblinking, not quite accusing. Then he thought this but a trick of his guilt, and he turned away so he might go on.

"This is necessary," he said. "I can't alibi it; I'm not sure I can really say it."

"Don't."

She confused him, amazed him. He searched the pale face; where was his relief, his glory of confession?

"If I'm not mistaken," she said, "this is to be about Mrs. Birdsong. I've been waiting. But now I don't want to hear it."

370

"How long have you known?"

"Please, let's don't get into it. Not today."

"Beth. I have to find out."

"All right. I've known since you painted the barn. Mrs.—that woman telephoned me during the night. You'd just left her apartment, she said."

Moon sought to rouse his mind, to prod it up through stupor and shame. "She called you?"

"Do you find it hard to believe?"

"Yes. I mean, I don't know."

There was Teddy Birdsong, in drunken prayer at Cecil Munger's old couch. The painted ruthless face, so suddenly all remorse and agony. He even brought to his lips, now, his term for it. Teddy of the reverse inhibitions, the horror preparing to occur. . . .

"She sounded sodden with drink," Bethel said coldly. "She told me she needed to—to 'get straight,' I believe that was her phrase."

He said, "She's that way."

"And of course, you would know."

He caught the malice that edged her tone. He welcomed it. Until now, such impersonal calm. All this emotionless discussion of a crime meant for screaming. If she'd but reach across, claw him blind—

"Yes, I do know!" he told her. "She is the unhappiest person alive. You, I, no one ever had such torture. And I'm not saying this as the reason I went to her! I went for me!"

"You're shouting, Richard."

"All right!"

They sat looking ahead, he through the windshield at an idle carhop who had turned to ogle them. He glared at the girl, and as she turned away, he snatched out a cigarette. When he spoke to Bethel, it was softly, and without facing her.

"So, now?" he said.

"It's hurt for several weeks, Richard. Lately it hurts less."

"God, I'm sorry."

She tried to laugh. "This way, I've had time to think. The

371

truth is, I thought a lot; I had a speech ready for this occasion. Had it all canned up in my mind, precooked for you. But I don't want to make it."

"Go ahead."

"No. But I ought to tell you how it was for me. You're going to need to know. The night she called—that first night, I hated you. Hated you for the cheap rotten dirty sex of it. Then I hated you for myself. If our marriage was so—so despicable a tie, then I'd hold you to it. I swore to rub your nose in it; I meant to smother you a little more every day. Women are like that, Richard. Even my kind. But, all that was the first night."

"Bethel—"

"Wait, you wanted this. I ran through all the ideas wronged wives are supposed to have. I thought about dying, I even thought about trying to—to walk in on you at just the vilest moment. That is a stage, I guess. I considered all the schoolgirl things. Some of them I really did. I stood and looked at myself in the mirror; I tried to see if I was so poor a creature as all that. Being an ugly duckling, that seemed like a reason. But I didn't *feel* ugly, or cold—oh, look at me, Richard; I want to know you hear me. I—where was I—then I turned everything inside out. The magazines say it; the wife is usually to blame.

"There was the movie equipment you wanted, the Mean Weeks, all the rest. I loved you again when I remembered, and then I could have whipped myself for letting it happen. For making it happen. That lasted and lasted, Richard. Then something else occurred to me, and I got very happy about it. It's true, I was really, honestly happy. Now, today, it hurts awfully to recall that. But at the time, I was glad about your—your mistress."

Her voice caught. "Do you remember the day you stayed home and we did the iris bulbs? That was one of those happy days. I kept saying, oh, how wonderful, my husband has been to bed with Mrs. Birdsong. I said, that means my husband isn't in love with my sister, because no man could ever cheat on China. So my husband doesn't lust for my pretty sister, hooray. It sounds silly, doesn't it? But I said it a hundred times. Laska

372

and I used to have a game, where we said something a hundred times, so we could believe it. Papa loves his little snotters, loves his little snotters, loves them, loves them—"

"Beth, let's go home."

"Don't get me off track. There was another attitude, after that was finished. Where you separate love from sex. I said that woman was just sex, and if I had a Kinsey husband, then I was like millions of other women, wasn't I? The only difference was, the others didn't know about it, and I knew. So I needed only forget, to be back where I was before. Oh, I never convinced myself of that, not for a minute. But it gave me time, and it gave you time I wanted you to have, though I don't know what for. Unless I wanted you to come to me with it—oh, get us some more coffee. You always smoke with yours, as if that made it twice as good. I wish I smoked. . . ."

The coffee came, and they drank it in an air that seemed almost ceremonious. Moon was numbed, unable to taste, or to make his lips sting with the heat. He kept thinking, of all the times to need a bathroom.

"It's all very odd," Bethel said. "I hardly considered leaving you. But my whole family is odd. Everyone says so."

He waited, but she offered nothing more. They finished the coffee and he signaled a girl to take away the tray. As he reached for the ignition, she said, "Richard—I think, now, I want you to tell me."

"I have."

"Not directly. You said you wanted to get clean."

"All right. I cheated on you, with Teddy Birdsong."

"Thank you. For saying it."

"Should I try the explanations, Bethel? It wouldn't improve anything, would it?"

"I don't think so."

Lost, she became more desirable than breath. "Maybe I should —I feel like pleading with you."

She smiled at him. "Didn't I tell you, Richard? I've made adjustments to this. Of a kind."

"Beth, let's stop this, please."

She leaned toward him, braced on one slim hand that crushed the veiled hat, and she said, "You can kiss me, if you like."

He twisted to meet her, then froze at sight of the pale icen eyes. He heard her teeth grind, felt a strong arm reach behind his neck. She hissed, "Come on, Mr. Hot Pants, kiss me!" Her mouth crushed to his. She held it there, bruising them both. He knew her teeth yearned to bite. Then she slid aside, her cheek hard and hot against his, and she whispered harshly, "How was she, dear; how does it feel when you do it with her?"

He shoved her away. He wrenched the car out into the street. They drove wordlessly home.

They sat several minutes at the curb, looking at the little house as though it were strange, or a place often seen but not understood before. Too much on the brink, Moon thought. Now, too much knowledge of each other, and with it the realization that there is never the ability to forget. The car seemed full of a special, necessary formality. Not good, yet better than what might have been. At last, Bethel sighed and opened her door to alight.

"What about Frank?" he said carefully. "Do you still want me to go find him?"

She turned as if to lash him with a terrible fury. Suddenly she controlled herself, and she said, "Spain may have thought to see about him. But if you don't mind, Richard, perhaps you should make sure. China would want that."

Up from his mire, he gazed in awe at his wife. In a stroke, she was finished with this picking of the dirtiest bone. Her inning deserved, claimed, and had; her mind fighting, now, to push it farther behind. He watched her move slowly up the walk. As she climbed the three steps to the house, she became more than just a tall fair woman spent and heartbroken from having buried a baby sister. She was someone he needed.

Then, Moon shuddered. Wouldn't this, too, be your matter for your board to lay its solid front to?

The day after the funeral, John Remo and June Munger sat on the porch of The Old Place and watched a car and trailer come up the road. Now that his bags were almost packed, Remo was impatient to be away. Time, destination, and purpose remained indefinite with him; they were matters to be let slide as altogether unimportant. Beside him, Brother kept rubbing fat thumbs together, and he seemed to pant, like an animal, from the heat. The happiest Munger wore fresh overalls for this occasion. His rim of gray hair was oiled down, the snarl of copper eyebrows was up out of his line of vision. He had put on his dress shoes, these sturdy new Thom McAn's bulging at their bunion slits, and about his throat was tied one of Spain's white scarves.

"Mister Remo," he whispered, "ain't China an' all them comin' out, Mister Remo?"

"Not today."

"Well goddam, Mister Remo, how come—"

"Stop cussin'."

They watched the big sedan swing wide for its pass at the cattle guard. Still the driver had to halt and back twice, then maneuver with screaming engine and creeping gears to bring the trailer house safely across. Sun glinted off the trailer's aluminum shell, and Remo had to squint to read the red lettering on the side. Judo Jack Bloodstone, Champion, it said.

The man's name was in fact Lois Bloodstone—Lois like a woman, Spain said on the phone—and with Essie, his wife, he had wrestled professionally for almost twenty years. Brother and The Old Place were to be their retirement.

The car came upslope and onto the gravel parking area. The driver was a T-shirted giant and the woman beside him looked as ample. Both had long hair startlingly peroxided. Judo Jack pushed open a door and two small black dogs popped out. "Them's my cocker spaniards," Judo Jack yelled. "That stupid one there is Joe, and that nutty one yonder is Ollie. This here is Essie, my Missus."

Remo met them on the steps and put out his hand. "I'm John Remolewski," he said, and was shocked at how the unfamiliar whole name leaped to his mouth. "Glad you come; I kind of looked for you yesterday."

Judo Jack had one cotton eye, opaque and milky and apparently sightless. He wore elevated scars on both brows where, in more than a few rings, his opponents must have missed their cues or else gotten carried away. The cloudy eye blinked. "Well, I was in town, but them folks had a funeral or something, so's I had to wait to get the dope—"

Remo whispered, "June ain't supposed to know about that yet."

"Yeah, I forgot." Judo Jack looked up at Brother. The baby eyes were staring at them as at some indescribable catastrophe. "Is this here the vegetable?"

"This is him."

Essie, who snatched up a squirming cocker for draping over one arm, winked at the fat frightened face and said, "We're gonna get along real fine, aren't we?"

Brother swallowed. A drop of tobacco juice was drying on his chin. "Hell, speak to her!" Remo shouted. Damn the ox, he'd moped around all morning. No golf sticks, no hole-borer, no "Jesus Loves Me," no nothing.

"You got a bad cold, Mr. Munger?" Essie said.

June gulped, his belly rolled spasmodically, and he began making hiccups.

Remo said, "No ma'am, he ain't. His folks just want him to wear his scarf all the time."

"Nuts," Essie said, "I have a couple of tattoos myself, though I won't say where," and she laughed heartily.

Remo frowned. "No harm meant," he said, "but I didn't know you was bringing Mrs. Bloodstone, on the kind of job this 'un is."

"Sure," Judo Jack grinned, "that's part of the deal. Ess, she's climbed many a hump with me." He slapped her great ungirdled behind. "Now babe, you find the kitchen and scare us up some lunch."

The woman sprang up to the porch, so quickly and powerfully that Brother shrank from her. She gave him a grin and as she got into the house she yelled, "Whew; we'll need to fumigate!"

Judo Jack drew a billfold out of his rear pocket. "The boss

man sent your check out with me. Says it gives you an extra week, and if that don't suit you, you can stop by and see 'im when you get to town." He held out the slip of Munger green, but pulled it back as Remo reached for it.

"Man," said Judo Jack, "they didn't pay you enough to spit at, did they?"

Remo's heavy textures awakened. "No, by God; they didn't." He took the check, enraged at the implication that the Bloodstones would be paid more. Still, there were two of them. And Spain wouldn't have changed. A cowboy is a cowboy.

The wrestler was saying, "Mr. Munger said you'd show me the place—Kee-rist, look at them Cadillacs!—and gimme all the pitch. Said you'd gimme the moneybelt, and stuff like that."

Brother padded up behind Remo, crowding close enough that Remo felt his fast breath. In grating whisper June said, "Mister Remo, you're a good sonofabitch; sure enough, Mister Remo!"

"Lemme see your neck," Judo Jack said.

" 'Scuse me, Mister Remo, but I sure ain't goin' to stick your tit in no more wringers, I'll say that, Mister Remo! China an' me, we'd just as leave you wasn't going off nowheres, if you'd just as soon as, Mister Remo!"

"Here," said Judo Jack, "let's peel that neck rag off a second."

"Mister Remo—"

"You do like Mr. Bloodstone says, hear me?"

Brother untied the scarf with slow unclever fingers. The tattoo hung on him like a broken blue grin. Judo Jack gaped. "Cut here!" he bellowed, and he whipped himself and whooped for Essie to come and see.

Loudly Brother said, "China, she don't care none!" and he pushed harder against Remo.

Remo stepped aside. "Quit scrounging up agin me, dammit."

If China were alive, Remo thought illogically, he'd be staying on despite everything. He seemed to remember that she'd always battled for him. But China was gone; his mother was equally dead to him. Through the nights since Saturday, he had ached for them; they became the only reason he'd held on.

He was being morbid, he knew. Maybe, away from The Old Place, this would change. A man needed peace and quiet and rest; he got tired of having heartburn every time Spain Munger ate a radish.

Brother said, "Boy, Mister Remo, them's the last pennies I aim to put in the john, Mister Remo, and you ain't got to go off, not on account of that, Mister Remo!"

Remo closed his fists behind his back and stared at the white road. "Mr. Bloodstone, I'm taking that new Cadillac to town with me; time for a tune-up. I reckon you can get somebody to bring it back."

"Go ahead," Jack said. "Tomorrow or the next day?"

"Quicker'n that."

The wrestler nodded, and he turned an appraisal upon June Munger. "Now Tubby," he said, "you listen to what I say. You don't know me yet. But I'm easy to get along with. We're gonna make some trips and spend a lot of money and all that, you and me and Ess. You're gonna like me just fine, long as you mind your onions. But when you don't, Bucko, I'm gonna kick your ass till your nose bleeds. You ain't gonna wreck this house with no more holes, and you ain't gonna sneak around here knocking chickens in the head. You ain't goin' to mess around under the house, and you're gonna wear your clothes right, like a gentleman, see? And another thing, while it's on my mind—first time I see you tampering with one of my dogs, I'm going to brad you. Now, you understand that, and we're off to the races. We'll have us a ball, all over the country, and Ess'll feed you better than you ever et. You don't horse around, and everything goes good, see?"

Brother stood trembling before the frosty, white eye and the bleached head of this, the new regime. He seemed unable to speak into the face of tyranny. Remo thought, good enough for him, the slob.

"If it's all the same to you, Mister Remo—"

"Chow!" yelled Essie.

"Me, I don't want no more Grape-Nuts throwed out, Mister Remo—"

"Go get washed up," Remo growled. Brother went at a trot. Remo followed Judo Jack inside.

"Hell, this ought to be pretty good," Jack said. "That Spain Munger, he's a good man to work for, huh?"

"Fine," Remo said.

"Around town, I notice, they say he's worth about two hundred million. Do you think there's anything to that?"

"I don't know."

"Damned sloppy old house, ain't it? Which is the best rooms? Ess can stay in the trailer tonight, but I guess we better move in and get settled tomorrow."

"June sort of wanders around at night. So you better take my room, downstairs. I got a hole, where you can watch 'im."

"Well, maybe I better just stop his wanderin'," Jack grinned. "There's times when I'd get put out at him looking in on me and Ess."

Remo stopped him in the dining room. "He don't know about his sister dying, not yet."

"Was that it? I didn't get straight who died."

Remo wanted to explode. Not straight *who* died! "Well, it'll bust him to pieces. Some of the family will tell him, later on."

Judo Jack shrugged. "Sounds silly," he said, "but okay."

They ate an omelet Essie had prepared in a bounty that heaped every plate. Except that Brother did not eat at all, until Judo Jack barked at him.

Afterward, Remo showed them around the place, from the tricky button on the automatic washer to the way you had to kick the bottom of the chicken house door to get it open. With Remo, it was to be accomplished in a hurry. He wanted badly, of a sudden, to have this night in his town. Maybe to hunt up old friends, perhaps even to drop by the station and badger the night captain. He wanted to walk the downtown streets, to drink a few beers, to see how it was his town had continued without him. He might, even, see Moon as he had promised. But most of all, he'd be getting away. Out of the tall Munger shadow under which he had lived two lonely years.

"Satisfied about everything?" he said.

Judo Jack nodded. "How come, with all that dough, it's such a junkpile?"

Remo finished packing his bags and closed them. As he carried them out, Brother followed, his hands plunged beneath the bib of the overalls, his eyes pleading and frightened.

"Mister Remo, I ain't gonna pee under them windows, even if it snows, I ain't, Mister Remo!"

"You better not, or Judo Jack will tromp you."

Remo kept his gaze away from the round face. Big tears, like crepe, dropped from the baby eyes. "You're a good sonofabitch, Mister Remo!"

Judo Jack came out on the porch, nudged Remo's luggage with his toe. "Can I give you a hand?"

"No, I ain't got much."

"Boy, Mister Remo, you crave one of my Cadillacs, why I don't care none, Mister Remo!"

"Hell, I'm leaving it at the garage."

"You want to have it, Mr. Remo, I don't care!"

Remo put his bags in the car. Judo Jack followed him out. Then, trailing at a distance came Brother, one hand dragging a battered golf club, and his voice trying to sing. When Remo was ready to get in the car, he turned and looked at them.

"Mr. Bloodstone, if you don't mind me saying, they's just a couple of things to think about, and the rest is easy. He copies whatever he sees, so you watch out what he gits a look at. The other thing is, he's high on his folks. Likes to have them out here for Sundays. If there's a spell they don't come, then you better watch out. And that's all; outside of that, he ain't much bother."

"I'm ready for him," Judo Jack said. "I just won't start out mothering him."

"I ain't mothered him any."

Jack grinned, but nodded. "Then he won't notice much difference."

Remo opened the car door, then turned again, compelled by the doom on June Munger's whitened face. "Come here," he said gruffly. The Beloved of China came slowly. Remo glared at him.

"June, you behave. You'll have it good, now. Mrs. Bloodstone says she'll fix plenty of Jello—"

"I don't care none how sorry you cook, Mister Remo; me, I like ole greasy cookin', honest, Mister Remo!"

"Goddammit; don't butt in when I'm talkin'!" Remo slapped a rough hand down on one of the pillowy shoulders. "So long," he said, and he started getting into the car.

As he bent he heard a hiss. The blow burned across the back of his neck. He went to his knees; the sun appeared to burst before his eyes. He shook his head to rid it of the lights, and an electric shock bolted down his spine. In a corner of his misty vision he saw the golf club. It lay on the ground beside him, its chrome steel shaft sharply bent.

"You ain't no good sonofabitch no more, Mister Remo!"

The sudden paralysis tingled and faded, and the pain began. Remo twisted slowly, stiff-necked. Judo Jack had Brother. The hairy arms seized a leisurely quarter-nelson, and with an easy shrug, Jack dumped Brother heavily to the ground. The ox, the happiest Munger, struck with a sob. Jack put his foot across the soft face as if leaning on a bar rail and pinned him there.

"You hurt?" he said.

Remo pushed up to his feet. "Hell no," he said, "it felt good!"

Jack grinned. "You go ahead, I got 'im."

Remo shook himself again; he began to see clearly the big shoe across Brother's nose, the clumsy flailing of all the fat limbs. "Git your foot off him," he said.

"Man, I thought for a minute he'd killed you," Jack laughed. "If you're okay, go ahead and shove off; I can handle him. Looks like I might as leave school him a little right here and now; I don't want him clouting me one of those."

Brother moaned and stopped struggling. His belly pumped rapidly, laboring for breath that had to be whistled in beneath Jack's shoe. Remo said, "Get your goddamn foot off him!"

The wrestler's head cocked. "Huh? It was him clobbered you; not me."

"I know it."

"Well, hold on. This here is my show now. You better get on, hit the road."

Remo had the revolver in the palm of his hand. He swung it; hazily he saw Judo Jack drop as though sitting too hurriedly. He landed on Brother's stomach. "Hey," he rubbed his ear, "what you think you're doing? You crazy too?"

"Git off him," Remo said, and he kicked him off.

The wrestler bounded up, he squared off with arms dangling. Remo leveled the pistol with the snub muzzle a foot from the cotton eye. The wrestler looked at it amazedly. "Good God, man, you whacked me with that!"

"You grab your wife and your dogs and leave. Right now."

Judo Jack jumped up and down, stomping the earth. "Mr. Munger's gonna get an earful of this, and you lemme catch you without that gun—!"

"Move."

"Shoot 'im, Mister Remo; boy, kill him, hot dog, the sonofabitch!"

"Dammit, you shut up!" Remo said.

He followed them about with the pistol as they collected the several items already brought from the trailer. Essie kept asking what was the matter, and neither man answered her. Jack sent her into a prolonged chase, around and around the house, to trap the dogs; they appeared too retarded to respond to their names. When the Bloodstones were loaded, they yelled their threats and sped away. The big trailer sideswiped a post as Judo Jack cut it onto the road.

"Boy, Mister Remo, I knew you was goin' to hit him one like you done, Mister Remo! If we went and ketched up, me, I could whop him agin, Mister Remo!"

Remo sat down on the porch to rub his head, to combat the wavering streaks of light that yet crossed his vision. He groaned; now what had he done? And why? He must have been thinking of *her*, of Brother as her pet, her Beloved, the infant she didn't have. It startled him to find this wasn't true. Nothing so generous, nothing in memoriam was involved; he couldn't draw from it any shred of self-approval. Oh, hell. He'd only wanted to look after the slob, and that was all. Just like he was blood kin, or something.

"Boy, what we gonna do now, Mister Remo?"

"Sit here and wait for Spain to bring the sheriff, I reckon. You got my tail in a sling for sure."

" 'Scuse me, Mister Remo. But you an' me, Mister Remo, if the high sheriff comes out here, you an' me we'll kick his ass till his nose bleeds, won't we, Mister Remo?"

"No, by God, we won't. And Christ, how come you swattin' me with that golf stick? Yu' near broke my neck. I got a notion to pick up that plank and tan your hide. . . ."

But already, June Munger was teeing up a row of new and costly golf balls, and as he chose a new club, he was humming that Jesus loved him.

The Munger enterprises had resumed operation at eight Tuesday morning. Briskly, chins-up, they ended the funeral holiday without any direct order from Spain. The employees reported tentatively, found their work piled up and waiting, and fell to it. The black wreaths came down from the doors, and your shoulders went to your wheels. The Estate people maintained a hushed reverence, but they moved about the suite in something of a trot. They found themselves with only the one day in which to prepare for the most significant board session of them all.

Richard Mooney reached town shortly after daybreak. He had searched until very late without locating Frank Wallace. Then he had gone home reluctantly and found his house dark. He tried vainly to smoke himself to sleep. He had lain out the night, staring through the dark at his wife. Beside his own pallet of spikes, her bed seemed dignified and lofty, the couch of a wronged queen. Finally he had risen, dressed quietly, and left. He got a tasteless breakfast at Georgie's. Now he sat alone in The Camera House, drinking the bitter coffee of his useless-ness, and scratching steadily at his hand although it hadn't begun to itch.

Shortly before nine, Teddy Birdsong called: sick and won't be in today; that's too bad, what's the trouble; oh thunder, any inky-pank ought to know better than ask a woman that; well, I'm sorry, we'll expect you tomorrow. As the call finished, Moon was reminded that his sex adventure might go before the directors tomorrow, along with the matters of the expiring trust and China's will. At least, Teddy Birdsong was no longer a secret, no longer beyond dismissal. If she were out of the store, her astounding figure out of view, might he not be more secure in his hard resolve against her?

Of course the idea was cowardly. Perhaps a man grew cold when desperate to reclaim his wife. He knew he would not fire Teddy; he realized, even, that when the Mungers did, he would fight for her. He wished he might explain that to Bethel.

He shook his head. Brain surgery, perhaps that was what he needed, and had always needed. Something special, to dissect memory, to remove the tiny white bean of conscience that must force him, always, to condemn immediately whatever would work practically toward his rescue. So, he must battle for Teddy Birdsong. Otherwise, he could never excuse himself.

Wow. At thirty-five, a man who misses his sleep misses it.

At mid-morning, Frank appeared. He came in through the rear, noisily. The florid face was puffed, its net of small veins was less definite under the exhaustion and dissipation. He said "Eeyo," lifelessly, and served himself coffee.

"What became of you last night?" Moon said. "I looked all over town."

"Why? Was I supposed to be out shooting myself?"

"Take it easy—"

"Don't worry. I won't shoot myself today, either."

Frank sat down. The coffee steamed his pink glasses, and he took them off and polished them on his sleeve. Moon thought it far past time for Frank to "break," as the Munger women felt sure he must. They could not see that Frank had "broken" years ago, that he had crumbled slowly ever since.

"I saw Spain this morning," he was saying. "Looks like they aren't sure what to do with me. I'm an heir, you know."

"Oh, can it, Frank—"

"I came to talk to you about it. I'm a multimillionaire—before taxes, anyhow."

Moon stared at China's husband—no, her wretched survivor. On this first day after her funeral, it was difficult not to greet him with outrage. But Moon recalled, suddenly, an old idea he had once transposed from English Literature II to his perpetual study of Davis & Scarborough. To a maggot deep in one of the carcasses, the whole world is flesh. Perhaps to Frank, buried under sudden new millions, the view was no more broad. Moon felt sorry, not angry. He said, "Aren't you a little bit drunk?"

"Yep. But you should have seen me a couple hours ago. Let me tell you—here, give me one of your cigarettes—I'll tell you what's happening up there, Moon. Spain—that bastard, he's making a triumph of this! I mean it. I lose my wife, and he turns it into a trophy for his damned big picture."

"Don't be stupid, Frank."

"You know what I'm talking about; has it ever happened any other way? God, I don't even think Spain knows he's doing it. But he's sitting up there with all those telegrams on his desk. He's got all the VIP's placed in order, from the governor on down. Hell, any sister of his is expendable, if there's to be such a net—"

"I can't listen to that!"

Frank looked up quickly. "I thought you could. If you can't, who can?"

Moon said, "Why don't you go home, get some sleep?"

Frank smiled humorlessly. "I'm through with this place, Moon. I'll pull out of it, and I won't apply for travel papers from the board. Do you understand that?"

"Maybe you need a vacation," Moon said. "But they want you up there tomorrow."

"They sure do," Frank said. "Funny, ain't it? It'll be the day. But to me, it doesn't count. Spain showed me the will, this morning. So it doesn't count. They'll do something, one way or another about the trust, and I won't even care!"

"You're repeating yourself," Moon said. "Drink the coffee."

"Hell, Moon, listen to this. All the wills are exactly alike, I found that out. Fact is, they're all in one file up there. You know what I get?"

"Millions, you said."

"The community property—house and cars and all that—those are mine. China's share of the estate, and her stock in the companies, is divided into sixths. One part to each of them—including that fruitcake out there on the farm, by damn. But the other sixth is mine." Frank laughed. "They've got them a partner, like it or not!"

Until now, Moon hadn't considered China's death as a business problem, as possibly, the destroyer of the one-minded Munger solidarity. He drew neither gloom nor cheer from the thought.

"You see it, Moon? Could be a break for you and old Sid. They might bust up, rather than let me in."

"I doubt it."

"It doesn't matter to me. The trust is over, and I'm in. They might organize Estate property into some kind of holding company, and issue stock to each other just like with Big Plains and Panhandle Green. The new outfit could go on leasing the oil land to PGP, the way Estate always has, and everything would go on as before. Except, they couldn't keep me from being a shareholder. Or—and I talked to Cicero Williams, so I know what I'm saying—they can divide everything, and cut everybody loose on his own. That way, I'm still in. The only other thing—they might hold together and buy me out. Hell, Moon, I don't care which it is. But you—I'd just as soon pull them across the barrel the way you prefer 'em, boy. What do you want?"

The cloying, almost lecherous fatherliness had crept into Frank's voice, into the way he leaned across the desk. Moon felt sick. He said, "I want you to stop sounding like a vulture."

Frank chuckled. "You think old Spain ain't sweating? I didn't tell 'im the time of day! I've got a thirty-sixth of the whole kaboodle, whatever he does, and that bony bastard knows it!"

Moon was wincing at every word; each struck him as a desecration of China's new grave. Such knowledge of the Estate had been deprived him for years. Now that it came, it was

386

rotten to listen to. Suddenly he thought of the frumpy burial dress on China as a part of Frank's retribution. He chilled as he watched his partner-in-law, now the heir, perhaps even the new member of the board, take a bottle from the desk and pour into a cup.

"Frank, have you forgotten her already?"

"You're like the others, huh? You want me singing sad songs and moaning at the bar and tolling the chimes and all that? All right, I'm doing it. But it's different than you think. Everybody, including you, tells me how lucky I was to have her. Maybe you don't know what you're talking about."

"Let's close up, and I'll take you home."

"Listen, Moon. I know I'm full of whisky, all the lights are burning. But I know what I'm doing, and there's things you ought to know about China, the way you've always shined to her right under my nose—"

"Drop it, Frank."

"Boy, if you don't want to hear it, I can write it down."

Moon was remembering China as she looked after the struggle with Brother. He realized he wished Frank to go on, and he was ashamed of it. He said, "Don't tell me anything that's none of my business."

"Hell, everybody loved China, so it's everybody's business. You're the one I want to tell. I've always felt—I know you hate my guts, Moon, but I've tried to be your friend. You don't believe it, but I'm being your friend now: I'll get you off the hook with her. For instance, why you suppose a girl like China wanted to marry an old crud like me?"

"Right now, I'm thinking she must have pitied you."

"Okay, I'm a sonofabitch. Maybe that's why she never cared any more for me than she did you, or the Baptist preacher, or the milkman. She loved everybody, all of them the same. Nobody special, unless it was that fat dodo; made me sick, how she mothered him. Don't get sore, Moon; I'm telling the truth. I never got one thing more from China than you did."

Moon went forward in his chair; he thought of smashing the drunken face.

"Hit me, if you want to," Frank said. "I take a licking real well, I don't even try to hit back."

Moon watched him drink directly from the bottle.

"One of those things," Frank said. "You know, Texas has to shave, Laska is like a bricklayer. Hell, you got the only whole woman in the bunch. Now wait—I ain't saying China was stone cold. Maybe if she'd married a young man, maybe if she'd not been so busy loving everybody—once I took some films home to show, thinking maybe—"

Moon bolted to his feet. "Are you telling me *she* was expecting someone else's child?"

Frank looked up and sighed. "No. There wasn't any child. *Pseudocyesis*, they call it. Phantom pregnancy. I guess she wanted bad to be a real woman. Hell, she put on all the real symptoms, and she just blew herself up with air like a frog. You never saw such a thing; she—"

"You're a damned liar!"

Frank shrugged. "Not right now, I ain't. The doctor knows; he'd just got through proving it to her when she left the office. You still don't see what happened, do you? My God, boy, don't you think she knew what she was doing when she jumped in front of that truck?"

Moon sat down. "You don't know that," he said hoarsely.

"No, I don't know. Maybe it was an accident. Or maybe she didn't mean to be killed; maybe it was just to get hurt so she could appear to have an abortion. But—well, what do you reckon she thought when she found out there wasn't any baby, when she knew she'd have to admit it to that board, when she woke up to the trick she was pulling on herself?"

Moon shut his eyes.

"You never saw anything like it," Frank said softly. "She went flat as a fritter before she died."

"Can't you stop it?"

The old druggist drank, then wagged his head. "I'm finished. You're the only one who'll ever hear it, Moon. It's not going up there to get kicked around in the board like Sid's trouble was. I didn't tell them three months ago, and I won't now. Only one

388

thing about how it was—I never made it mean for her, I swear it. She treated me like she did her old man, sort of kind and neuter, and except for a couple of times, I let it go. Seventeen years of it, and I didn't explode. You'd never have thought I could do that, would you? Me, the crumby old bastard?"

Moon couldn't doubt. He tried to catalogue it, to piece together toward a final assimilation that could be understood and then forgotten. This, then, had been China the sweet child; this was the imperfection he'd sensed the day before she died. Somehow he did not pity her. The secret, in its way, seemed to prove she had been, in fact, almost an angel.

Frank got up. He capped the bottle and put it in his coat pocket. His face sagged, the lower eyelids hung loosely so that the red inner crescents were exposed. He looked old, yet in this aura of the long-kept secret, he was all of a man.

"Where are you going?" Moon said.

"Out on a mission," Frank grinned suddenly. "I'm a rich fellow thinking of doing you a favor."

Moon sat a while as if part of a fantasy. Then, before thinking why, he telephoned Bethel. When she answered, he stammered, and he could only tell her he was sorry to have gotten off today without seeing her or the kids.

XXIII

The Old Girl typed away on the last draft, in six flimsies, of the board agenda as most recently amended. All about her, Estate rumbled and hurried and droned. In glassed-off office, Mr. Williams-the-lawyer browbeat underlings while arranging his mountains of freshly drawn documents. The blue-backed papers seemed to begin at Last Will and Testament of Cecil Munger, In His Own Hand, and to extend through Petition for Probate, Last Will and Testament of China Munger Wallace, with all the corporation charters, briefs on corporate law and trust dissolution, his own distinguished paper entitled "Statutory Controls upon the Family Partnership," and God knew what else sandwiched in between.

Mr. Jacobson, his ulcer buzzing and his complaints linked together in endless chain, drove loose-collared bookkeepers onward toward the tardy completion of his Detailed Statement of Immediate Condition and its equally detailed Summary and Definition of Properties, Appraised. Clerks dashed in and out of the file rooms, bumping one another yet keeping the essential folders in unbroken flow.

Something was prepared for every eventuality. Those few

who stood outside the mammoth assignment, particularly Mr. Williams-the-engineer and his staff, gathered in back offices to speculate which of the documents would be used. There was rumor to the effect that a pool had been started in the drugstore three floors below. The meeting would start at eleven.

The Old Girl paused in her typing to look about her. There was the green carpet, the tricky shades, the old faces. But no longer was it her domain. She felt outside of it, even while remembering she was its senior part. Mr. Munger had scarcely spoken to her through many painful days. No lunches "in," no "little visits" to put the Estate's ear to the ground. Since the day of the Children's Home gift, all had been restricted to business formality. She tried not to think about it. She might have, with less distress, given up an arm. If Mr. Munger would ask it, she'd tear one off and hand it to him. But lately, he'd asked so little that for hours each day, she sat idle.

Had she not sensed the change so readily, she would have known it anyway. Mr. Jacobson had hinted, with pleasure, that she might soon have much time to devote to her parakeets. To him and many others, she wasn't the hub any more.

She put herself back to her work. Mr. Munger was so busy. So much misfortune, so much to deal with. Soon, in some noontime, he would ring her in. There would be the old confidences. She must believe that into happening. And it would. Good things, her father always said, do not end. If they pause, it is only so that they may refresh before resuming in greater richness than before.

She finished the agenda and took it carefully out of the typewriter. She put a copy aside for file, and took the others into the board room. She placed one at each place, exactly square with table and chair. Then, before leaving, she made her inspection. There was the chair that would be vacant for the first time, and she pondered on whether to draw it away from the table or leave it in place. She decided upon the latter. She patted the flowers into flawless arrangement, and tears came to her eyes. White carnations, long-stemmed but lying in flat spray upon a shallow black dish, in mourning for Mrs. Wallace. Poor, lovely China. . . .

As a last matter, Miss Northington went to the head of the table and drew out Mr. Munger's chair. She lifted her skirt, and with her slip wiped the seat for any lately settled dust. When she returned to her desk, she found the office almost still. Mr. Williams-the-lawyer and Mr. Jacobson had finished in a dead heat. Everyone waited; there was a half-hour to spare. Then Mr. Munger rang for her.

She fled down the corridor, pad hugged to her breast, pencil in her hair and another in her hand. Mr. Munger opened the door for her.

"Uh, sit down, Miss Northington."

"Oh, Mr. Munger, if I may—I haven't had the chance to say how sorry and heartbroken I am about Mrs. Wallace."

"Thank you."

He went to his desk, took his seat, and put his chin upon the thin pallid hands. She thought he looked thinner, less straight. His hair was poorly combed; he seemed to her infinitely haggard. Her heart ached for him.

"Uh, your board will be here soon, and we've all been in such a bundle of feathers. But, uh, I have some good news for you, I'm glad to say, and I thought we might seize the spare moment here and discuss it. Uh, if you're comfortable—"

"Oh, yes!"

His eyes looked palely beyond her toward the door. He was martyred; she had to imagine he was thinking that his sister was gone, that she'd never pass through it again.

"Well, Miss Northington, to fire right off, I want to say I appreciate—and we all do—your good service to the Estate and your board. You've carried your burden, that's why I feel free to say you'll always have a place with your Munger enterprises, just as long as you want it. If—"

"Thank you, Mr. Munger. That's the kindest thing—"

"—uh, if that's clear to your mind, I want to get to your changes the board is going to have to make under the new concept here. The giz is, your new company to be organized today will cause an additional office load that's going to be your real jaw-breaker, and you can bet your lucky stars on that. Well, I know you see this, uh, just boils down to magnified records and procedures demanding your extra personnel. A part of the plan —and I know you'll agree this patch is overdue—is to split several positions here down the middle, to get a full-time secretary and on your other hand, have a full-time PBX operator and receptionist. Now, since you follow the line of thinking there, I want to ease your questions about Mr. Mooney."

"Mr. Mooney?"

"Uh, yes, I wanted to say he's your highest type person to work for, and at The Camera House, you'll find your work is certainly a lighter piece of cake. And I hope you understand your board has to stare the facts in the face in picking which paths to climb. Now, in case you think we were behind the barn door when the loyalty was passed out, let me say your normal salary reduction you might expect from your transfer— well, that's going to be by-passed. Which I know comes, from your view, as a compounding of good news with more good news. Uh, I'd like to make clear as a final thought how, uh, pleased I am to be able to outline these details in such a happy light. . . ."

She was dumfounded. Feelinglessly she watched him take down his hand bridge and crack the prominent white knuckles. Then she had the sudden thought of something forgotten. Those words of Mr. DeMarco's on the day he left: Ah, the ax falls so gently! For a moment, she sorted phrases and put them in order. Mr. Munger, I've heard an ugly rumor. There's a rural mail carrier, and he tells people that at The Old Place last Friday, your Brother June tried to rape your sister China; have you heard of that?

She did not say it; Corrine Northington could die for Mr. Munger, and although what he asked now hurt worse than death, she was sure he did not know that. She said, "Thank you," and she got up and went out.

Spain looked at his watch. Its black, shockproof waterproof face—actually a hated face because its military style reminded him that he'd been 4-F, which was a misfortune people never forgot—indicated there were twenty minutes to spare. He crossed to his window. He stood with arms folded behind his back, and squinted down at the street. Despite Mom's solicitous warnings, he thought at once of China. She the sweet one, the tender force that made the board's cogs mesh and go. She seemed to die again each time he remembered her. He missed her, he would miss her forever, and part of this lay on him very much like blame.

He could think, at times, that Papa had sent for her behind his back; that such a thing could happen only because he'd fallen asleep at the throttle. Did Papa punish him so often, so long, for pleasure or for cause; was it that business about ignoring a delirious old man's request for an odd-ball funeral, was it some other essential of the big picture that Papa disapproved? Spain shuddered. No, he had only dozed for a moment and aroused to find China gone.

He must put these ponderings aside. Your mental and spiritual health could become your problem if you dwelt on your stuff already gone over the dam. Rather, you gathered the tips toward a better wisdom, and only to that degree did you keep your memories.

Of course, if that T. J. Cowles would keep his mouth shut, then you'd not have to consider how she stepped under the truck after looking directly at it—if this wasn't just another dirty lie, which no doubt it was.

It surprised him, then, how calmly, how curiously, he imagined himself falling from this window to that street. There was nothing strange about it, not actually. In books covering such subjects, you discovered your speculation of this color was no more than your natural occurrence. No one ever stood atop a high building without at least one thought of how it might be to plunge over. With him as with any ordinary person, it didn't mean a contemplation of suicide. He had stood here so often, looking down, that he had come to understand that curiosity is safe, up to the point that it begins to hypnotize.

He took a step closer to the sill, and smiled. If one of his sisters should arrive at this instant, she would be horror-stricken.

She would think him irrational when he'd never been more sane. If he were really going to do it, this wouldn't be the way. In going out a window, you'd carry a crime with you, and you'd leave its stain on your name. Wouldn't it be better to put yourself in a hopeless situation, so you might fight to survive? You could, say, plunge into a deep lake too wide to swim, then fight the water to the end. You would then be as honest as the man who knows he must retire or die yet keeps on working. Men who'd made such choices filled executive offices in Amarillo every day. And when one died, everyone spoke highly; your public often put the garland of heroism around him. For devotion to duty, for selflessness toward the security of a widow.

The more you had the thought. . . .

He turned away from the window. The telegrams lay on his desk. He looked at several without touching them. "The Honorable Spain Munger," the governor began. China had brought these. Every one an upswing in the graph. Your plus fed off your minus, downs are very close to ups, stars also shine over your cemeteries. He experienced a sudden, brilliant sense of conquest. Except the back part of his brain felt chilled, and something in his chest seemed to be stalking him.

Mr. Williams-the-lawyer came in without knocking. He closed the door hard. "Excuse me, Mr. Munger—"

"Are they arriving?"

"I beg your pardon? Oh, yes, Miss Munger is here, and I think Mrs. Mooney was just coming in."

"Uh, have you located Mr. Wallace? As you know, it's vital that he be on hand. I hope you've kept digging in on that."

Mr. Williams looked pallid; his eyes blazed peculiarly. Spain watched him take a chair and frown down at the memo pad he held before him. "Mr. Munger, I hardly know how to put this. But I came in to tell you I haven't found him. But we just received a long distance call from New Mexico, bearing on this, and I thought—"

"Uh, can't Martin call back tomorrow? Your board will need your entire day, without any interruptions from the switchboard; I think you'll agree it'll all take time."

"Sir, it wasn't Martin. I think you'll want to hear about this."

Spain caught the dread in the tone, the hesitancy in Mr. Williams that had, in times past, meant some new upset in the alignment, some difficulty needing to be seized by the horns. He wondered why this critical day had to be confused by even one loose end.

"The call," Mr. Williams said, "came from an automobile dealer over at Albuquerque. Miss Northington put it through to me, although the man insisted on making contact with you personally. He wanted to confirm Mr. Wallace's credit."

"Uh, why would he be concerned with that?"

"I'm afraid Mr. Wallace is in over there now. He is buying a car, a Cadillac. The dealer says he appears to have been— well, stimulated, so that he wasn't exactly himself. Mr. Wallace wants to charge the car, and the dealer wanted to be sure of his connection with the Estate."

The lawyer made it all a question.

Spain stiffened; he tried not to be angry. There'd been occasions when he suspected Frank of taking drink. "Uh, what is Frank doing over there, for heaven's sake?"

"This is all I know about it."

You have to keep nimble feet; hold your wit and make speed slowly, that's the only ticket when your sisters' husbands get so handy about sticking your tail in the grinder.

"Uh, is that man still on the line?"

"Well, no sir. Under the circumstances, it seemed best to react quickly. I knew you'd want no issue made, so I simply confirmed that Mr. Wallace—that the car would be paid for. I'm sorry if—"

"Uh, no, you were right there." Spain thought back; he could remember how, years ago, Frank put up frequent to-dos about moving to New Mexico to fish, which was the type of nonsense you had to nip at the roots. But China was dead, and in grief a man sometimes ripped his seams. "I wish you'd make a few calls, Mr. Williams, if it won't botch up whatever you're doing, and if you get Mr. Wallace nailed down on the line, I'd appreciate it if you'd pipeline him right in here to me."

396

On the intercom, The Old Girl said faintly, "Mr. Munger, the board has arrived."

"Uh, thank you. Ask them to, uh, go on in and be seated, and if you'll have some coffee sent in to them, I'd be obliged. I'd appreciate it if you'd say I'll be held up here for a couple of minutes."

Mr. Williams was at the door. Spain said, "Uh, I hope you'll tackle this full-steam forward. Your board will need information—"

"I will."

Spain waited. He punched out the high crown of the Western hat, then recreased it. He gathered the sympathy telegrams and put them in a file folder. Twice Mr. Williams burst in, reported, and hurried out. Spain's face tightened, it faded to a deathliness.

Mr. Williams worked in his own cubicle. One call stumbled over another; sweat broke out and filled the grooves of his forehead. The outer office watched him through the panel of glass until he finished a final call and hung up the phone with a hand that moved very slowly. He came out into the corridor and started toward Spain's chamber. Then he appeared to change his mind. He seized an agitated young clerk, armed her with ten cents from petty cash, and dispatched her on an urgent errand. He paced away the five minutes until she was back to deliver him a newspaper. He returned to his office, he sat hunched over the columns of the Albuquerque daily. Then suddenly he stopped chewing his cold cigar. He got up with the newspaper under his arm and went plodding down the corridor.

It was past eleven and Moon was at The Camera House alone. He had dropped Bethel off at the Baldwin Building, had taken his cruise along movie row, then arrived at the store to find it unopened. He hadn't expected Frank, and he felt foolish over having forgotten Teddy Birdsong's indisposition.

He switched on the lazily awakening fluorescent lights, opened the front shades, fetched the coin bag from its locked file drawer and sorted the change into the bins. He was as vacant as the building; perhaps this was an emotional hangover.

The tensions kept over so many days created a malaise; he felt used and sapped and dried out. Physically, he had felt so before, in the Pacific jungles. Only now, his mind also seemed to be dry.

This morning before his mirror he'd observed the whole effect. His face looked leaner and older; it struck him that even the color of his eyes was different. They were darker and more shadowed. He neither liked nor disliked the change; it was just there.

He went back to Frank's office and set off a pot of coffee. He used Frank's chair. In front of him hung the awful Christ's head, which assured him that on the wall behind would be the white shotgun. These were Frank's farewells to the make-believe responsibility, the toy usefulness of The Camera House. Maybe Frank thought them a rowdy hello to his honest new idleness, or maybe he'd hung them as just a test of the new muscles he intended to flex at the Munger board.

As the coffee perked, Moon took the gun and picture down. He stood the weapon out of sight behind a file cabinet. He had an impulse to destroy the picture. Instead, he carried it far into the back and leaned its face against the wall. As he returned to the office and began wiping the dust out of a cup, Bethel's call came.

"Richard, you must come up here!"

"There's no one for the store."

"I know that. Come now, Richard, and hurry!"

Her voice was less audible than her breath; he knew the echoes. His first thought was of Brother with a new keeper. The happiest Munger might have greeted the man with some hideous caper. Then it occurred to him Frank could have gotten angry with the board; that Frank, if drinking, could have told them about China.

"Tell me," he said.

She was crying, blurting.

"I can't understand you, Beth."

"Just hurry. I—Frank has eloped!"

Moon asked for it again.

"Oh, he has! He's married—that woman, that Mrs. Birdsong."

Moon trotted, dodging between the people who turned to stare at him on the street. Frank and Teddy, who hated each other! And God, count it on your calendar, or on your fingers, or on your toes, and it came out the same. China had been dead only five days.

He darted across Polk against a light, ignoring an officer who yelled "hey!" and he raced on down the block in a rage. If he were to be the errand boy, let the assignment be violent; let them say, find those two, beat them, kill them. Suddenly he knew that was all wrong. Who was he to pity, but he did pity them. Frank, the forlorn wreck, and Teddy the impending disaster. This seemed the explanation, this must have been the affinity. They understood each other and themselves; like drowning people, they must cling together a while before sinking. Now he wondered only when they decided, why they'd not waited. What was it Frank said the other day?—no, just yesterday that was. Something about "doing you a favor."

In the last block, Moon slowed to a walk. His jacket was open, he was panting. He wiped with his handkerchief, and thought now that he might have driven over and double-parked and gotten to Bethel a minute sooner, the traffic citation be damned. He cut into the lobby, halted a departing elevator with a shout, and squeezed in. Sid Glass met him at the landing.

"Where are they?"

"They've started the meeting, just now."

They went through the offices where employees stood in groups as if to protect one another from a freezing wind, and on into the small, arched anteroom that was a threshold to the high boardroom door. Moon said, "Bethel sounded bad. Do you think we ought to break it up?"

"I don't know; Laska and I just got here. I guess it's all right. Mr. Williams is in there."

They sat down on a low, velvet upholstered bench against the wall. Moon said, "How much is definite?"

"All of it, I think. It started with calls about Frank's credit. He bought a car, and then two other fellows called. They were buying a house trailer and a lot of camping stuff, and she was getting clothes and a six-thousand-dollar mink coat. Then they found the marriage license in the New Mexico paper. Turns out they got a JP out of bed last night."

They heard voices behind the big door, and Moon strained to hear. He thought of Bethel, again a tortured pincushion, and found himself rooting for Spain, hoping the chairman was entrenched as ever to beat this back from her, and from them all, with one of his solid fronts.

Sid said, "I saw him yesterday. Poor guy, he's been drinking steadily since China died."

Moon shook his head. There was nothing to say. It occurred to him that he must go on saying nothing for the rest of his life.

They alternately sat and stood, they tuned their ears to the door. Through it slipped fragments of Spain's thin voice. He seemed to speak in mounting waves. In the occasional interludes, they heard nothing, and the foyer was silent. It appeared the women were saying nothing at all. Both men jumped when the door opened and Mr. Williams came out.

He was sweating, rushing, but he stopped as he saw them. He looked a little wild; he held a great stack of papers under one arm. "Glad you boys got here," he said. "It's pretty rugged."

"What are they doing?"

"Busting everything up, just one-two-three by the numbers. If you'll excuse me—"

Moon and Sid looked at each other. Sid heaved his small shoulders, turned his back and gazed up at the ceiling. "Well," he said, "I guess Frank has done it. And damned if I ever thought he'd even try."

Moon said, "Do you want this?"

"There was a time," he said. "But I suppose I want whatever suits Laska best. I know how that sounds, Moon, and I don't mind. Whatever pleases Laska. Me, I'm all right, either way."

"Business-wise, Sid. Is it good?"

"No. Taxes will slaughter them."

Moon studied the little man. Somehow, Sid had never gotten around to rebellion, or even to sympathizing with himself. Perhaps this was his tranquility, the reason the Munger art of

400

gentle destruction had never quite hurt him. Moon envied him. As for himself, he was shattered.

His heart sped, he thought of much money, of free choice, free risk, and free action. It beckoned him irresistibly, it glowed before him on every wall of the little foyer, this great opposite to his past thirteen years.

"What will you do, Sid?"

"If they split? I'll take care of sick dogs."

They could hear Spain speaking more rapidly. Moon paced a circuit around the room, and abruptly he knew he couldn't wait; all the years of waiting were enough, and he was going inside. "Come on, Sid," he said, and he opened the door.

The blond women sat uniformly, elbows on the long mirroring table, faces in their hands. At the head was Spain, the absurd hat beside him and crushed; deathly face supported by trembling bridge, his pale squinting gaze fixed upon the chair that had been China's. He spoke through the cotton of many words, now a paste on the thin lips.

"—and now that we're a hundred per cent on that point, I may as well let you know about a few more rabbits in the brush. I trust I can speak, uh, straight out from the hip—take things like your road paving falling flat on its face, you get those dropped on your neck without making one single mistake of your own."

Spain's voice had risen; his thin knobby wrists kept flexing beside his jaws, so that his hands pumped his face up and down, and his narrow eyes were not blinking. "Uh, that's not all I've got to say, either, and I know you want me to feel free before we get our beggars up on horseback and all go riding off in all directions, so to speak. There's things you learn good in running your family corporation, and you can stick your finger up in the wind every time your rooster crows and your last straw will fall on you anyway; I can vouch for that. It's because you've got to depend on your Remo types that'll fry your goose behind your back before you can turn around!"

Spain paused to suck in breath; he glared about the great paneled chamber as if following the course of an insect. Before him were the two thick files. Mr. Williams had outlined division of the Estate in a red folder; the reorganization procedure was encased in green. Like danger and all-clear; like stop and go.

"And then there's your Old Girl, where your loyalty turns turkey on you and stabs you in the back so that before you know it, you're screwed up like six-bits. But, uh, I want to get your minds clear of cobwebs at the beginning, and you make no mistake about this: your chairman isn't the Snake in the woodpile when you have to deal with plumbers that go around killing innocent women. And you take your chickens out there, that's a perfect example of your dirty trick I'm talking about, and it's exactly how you get your cheap backfence tone of voice going around about you, and just as soon as you give away a fortune in hard money, the wolves bunch up and start snapping your heels right to the funny bone, and that's a bunch of apples you can count on, and I'm just the jazzbo that knows!"

Spain whipped off the thick glasses, gesturing with them. The pale eyes looked like sightless slits. "Now—while we're ironing out your ancient history, I want to say having your funeral the way *he* wanted would have been your heathen exhibition and when you love your father you do your duty on that score, whether you're tickled about it or not. If you think your chairman is the lowdown Snake on that, then let me ask you how you expect to deal with your general public, can you tell me that? Take your drouth, and your disaster area in your mind, and still they turn their snotty noses up at your beans. And that's not one bit different, either, from your roof that falls in because your own board has icebox babies that corner little girls in the barn behind your back! The crux is, you've got your Mrs. Casey and your birds of that flavor telling your fuzzy lies, and before you get your barn painted, you've got your tattoo staring you between the eyes! And if you want your responsibility just to fall where it may, then I want to say at this point that this board approved your nasty little Indian whore for your payroll, and your vote there was unanimous, too! There's where you drive the nails in your own coffin, and I don't know how you expect me to keep my ear on The Camera House when there's a jillion nuts to be cracked right up here every time you turn around, and you'll all go along with me there, I'm confident of that!"

Moon went forward. "Spain—"

"—and you commence with your queer reputation already rigged up for you, and right off your snipers sharpen up their gigs to hit you with every mattock they've got, and I want to say I'm getting pretty sick and tired of your goddamn in-laws that want to flag your money around and knock your leeway in the head while you aren't looking!" Spain was shouting; a string of his mouth's cotton moved down his chin. "That's not mincing your punches, but when you've got your slimy little sneakthief like your Frank Wallace not letting your sister get cold in her grave and cramming your face down into your cowpiles and rubbing your nose for you, and your old drunkard sticking his hand in with both feet, then I say you can have the whole sonofabitch, the whole stinking sonofabitch, and every snotbox of you can plow his own furrow and don't look for your chairman to come honking the first time it hits the fan!"

Moon took hold of the bony shoulders. The pale eyes came up, squinting without recognition. The star chamber was utterly quiet. Then Spain Munger shuddered. He groaned, and lowered his head to the table and began to cry.

Bethel came quickly. She put her arms around him, she took her brother's head and held it against her breast.

Moon turned. Laska leaned stonily, expressionlessly against Sid. Texas still sat in her chair; she stared at Spain in a horror that was frozen and white. Moon thought, how much they love each other!

"Everything is all right," he said. "We're all going home."

XXIV

The sun was out and hot. Still, you could look at it and not sneeze, for the wind had lifted so much of the Golden Spread's arid land into the air that the light was tinged a dusty green— bilious green, Old Cecil Munger used to call it. Moon steered the Chevvy up to the curb before The Camera House and got out. He went inside just long enough to find the "Closed" sign and hang it on the door. When he returned to the car, Bethel was laughing at the plump, black-faced boxer puppy that tumbled in her lap.

"His teeth are like needles," she said. "What should we name him?"

"June will want to do that."

"Richard, you know, don't you? Why we never let Brother have a dog before?"

"I think so."

The pup staggered about between them, his stubby nose following her hands wherever she moved them, his small tongue licking wetly. "He'll be crazy about this cutie."

"Unless," Moon said, "you've stolen him before we can get him delivered."

404

They drove out through gusty warm wind and the dust. Grit collected on their faces despite tightly shut windows that made the car suffocating. The pup tried twice to climb up for a look at the weather and the world; it fell back and nestled down against Bethel to sleep.

She said, "How will we tell him? It'll be terrible."

"He has to know. I was thinking of the way we told the children—no, the way we should have told them. At least, we didn't just say, 'China is dead.' "

"Of course, but—"

"Beth, you wouldn't want to wait until he hears about it from someone he doesn't even know."

"Oh, you're right. But I dread it."

They reached the highway, then the turn-off on the old caliche road. The uncovered earth between the Munger fences was blowing out. The wind must have swept first across the river bed, for the air was filled with coarse grains that drummed a tinny ring from the car as they struck it.

"I feel proud," she said.

"Of what?"

"The new president of the Munger companies."

"I feel scared, Beth. What do I know about oil?"

"You'll learn—oh, that reminds me, you've not thanked me for nominating you."

He smiled. "Later, when I've messed something up, you won't admit that."

"No, I'll deny everything. But today, I'm proud. The way you—it seems so right, how you started off. About Miss Northington, I mean. She's been so faithful, and she hadn't understood that Spain wasn't well. And bringing Sid to the board, too—"

It had been only three days since Moon guided them out of the stricken board room, since he called cabs and sent them home, since he chose the green file and, as if in authority, instructed Mr. Williams to rush along toward the new holding company; since he directed that Frank's bills be paid and saw how quickly, strangely, the Estate people acknowledged him and fell to it. And now, only thirty hours had passed since he'd told Spain's board there must be no more unanimity, that family forums were finished, that holders of empire—couldn't they see?—are so few they can never make themselves ordinary or obscure, never unenvied or even unfrightening. All had occurred too fast, almost irrationally. He felt sure and mature and alive, yet the reasons eluded him. Where was all the memory, all the bitterness?

"Dear, did you notice Sid with this puppy?"

He nodded. They'd watched Sid as he selected the dog, they saw how he soothed the quaking little body; how gently he teased and mollified. There, Moon thought, was a part of it revealed. Better than to work or wait or dream was to give. This was the simple, painfully learned bit of wonder.

He glanced aside at his wife. She was looking down at the sleeping pup, her hand lightly scratching its ridge of spine. As he saw her, she was no less tall, no less pale, and he liked this; he liked being impelled along on truth's own tireless momentum. She pretended no forgetting, nor did he. But the need for it wasn't great; he thought they shared instead an eagerness for the future.

"Didn't you talk with Selma this morning?" he said.

"Yes, I meant to tell you. Spain feels fine; they're making plans. I didn't talk long. The travel-bureau man was there."

"So soon?"

She smiled. "They're in a wonderful hurry. They'll go to Spain first—Madrid and Barcelona, I think. Papa always wanted to go there, and to Alaska and China—he wanted to go everywhere. Bullfights and things, that's all Spain's own idea. Of course they'll see Paris and London and all the rest." She laughed. "I doubt if Spain himself knows that yet, but Selma does."

Moon said, "I'd counted on him for a lot of schooling."

"Don't ask him, Moon. Not until they get back."

"All right."

"I—"

"Say, didn't you call me Moon?"

406

"Well, I suppose I did." She frowned in seriousness. "I was about to ask—I can't help it, I'm bothered about Frank. Do you still mean what you said?"

"I do," he said. "I want him to have all that's his. I wish I could organize myself and state things as I feel them. But for now, try to believe that Frank was me, and I have been him. At this minute, there's only the thread of difference. . . ."

The dust around them was becoming almost white; it cut his vision like a hot blizzard. He slowed the car on the section of road he remembered as the roughest, and he felt the shy touch of Bethel's hand on his neck.

"Richard, there's something you haven't noticed, and I'm hurt about it."

"Like what?"

"Well, like me. Don't—don't things seem better?"

"Lord, Beth; I can't say how much."

"Thank you. But I'm speaking of the time."

He glanced at his watch: 11:20 A.M., May tenth, and a Thursday. He announced it.

"Also," she said softly, "it's Mean Week."

He looked at her, and she met him with a pout, then a smile. He stopped the car. The puppy rolled from her lap and struck the floor with a yelp as he kissed her. After a moment she told him smoke was coming out his ears, and he put the car in gear and they moved on.

"Do something for me?" she said.

"Yes."

"See the allergy doctor about your hand."

"Well, jungle rot is permanent, it's a—"

"I know, a leprosy. But I'll make you an appointment."

They climbed the last rise of the road. The dust and the wind which, so far from the city, claimed the privilege of whines and sighs, permitted them only the dimmest view of the house. Moon said, "What's this new man's name, again?"

"Mr. Bloodstone. I guess he's a good one. He and his wife will have been out here several days now, and nothing seems to have gone wrong."

"I'm sure he's as good as any," Moon said. But he was thinking, Remo will be a hard one to forget. It would be a perfect day for me if we could drive in there and have that ugly guy come lumbering out to meet us. Aloud he said, "Remo didn't check in with me before he left. I wonder if he went to Pennsylvania?"

Then they turned onto the cattle guard, past a recently bent post. Through the duster that now caught them broadside and rocked the Chevvy on its tough and flattened springs, they continued upslope to The Old Place.

AL DEWLEN, an award-winning
novelist, magazine writer, and newspa-
perman, is also the author of *The Night
of the Tiger* and the international best
seller *Twilight of Honor,* both of which
became major motion pictures. His
short fiction and articles have appeared
in numerous publications, including the
Saturday Evening Post and *Look*.

DOUBLE MOUNTAIN BOOKS

RELATED INTEREST

**Through the Shadows with
O. Henry**
$17.95 paper
ISBN 0-89672-480-8

Alkali Trails
$15.95 paper
ISBN 0-89672-394-1

The Story of Palo Duro Canyon
$17.95 paper
ISBN 0-89672-453-0

I and Claudie
$15.95 paper
ISBN 0-89672-429-8

Quincie Bolliver
$19.95 paper
ISBN 0-89672-449-2

Texas Panhandle Frontier
$17.95 paper
ISBN 0-89672-399-2

The Big Ranch Country
$18.95 paper
ISBN 0-89672-416-6

The Quirt and the Spur
$17.95 paper
ISBN 0-89672-441-7

Texas Tech University Press
Box 41037
Lubbock, TX 79409-1037 U.S.A.
1-800-832-4042
ttup@ttu.edu
www.ttup.ttu.edu